GREG MCLEOD

KING OF DREAMS

VERELDAN

ISBN 978-88-940221-0-0

For Laura, Sybille and Anna-Faye, faithful test pilots.

Part I – Icebound

Dreams are true while they last, and do we not live in dreams?

Alfred Lord Tennyson

1

After fifteen endless days the storm let up, but not the sense of foreboding that had begun to haunt Anuun already long before the
massive front rolled in from the west, the air thrumming with violence, the light diseased, the sky heavy and roiling with menace like
nothing he'd ever seen before, not once in all his many years.

This far north, blizzards could strike in any season, even at the
height of the short Arctic summer, and this one was only slightly
early for a first serious blow heralding the onset of winter. What set
it apart was that it raged for two weeks straight without a break,
howling with a cutting, rending ferocity that for the middle of September was unusual even in these high latitudes – which was why
Anuun didn't notice the disruption in the pattern until it was too
late.

When the high winds finally did relent and he became aware of
the intrusion, he immediately set off, deeply disquieted, taking the
shortest route to the place where his finely attuned Iceling senses
had detected the disturbance. Traveling underice, he flowed swiftly
through the blue-green depths, now a fleeting shadow, now a streak
of livelier color, now a whitish string of icebound bubbles freed by

elemental magic to move with ease through compact matter.

Only when the offshore ice became too fragmented to allow him smooth passage did he surface. His essence pouring into form like water into a sturdy-sided jug, he assumed his bodily aspect: a head shorter than an average human, stocky, broad-shouldered and immensely powerful, his curly hair and beard the silvered grey of finely spun frost, his eyes the profound ultramarine of deep-core ice.

At the site of the disturbance he found an Orrian ship, completely imprisoned by the pack ice. *Albatross*, she was called, but her days of flying before the wind over sun-sparkled waves were forever over. Massive floes piled up three and four deep all around her creaking, groaning hull had already begun their slow, relentless work of destruction, crushing, grinding, splintering until, come spring, nothing would be left of the once-proud vessel but a handful of flotsam, free to drift off into the vastness of the northern sea once the strengthening sun beat back the ice.

Inspecting the ship and its cargo, Anuun reckoned that the purpose of her voyage had been to trade with the Nordsmen, probably for pelts and the odd bit of gold. Blown hundreds of miles off course by the storm, she'd never reached Nordsmen shores, that much was clear from her hold still filled with Orrian trade goods – and with nineteen seamen huddled together under decks in a clump of frozen bodies, their faces blued and rimed with hoarfrost. Snow had drifted in through a broken hatch, and the deck was scorched and charred where they'd tried to start a fire, so desperately cold they'd risked burning down the whole ice-bound ship around them for a bit of warmth. For whatever reason, they'd failed to keep the fire going, and died a little faster for it.

Anuun couldn't help a breath of relief. Tragic as the death of these men had been, it had likely served to prevent an incomparably greater catastrophe. For their ship had come to rest worryingly close to the Forbidden, a place no man must ever be allowed to set foot in, a locus inhabited by something far beyond any mortal's, and even an Iceling's, grasp, something buried under the ice thousands of years ago for a very good reason.

Ages past, Icelings had been assigned to guard against any living being intruding on this place, deliberately or otherwise, and they'd faithfully fulfilled the task to this day – though the passing of so many eventless centuries had perhaps begun to dull their vigilance a mite. Maybe earlier times would have seen one of Anuun's predecessors brave a storm similar to the one just past, doing the rounds regardless of the inferno outside instead of sheltering underice until the weather cleared. And maybe not.

At this point, the question was already entirely moot.

What Anuun had no way of knowing was that the ship's crew had originally numbered twenty-four. Four had been taken by the storm, swept overboard by waves that towered higher than the masthead before they came crashing down and cleared the deck of anything that wasn't twice and threefold battened down. Maybe the four went in silence, or maybe screaming for help – with the howling wind and thundering waves it would have made no difference. And whether it was the water or the cold that claimed them first was anybody's guess. The deep took them either way, with a swiftness that was close to mercy.

9

Twenty-four. Four drowned, nineteen in the hold.

One was missing from the count.

That one had come through the storm alive. Owing perhaps to an exceptional constitution or to one of those twists of fate that border on the bizarre, he'd survived the cold as well, at least long enough to leave the stranded ship and head off across the pack ice to where he hoped to find land, the storm erasing his tracks almost as soon as he'd made them.

But Anuun was nothing if not thorough, and he was warned. Near impossible as it seemed, his questing Iceling senses found the feeble traces of the human's passage. When they did, and when he realized where the man had gone, his heart went colder than the deepest ice cave.

This should never have been allowed to happen. Not on his watch. Storm or no, he'd neglected his duty, broken the trust placed in his kind, risked bringing shame on the whole Iceling nation. Only one thing he could do: find the man before it was too late and untold horrors were loosed on the world.

Desperate, he plunged back into the ice, a streak of white lightning ripping landward.

*   *   *

Now skidding over patches of wind-swept ice, now laboring through waist-high drifts of fine, powdery snow that crept into his boots and melted down his shins in icy trickles, Nudd Wiggin repeatedly cursed fate, the gods, and anyone else who'd ever done him an injustice.

Since that list included practically everyone he'd ever met, it made for an impressive litany, with the captain of the *Albatross* currently ranking second only to the filthy, whoring slut who'd given birth to Nudd between turning tricks, followed by his drunkard, layabout father and then by a long string of masters Nudd had been apprenticed to, a bunch of narrow-minded, nitpicking fools none of whom had owned the sense to recognize his true potential.

Looking back, he felt nothing but contempt for the lot of them... and, hell yes, a level measure of hatred as well.

The last of these masters, a furrier named Brychan, was the reason Nudd had started keeping the list in earnest, and the reason he'd begun to hate with a dedication he otherwise seldom saw the need to muster: Brychan, and his daughter Dilys – Amut take the vicious slag.

For months, she led him on, acting the bitch in heat when neither her old man nor the journeyman she was bespoken to were looking, until Nudd finally decided to give her what she so clearly wanted. But the moment he tried to jump her the stupid cow started screaming down the house, and suddenly he found himself cast in the role of the faithless fiend who'd tried to rape his master's precious daughter.

Brychan, the craven arsehole, let his other three apprentices beat Nudd to a bloody pulp before calling in the city watch and having him arrested for a deed Nudd told himself he'd never intended to commit and hadn't gotten round to in any case. Choosing between the noose and three years on an Orrian war galley was the easy part. Serving his time and getting through it in one piece was another matter. As an alleged rapist, he was scum to the scum that manned the huge ship's one hundred and twenty oars, and he was treated accordingly, as likely to accidentally run into a fellow oarsman's fist as catch a couple of – entirely unwarranted – lashes from the overseer's cat o' nine tails. He consoled himself with vivid fantasies of the terrible, painful things he'd do to every single one of them, once he was good and ready to strike back.

Just thinking about the bloody cocksuckers made him fricking mad all over again. *Their* fault, all of it. *Their* fault that he was stranded in this freezing shithole. *Their* fault that he had to wade through all this godsdamned, bleeding white shit. Seething with anger, he came to a sudden halt. Sucked a gob of brownish-pink spit from rotting teeth and bleeding gums and used it to mess up the godsdamned snow that was so fricking pristine it made him want to puke. Wished he had a load of piss to add to it, but the bloody cold seemed to have sucked all the moisture out of him and left him drier than a hag's cunt. Satisfied that he'd done what he could, he screwed up his muddy, close-set eyes against the overwhelming brightness and trudged on, still far from finished with the past.

When his three years were up, for want of a better plan he took hire on a merchant ship, the *Dauntless*. His list went with him, grown by over a hundred names but with room for plenty more, and a good thing, too. It took him less than a day aboard the *Dauntless* to figure out that her captain and crew were dead set on making his life as miserable as they could, giving him all the lowliest, dirtiest jobs and no doubt acting at the behest of the fricking gods, who'd had it in for him since the day he was born, or maybe even longer.

Let them, he thought to himself. *Let them go on digging their own graves. Though it's still too early to say when exactly it'll hap-pen, they've got a big surprise coming. Nobody messes with Nudd Wiggin and gets away with it – not in the long run, they don't, that's for bloody sure.*

At the *Dauntless'* first port of call he jumped ship, and so began a series of hires that ended with the ill-fated voyage on the *Alba-tross.*

And to think that, this very fall, he'd actually considered hang-ing up his oilskins and trying his hand at something less strenuous than seafaring. But then he'd heard that the captain of the *Albatross* was offering double pay to any man willing to sail north a good three weeks later in the season than conventional wisdom deemed prudent.

There was some talk about a fashion war having broken out be-tween the two leading houses of the Orrian Dressmaker's Guild, Orid and Lechan; something to do with a battle over fur of the arctic fox and prices having gone through the roof, which in turn promp-ted the *Albatross'* owners to send the ship on a late voyage north to trade for the stuff.

Nudd gave a rat's ass for the reasons. The only part that interest-ed him was collecting double wages, and then taking the winter off to figure out what he wanted to do with the rest of his life – aside from paying back his enemies with interest, that was.

And then the fool captain steered them straight into the worst fricking storm in history, and everything went to hell in a fricking handcart.

Now everyone was dead except Nudd.

No big surprise there. The idiots he'd sailed with had gotten exactly what they'd asked for, answering to the death god's call like they did: limp-dicked, spineless chickens lining up at the chopping block even before the axe was sharpened, instead of fighting it like men.

But then, *he* had a righteous anger burning in his gut to keep him warm. *He* had his list, had accounts to settle, and he'd be damned if he let a bloody storm get in the way of the revenge that was his rightful due.

At least the godsdamned blow had finally died down, though his eyes were still half blind and stinging from the whipping snow, and his face felt cut to bloody ribbons. But he was alive, no thanks to anyone but himself.

And so he plodded on, his imagination hard at work torturing, maiming and slowly killing his enemies one by one, until suddenly a fricking crevasse had the bloody cheek to open up right in front of him. Too late, he tried to stop, his skidding feet finding no purchase on the mirror-smooth ice. Inexorably, his forward momentum delivered him straight into the arms of gravity, reaching out to him from bluegreen depths that looked as beautiful as they were deadly.

Fricking gods again, he thought angrily. *Bugger the lot of you. I'm not ready to die.*

Then he was falling.

The drop was short.

Not six feet down, the seat of Nudd's pants made contact with the ice, his free fall abruptly turning into a high-speed toboggan ride along a bumpy, madly twisting tunnel. Thankfully, what began as a frighteningly steep incline gradually flattened out until he was spit

14

out onto the floor of a spacious gallery deep under the ice. Sliding down the entire length of it on his butt, he finally came to a stop at the foot of a wall that looked suspiciously like it was man-made, its dull, black stone seeming to swallow the little light that filtered down through what had to be at least thirty feet of ice.

Nursing his bruised backside, he climbed to his feet, unsteady in the blue gloom, the slippery floor nearly throwing him right back on his face again. Looking back the way he'd come, he wondered how the bloody hell he was ever going to get out of this place. His only chance, he decided after a moment's thought, was to somehow climb back up the tunnel. But for that, he needed something he could use to hack foot and handholds out of the sheer ice. Reaching for his knife, he cursed. The sheath was empty – how else could it be? Just his fricking luck again. What else…

The wall. Maybe he could find a loose stone, work it free and use it as a tool. Bloody crude, but better than nothing.

Taking a closer look at the wall, Nudd realized two things: one, the damned thing was made of a single piece, most likely hacked out of the bedrock, seeing as it was far too smooth and straight to be natural; and two, he was going to die down here.

Torn between wanting to collapse on the floor in a blubbering heap and the urge to scream out his rage over this totally unfair turn of events, he chose the latter, raising his face skyward and directing a stream of the vilest invective he could muster at the whole buggering lot of rotten, spiteful, scheming men and gods, all of whom kept on stubbornly refusing him even the smallest of breaks. For good measure, he gave the bloody wall a kick as well, hitting it full on

15

with the flat of his boot.

With a groan like a ship's hull scraping against dockside pilings, where he could have sworn that moments ago there had been nothing but seamless rock an eight-by-three-foot slab of stone detached itself from the rest of the wall, sinking into some sort of recess in the floor and revealing a dark, narrow passage.

Briefly, he wondered whether going in there was a good idea. Who knew but the stone might rise back up behind him, trapping him forever in a lightless prison deep underground. Then another thought struck him: what lay at the other end of that tunnel might well be some long-forgotten king's tomb, brimful with gold and gems. Riches beyond imagining. The more he thought about it, the more sense it seemed to make. On the other hand...

In the end, curiosity and greed got the better of him. Pushing aside any lingering doubts, he stepped over the sunken stone and into the passage.

The tunnel zigged and zagged through the rock for a stretch, as if whoever had made it hadn't been able to make up their minds which way they wanted to go. Or maybe they'd been falling-down drunk throughout the many weeks it must have taken to hack the bloody hole out of the bedrock.

When he reached the other end, Nudd found himself staring out into a large, six-sided chamber walled in the same, dull-black stone. There was no ceiling as such, only a natural, high-domed roof of ice. In the dusky, blue-tinted light that trickled down from above, he saw openings like the one he was standing in cut into each of the other five walls. Five chances of finding another way out – though he was almost a bit hesitant to set foot on the chamber's spotless floor. Blacker even than the walls, it was polished to a high gloss, slicker than the finest marble, the kind of floor Nudd associated with the whispering, slippered feet of priests and highborn ladies – not that he'd ever seen one of the uppity cows except floating by in a curtained litter or gazing down on the common folk from some palace's safe, high window.

There was nothing in the chamber, though. No dead king, and no treasure. But then, the good stuff might well be waiting down one of the other five passages.

His confidence renewed, he stepped out into the chamber – and found that the floor wasn't polished stone at all but some kind of thick, oily liquid that sucked at his boots and shivered in slow, wavy ringlets around his feet. It was hardly half an inch deep, though, so nothing to worry about, unless the floor underneath sloped downward farther out.

Just take it slow, feel your way as you go.

Three steps out, overcome by a sudden, unaccountable fear, he stopped. Realized that he didn't care anymore what lay behind those other doors. Tried to turn back. And found that, in the two short heartbeats he'd stood still, his feet had somehow gotten stuck to the floor.

Suddenly he was sweating despite the violent cold, his hands clammy, his pulse hammering so loud he thought he could hear it echoing off the walls.

All right, then. So I'll just slip out of my boots and make a run for it. It's only three bloody steps. Piece of cake, as long as I don't stop.

But, try as he might, he couldn't seem to pull his feet free of the boots. Couldn't even feel his feet, actually, only a cold, tingling sensation somewhere upwards of his ankles. Looking down, he saw that he'd sunk into the gods-cursed stuff up to his shins.

Which was impossible, seeing as it was only half an inch deep and there was solid stone underneath. Could the nasty black shit be rising? But no – the sill of the doorway he'd come through was still free of it, clearly visible. So maybe some sneaky, hidden mechanism was cranking down the floor under him? No matter, he had to find a way out of this mess, and fast. Even while he'd been standing there wasting time on useless thoughts, he'd dropped another six inches, the stuff rising up to his knees, all feeling gone from his lower legs.

By the time he finally understood what was really happening to him, the black crap and the cold tingling were already up to his arse. It was then he started screaming – screaming, and wildly thrashing about, suddenly caught in the grip of utter madness, trying to claw his way out of a nightmare that cruelly refused to be anything other than real.

The moment his uselessly scrabbling hands touched the black liquid's surface it started eating them away as well, just like it had done with his legs, dissolving skin, flesh, and bones like some impossibly concentrated acid and consuming what was left of him with unearthly speed.

The last part to go was his head, his mouth stretched wide in a continuously rising scream that only broke off when the stuff reached his vocal cords, his face staring up from the floor in a frozen rictus of horror, distorted far beyond anything that might have still been called human.

*   *   *

Some time later, a shudder went through the liquid covering the floor. Here and there, puckers and dimples appeared, multiplying and spreading out as if a wind were rippling the shiny black surface. Whorls and eddies formed, gradually joining into a single, purposeful current. Then, with a sudden quickening, the viscous stuff drew back from the chamber's edges, baring a rapidly widening margin of the underlying stone as it coalesced into a large, amoebic blob centered over the very spot where Nudd had been consumed.

For a while the accreted liquid simply hung there, wobbling, heaving, collapsing and reconsolidating, an amorphous mass obviously striving towards organized form, oozing its way through a painstakingly slow series of failed attempts as it sought to mold itself after some as yet indecipherable pattern.

Finally, contracting once more and further than its mass would seem to allow, it reached the shape it had been seeking. There, feet planted wide, stood a perfect copy of Nudd Wiggin, resurrected from the sludge, faithfully reproduced in every detail and black as the devil's arsehole on a moonless night.

Almost hesitantly, the Wiggin-thing looked around, moving slowly as if it feared that any rapid movement might cause it to dissolve in a large puddle on the floor. And indeed it was still far from stable, the stuff inside it not yet settled, its outline warped, buckling and

19

bulging like a sack full of angry weasels as it strained to hold itself together.

For the longest time the Wiggin-thing stood still, waiting with seemingly inexhaustible patience for the inner turmoil to subside until only the odd, wandering bump or hollow still occasionally distorted its outer skin. When even those had ceased to appear, it raised a foot and took a slow, careful step forward. And another. And a third. Heading back the way the original Wiggin had come. It wanted out, that much was clear, and it no longer looked as if anything could keep it from getting there. Gradually, color began to seep into the black, skin and hair and clothes beginning to look like they had before.

Once, just before it reached the tunnel entrance, one leg gave a sudden wobble and shed a large gob of black goo on the floor. Stopping to reclaim it, the Wiggin-thing scraped it up with a booted foot. Then it went on, single-minded, unswerving in its purpose.

*   *   *

2

A thousand miles farther south, Laurin, son of Sem, was running for his life. Not an easy thing to do if you stood just under four feet tall in your boots and had a dwarf's bandy legs thrown into the deal. The torrential rain blurring his sight and slicking the cobblestones didn't help either, nor did the heavy pack bouncing up and down on his back, nor the fact that the man chasing him was not only a big person but one who moved with uncanny speed and grace, swift and inexorable as the dark water rushing down the gullies on either side of the street.

Suddenly the street was gone, wiped away like chalk marks by a giant sponge, and, with no noticeable transition, Laurin found himself caught up in absolute darkness.

It was then he realized he was dreaming, though he found himself thinking that by rights no dream should feel so damnably real. There was substance to this darkness, a feel of cold, a smell of dust, an 'up' and a 'down'. Shifting a foot, he felt his boot scrape over solid rock, a faint, lagging resonance suggesting that he was in a large, enclosed space.

Someone groaned, and Laurin's heart skipped a beat as manifold echoes stretched the tortured sound to painful length.

'Who's there?' he asked nervously, his words coming back at him in an overlapping multitude of splintered fragments that seemed to nest in every nook and cranny and go on softly whispering there forever.

'I am the King under the Mountain,' the answer came from somewhere in the dark, the voice sounding thin and distant, like wind blowing through reeds. 'Who else would I be, given where we are? And you. Come closer, fellow, so I can see what manner of fish I've netted.'

Laurin didn't much like the sound of that.

Then he remembered it was all just a dream, and took a few shuffling steps forward until his shins met with something hard.

'Ah.' The king – assuming he really was a king – sounded disappointed. 'Just my luck, to catch a dwarf.'

'I may be short,' Laurin said, stung, 'but I can fend for myself as well as the next man. I'll also have you know that I don't take well to belittlement. And now, if you'll just point me to the door, I'll be on my way.'

'Not so fast, little man.' The king sounded faintly amused. 'I've called you here for a purpose. Because, you see, I need you to run an errand for me. So you'll kindly stay until you've received your instructions. And be advised I meant no slight by what I said just now. I've known a few dwarves in my time, stalwart fellows all of them and held in the highest esteem by my royal self. It's just that, in this case, a slightly longer pair of legs would have come in handy, seeing as you'll likely have a lot of ground to cover. Now – '

'Hold it right there,' Laurin said, raising a cautionary hand, the gesture feeling pointless in the impenetrable dark – though the king seemed to be able to see him well enough. 'What makes you think I've got nothing better to do than play your errand boy? I've got a job, in case you didn't guess. I have people to report to, I have – '

'Pettifogging,' the king interrupted. 'Irrelevancies. Whatever it is you do for a living, it can't possibly be more important than delivering my message. In fact, *nothing* is more important. Thousands of lives may depend on whether it gets through or not. Tens of thousands, perhaps. So listen carefully.'

'Just so we're clear,' Laurin interrupted once more. 'You *do* realize this is just a dream? I might wake up and not remember any of it. And even if I do, I might not give a fig.'

'Oh, you'll remember all right,' the king growled. 'And you'll give more than just a fig. Here.'

Laurin heard a rasping of steel on steel, and suddenly there was light, emanating from an object that seemed to float in the air before him. It was a sword, he saw, its half-bared blade glowing with a soft, amber radiance, the edges looking sharp enough to cleave downy feathers. He was no judge of weapons, but even he could see that this was an exceptional specimen. From the finely wrought pommel to the hilt wrapped with artfully braided silver wire, to the scabbard chased in gold and silver, it spoke of masterly craftsmanship – and of something more. Magic, perhaps.

Next, he became aware of the hands that were holding the sword: desiccated, leathery claws, bloodless skin and bones. The hands of someone who couldn't possibly be alive. Fearing what

23

he'd see, he steeled himself and raised his gaze. But before he could catch a glimpse of the king's face the blade was thrust back into the scabbard, the cross-guard kissing the rim of the sheath with a ring of finality, the light winking out.

'Take it.' There was a rough edge to the king's voice, hinting at a wealth of pain, and Laurin's heart responded with a spontaneous twist of sympathy. Guessing in the dark, hoping not to touch those bony claws, he managed to grasp the sword midway along the scabbard.

'The sword is called *Altingal*,' the king said. 'Which means Wild Thing in the old tongue. It is named thus because it's apt to bite the man who wields it, if his purpose is anything less than pure. I charge you to deliver it to a person who will soon find himself in desperate need of it, if he is to fulfill the task that fate is about to set before him. For he is of the Blood – the first after all these years who looks to be deserving of the honor – and long has the Blood been singled out in dire times to bear the burdens no one else will shoulder. Guard the weapon well, needs be with your life. Should it fall into the wrong hands, all will be lost.'

'Why me?'

'Because I can reach you, shortling. Either because you're somewhere close, or because you're simply the responsive kind. Him, I can't get through to. Thick as a brick, that boy.'

'All right,' Laurin said, suddenly wondering how sane this King under the Mountain was – and whether it might not be a good idea to wake up rather quickly, before he got himself neck-deep into trouble. 'Assuming I'd be willing to do as you ask: where would I find this person?'

'North and west,' the king said.

'North and west?' Laurin asked incredulously. 'That's the best you can do?'

'Well, no. It's somewhere in... Ardath, I think. Here, let me show you.'

An image appeared in Laurin's mind.

Almost as if he were there himself and standing only a short distance away, he saw some minor noble's modest keep sitting on a knoll surrounded by a gently undulating landscape of woods and farmland. It could have been anywhere in the Seven Kingdoms. Or in the Empire, for that matter.

Then the scene was replaced by another, this time the interior of a barn. Laurin saw a hazel-eyed youth with bits of hay in his light, curly hair and dirt on his square-jawed face, crouching in the straw beside an enormous sow. The massive animal was lying on its side, every teat occupied by what looked to be close to a dozen suckling piglets.

'A farm boy,' Laurin said, his doubts as to the king's state of mind redoubling.

'Among other things,' the king said. 'Don't let appearances fool you. There's more to him than meets the eye.'

'So I'm supposed to find this lad and hand over the sword to him.'

'Exactly.'

'Do you have any idea how many keeps like this one there are apt to be in Ardath? It's a fairly big place, you know.'

'I know. I've been there.' Sounding slightly embarrassed, the

25

king gave a phlegmy cough. 'But I trust that, employing a modest measure of brains and goodwill, you'll have no trouble finding the right one.'

Laurin sighed. *Time to wake up,* he told himself. *We're flogging a dead horse here, and I've another long day's work ahead of me.*

'Does the lad at least have a name?' he asked for completeness' sake.

'Avellin,' the king said, and for once it sounded like a certainty.

Avellin? Laurin wanted to ask, incredulous, but suddenly felt the morning sun warming his face and realized he'd woken. *Avellin, as in... No, it can't be. Surely not in Ardath.*

Far from slipping his mind, the dream stayed with him – didn't leave him much of a choice, actually, seeing as upon waking he found himself clutching a sword to his breast, though it bore no resemblance at all to the one he'd seen in his dream. This one was a ruin, its hilt gnawed to a finger's thickness by rust, shedding large flakes when he tried to draw it – only to find that the sheath and blade were fused into a single lump of hopelessly corroded metal.

Last night I must have bedded down right beside the thing, he told himself, *and somehow gotten hold of it in my sleep.*

Looking around, with a bit of imagination he could almost see how the stones scattered along one end of the flat piece of ground he'd made his camp on might have once been heaped into a small cairn.

Some poor sod probably lost his life and sword here centuries ago, perhaps in a long-forgotten skirmish or through some sort of accident, and it's been lying here ever since. And my dreaming mind made up the rest of the story to go with it. That's how dreams work, isn't it? Like when a full bladder makes you dream about pissing. Yes, that's exactly what must have happened.

He piled up a few stones, enough to support the sorry excuse for a sword in an upright position, and left it standing there with a short prayer for whomever it had belonged to.

And still the dream continued to haunt him.

Brewing a pot of morning kaf, filling his pack pony Dag's feed sack with a few handfuls of oats, chewing hard waybread and stale cheese for breakfast, striking camp and readying to move to another site, he couldn't stop himself from dwelling on it, silly as it seemed to go on worrying over something he'd already found a perfectly satisfying explanation for.

Except the more he thought about it, the less satisfying it felt, for no reason he could put his finger on. Finally he was forced to admit that the whole thing scared him, plain and simple. It weighed on him, pressed him, urged him, filled him with a crushing sense of guilt for not having rushed off on the king's errand the moment he woke up, no matter the idea was entirely ridiculous. Mad, actually. Now *there* was a worrying thought.

Though he tried to keep his mind occupied with seeing to the everyday necessities, by mid-morning he was close to panicking, and thoroughly angry.

Neither feeling was new to him.

Born a runt among normal-sized people, he'd learned early on to deal in the long term with issues that ceased to be a problem for other children as they grew older and taller: objects that were too large, too high or too heavy; chores that taxed his small body, and sometimes even his inventive mind, to the limit or beyond; big people who all seemed to have a singular knack for overlooking him and putting their large, clumsy feet in the exact same space he happened to be occupying.

But none of that made him angry, though it was far from easy to watch his peers grow tall and distant, leaving him behind, a sad, quiet child who became sadder still once he realized what a burden he was to his parents.

Like every tenant farmer's life, theirs was a constant, daily struggle to pay the lord's tithes and still feed seven hungry mouths, even with all the children helping out from the day they were old enough to reach a cow's udder or hold a rake.

'He works for one and eats for three,' Laurin's da used to say about him, only half joking. What he really meant was that, try as he might, his stunted youngest managed to do only half the work it would have taken to earn his keep.

With a start, Laurin realized he'd been sitting there staring at his hands. Small hands, scarred and calloused, short, stubby fingers, cracked and dirty nails. Not pretty or impressive by any standards. But, dammit, they were *his* hands, strong and nimble as he needed them to be. Good for earning his keep now, though probably still not strong enough to save him from big men harboring cruel intentions.

The first time he'd known real fear was when the men from Orr came riding up to Sem's farm one hot, dusty afternoon some weeks after his tenth nameday. Two of them were armed and mailed, strong, rough men whose unsmiling faces and hard eyes frightened him – though not nearly as much as the third member of the party did. A grey-haired, weathered man on a pint-sized palfrey, he looked to be only half a hand taller than little Laurin, who stared at him in amazement, never having considered the possibility that there might be others like himself.

He's just like me, Laurin thought. *I'm not the only one. I'm not alone.*

It was shortlived sentiment. There was no hint of recognition in the gaze with which the man scrutinized Laurin, no sign of kinship, charity, or mercy.

'I am Guildmaster Crowlin,' he proclaimed before the dust had even begun to settle, 'of the Orrian Glassmaker's Guild. This writ' – he pulled a rolled-up parchment from his saddle bag but didn't bother to open it, knowing full well that none of them could read, – 'is signed and sealed by the Council of Landing, and it assigns me the power and the right to conscript into the services of the Guild whomever I see fit.'

As if she sensed what was coming, Ma laid a protective hand on Laurin's shoulder. Da looked ready to put up a fight, writ or no. One of the men-at-arms laid a casual hand on the hilt of his sword and gave Da a long, hard stare, and that was all it took to take the pluck out of him. His big hands falling limp and powerless to his sides, he lowered his eyes in shame and resignation.

That was when Laurin made his first acquaintance with real anger – not the sudden fit of temper that passed and was forgotten but a deep, corrosive ire much too large and inexpressible for a ten-

29

year-old to handle.

Nonetheless, it stayed with him, changing him in ways he wouldn't begin to understand until many years later.

'You there,' Crowlin said, pointing at Laurin. 'The little one. You'll come with us.'

'No,' Ma breathed. 'Please, no.' Her grip on Laurin's shoulder tightened momentarily, but when one of the soldiers kneed his horse past Da and crooked a finger at her, she picked the boy up and handed him over quickly enough. 'Don't forget, your Ma loves you,' she whispered in his ear, her hair smelling of hay and freshly baked bread – or so he preferred to think in hindsight. It could as well have been old sweat and cow dung, for all he remembered.

Thus he learned another thing that day, namely that love bought you nothing. No security, no protection, no reprieve. Nothing at all.

Parted from his home and family at an early age, Laurin was lucky in other ways. Instead of sending him to the mines like the rest of that year's cull, the Guild apprenticed him to a Waylen, one of the mysterious, fabled seekers of rare minerals, precious, secret ingredients that enabled the making of clear, flawless glass – and hence of mirrors, an outrageous luxury much sought after by the mighty and the rich and fetching several times their weight in gold. The purchase of a small hand mirror could drive a lesser lord into bankruptcy, and a full-length wall mirror was worth a king's ransom.

So it was no wonder that the nature of these minerals was jealously guarded knowledge, as was the process in which they were used. Everyone who was in any way involved, be it in the gathering of materials or in the making of glass, was made to swear on his life

30

and on the lives of those he held dear to never so much as hint at what he did for a living, and promised a terrible death should he even dream of revealing what he knew.

Guided by his master, Laurin learned to read and write, studied mineralogy, botany, and alchemy, was taught to read the subtle signs that spoke of a nearby trove of minerals: the color and feel of the soil, the taste and smell of the water, the presence or absence of certain plants. The last piece of knowledge revealed to him when the master judged him ready was the secret of the Waylen signs. Then he was sent off on his first trip into the wilds alone, and alone was how he'd plied his trade ever since.

Twenty years Laurin had given in service to the Guild: three as an apprentice, two as a journeyman, and fifteen as a master Waylen, one of the best the Guild had ever had. Twenty years of long, lonely treks through wild, wayless country, of clambering through dank ravines and scrabbling up steep slopes, of balancing along dizzying ledges and crawling into caves and subterranean passages so dark and narrow even a dwarf sometimes risked getting stuck in them and never seeing the light of day again. Twenty years of searching for deposits of brownstone and cobalt, leaving Waylen marks chiseled into rocks or cut into tree trunks, signs to guide the miners – all of them dwarves like him – to the lodes he'd found. Twenty years of sweltering heat and freezing cold, of rain and hail, snow and ice, thunderstorms, flooding streams, mudslides, rock falls, avalanches. Twenty years of hardships and solitude.

He endured, not least because they'd promised him that twenty years would buy him freedom.

This last thought sparked an inspiration.

The dream was trying to tell him something. *Him*, Laurin, and not some imaginary farm boy in Ardath. With this insight, things began to fall neatly into place, and he breathed easier again.

His twenty years were up, a fact he'd almost forgotten over the daily grind. *That* was what the dream was supposed to remind him of. Standing there holding Dag's lead, ready to leave, he was overcome by a sudden excitement, causing him to sit down once more by the cooling ashes of the morning's fire to try and think things through properly.

It was true: in theory he was done with the Guild, his contract fulfilled, already working overtime. All he still needed to do was report this last trip's findings to the master miner at the Guild's Kingskeep branch, hand in his notice, and then he'd be free. Oh – and he'd have to check on his savings, a tidy sum by now, even though he'd regularly sent half his wages to his family. Still, there should be more than enough to start anew, perhaps open a small gem shop or a tavern. He might even decide to follow another dream he'd secretly nourished ever since he heard a rumor that...

But he was getting ahead of himself. First things first.

Greatly relieved, he stood and dusted off his hands, ready to set out on the long journey back to Dunmark. Now that he knew someone had likely died here in this dismal, steepsided valley that was no more than a tiny wrinkle in the vastness of the southern Caerrocks, he was glad to be away. Even Dag seemed eager to show the place his plump backside. Would that it had been so easy.

They'd gone less than two hundred paces when Laurin suddenly stopped dead in his tracks as if he'd reached the end of an invisible tether. Almost simultaneously, he heard the swish of many wings fast approaching from behind, and a murder of crows passed low overhead. In a flurry of flapping wings and raucous caws, they settled on a pair of stunted trees not fifty yards down the trail, a bunch of dark-feathered sentinels taking up station. Laurin could have sworn that every single one of their black, beady eyes was fixing him with a reproachful stare.

Though he wasn't given to superstitions, he did know a sign when he saw one. Reluctantly, he turned around. Looping Dag's lead over a low branch, he retraced his steps back to the campsite, Dag giving a quizzical snort as if to say 'Are you sure about this?'

No. I'm not, but it doesn't look like I have much of a choice.

For long moments, he stood staring at the sword. Then, heaving a heavy-hearted sigh, he pulled the rusty thing from its pile of supporting stones, carried it back to where Dag stood waiting, and stored it in one of the panniers.

He'd barely closed the flap when the crows took flight again, heading off down the valley like an airborne vanguard marking out his path for him – and possibly a future unlike anything he'd ever imagined.

*   *   *

3

The boy was late again.

Always in a hurry, and never on time. Bowen Threehands sighed, running age-knotted fingers through his grizzled beard. *Gods know I don't expect the lad to be flawless. But there are faults – and then there are faults. Some you can live with, even happily if you're that kind of man. Others are liable to get you killed. Sometimes I wonder how I survived mine. But then, I learned the hard way to recognize my weaknesses and forge them into something less deleterious, possibly even useful.*

It's the single most important thing I've been trying to teach young Bryn all these years, and the one I fear he's still not understood. Perhaps because it's something that simply can't be taught, a lesson a man can only learn by way of going through his own hard and bitter experiences. Perhaps I'm getting soft in my old age. Perhaps I'm a fool to wish I could spare him at least the worst of it.

Ah, well. It will go as it will, whether I like it or not. I should give the pot a stir – though burnt or no makes hardly a difference with my cooking skills. Can't even make a decent meal of what Nan prepared. I do wish she'd get back soon. Another day or two of this, and we'll likely be going hungry.

Nan the cook, who doubled as the shire's midwife, had taken leave to go and help with the birthing of what must be her fifteenth grandchild. A day without her, and she was already sorely missed. Unlike Bowen, she was a damned fine cook. And, to his knowledge, nearly all of the weans she delivered survived, which spoke for her skills as a midwife as well.

What was I...? Ah, yes. The pot.

Still, Bowen didn't get up from his place at the long table in the great hall. Instead, he sat staring into a beam of late afternoon sunlight, the motes dancing in the golden rays reminding him of another time and place, an old man traveling back in time and losing himself in the past.

Unbidden, a faded scene intruded on his mind's eye.

It was of another great hall, a place he hadn't set foot in for nigh on twenty years, and likely never would again. Time had washed out the colors, and repeated handling had frayed the image around the edges, but the feelings it stirred in him were still fresh as the roses sitting on the table where Nan had placed them before departing early this morning.

The hall he was seeing was that of Kingskeep Castle, the late-afternoon sunlight that filtered in through a high lancet window casting a fair-haired woman in a soft, golden halo. Head bowed over her needlework, she was sitting among her ladies-in-waiting, a pearl surrounded by dull pebbles. It was the first time Bowen saw her, and the last time he knew the peace of mind that comes with the carefree lightness of an unbound heart.

36

Appointed weapons master by the king of Dunmark at twenty-five, Bowen was young for the job, though he'd already been awarded the surname Threehands, folks saying that a man had to have more than two hands to fight like Bowen did. Young he was, but then so was King Seorus, barely a year on the throne. A friendship of sorts connected them since first they met – of sorts, because friendship with a man of such power as the King of Dunmark wielded went only so far, and then birth and breeding kicked in to raise a clear and insurmountable barrier, one that no amount of goodwill and commitment could remove. All the same, there was sympathy, and trust, and oftentimes an easiness to their converse that made Bowen more enemies than friends at court.

And then there was Helise.

She was Seorus' queen, and Bowen loved her from the fateful moment he set eyes on her. That was his quandary in a nutshell, though he often felt as if all of Kingskeep wasn't large enough to accommodate the silent inner agony that marked his days, beginning with that first sight he'd caught of her in the royal castle's great hall.

What made it so much worse was that Seorus was an unchecked philanderer, his frequent, poorly disguised affairs no secret to anyone. And Helise felt for Bowen as well. The bittersweet, torturous shocks that passed between them whenever their eyes met by chance left no doubt at all that, had the circumstances been different, theirs might have been a union in a million.

As it was, they were both bound by honor and duty, and the odd, accidental collision of glances was as far as things ever went between them.

And so for twenty years Bowen lived with a constant, two-fold sense of inadequacy and defeat: to his king he was a friend with a guilty secret, and to Helise a lover who might as well have existed a thousand leagues or centuries removed, for all the hope there was of ever seeing their love fulfilled. Truth be told, thinking of her still hurt something fierce. But, difficult as all that was, he'd suffered his most bitter defeat at the hands of another person – bitter in that it was so unexpected, and yet so inevitable.

It was this last defeat that had seen him banished from Kingskeep. But it had also brought him here, to Bailon Keep, and with it had come a second chance.

'Sorry I'm late.' Bryn plumped down in his place, then got right up again. Grabbing both their bowls, he carried them over to the hearth and filled them with stew from the pot.

Bowen came out of his reverie with a mild start. Dammit, he'd been woolgathering again. But the stew smelled only slightly burnt. Not too bad, then.

'Em finished littering half an hour ago, and I wanted to make sure all the piglets are suckling properly. Ten, can you imagine?' Bryn set the bowls on the table and sat down again. He'd taken the time to wash his hands and face in the trough outside, Bowen noted. And he'd combed back his unruly locks with wet fingers, his idea of neatening up for supper. There were still bits of hay in his hair, though, and he'd missed a wide streak of dirt on his neck.

'Hurn can't get along without you?' Bowen said.

'No – I mean yes, he can,' Bryn said defensively.

'Good. Because farming is *his* job. And yours is studying. Unless next All Gods Gathering you aim to impress Meris Conlin with your profound knowledge of suckling pigs, that is.'

'I don't care what Meris Conlin thinks of me,' Bryn mumbled, his reddening ears saying different.

'As you say. But, like it or not, you're a lord. And the Bailons have a long tradition of being educated men. Men whom their king could always rely on when he called them into service.'

'To go to war for him, yes. How is reciting sonnets supposed to help in a battle?'

The lad was getting worked up over nothing.

He loved to learn, actually – just not the things he was supposed to. Give him a treatise on medicinal plants or animal husbandry and he'd devour it as if it were a plate of sweetmeats. Ask him to read up on battle tactics or siege engines and he'd likely fall asleep on page one.

'You'd be surprised,' Bowen said mildly. 'Poetry and strategy have a lot in common, as do dancing and swordcraft.'

'Or courtship and laying a siege,' he added with a twinkle.

'I hope Nan gets back soon,' Bryn said, abruptly changing the subject.

'Aye,' Bowen said. 'So do I. With Nan in the kitchen, maybe I can get you off pigs and back to the stuff you really need to know.'

'Pigs are important too,' Bryn insisted. 'And it's not every day a sow casts ten piglets.'

'Looks like we're all set for pork, then,' Bowen said drily, noting how Bryn's enthusiasm visibly faded at his words. The lad tended to get a little too attached to animals. The way he looked after them would have done any farmer proud, but when it came to butchering it was always Hurn who wielded the knife.

'Actually, we'd be better off eating less meat,' Bryn said. 'It sours the blood.'

'Been reading again, have we?' Bowen asked.

'Solenon the Great,' Bryn said. 'The emperor Antherion's physician. And Antherion lived almost to a hundred and eighty, so maybe Solenon had it aright. It's something worth thinking on, at least.'

'Right,' Bowen snorted. 'A hundred and eighty. You do realize people can say anything they damned well please in books, whether there's a shred of truth to it or not. Now *that's* something worth thinking on.'

'I had the weirdest dream last night,' Bryn said, apropos of nothing. 'Only I can't remember what it was about, except it was strange, and scary, and it felt like I'd dreamed it before. It was as if someone was trying to tell me something important but I couldn't hear what they were saying.'

The lad looked troubled of a sudden, the light in his eyes dimmed by whatever cloud was passing through his mind.

He's so bloody young and innocent. His face is an open book, a faithful mirror of what goes on inside him. An endearing, an admirable trait, if it weren't so bloody dangerous. Gods give he never has to play the Game of Secrets against powerful men.

'Books, dreams, pigs,' Bowen said with as much briskness as he could muster, pushing back his chair. 'You ask me, it's high time you got some exercise and cleared your head. I can think of several of your forms that still need some serious work. So I'll be expecting you in the courtyard after you're done washing up.'

Soon I'll have to tell him, Bowen thought as he went to fetch a pair of weighted practice swords from the armory. *His eighteenth nameday is coming up, and I promised her I'd tell him then. Gods know I fear that day. But a promise is a promise, and I won't shirk my duty, be it to the living or the dead. She and Bailon took me in when I was exiled and homeless, and for that alone I owe them more than I can ever repay. So I'll do what I have to, and hope I've trained the lad well enough so he can swallow a dose of bitter truth without completely losing his footing over it.*

*   *   *

4

For being the smallest of Kingskeep Castle's council chambers, the place was still too damned big. And bloody cold, at least this end. Standing in his usual place by the door, Macsen Redbreast, First Sergeant of the king's personal guard, caught none of the warmth from the huge fire roaring in the great hearth and all of the icy draft whistling through the cracks, drawn in by the hungry flames.

The end of September, and already cold as witches' tits. Frost on the ground this morning, and a smell of snow in the air. Times were, I'd have gone for a swim in the river in weather like this. Not anymore. I'm getting too old for this. No, I am too old for this. I should have retired years ago. Should be sitting at home nursing my aching joints in front of a fire of my own. But, whatever his reasons, the king demands my presence, so present I am.

And so he stood, wishing for a spear to hold on to like the men standing watch outside the door had. Although, knowing himself, he'd probably refuse to lean on it anyway, endure the pain in his back and knees rather than give anyone the satisfaction of seeing him weak. Oftentimes, come the end of his shift he was too stiff and sore to sit down and eat, just glad if he made it to his bed without something or other seizing up on the way there.

As punishment went – if that was what this was about – there was worse. Much worse, as scores, nay, hundreds of men who'd stepped wrong with the king could have borne witness to, had they still been around to do so. A few women, too, come to think of it – possibly even Macsen's own daughter Megin among them, though he'd likely never know for sure.

Eight years, and he still hadn't figured out whether he was a man condemned or a man redeemed, or perhaps just too bloody unimportant for anyone to bother either way.

Watching the king rise from his chair and stand close to the fire, the massive, barrel-chested figure with the overlarge head and the comparatively short legs a stark silhouette against the flames, Macsen thought once again how near impossible to read the man was, always had been, a mystery to all those around him practically from the cradle.

Dour, utterly without humor, often brusque to the point of being carelessly and sometimes brutally insulting, Edric Avellin kept his secrets close to the heart and his enemies closer still. For certain there weren't any friends or lovers to occupy the position, not that Macsen had ever seen. Not since the queen had died in childbirth, and he doubted Edric had ever seen more in her than a means to an end, a convenient alliance, a womb of sufficient pedigree to plant his seed in.

There was a daughter, Wilda, a pale, fey creature seldom seen outside her rooms. Rumor had it she wasn't quite right in the head. Moonstruck, or some such thing. If Edric felt anything for her, he

44

certainly didn't show it, completely ignored her on the rare occasions when she chose to make an appearance, sitting silently at table or hovering wraithlike in some shadowed corner of the great hall for a spell, watching the comings and goings with impossibly large, dark-liquid eyes that tended to remind Macsen of a deer cornered by a pack of baying hounds.

Inscrutable as Edric was, the man sitting to the right of his now empty chair made the king look like a leaky sieve – though at first sight Corwin Gale appeared to be Edric's exact opposite. Sandy-haired, large-girthed and jolly, the Lord Treasurer had the winning air of a benign uncle, the sort who was never at a loss for a well-timed jest with the lads, a gracious compliment for the ladies, even an occasional kind word for the help.

And the uncanny thing was, not even the eyes gave him away. He was that good. Or that bad, however you wanted to look at it.

Still, it was a very long time since Macsen had let himself be fooled by the man. Since then, he'd had ample occasion to study the Lord Treasurer, and what he'd seen and heard all boiled down to the one certainty: in all these years, the only thing he'd learned about Gale was that the face he presented to the world had nothing at all to do with the real man. With him, you definitely didn't get what you saw. Nor did you see what you got. Didn't see it coming until it hit you, most often square in the back.

Other than that, Corwin Gale remained a riddle – except to his many enemies, all of them undeclared, who called him The Snake behind his back and held him responsible by default for every atrocity committed in Dunmark, the Seven Kingdoms, and beyond. No doubt Corwin knew who every single one of them was, seeing as his other job, the one very few people, if anyone outside this room, knew about, was overseeing Dunmark's network of spies, a good part of whom Macsen suspected did their dirtier work in Dunmark itself. Enemies close, and so on.

Gale, sitting with his back to the fire and probably close to well done by now, got up to stand beside the king, stretching his hands out to the flames.

A coldblooded pair, forsooth, the king and his spymaster. The Lizard and The Snake.

Not a heartbeat later, fat, beetle-browed Algar Stonebridge, occupying the chair across from Gale's, rose to join them. As if he might miss something important from four feet away.

A different kettle of fish, this one.

Pompous, garrulous, mean-spirited to a fault, the Duke of Dalborn was said to never forget a slight, and to always pay his detractors back in kind and with double and three-fold interest. Stonebridge had his place at the table by dint of heading up the faction of nobles most supportive of the king, though Macsen was sure their backing went only so far as it suited their own interests, and not a midge's fart beyond.

Which left the fourth member of the party sitting alone at the table, looking a bit the odd man out, like the one with the disfiguring disease the others feared might be contagious. And in fact most men tended to give Albin Pryce a very wide berth.

Born a commoner, he'd started his career as a henchman and done his bloody work with such admirable efficiency that he'd caught the king's notice – inevitably, one might say, seeing as Edric with his by and large bloody approach to keeping the peace had an ongoing need for such men. Which was perhaps why he'd created a new office for Pryce, made him Dunmark's first Lord Executioner and raised him to noble status. Pryce was also responsible for founding the Dunmarkan chapter of the Headhunters' Guild, modeled after the Orrian example but with a marked tendency to bring the wanted in dead rather than alive, if at all. Rumor had it that he was behind the disappearance of scores of so-called 'enemies of the realm'. True or not, the man carried the scent of death on him like a rank perfume, a disquieting whiff of sudden terror, of smothered screams and unmarked graves.

'The north,' Stonebridge said, starting to sidle up to the king like he was wont to do with those he deemed worthy of his attention, but prudently changing his mind. Edric hated it when people came close. And Stonebridge wasn't even talking to the king, had his beady little pig's eyes fixed instead on Gale, his eternal rival for the Edric's attention in an endless string of skirmishes he most often lost.

'I've heard quite a few of those ugly smearings have been showing up there lately. You know, those broom things. And reportedly Garamon was seen, once in Whitelake and once in Redfern.'

That made Macsen listen up smartly. The broom-graffiti were the mark of a secret society who called themselves the Sweepers, allegedly made up of a growing number of people fed up with being taxed out of house and home to no reasonable end they could see. Commoners, mostly, but, if rumor had it right, impoverished and embittered members of the lesser nobility had begun to join their ranks as well. Their declared goal, announced in boldly painted symbols and in handbills secretly circulated, was to sweep out the kingdom with an iron broom – hence the name – and rid it of every last corrupt, self-serving official living the good life at the expense of the poor and the powerless.

The part about the infamous Garamon showing up was probably nonsense, though. If even half the sightings of the Sweepers' elusive, shadowy leader reported from all over the kingdom were true, the man had to possess several miraculous capabilities: traveling faster than thought, being in several different places at once, and changing his appearance more often in a day than a chameleon did in a lifetime.

Silently cursing age and the frailty of human flesh, Macsen eased some of the weight off his bad knee. Worse knee, actually. The other one wasn't in much better shape. Predictably, after a few minutes his back began to cramp, as if to remind him there was no escape: not from the pain, not from the past, and not from a duty that was beginning to look more and more like time served in prison.

Garamon. In Macsen's opinion the man was a myth created by the Sweepers, not a person of flesh and blood. The Sweepers were also the people Megin and her husband Alfred had gotten mixed up with. Macsen suspected it was the reason the two of them had ended up missing, likely dumped in the bogs south of the river. Anything went in there never saw the light of day again. If the place by some miracle ever dried out and somebody decided to dig there, they'd probably find bodies stacked ten or more deep under the surface, the

48

way Gale's and Pryce's people had been going these past fifteen years.

And, to cap it all off, last year Rhea, the granddaughter he'd so conscientiously raised since she was ten, had decided to join the Headhunters, of all bloody things, stubbornly ignoring his advice as well as his pleas, not to mention his abortive attempt to simply forbid her. Hardly saw the girl anymore. Missed her something fierce. Though to be honest, she did come by whenever she could. Just wasn't that often.

So yes, Macsen was listening.

And clamping down hard on all the old sorrow and bitterness that suddenly burned like acid at the back of his throat.

His eyesight might have known better days, but his hearing was still fine. Excellent, actually. Good enough to make out what was being said nearly ten yards away even with voices kept low and the fire roaring and crackling. Not for the first time, though, he wondered why Edric insisted on having him in the room instead of outside like the others. Especially when, as now, matters of a sensitive nature were being discussed.

Does he trust me that much, even after the business with Megin? Could it be that he had nothing to do with her death? Or did he have everything to do with it, and this is some sort of ongoing test of my loyalty? Could he still be waiting to see whether I'll betray his secrets, eight years later? Ah, for the love of the gods, there's far too many of those being hoarded in this place.

Too many truths unspoken. Too many questions unanswered. Too many things hidden away in the dark and left to fester there until they turn so damned poisonous nobody dares touch them anymore.

'Have you now?' Gale said lightly, as if Stonebridge were discussing the weather. 'Wherever did you get that from, I wonder?'

'I have my ways,' the duke said importantly, trying to match Gale's easy tone and poise but failing miserably on both counts. 'Little birds, and such.'

'Is it true?' the king asked Gale, speaking over Stonebridge's head as if the fat man were merely a forward child butting in on an adult conversation.

'As a matter of fact, apart from that rubbish about Garamon, it is,' Gale said. 'I've been getting reports of late that seem to point to a certain... resurgence, you might say, of the bothersome fools. It would appear they've found friends in Ardath. Some of them have reportedly been seen frequenting the halls of Castle Cullamor. Seems Aeron himself is, if not helping them outright, at least not going out of his way to put a spoke in their wheels.'

'Why, that's good of him,' Edric said with not a hint of humor, 'handing me a reason to go pay him a visit and muck out that pigsty he calls a kingdom.'

'Ah,' Gale sighed. 'A lovely idea. But alas, we have no proof. Rumors and hearsay, all of it. The facts, on the other hand, are all on our side of the border. A tax collector attacked and robbed in Longwood. A bailiff in Whitelake tarred and feathered. The market in Far Greening twice disrupted by bands of masked ruffians. Two tollmen thrown from the Colver bridge in Dalborn. Every incident a loss to the royal coffers.'

Macsen saw Stonebridge give a start at the mention of his own duchy. Not so well informed after all, the Duke of Dalborn.

'The Sweepers may be a misguided bunch of fools,' Gale went on, giving the ghost of a smirk at Stonebridge's discomfiture, 'but word on the street is, the general mood is beginning to swing their way. Meaning, things are getting to a point where we can hardly afford to ignore them any longer. What we need is something tangible, something we can use to pressure Aeron with. Put his dick in a vise, so to speak.'

'*Royal* dick, that would be,' Pryce offered around a nail chewed to the quick, the firelight making a landscape of shadowed craters of his pock-marked face. 'And talk's not going to get you anywhere with Aeron.'

Once again, Macsen marveled at the man's ability to slouch in his chair and drawl as if he were about to fall asleep from sheer boredom while at the same time giving the impression of something coiled and deadly, ready to strike at a moment's notice.

'I'm not thinking talk,' Edric said, his dark, heavy brows and down-turned mouth set in a habitual frown. 'What I'm thinking is, we burn a few villages along our side of the border, make it look like the Sweepers did it with Aeron's help. And there we have our proof.'

'Why, that's brilliant,' Gale said, beaming like a proud uncle. As if he hadn't been leading up to something like this all along. 'What better way to cure the common folk of the Sweepers' mad ideas than burn a few of their compatriots? The perfect distraction.'

'I agree, your majesty. Absolutely... brilliant.' Stonebridge's fawning smile looked about as genuine as a lead gilder.

'We'll do more than that,' Edric said, 'seeing as there's nothing like a bit of mayhem and bloodshed to distract the commons. But first things first. Gale, Pryce, have your men light a few fires up in the North. They should make sure the blame falls squarely on the Sweepers and on Aeron. Meaning, leave no survivors to tell a different story. Are we clear?'

'Absolutely, your majesty.' Gale was rubbing his hands, and not for lack of warmth.

'Tondern won't be happy at all,' Stonebridge said, looking quite happy himself. He hated the Duke of Redfern, who by Macsen's reckoning was as straight a man as Stonebridge was crooked. 'It's his villages we're talking about.'

'Good,' Edric said. 'A fine incentive, then. Burning them, we'll light a fire under his grace's arse as well. I damn well want him ready to do his part when we move against Ardath.'

Please gods, not another war, Macsen thought as he made his way to the kitchens after the meeting had broken up and Edric had dismissed him with a curt nod. He wasn't hungry, but after what he'd heard today he needed a drink. Or three.

Since Edric took the throne, I've seen enough battles to last me a dozen lifetimes, and none of them even close to a cause worth fighting for. I should have quit when the old king died, that's what I should have done. Now there was a man it was a pride and an honor to serve. Not like his son at all, King Seorus was. A man of peace, a man of patience and of reason. Only took up the sword when all else failed, and then it was clean, honest fighting, no sneaking around in the dark, no backstabbing, no underhanded maneuvering. Oh, to fight beside men like him and Threehands again!

But what am I thinking. Times past. Past, gone and buried. These days, I call it a victory if I get through a shift without falling on my face. Be that as it may, Edric's king now, and he'll do as he sees fit – though I can see no good coming of this. No good at all.

*　　*　　*

5

No matter whether one approached Kingskeep from the south, the west, or the north, the capital of Dunmark was ever a breathtaking sight. The Godswall, a high, miles-long cliff of light grey limestone, made for a dramatic backdrop to the neat rows of whitewashed houses ringed by the town's massive fortifications, dark, defiant walls bearing the marks of many a failed siege. The town was built on a gently sloping hill at the foot of a spur jutting out midway along the Godswall and descending in three great tiers, fittingly called The Steps, with Kingskeep Castle sprawled on top of the lowest: a thousand years' worth of extensions and annexes, gatehouses, battlements, towers, turrets and curtain walls spread out like the trailing robes of a weighty but somewhat disheveled dowager queen impressing authority on her subjects by dint of sheer mass rather than beauty or splendor.

From the castle's eastern gate, a cobbled road snaked along a narrow ridge to the base of the second Step. From there it wound up a steep cliff in a series of dizzying switchbacks, sometimes clinging to the sheer face seemingly by imagination and willpower alone, sometimes disappearing into galleries hewn from the rock for a stretch, until it reached a massive, fortified watchtower that commanded a spectacular view from the second Step's rocky summit.

But the road didn't end there. Crossing a bridge that spanned a deep chasm separating the second and third Steps in one elegant, heart-stopping leap, it wound its way up to a grim, grey-walled fortress perched on the Godswall's rim like an armored giant turned to stone: High Keep, Dunmark's last refuge in desperate times.

Any other time, Laurin would have enjoyed the impressive scenery, but today he took little note of it, hardly registering the guards' curious stares as he passed through the gate into Kingskeep Town.

The journey down from the Caerrocks had given him ample time to ponder his immediate future, enough time to become increasingly worried that resigning from the Guild might not prove all that easy after all – twenty years or no, promises or no. Enough time to remember a few hints he'd picked up here and there over the years, nothing more than vague intimations and unspoken undertones, stuff read between the lines rather than actually heard but disquieting nonetheless. Not to mention the longish lump of rust tucked away in Dag's left pannier, out of sight but nowise out of mind. It had begun to weigh heavier and heavier on him, so much so, he'd actually found himself checking Dag's gait from time to time, fearing the sword might prove too cumbersome a burden for the faithful animal.

Heavy or not, there was no helping what had to be done. Laurin's mind was made up. He'd see this through, one way or another. Get his business with the Guild over with, try and deliver the damned sword, and then find himself a nice, quiet spot and not stir from it for at least the next twenty years.

Before tackling the trek up the hill, he stopped at a stall just inside the gate, to buy an apple for Dag as much as for a moment to gather his courage and wits.

'Master Semson! Returned safe and sound, I see.'

Guildmaster Firth beamed at Laurin, his three chins aquiver with goodwill. 'Already been to see Master Cadoc, I hear. Said you brought him some very fine samples. Very happy, he was. Thrilled, I daresay. Not that a one of us here would have expected any less of you. Well then, to what do I owe the pleasure of your visit to these humble quarters?'

'Humble quarters' was about as bald-faced an understatement as you could make, short of calling the royal castle a tumbledown shack. The building housing the Guild's Kingskeep branch was one of the finest in town. High up the hill, it stood cheek by jowl with the residences of the rich and the noble, some of them only a small step down from palatial. Firth's office could have graced any of them, marble floors, high windows, precious wall hangings and all. The guildmaster's ornately inlaid desk could have easily accommodated a dozen scribes instead of the one pale, watery-eyed clerk scratching away at a desk of his own, a fraction in size and piled high with stacks of ledgers and parchments.

'To come right to the point,' Laurin said, hoping his voice didn't betray how very nervous he was, 'my twenty are up. I've decided to take them and retire. Quit while I'm still ahead of the game. It's not a job to grow old in, as I'm sure you're aware. Time for me to think of the future.'

There was an uncomfortable pause, the guildmaster's smile growing strained and then disappearing altogether, his chins sagging in dismay.

'Well, now. I must say this comes as quite a surprise. Bit of a blow, actually, should you really decide to go through with it. You're our best man in the field, Master Semson, an asset the Guild can ill afford to lose.'

Suddenly his mien brightened. 'But I'm sure we can find a solution to this... little problem. Reach an agreement between friends. I'd be more than happy to raise your pay, if that's where the shoe pinches. And, what the dickens! Let's not stint on a good thing. What say we double it? And a month off to go visit your family. Make it two, if you like. We live only once, eh? How does that sound?'

'I'm sorry, Master Firth.' Laurin was sticking with his decision, though right this moment he was feeling like an ungrateful son, dangerously close to a traitor. But the Guild's cause had never really been his, only a job to be done as well as he could. And the money didn't interest him. He had enough tucked away to get by, providing Firth didn't find some excuse to hold it back. Another disquieting thought, that.

Still he forged on. 'I've given the Guild twenty years, done the job best I knew how, and never regretted a day. But a deal's a deal, and my mind's made up.'

The guildmaster's jowls sagged, his face folding into an expression of sorrow that reminded Laurin of a dog he'd once seen somewhere or other, a sway-backed, bowlegged creature with sad, floppy ears and a look of long-suffering resignation with the world's incorrigible follies.

'And you're sure there's nothing can make you reconsider? It's a hard world out there, you know, without the Guild at your back and a steady income to rely on. Not to pry, but what will you do with yourself? You do realize you're forbidden by contract to do anything similar to the work you've done for the Guild? How great do you reckon the chances are of a man of your size and skills finding gainful employment out there?' Firth waved an arm at the windows, as if everything that lay beyond them was dangerous, unforgiving terrain, the world out there just waiting for a defenseless dwarf to stumble from the Guild's protective arms, an enemy poised to bowl him over and plow him under.

'Even so, I guess I'll take my chances,' Laurin said, struggling for equanimity. He was beginning to feel a mite put off by Firth's insistence. 'And then there's another matter still. My savings. I'd like to – '

'Why certainly.' To Laurin's relief, Firth's mien lightened. He reckoned the guildmaster had come around to accepting the inevitable and was now decided to see the rest of their dealings through in good grace. 'Though I'd suggest you take only a modest sum in coin. For the rest, I'll be happy to issue a letter of credit, valid anywhere in the Empire and the Seven Kingdoms. I'll have it made out in your name and add an accurate description of your person, that way you'll not risk losing everything should you encounter… a misfortune.'

A valid point. The roads in Dunmark were relatively safe, but the sparsely inhabited border regions were another matter. And it didn't necessarily take a deserted forest track to see you robbed – a skilful cutpurse in a tavern or a thief in a dark alley would do the job just as nicely.

'Provided you're not in too much of a hurry, that is,' Firth went on, producing a fat purse from a desk drawer. 'I'll need a day or two to go over the books and have the pursuant documents prepared.'

'That's all right,' Laurin said. 'No hurry at all.'

'Good. Well, not good, actually. I must say I deeply regret losing you. But the decision is yours, and I can't but respect it. Well, then. I trust I'll be seeing you day after tomorrow. And best of luck for the future and whatever you decide to do with it.'

*   *   *

Once Laurin had left, Firth remained sitting at his desk, his brow furrowed, contemplating decisions of his own he'd rather not have been faced with. Very unpleasant, this whole business with Semson. Thank all the gods this sort of thing didn't happen more often. It was a part of his job he intensely disliked. But there was no helping it. Policy was quite clear on the subject. The Guild's secrets had to stay with the Guild – no ifs, no buts.

With anyone other than a Waylen he might have tried the stick after the carrot had failed. But the seekers were a tough, self-sufficient, resourceful lot, and not easily cowed. Had to be, to do the job they did. Threaten a Waylen or his family, and you'd most likely end up with an implacable enemy, and unfortunately one who knew exactly where your weakest spot was. Push a Waylen, and nine times out of ten you'd be shooting yourself in the foot. Experience had shown as much, and policy reflected bitter lessons learned. *Step one having failed,* it said, *skip step two and go right on to three.*

I am not to blame for this, rules being what they are, Firth thought as he reached for a scrap of parchment. *Which doesn't mean I like it, not one little bit.*

Heaving a great sigh, he dipped his pen and reluctantly dashed off a note to the entity he employed in such matters, distasteful as he found that particular setup. Would that there was another solution to the problem. Would that there was a way to erase the knowledge the dwarf carried in his head. But there wasn't, and he couldn't be allowed to simply depart with it.

A pity. Firth actually quite liked the little fellow.

*   *   *

Stepping out onto the street, Laurin found it had begun to drizzle, the late afternoon sky dark with clouds that promised worse to come. He didn't mind, feeling instead as if a great weight had been lifted from his shoulders – until he remembered the bloody sword.

Oh, to hell with it for now. One thing at a time.

Swinging his pack onto his shoulder, he went around the back to fetch Dag from the stables, then he set off to find affordable lodgings for the two of them. Gods only knew how he looked forward to a bath, a good meal, a mug or two, and a real bed for a change. Turning into the street, he saw Firth's secretary talking to the guards at the front door and gave him a wave. The man didn't respond, quickly averting his gaze as if he'd noticed neither Laurin nor the friendly gesture. Odd. But then, who knew what went on behind that pale brow and those watery eyes.

61

Laurin found a vacancy at a boarding house he'd used before, a room under the eaves, tiny and cramped if you were a big person but entirely sufficient for someone his size. The landlady was a shrew, but the prices were reasonable and the sheets weren't crawling with bugs. And they had stables for a few horses in back where Dag got to share a box with another guest's palfrey. After making sure that the two of them were getting along, Laurin decided to take himself to a bathhouse up the hill before seeking out a tavern where they made an excellent stew – or used to, anyways. It had been some years since he'd last been to Kingskeep, seeing as he usually steered clear of human habitations, avoiding inns and taverns wherever he could. *The less seen of a Waylen, the better,* the code went, and as a rule he'd stuck to it as closely as he could. A dwarf already tended to attract attention just by being what he was, attention that unfailingly led to questions he was neither prepared nor allowed to answer. To common folk, the Waylen were fabled creatures steeped in legend – which was how it should stay. It was the perfect disguise, after all. No one would ever think to abduct and interrogate a myth.

Coming out of the bathhouse clean and refreshed, Laurin saw the scribe standing a ways down the street, talking to a tall man in a dark, hooded cloak. He couldn't be sure in the failing light, but he thought he saw the clerk give a nod in his direction.

A bit late for acknowledging my wave from earlier on, Laurin thought, nodding back. *But better late than never. Strange fellow, though.*

The tavern was still where it used to be, the common room packed, the stew even better than he remembered. Thankfully, a trio of musicians was striking up one lively tune after another, people singing along or shaking a leg even though there was hardly enough room to stand, and Laurin went pretty much unnoticed in the merry crowd. Still, he allowed himself only a single mug of ale. Though strictly speaking he was no longer a Waylen, he remained bound to the oaths, and one mug was all he could afford, seeing as secrets and drink were ever a dangerous combination.

Sobriety soon turned out to be a blessing, for it was on his way back to the boarding house that trouble caught up with him.

He couldn't have said what exactly made him look around.

Not anything he heard, seeing as the rain had begun to fall in earnest now, the downpour drowning out even his own footfalls. When he turned his head, he saw a tall man in a dark, hooded cloak maybe fifty yards back, walking at an easy pace as if he just happened to be going the same way Laurin was. Which was already suspicious in itself, considering that everyone else left on the streets was in a hurry to get out of the downpour. Seeing the man, Laurin's mind immediately flashed back to Firth's scribe talking to a cloaked stranger in the street outside the boarding house, and suddenly things came together and appeared in an entirely different light: the whispered rumors of Waylen who had retired and thereafter never been seen or heard of again; Firth trying so hard to keep him from resigning, and then giving in all of a sudden; and, in hindsight, the normally tight-fisted guildmaster offering to double Laurin's pay seemed almost absurd. Now that he thought about it, he should have seen it for what it was: a clear sign of danger. Instead, fool that he was, he'd allowed himself to feel flattered by the high value the Guild apparently placed on him.

High enough to have him permanently removed, perhaps.

Another look behind told him the stranger was still there, still keeping his distance. For a moment he considered taking a more circuitous route, just to see whether the man was really following him, but quickly discarded the notion. Rain or no, there were still a few people about on the larger thoroughfares, whereas in the side streets and alleys it would likely be only him and the stranger. Turning off into unlit byways might well be an invitation to sudden and terminal violence.

His heart suddenly pounding so hard it felt like the whole of him was shaking along with it, he quickened his steps, pitifully short as they were compared to those of the man behind him, and hastened on to his quarters.

Back at the boarding house, he hurried up to his room, grabbed his pack and the sword, and then crept on to the far end of the corridor and the head of the back stairs as silently as he could. Crouching out of sight a few steps down, he peeped through the banisters, listening hard for anyone coming up after him.

For a while there was nothing.

Then he heard it: the slow creak of a tread, followed by a swish and the soft slap of wet cloth. A moment's silence. Another squeak. A guest climbing the stairs on the way to his room would perforce make a lot more noise. But not someone sneaking up step by careful step with mayhem on their mind.

He should have run then, but some stubborn part of him wanted to be certain. So he waited, hardly daring to breathe, hands sweating, pulse hammering in his ears.

Another creak, this one louder, and then a tall, cloaked figure turned into the corridor, the hood still up, the face cast in shadow.

Stopped outside Laurin's room.

Lifted the latch.

Run, you idiot! Laurin told himself, but remained rooted to the spot. With a loud clatter, the chair he'd placed just inside the door fell over.

'Master Darnby, is that you?' The landlady, shrill-voiced, coming up the stairs. 'How many times do I have to ask you to clean off your boots before you come in? You've tracked mud all over the stairs again.'

The stranger froze, then slipped into Laurin's room, leaving the door slightly ajar, no doubt watching the corridor through the crack.

Laurin rose. Placed a tentative foot on the next lower step. Carefully shifted his weight. And then the damned thing had to go and creak loud enough to wake the dead. A panicked glance backward showed him the door swinging open. Giving up any attempt at stealth, he clattered down the stairs, skidding through the turns, twice nearly going head over heels as he took the steps two and three at a time. Heavier, more measured footfalls followed not far behind.

Banging out through the back door, he nearly collided with someone on their way in. Whoever it was reached out a steadying hand, but Laurin was already past, running full tilt now, his mind racing through nonexistent options.

No time to apologize. Can't risk stopping to ask for help that might not be forthcoming. No time to fetch Dag. Off into the night, and hope it swallows me whole.

Moments later he was running for his life, the rain pouring down in buckets and turning the cobbles dangerously slick, his pack bouncing up and down and the sword he'd hastily shoved into it painfully digging into his back with every desperate step, the big person still on his heels and moving with an uncanny speed Laurin had no hope of matching, swift and inexorable as the dark water rushing down the gullies on either side of the street.

All of it happening exactly like in the dream he'd had. Only now it was for real.

So far, he was the only one actually running, his short legs pumping as fast as he could make them go. His pursuer kept up easily. Walking with long, unhurried strides, he allowed a gap to remain open between them, though never wide enough so his quarry could turn and slip off unseen into a doorway or an alley. A man who knew his business, and enjoyed it. A cat playing with a mouse, a hunter sure of his kill.

Laurin hated being the mouse, and he definitely wasn't ready to die. Terrified as he was, he also felt a knot of anger slowly tightening his chest. No way was he going to hold still for the axe, or dagger, or garrote, or whatever else his pursuer intended to use on him. Too bad the sword was useless – though even if it hadn't been, wielding it he'd have probably been more of a danger to himself than to anyone else.

With a shaking hand, he felt for the knife sheathed on his belt. Given the circumstances, it seemed pitifully small.

Rounding the next corner, he risked a backward glance to see how much of a lead he had left – which was why he didn't notice the oncoming traffic until he bowled full tilt into someone's legs and sent that person stumbling into more people coming up behind them. Rolling and skidding across the wet pavement, he heard angry shouts and saw a palanquin tilt over on its side in a welter of thrashing limbs, the bearers gone down in a heap, the litter's occupant spilled onto the cobbles. The guards accompanying the litter, three of them, were up in a trice, swords drawn, turning this way and that, looking for the man who'd attacked them. Amidst all the confusion, none of them seemed to notice Laurin, which was fine with him.

His pursuer on the other hand, likely having heard nothing of the scuffle over the driving rain, turned the corner and walked right into them. A fight broke out, blades flashing in the light of a guttering torch one of the men had dropped when he fell. Someone uttered a muffled cry. Someone else cursed. The litter's curtains caught fire.

Meanwhile, the hunter had managed to extricate himself from the fight. Laurin caught a glimpse of him retreating around the corner with two of the guards hard on his heels.

This is it. Perhaps my one and only chance to get rid of the blighter.

Sticking to the deeper shadows, he stole off. With no alternative route to choose from, he went in the direction he'd been headed anyway.

Once he was safe in the shadows beyond the circle of light cast by the burning litter, he looked back, just in time to see the two men who'd gone after his pursuer return. It seemed they'd given up the chase, but now they were shouting and pointing in his direction. The only words he caught sounded like 'two of them'. But then, it might

67

have been something else entirely. Impossible to tell with the rain coming down so loud you could hardly hear yourself think. In any case it was high time he disappeared. One thing he didn't need was more people hunting him.

Determined to shake off any and all pursuers, he turned left at the first crossing, and immediately right again into a dark alley, uttering a silent prayer that it wouldn't end in a blank wall. It didn't, and he forged ahead, alternately turning left and right and throwing in the odd, random double turn for the sake of confusion as he sought to put the greatest possible distance between himself and the man who was chasing him.

The *assassin* who was chasing him. He no longer doubted the nature of the beast he was dealing with.

He avoided streets except to cross them, sticking to back alleys and narrow passages, some of them so dark even his excellent night vision deserted him and he was forced to feel his way along the walls. Finally, when he reckoned he'd gone far enough, he started looking for a shelter to spend the rest of the night in. It didn't look like the rain was going to let up any time soon, and in any case there was no way out of the city until the gates opened in the morning. There was a good chance that was where they'd be watching for him, but that was tomorrow's problem. Right now he needed a hideyhole.

As luck would have it, he found an unlocked door at the bottom of a short flight of steps. Behind it lay a pitch-dark chamber. Testing the air, he decided the place felt empty. It also a smelled like it was rea- sonably dry. Closing the door behind him, he shuffled forward. After a few steps his shins met with an obstacle – not hard and bruising but rather something with a give. Reaching down, he felt a rough weave, like burlap, and caught a whiff of turnips.

Sacking. A whole pile of it. Then his hand found material that was softer still. Wool, by the feel of it – an old horse blanket perhaps. Slipping off his pack and sodden cloak, he lowered himself onto the pile of sacks and reached for the blanket.

His searching hand came to rest on fabric – but not on wool.

Instead, it felt smooth, like finely woven cloth. And underneath it was something warm. Alive. Soft and rounded, and somehow... thrilling.

Snatching his hand back as if he'd touched a hot stove, he heard a hissing intake of breath and a quick rustle of cloth.

A tiny draught of air brushing his face was the only warning he got before something hard and heavy came rushing out of the dark and crashed into his head. Briefly, his vision was lit up with whirling lights. Then the lights winked out, and the world went on without him.

*   *   *

6

The storm was over, the child delivered.

Wanderer, shaman and by far the oldest living member of the Snow People, carefully wrapped the sacred Four Winds Drum in soft caribou hide before sliding it back into its sealskin pouch, a slight trembling of his age-gnarled hands the only outward sign of the bone-deep fatigue that made his breath come up short and his heart wobble around in his chest like a ladleful of whale blubber. But his face remained impassive, a landscape too deeply rutted and criss-crossed by the hard northern weather and a lifetime's worth of emotions for anything more to find room there. These days, he relied on his eyes to speak what he felt, and seemed to have no trouble making himself understood.

A long storm, and a difficult birth, but now daylight fell through the entrance of the snow house for the first time in fifteen days as his grandson Raven and Raven's son Strongest-of-All finished digging through the snowdrift piled up outside. Feather, his granddaughter-in-law, sat cradling the head of Younger Sister, Strongest-of-All's wife, who lay exhausted but happy in a heap of pelts with the newest member of their small band suckling on her breast. Rainbow, the little one was called, after her great-great-grandmother, Wanderer's wife, passed away sixteen winters ago at a venerable age.

Wanderer had been prepared to join her for a long time now, but death steadfastly continued to ignore him. He could only wonder at what the gods might be thinking, letting him live so far past a man's normal span of days. Could be they were saving him up for something, unlikely as that seemed. Or maybe they'd just plain forgotten him. Either way, the ancestor spirits refused to speak on the matter.

As for the child, Wanderer had gently insisted she be named right away rather than in a few days' time, arguing they'd be weeks on the move before they reached the rest of the clan at the winter hunting grounds, so they might as well get it done now. His real reason for pushing the issue he kept to himself. The trip south was long and dangerous enough without having everybody scared and on edge.

Already weeks before the storm, Wanderer had gotten a very bad feeling, a creeping sense that something dark and menacing was afoot in the north. He'd tried asking the ancestor spirits about it, but all they said was *make haste, make haste,* and otherwise seemed to cringe away from the subject as if it filled them with a nameless terror. Which was neither reassuring nor helpful, seeing as traveling in such a mother of a storm with Younger Sister so close to giving birth was out of the question.

They'd had no choice but to dig in and wait it out, and all the while Wanderer's feeling of foreboding had slowly crept from bad to worse.

The Four Winds Drum was an object of great power, and neither a bad storm nor a difficult birthing was reason enough to sound it, but some deep inner certitude had made him bring it out all the same – little as he knew what the nature of the beast was, or what shape it might choose to show itself in.

Once the dogs were fed and Wanderer, Younger Sister and her child had been bundled onto the sleighs, they set off. South, they went, ever south, until near mid-afternoon they took a sharp turn east, giving that stretch of the coast a five-mile berth before heading in a western direction and then south again. It made for a long detour, but with good reason. The place they so carefully skirted was cursed, taboo, painstakingly avoided by the Snow People for as long as their collective memory reached back into the shadowy past, and probably longer.

As they turned south again, their route coincided with a set of tracks coming straight out of the Forbidden. Human footprints, made by boots such as the southerners wore.

His old heart suddenly beating harder than could possibly be good for it, Wanderer reached for the Four Winds Drum, his hands shaking as he fumbled with the ties on the sealskin pouch.

'Stop,' he told Raven, Strongest-of-All pulling up behind. Wanderer climbed down and went to stand in front of the lead sleigh, the dogs suddenly cringing and yapping as if they'd caught a scent that scared them something fierce.

'Shush!' Strongest-of-All told them, to little avail.

'What is it?' Raven asked, looking around and seeing nothing.

Wanderer didn't answer, studied the terrain around them instead.

Pack ice to the right, a wild jumble of huge, piled-up floes, jutting and teetering every which way.

More ice on the left, a maze of huge blocks and narrow crevasses carved out by the wind, flanking a steep ridge.

Ahead, a passage no more than twenty paces wide. No way around.

They couldn't go back – though everything in him screamed to do just that. But they couldn't go forward either, not with what he sensed waiting there: something that made his blood run cold even as his heart threatened to climb up his throat. Something beyond terrifying.

Then it stepped out from behind a tall serac, and it was too late to do anything but pray and sound the drum.

A southerner, wearing a sailor's oilskins.

At first sight he looked like an ordinary man, if not a very pleasant one: long, greasy hair, coarse features, furtive stance. A shifty expression that came across as both stupid and cunning. Something about the eyes seemed off, though. Wanderer couldn't tell for sure, seeing as the man was squinting against the snow-glare, but he thought there was nothing but black in those eyes. This was no man, he realized. Not anymore. Useless the shaman who couldn't figure that much out.

'Get back,' Wanderer told Raven and Strongest-of-All, both of them come up to stand beside him, spears gripped in strong, competent hands. Not strong enough for this, though, not by a long ways.

'It's not what it seems,' he told them. 'Spears can do nothing against it. You can do nothing. Take the women and leave. Now.

Run for your lives. I'll hold it up for as long as I can. Go!'

Not waiting to see whether they did as he'd said, he took another step forward, holding the Four Winds Drum before him like a shield and beating out a slow, measured rhythm with his fingers.

The effect on the stranger was... interesting. As soon as the first low throb sounded, his whole face seemed to flatten out as if hit by a gale-force wind. Driving him a step backward. And another. His whole form rippling.

Then he rallied, stood fast, opened his mouth in a wide, horrible grin. Wanderer saw black, oozing liquid dripping from teeth and a squirming tongue rudimentarily formed out of the same black stuff. As if the man's skin contained neither flesh nor bones, was filled instead with nothing but black sludge.

Wanderer beat the drum harder, faster, and faster still, calling up all of its ancient magic.

The stranger's grin only widened.

Then he coughed, his throat convulsing. Hawked. And spat a gob of black goo at Wanderer that hit him on the shoulder with the force of a fist, spinning him halfway around.

Immediately, a cold tingling began to spread out from the spot, and Wanderer found to his horror that he couldn't move anymore. As the Four Winds Drum slipped from fingers gone completely numb, he felt the black stuff come knocking, prying at the cracks, looking for a way in. Terrified, he threw up everything he had against it, his eyes threatening to pop out of his head with the strain of it. He thought he might be able to hold it back for a while. Not forever, though.

Helplessly, he watched as the stranger raised a hand and with three quick movements threw gobs of black at Raven, Strongest-of-All, and Feather. Saw their faces go slack with shock, and then just slack, eyes dull and empty as if their minds had been smothered under six feet of snow. None of them had a shaman's resources. With nothing to set against the stuff, they were gone in the space of a heartbeat.

Going over to Strongest-of-All's sleigh, the stranger stood looking down on Younger Sister and Rainbow. Hawked up another gob and spit it in Younger Sister's face. Lifting Rainbow out of her mother's limp embrace by one tiny arm, he held her dangling for a moment, inspecting her. Apparently dissatisfied with what he saw, he dropped her onto the wind-packed snow. Useless. Discarded.

Seeing him handle the child, Wanderer felt a sudden rage take hold of him – and realized with a wrench of dismay that anger only opened the door for the stuff. Catching a first glimpse of its nature and purpose, he teetered on the brink of defeat, overwhelmed by a crushing, suffocating dread that seemed to suck everything worth living for out of the world.

With a tremendous effort, he stamped down on the anger, slamming down a second line of defense – for whatever good it would do him in the long run.

For now, though, he was going to fight. To the last breath. Better to die than become what the stuff was trying to turn him into, what it had already made of the man from the south, and of Raven, Strongest-of-All, Feather, and Younger Sister. He doubted there was any way to save them. But if there was, then he, Wanderer, was their only chance.

An open crevasse.

One set of tracks leading up to it, one leading away. The same man, walking in the same pair of boots, and yet there was a marked difference. What was left of the tracks coming in, preserved from the wind in the lee of a ridge, was what one would expect to find under the circumstances: a slightly wavering line of short, dragging footprints left by an exhausted man near the end of his endurance.

The ones going out were a different story, weaving all over the place for the first twenty yards or so, as if the man had stumbled on a cache of firewater and gotten falling-down drunk. But from that point out, his strides had suddenly turned purposeful. Long, as if he'd started to run. And then longer still, great, leaping bounds beyond anything an ordinary human body could be made to perform. The tracks told Anuun the devastating truth: he was too late. The Forbidden had already been breached, and whatever had been imprisoned there had finally broken out. This was terrible. A disaster of untold proportions. He didn't dare imagine the consequences. They might well turn out to be beyond horrific.

For a few, brief moments he hesitated, considering what he should do. Alerting his Iceling brethren to what had happened was one option. Getting help. But they were few and far apart, scattered over the vastness of the Ice Wastes like a handful of pebbles thrown from a very high mountain. By the time he reached even the nearest of them, the sailor could be anywhere, his trail lost forever in another storm.

Besides, he doubted there was much any of them, himself included, could accomplish against the man and whatever had come out of the ice with him, except stay on his trail and hope for some kind of miracle.

Thinking of miracles stirred a vague memory, something to do with... something... No. Some*one*. Gods, it had been so many centuries since he'd last thought of it. But there *was* someone who needed to be told if something like this ever happened, someone who could help. What was the name again? Grey something. Grey... Greytower! That was it.

Slowly, the attendant information began to unwind itself from a dusty corner in the back of his mind, and suddenly he remembered old Tikaani showing him a map with the name Greytower written along the lower edge in Iceling runes. A map that said where he could be found in case he was needed.

With an effort, Anuun brought up an image of the map before his mind's eye, his heart sinking when he saw how very far it was to the place. Eight hundred miles, as humans reckoned distances. And what was worse, hardly a fifth of the way there he'd be running out of ice. Meaning, he'd have to walk from there on. Meaning, he'd be no faster than any other being that walked the earth on two legs. But there was no helping it. His path was mapped out for him by recent events as much as by an old piece of parchment: track the sailor and his dread load, and try to reach Greytower. Gods give he wouldn't have to tear himself in two to do both.

When Anuun reached the site where the sailor had happened upon the Snow People, his heart dropped what felt like another ten feet. The two abandoned sleighs were the least of it. Both strings of dogs

78

had been brutally, senselessly slaughtered, the snow all around stained red, strewn with body parts and hanks of bloody fur and madly looped with ripped-out intestines.

He found what he was seeing hard to believe. Apart from family, nothing was closer to the Snow People's hearts than their dogs. The animals *were* family. The Snow would never, ever do this to them. His fault. All of it, his fault.

Suddenly there was a sound, a strange, gurgling cry coming from behind one of the overturned sleighs. Could one of the poor beasts still be alive?

Anuun's breath caught as he dragged aside a tangle of fur blankets fallen from the sleigh and saw what lay on the snow underneath. A child! A Snow child, and barely a few days old, as far as he could tell. Carefully, gently, he lifted it up, held it in the crook of his arm, looking down at it in wonder and dismay.

Wonder, because he'd never seen such a tiny little thing, and dismay because he realized that all of a sudden his mission had become infinitely more complicated.

What to do with it? He knew nothing about children, seeing as it had been centuries since a child had been born to the Icelings, and he knew less than nothing about human infants. What did they need? Warmth, he supposed, and food. Milk. A mother, ideally.

He'd have to find another band of Snow People willing to take the child in. But all of them would be far to the south by now, on the way to their winter camps or already there. Which wasn't his biggest problem. He was going south in any case. Only he was in a hurry, had to catch up with whatever horrors were ahead of him. Judging by those long, bounding footsteps he'd seen farther back, they'd be traveling at one hell of a pace. He was likely faster through the ice, but he couldn't take the child that way. It took Iceling magic for that, and even an Iceling child stayed overice for several years, which was how long it took to develop the skill in the first place.

And milk. He had to find milk for the little one. Where in all the gods' names was he supposed to find milk? Not to mention the fact that he absolutely didn't have the time for this.

'A fine, fine mess we've gotten ourselves into, Snowchild,' he told the little girl, who looked at him with grave, ageless eyes as if she perfectly understood the gravity of the situation. Anuun suddenly felt utterly overwhelmed by the sheer impossibility of getting so many disparate things lined up in a row.

Forget tearing himself in two. Half a dozen, was more like it.

*　　*　　*

7

Working the pell was one of Bryn's least favorite pastimes.

There was hardly anything more boring than hacking away at a thick, six-foot pole with a double-weight practice sword, sweating like a pig despite the unseasonable chill, muscles aching, arms getting heavier by the minute. No fun at all. Especially not with Bowen sitting there, seemingly half asleep but watching him with a sharp eye and sporadically giving instructions like, 'Mind your feet! Just because you're clobbering a piece of wood doesn't mean you should shuffle around like you're facing a girl at the dance.' Or, 'Stop fondling the damned thing and hit it, for mercy's sake! And you've got two arms, not just the one, in case you forgot. Blade, shield, pommel, shield, blade. There you go.'

So it felt close to a godsend when old Andras leaned over the gatehouse battlement and shouted down into the courtyard, 'Oy, down there! Couple of riders comin'. King's men, by the looks of 'em. Should I let 'em in?'

'I'll get it,' Bryn told him, walking over to the gate as Andras winched up the portcullis. The riders were still a few hundred yards away, but there could be no doubt they were Aeron's men, one of them carrying a pennant showing the Bear Rampant, Sable on Argent, the arms of House Terengil. Royal men-at-arms, and a hard-looking pair, as Bryn saw when they drew closer. Grim-faced, weathered and scarred, they looked like they'd seen their share of fighting and were used to coming out on top. Not the kind of men you'd want on the other side of a battle.

'You aimin' to clobber someone with that, boy?' the older of them said, reining in his mount and nodding at the blunt practice sword in Bryn's hand.

'Oh. No. Just been practicing.'

'Right, then. How 'bout you run and fetch yer lord for us. Tell him a message from the king, and sorry 'bout the niceties, but we ain't got time for 'em. So we'd be much obliged if he'd step out fer a moment.'

'You're talking to Lord Bailon,' Bowen said, coming to stand beside Bryn. 'So at least try and act like you had some manners, Dai Flatside, you old sinner. And you, Catch. It's been a while.'

'Threehands,' the soldier named Flatside said, while Catch merely nodded. 'Good to see you too. And beggin' your pardon, m'lord, but it ain't every day a lord comes answerin' his own door.'

'I'd a done it,' Andras shouted down from the walkway, '"cept his lordship beat me to it. Times were, younglin's used to show some respect for their elders.'

'Aye,' Flatside said. 'Times were, you was the cheekiest bastard o' the lot, Andras. How you been keepin'?'

'Good, good.' Andras gave a wide, mostly toothless grin. 'Still whup you young whippersnappers with both hands tied behind me back, needs be.'

'Afraid we'll have to leave that for another day, old man. King's business won't bear no delay.' Flatside turned to Bryn. 'Reason we're here, m'lord, there's lookin' to be war with Dunmark. Damned Sweepers burned a bunch o' villages down Redfern way, and now Edric's marchin' south, cryin' murder and blamin' Ardath for shelterin' the stupid buggers. So King Aeron's callin' his bannermen to arms. Muster's at Bentridge, a week from today. Bring what you can, Aeron says, and don't be late.'

'Right,' Bryn said. 'Bentridge. In a week. We'll be there.'

'Good, then.' Flatside gave a one-fisted salute, already bringing his horse around, Catch following suit. 'See you all at Bentridge.'

And off they went in a trail of dust, leaving Bryn dazed and still trying to come to grips with what had just happened. A part of him had always dreamed of this moment, of going to fight for king and country, of acquitting himself bravely and honor, of making a name for himself in the world beyond the Bailon lands. And then there was also the other part, the small, ugly, fearful one he usually did his best to ignore, the one that wanted to stay home, bar the gates and hope that whatever storm was brewing out there would give Bailon Keep a wide berth. Now, it refused to be silenced, and of a sudden he wasn't sure anymore where he stood between the two. Not sure at all.

'Best start thinking about who we're going to call in,' Bowen said, once Flatside and Catch were gone. He didn't look happy. 'At least harvesting's done. Nothing left the women can't take care of while the men are gone.'

He didn't say that some of the men might stay gone. Didn't have to. Bryn could see it in his face, was thinking the same thing. Sometimes, like now, he wished he hadn't been born to the responsibilities of a lord. But then, being the son of a farmer didn't save you from having to go to war and risk your neck for other men's causes either.

Bryn sent Hurn round to the farms and the village, and the next morning they held their own little muster in the keep's courtyard. Ten men answered the call. More than he'd expected, and twice as many as Bailon was required to field. Under Bowen's approving eye, he pared them down to four, choosing the ones he thought were most likely to hold their own in a fight – meaning the ones most likely to make it home in one piece: Daven the hunter, a wizard with the bow; Ham the butcher, who'd fought under Bryn's father and reportedly put the fear of the gods into the enemy; Hurn's eldest son Arlie, a woodsman by trade, who knew how to handle an axe and could double as scout; and Little Tom, Lorin the smith's chosen successor and soon-to-be son-in-law, a bull of a young man who Bryn reckoned would prove himself as good at bashing in helms as he was at making them. Most of the others were farmers, and Bryn could see how relieved they were at not having to go. Shamefaced as well. It wasn't the kind of thing sat well with a man.

Looking to Bowen – who prompted him with a slight raise of his chin as if to say, *Go on, you're not done yet* – he realized that he needed to give them something more than a bare-boned dismissal.

'I'm sorry to say we're low on armor and horses,' he said. 'And in all honesty, I'd rather have four men properly outfitted than put more of you at risk for the sake of numbers. And besides, who knows where Edric will end up? Someone needs to be here and look

84

out for the womenfolk and children, else the rest of us need not go at all. No use going out to fight if there's nothing left to come back to.'

It wasn't much, but enough all the same. Faces were saved, tasks assigned, shoulders squared.

Hurn was another story, reluctant to let Arlie go to war without him. 'Nan would kill me if I took her son and her husband,' Bryn told him, a notion Hurn could hardly argue with, though he did grumble that she was apt to do the same to him for not going along to watch out for their eldest.

And then there was Andras, all set and raring to go, even if the first thing he did at the gathering was settle down on a bale of straw and slip the boots off his badly swollen feet with a groan and a sigh. In Bryn's opinion, if the old man went to war he'd likely be using his sword to lean on rather than for cutting and stabbing, and he didn't see Andras doing much damage by clobbering his foes with sharp words and a buckler. But he wasn't about to hurt the old man's feelings by saying so.

'I need a seasoned man to look after the keep,' he told Andras instead, 'and you're it. Hurn will give you a hand if needed, but it's your experience that will keep everyone safe if there's trouble.' It left Andras looking mightily pleased, and got Bryn an appreciative nod from Bowen.

That was it. The day after, with everyone outfitted, they departed for Bentridge, though not without a stern admonishment from Nan that they had all better come back safe and sound. 'I helped bring more'n half o' you rascals into this life with my own two hands,' she said, fists on hips, 'and not so's to see you wastin' it on some stupid war. So be warned. Anyone comes home with a hole in his hide, I'll give him another one to even things out.'

Even Bowen ducked his head a fraction under the onslaught, though he did so with a smile. Then they were out through the gate and off to gods knew what awaited them, Andras shouting a last send-off from the gatehouse battlement. 'Give 'em somethin' they'll remember, lads! And don't forget to knock a couple o' heads for me!'

Judging by the way Bowen had gone all grim and silent, Bryn reckoned they were in for more than just knocking a few heads.

It was a long ride to Bentridge.

With the Bailon lands lying at the kingdom's far western edge, they couldn't afford to dawdle if they were to arrive in time for the king's muster. It meant five long days in the saddle, riding at a brisk pace from sunup to sundown. But it also gave Bryn five days to drill Bowen with all the many questions weighing on his mind, and no quarter given to the fact that the old man obviously wasn't in a talking mood. It was all of it simply too new and strange and exciting to keep quiet for long.

The farthest Bryn had ever been away from home was Cullamor, Ardath's capital, an easy two-day ride east of Bailon Keep. Once, when he was five or six, his parents had taken him along to see the king, though he didn't remember much of the trip beyond the huge, forbidding castle crouched above the city's houses like a giant watching over midgets, and scores of small lakes that dotted the surrounding countryside, reflecting the sky's deep blue like so many

86

twinkling eyes. The then king, Aeron's elder brother Arnold, was a big, black-bearded man with a booming laugh and eyes just like the lakes outside his castle, though to Bryn's disappointment he hadn't worn a crown, leaving Bryn with only his father's word to confirm that this was a proper king at all.

Bryn's father and Bowen had fought at Arnold's side in the War of Eight, a ten-year campaign in which the Seven Kingdoms for once put aside their constant bickering to unite with the city-state of Landing behind a common cause and win free of their imperial overlords after nearly three hundred years of occupation. The bards loved King Arnold, made song after song about the great warrior king who'd led his men into countless battles and never come out with more than a scratch, called him Arnold the Strong, Favorite of the Gods. But peacetime didn't seem to agree with him, or he with it, and instead of finally marrying and begetting an heir he went and got himself killed on a bear hunt not three weeks after the peace treaties had been signed and sealed, leaving the throne to his younger brother Aeron, of whom Bryn knew next to nothing.

'What's Aeron like?' he asked Bowen, riding knee to knee with the old man who seemed to be bent on ignoring him and everyone else. 'I mean, as a king, and all?'

'Way I remember,' Bowen said, 'he was always a quiet one. Devout follower of the old gods. Which is fine, as long as he doesn't believe he can rely on their help when it comes to battle. Otherwise, he's chary. Reclusive. Bookish.'

'Bookish isn't necessarily a bad thing,' Bryn flared out of old habit.

'Didn't say that, did I?' Bowen went silent again.

'And?' Bryn asked before he clammed up altogether.

'And nothing. He's an excellent administrator, from what I hear. Good at making plans and seeing them through. Whether that makes him any good at fighting a war remains to be seen. Like as not, we won't know until we're in the thick of it. That's where even the most carefully laid plans tend to fall apart. And it's where a man will show whether he's got what it takes, or not.'

'What if he doesn't? Have what it takes?'

'Then we can only hope he has the sense to listen to those who do.'

'Like who?'

'Well, there's Lyr Longshanks, captain of the Guard, learned the trade from Arnold himself. Eilian Strong, the Duke of Greld is another, though he's getting on in years and might not even be there. If not, his son Iefan will. A good man, levelheaded as they come. And in my experience it always pays to listen to the sergeants. Men like Flatside can often tell you more about how the war is going at any given time than a command tent bursting at the seams with generals.'

'What about you?' Bryn asked.

'We'll see,' Bowen said. 'We'll see. Should I have anything worth saying, I'll make sure they hear about it. Whether they listen or not is another thing.'

'I hope they do. They should. I bet you know more than all of them put together.'

'Lad,' Bowen sighed, 'I'm flattered by your trust. But if there's one thing I've learned in the Bloody Business, then it's this: when it comes down to the nitty-gritty, nobody knows anything. Except maybe what the men to the left and right of you are doing. A general with a good view from a hilltop might have a notion of what's going on, but nine times out of ten what commands he sends down the line will come way too late and probably do more harm than good.

'Best you can do beforehand is try and imagine all the things that might go awry, and then think of what you can do to guard against them. Like as not, you'll find you never thought of the stuff that actually does go wrong, but at least you've got an idea of what your options are. Doesn't guarantee success, unfortunately. Doesn't guarantee disaster either, though, and that's as good as you can hope for. War is an ugly beast, and fool the man who thinks he can tame and ride it.'

'Why do people have to go to war in the first place? Why not just sit down and talk things out?'

'Boy,' Bowen said, 'someone ever figures out the answer to that one, it'll be the day mankind finally starts growing up.'

Done talking, the old man kneed his mount to a trot.

They were among the last to arrive at Bentridge, a homey village on the only road to northern Dunmark, snugged into the crook of a long, curving hill less than twenty miles from Ardath's eastern border.

Aeron's army was encamped atop the hill's eastern leg inside an ancient ring of fortifications, a ditch and earthen ramparts, defensive works that likely dated from times when men had still fought with weapons made of bronze. The early arrivals had spent the wait clearing a two hundred-yard perimeter of trees and brush and deepening the ditch. They'd also spiked it and the ramparts with rows of sharpened stakes. The sprawling, bristling fort reminded Bryn of a porcupine someone had accidentally flattened out by rolling a full thirty-gallon barrel over it. There was another hill the other side of the road, smaller, and rounded, a watchtower surrounded by a curtain wall sitting on its highest point. Bowen said the ridge was called the Bent, the smaller hill the Barrow. Together, the Bent and the Barrow made for a time-tested defense against invaders from the east, bottlenecking the road between them like a set of wide-open jaws. Bryn saw men up on the Barrow as well.

Bowen's expression as he eyed the whole setup was unreadable. Not disapproving. Not enthusiastic either. To Bryn, having fortified positions on high ground overlooking the road made sense, but then his entire knowledge on the subject came from Thalios' *Strategy and Tactics*. Deadly boring stuff, but now he wished he'd paid a little more attention and skipped a few less pages.

They were met just outside the village by an unlikely pair: a grey-haired, one-eyed sergeant who could have passed for a close relative of Flatside's and looked like he'd been in every battle fought in the last fifty years; and a pimply young scribe sitting on a camp stool beside him and appearing decidedly out of place with his ink jar, blotting sand, pen knife, quills, and parchment all neatly lined up on a writing board balanced on his knees. The sergeant gave them a salute and a welcome, after which the scribe noted down their names, head count, and relevant skills, if any. Then, consulting a neatly drawn plan of the camps on the two hills, he assigned them to the Barrow.

'His majesty's set up command down yonder inn, m'lord,' the sergeant told Bryn once the scribe was done with them, pointing along the village's single street. 'He's asked that all lords comin' in should drop by an' pay him courtesy afore they goes on up the hill.'

'Any word what Edric is up to?' Bowen asked in a casual tone.

'Not so's they'd tell the likes o' me,' the sergeant said with a shrug.

'Scouts?'

'Only sent 'em out this mornin'. Ain't none of 'em come back yet.'

Bryn saw Bowen raise an eyebrow at that, and the sergeant answer in kind.

'Flatside up there?' Bowen asked.

'Aye. An' I reckon he'll be glad to see you, Threehands. An' not just him.'

Looks like a lot of the men know Bowen, Bryn thought with a touch of pride. *Know him, and trust him. At least the old hands all seem to.*

Kneeing his mount onward, Bowen gave the soldier an appreciative nod, and got one back. A simple exchange, but to Bryn it seemed as if a lot more had been given and received than met the eye, leaving the sergeant standing a bit straighter and taller than before. Bryn knew the feeling. A nod from Bowen could seem worth ten times the praise of a king. For years now, Threehands had been teacher, friend and surrogate father to him – as well as a demanding taskmaster who could drive his pupil to tears of frustration with his relentless pursuit of perfection. Nonetheless, Bryn was unreservedly

91

fond of the old man, and knew well enough how lucky he was to have him by his side. Right now, in view of what lay ahead, he felt even luckier than usual.

*   *   *

The news Flatside brought to Bailon Keep had hit Bowen like a fist in the stomach. He'd been fearing the moment ever since Kendric Bailon died five years ago, making Bryn head of House Bailon at barely thirteen. The lad had been way too young to go to war then, and in Bowen's eyes he still was. Probably always would be.

Unlike some others he'd known over the years, Bowen had never been keen on the Bloody Business. He went and did his duty when called upon, and was glad when it was over. He'd liked the dance with swords when he was younger – which was probably why he fought well – though never the bloody end of it. But the older he got, the more he preferred the dance of minds, the matching of wits instead of blades. If done right, it tended to spare a lot of lives. Which still didn't mean he liked war, not one little bit. Never scared him either, though, until now. Now, he felt like Gara the Chosen must have when the old gods told him he had to sacrifice his only son to save the people. Gara went ahead, but the gods stayed his hand at the last moment, saying it was his trust and willingness to obey that counted, not the spilling of innocent blood. Unfortunately, as far as Bowen could see it had been a long time since the gods had cared whether the sons of men lived or died.

There was no helping it.

All he could do was stick close to the lad and try to keep him out of harm's way as much as possible. Which he knew would likely turn out a lot easier said than done. Bryn was good with a sword, very good, actually, but he'd never had to fight in earnest, never been put to the true test of a fight to the blood. Never would have been, if Bowen had his way – nor any of the other young men gathered on yonder hill, the sons of nobles, farmers, tradesmen, some of them eager to prove themselves, most of them wishing they were back home, all of them scared shitless whether they admitted to it or not.

It was for Bryn's sake and theirs that Bowen was scared as well. That, and because of an encounter he saw coming, inevitably drawing closer with the unrelenting force of something predetermined by destiny, a meeting he'd have given anything to avoid.

At least let it be me, he thought, and not Bryn. *That would be a twist of fate too cruel to even contemplate.*

*   *   *

8

Rhea, granddaughter of Macsen Redbreast, was in over her head.

In deep water wearing leaden boots, it felt like. Add a pounding surf and a razorsharp reef, a couple of sharks and some blood in the water, and you were getting close. Pretty much where Macsen had told her that joining the Headhunters would get her. He hated it when she called him Macsen instead of Grandda like she'd used to, something she'd started doing a while back for reasons she'd never bothered examining but that had a lot to do with him thinking she was too young to look out for herself and still needed his counsel and guidance, whether she asked for it or not. Most irritating of all was that he was usually right. Never said, 'I told you so' – didn't need to. He had that thing with the raised eyebrows that left no doubt as to what he was thinking. Made her feel young and brash and stupid. Besides, she wasn't sure she'd forgiven him yet for not being up front with her about how her parents had died, not right away, at least.

She'd been ten when it happened, and believed him when he'd said her ma and da had gone on a long trip and wouldn't be back for a while. To his credit, he hadn't kept it up for long. Sat her down one evening and told her the hard truth, or at least part of it: they weren't coming back. The gods in their infinite wisdom – infinite wisdom, what a laugh! Infinite cruelty was more like it – had decided to take them out of this life and scoot them on to another one. Entrusted them with some very special task only they could do because they were very special people. Like she was a very special girl who was brave and strong enough to go ahead without them, otherwise the gods would have surely chosen someone else. Even at ten, she felt her grandda's grief as keenly as her own, keener maybe, so she'd been brave and strong for him. Didn't want to add to his troubles by being weak and a burden.

A sorrow shared is a sorrow halved, they said, a piece of wisdom she'd come to doubt over time. Sharing grief could just as easily be a way of keeping it fresh and raw. Which, come to think of it, was probably another reason why she'd started calling him Macsen: she needed to put some distance between them, between herself and his pain. Between herself and her own pain.

The truth of the matter didn't come to light until she was fifteen. That summer she had a bit of a crush on the neighbor's boy, Ban, a childish puppy love that briefly flared and then stuttered along, guttering out before autumn.

Perish the thought, but for a short while she actually dreamed silly girl's dreams like all the other air-headed pretties, even went so far as opening her mother's dowry chest for the first time in years and going through the whole thing down to the last linen sheet. There, at the bottom of the chest, she found a thin stack of parchments written in her da's bold hand. Macsen had taught her letters,

96

and, like everybody else, she'd heard about the Sweepers, so she had no trouble understanding what she was looking at: treason. Certain death for her and Macsen, should these pamphlets ever be found in their possession.

Although it was a sweltering August day, she lit a fire in the hearth and burned them immediately. Only then did she allow herself to consider what else they implied.

Dinner that evening was a wordless affair.

Macsen knew something was up – could likely feel her anger burning right across the table – and she knew that he knew. But she wasn't about to give him anything at all without first making him beg for it. Which he did, sort of, once he'd pushed back his empty plate and lit his pipe with a piece of kindling from the fire.

'What is it, lass?' he asked, looking so bloody benign and concerned she could have screamed.

So she told him what she'd found, was perversely gratified to see the shock and alarm on his face, and something else: a hint of… regret. Guilt. He'd known. Not about the pamphlets, but about her parents' involvement with the Sweepers.

'What did you do with them?' was the first thing he said. Not, 'I'm sorry'; not, 'I should have told you earlier'; as if he still didn't understand she had a right to know.

'I burned them.'

'Good,' he said, and went back to sucking on his pipe in silence.

She let it build, but not for long.

'Why didn't you tell me?' she asked, startled by the coldness in her voice, when inside she was boiling with anger.

He sighed. 'Because I couldn't be sure. They were damned good at keeping it a secret, even from me. You can believe me when I say I didn't have the slightest notion of what they were up to. Wasn't sure until now, in fact, until you told me what you'd found. After they went missing, all I had was a suspicion, and no way of proving whether I was right or wrong.

'And besides, how would telling you your parents had been murdered – and for supporting the cause of a bunch of misguided do-gooders to boot – how would that have made things any easier for you? You were just a kid, for mercy's sake. Barely ten. You didn't need to be burdened any more than you already were, and with stuff even most grown-ups would have a hard time getting their head around. Gods' love, girl, I might as well have sat you down and told you the world was a bad, ugly place full of cruelty and injustice, the gods' favorite spot for taking a dump. Would *that* have made you feel any better?'

She couldn't deny the sense of what he was saying, but the anger burning inside her still needed somewhere to go. 'How *could* they?' she said. 'How could they put the people they loved at risk for something so... stupid?'

Macsen took a long time to answer. 'I reckon they really believed in what they were doing,' he finally said. 'Thought it was worth it, no matter the risk. Perhaps they were doing it for you as well, at least in part, thinking they could make the world a better place for their child to grow up in. They loved you dearly, you know. Never doubt that.'

'Except you can't make the world a better place,' she said

98

bitterly. 'Stupid to think you can. Stupid and careless.' They *had* loved her, if anything she remembered about them held true, though she wasn't sure she'd ever be able to forgive them for the choices they'd made.

'Lass.' Of a sudden Macsen looked so old and worried it almost made her feel guilty for being so upset with him. 'You can go ahead and be angry with me all you want. You can be angry with your ma and da, if it helps, though I'm not sure they deserve it. Anything, as long as you don't take any of it upon yourself. Because none of it's your fault. That's the one certainty in this whole sad business, and you need to hold to it. Promise me that?'

She nodded, grudgingly. It would prove a promise far easier made than kept.

She took what she'd learned and mulled it over for a few days.

And came back with a few more questions for her grandfather. Like who he reckoned was responsible for the death of her parents. At first he didn't want to answer, shrugging and saying it could have been a lot of people, the Sweepers themselves included. In a climate raw with fear and suspicion, where to misspeak could mean death and today's friends could become tomorrow's traitors, anything was possible.

But she didn't let up, kept on pressing him until he finally admitted there were two likely candidates: Pryce's Headhunters, and Corvin Gale's bunch of creeps. And he told her right away and in no uncertain terms that these people were untouchable. So she should put any ideas she might have of seeking redress right out of her mind, once and for all.

She should have listened. Instead, she'd started making plans. Preparing. Studying. She read Thalios' *Strategy and Tactics* until she knew most of it by heart. Then, two years ago, she joined the Headhunters. *Know the heart of thine enemy better than he knows it himself,* Thalios had written, and, *Should it prove impossible to strike from without, attack from within.*

Exactly what she aimed to do. And the Headhunters themselves would teach her how.

The Headhunters' Guild styled themselves a tough but on-the-level lot who happened to hunt down dangerous criminals for a living. Brought them in so justice could have a shot at them. As if. Two years in training, and all she'd ever seen them drag in were corpses – if they even bothered to bring anything back at all. And the stuff they taught should have gotten anyone thinking all by itself. Only, her fellow apprentices were too busy feeling so bloody full of themselves because here they were, learning a thousand ways to kill people instead of how to catch them alive. Clueless. Pathetic. Or just plain bad.

She despised the lot of them, kept to herself. Didn't make any friends, not even for appearance's sake. Trained twice as hard as anyone else, gave no quarter in weapons practice, pretended she took pride in the occasional pat on the shoulder from Pace, their teacher, even if the creep liked to leave his hand there longer than necessary. Couldn't keep his eyes off her either, her and Gwynne, the only other girl in training. Tall and dark, he was actually kind of handsome in a smooth and slightly nauseating way. Seemed to think he was the gods' gift to all women, with his arrogant sneer and invasive stares that always made her feel as if in his mind he were undressing her. Probably was. Slimy bastard, but fearsomely good with any weapon you could think of and some you couldn't.

And then suddenly it was Sweepers loose in the north and everyone off after them, every single Headhunter gone from Kingskeep except Pace and his little class of wannabe killers. She hadn't been sure what to think when Pace came and singled her out for a job, saying he'd gotten a commission from the Glassmakers to find someone for them, and that he could use a second, another pair of eyes on the quarry just to make sure he didn't do a runner. A dwarf, apparently, and pretty much harmless. Easy. Was the offer Pace's way of making a pass at her? Or was this her chance to see from up close how the Headhunters really worked?

She began to get a pretty good idea of what lay ahead when Pace selected daggers long as short-swords, garrotes, and a small, one-handed crossbow apiece from the armory. All that to run down and bring in a harmless dwarf? She reckoned the little man's chances of making it in front of a magistrate alive weren't all that good. Not much she could do, though, except leave the dirty work to Pace. She couldn't back down now, needed to worm her way a lot deeper still into the Guild's bowels if she was to find her parents' killers.

It was catching her first sight of the dwarf back in the tavern that made her change her mind. Looking in through the grimy window, seeing him sitting at a table close by, squashed onto the very end of a bench that was rocking with the other occupants' cheerful high spirits fueled by music and ale – a quiet, inward little fellow content to be alone with his food and drink in the middle of all the bawdiness, laughter, and singing – her stupid heart went out to him, willy-nilly. Just as she heard the nasty whisper of Pace's dagger returning to its sheath beside her.

'Not here,' the Headhunter breathed in her ear, suddenly making her feel like she needed a bath more than anything else. 'Too many eyes. I'll follow him back to his quarters. I want you to go on ahead and keep an eye on the back door. Don't let him slip away. The Glassmakers pay well, and there'll be something in it for you too if this goes right.'

That was when she knew without a doubt that Pace was planning to kill the dwarf, not bring him in – and that she couldn't let him do it. Whatever the little man had done to piss off the Glassmakers, it couldn't possibly warrant killing him out of hand. Murder, was what it would be, pure and simple. Not with her, though.

Now, standing by the boardinghouse's back entrance with the door held slightly ajar, listening for the slightest sound as if her life depended on it, Rhea desperately tried to think of a way to save the dwarf without getting both of them killed. Which kept coming up as the most likely result of any of the half-baked plans fluttering around her fevered brain like a coop full of startled chickens.

Suddenly she heard a bang upstairs, as if a piece of furniture had fallen over, and a muffled voice saying something in a nagging tone.

The creak of a floorboard.

A moment's silence, and then someone came clattering down the stairs.

Moving to the side of the door, she nearly knocked down a

shovel someone had left leaning against the wall. Instinctively she grabbed it as it started to fall over, the handle beginning to rattle along the uneven stonework.

Which was why the dwarf was already past her before she could do more than reach out for him with her free hand. Through the pouring rain she caught a glimpse of him slipping out into the alley, then Pace was there, hard on the dwarf's heels, one glance enough to tell him she'd messed up.

'Where is he?' he hissed angrily.

Mutely, she pointed towards the stables.

'Come on, then,' he snarled.

She let him take one long stride in the direction she'd indicated. Then she swung the shovel and brought it crashing into the back of his head.

Pace went down like a felled tree.

Lay there in the muck and the rain, unmoving, while she struggled to catch up with what had just happened. Of a sudden she was terrified, any ability to think shot to pieces by the dawning realization of what she'd gotten herself into. Forget having buggered her chances of revenging her parents. She'd just struck down a Headhunter, maybe even killed him.

She should make sure he was dead. Finish it if he wasn't. Instead, she found she couldn't even bring herself to touch him. With a muted sound somewhere between a wail and a curse, she dropped the shovel and ran.

With his short legs and the heavy pack weighing him down, the

103

dwarf wasn't all that hard to catch up with. Still, it wasn't far short of a miracle that she found him at all in Lowtown's maze of unlit, rain-drenched streets and alleys. She couldn't have said what made her decide to slip into a side street and shadow him on a parallel course, getting a ways ahead of him so she could catch a glimpse of his small, struggling figure every time he passed by the far end of a connecting alley. Maybe it was pure, dumb luck. Maybe it was instinct. Or maybe it was the gods holding a protective hand over her.

Whatever it was, the next time she paused and waited for the little man, she saw his hunched form hurry by – and moments later a tall, dark-cloaked figure walking with a long, loping gait she knew all too well. Pace.

In the two heartbeats it took the Headhunter to cross the open space between the two houses flanking the alley's mouth, she saw a quick flash of steel. He had his long-dagger out, ready for the kill, out for blood. Hers too now, as well as the dwarf's. What to do?

She hurried on to the next crossing, waited until the dwarf had passed and, after him, Pace. Unhooked the little crossbow from her belt. Fumbled a bolt into the groove. Snuck down the alley to get in behind the hunter, not sure she'd be able to shoot him in cold blood, and in the back to boot.

Risking a peek, she saw the dwarf turn left at the next crossing, into one of the wide thoroughfares circling the hill. Moments later, Pace disappeared around the corner as well.

She was about to sprint after them when the Headhunter suddenly came backing up around the corner, two men-at-arms with torches and bare blades coming after him. She saw steel flash in the torchlight, heard the faint ring of blade meeting blade over the hissing rain and the rushing, gurgling water in the gullies. Decided this was her chance to catch up with the dwarf, get both of them out of harm's way while Pace was busy fighting whomever it was he'd run into. A flitting shadow, she darted across the street behind the fighting parties and into the next alley over.

A right turn brought her back to the main street, where more men were clustered around a crashed and burning litter, two of them helping the fur-swathed occupant back to his or her feet while the others made half-hearted attempts at beating down the flames. Twenty yards to the left, a small, lumpy shadow moved off into the dark, unnoticed by anyone but her.

She needed to follow but was too close to the fire. If she stepped out from where she stood she'd be seen for sure, and chances were she'd be taken for another aggressor and met with steel. Backing up, she hurried through a series of courtyards and overbuilt passages running parallel to the street, desperate to get the little man back in her sights. A few turns later she ended up in an alley so dark she had to feel her way along the walls, not sure where she was anymore. That was when she knew she'd lost him for good.

Standing there in the pitch dark, halfway to lost in the city she'd grown up in and ought to know like the back of her hand, Rhea suddenly realized she was drenched to the skin, shivering, and not just from the cold. She'd risked everything for a child-sized man she'd never heard of before today, whose name she didn't even know, gods have mercy, and look what it had got her. In the time it took to swing a rusty shovel, she'd thrown to the wind everything she'd worked so hard for during the last two years, made herself an outlaw, and already she had a Headhunter on her heels, one with a personal stake in finding and seeing her dead.

How stupid is that? Grandda would say I'd taken leave of my senses, and right he'd be. But it's done now, and here I am. No use crying over broken crockery, as my ma used to say. Figuring out where to go from here, is what I should be doing.

I need to get out of Kingskeep, that much is clear, and then as far away as possible, somewhere they don't have Headhunters. Though the bastards will go just about anywhere if the pay is right. Meaning the kingdoms are out, and so is Orr. East over the mountains, maybe, or someplace the other side of the sea. But that's for another day. Right now I need a place to lie up, stay out of the rain and out of sight until the gates open in the morning. Daven Bury's cellar, that's it. He never locks it up, and it's close enough to Grandda's that I might be able to slip over and borrow a few things I'll be needing on the road.

Two alleys over, she finally figured out where exactly she was. Finding her way from there to Daven Bury's was only a question of not running into something hard and unforgiving in the sheer impenetrable dark. That didn't happen until she was safely inside the cellar and stumbled over an obstacle some idiot had left lying in the middle of the floor, painfully stubbing her toe and pitching headlong onto a pile of old sacking. With a smack that made her eyes water, her chin banged into another hard object lying atop the sacks, a length of wood by the feel of it. She was about to utter a curse – growing up with an old soldier you couldn't but learn a few choice

106

ones – when she heard soft footfalls on the cellar steps.

Terrified, not daring to breathe, she listened to them shuffle across the floor, coming closer.

Pace! How in seven hells did he manage to follow me all the way here? Does he have some sort of dark magic? I wouldn't put it beyond him, sick, murdering bastard that he is.

Something bumped into the side of the stack.

Hands felt around on the sacking, nearly but not quite touching her.

Without thinking, she grabbed hold of the piece of wood.

It felt good in her grip, solid and heavy. Nice and hard. Careful not to make even the tiniest sound, she sat up and swung it back over her shoulder, hefting it like a woodsman's axe. Heard a soft thump, like something being dropped onto the floor. Felt the pile of sacks shift beneath her as Pace put his weight on them, coming so close she could smell damp wool and leather and... horse?

Then a hand came out of nowhere, groping her breast, and she lost it. She let loose with a mighty swing and heard a satisfying, meaty whack! as hard wood connected with not so hard flesh.

Silence.

Not a sound beyond her own pent-up breathing and the muted hiss of the rain outside.

I got the bastard! Got him good. Only this time, I have to finish it. Can't risk him waking up. Can't have him coming after me any-more. Reluctantly, she reached for her dagger. *Maybe he's already dead. I should make sure. No use doing the job twice.*

She knew she was only stalling, putting off the inevitable. Went and felt for a pulse anyway. The first thing her searching hand encountered was a booted foot. A child-sized booted foot. Feeling her way up the prone, motionless body, she came up short. Way too short for this to be Pace. Way too short for it to be anything else but a child – or a dwarf.

It's the little man. Now wouldn't that be a hilarious twist. First I save his scrawny little neck, and then I go and kill him by mistake. Bloody gods must be cracking up: ha, bloody ha, just look at the dumb bitch.

She felt for a pulse. Nothing.

No. There. Weak, but steady. He was alive, thank the gods. But his skin was icy cold. Pulling half a dozen sacks from the pile, she spread them over him, a scratchy patchwork blanket reeking of turnips but better than nothing. Then she slipped in beside him. After a moment's hesitation, she snuggled up close. She was freezing too, godsdammit. Only sensible thing to do. Some time later, without quite knowing how, she ended up putting her arms around him, like a mother cradling a sick child. Weird.

Dead tired, drifting off, she felt a bit of warmth begin to build between her body and his. The next moment she was asleep, dreaming that she was running, running, running, though in the dream she had no idea why.

*   *   *

Laurin was back on the farm, a child again.

Lying in bed sandwiched between his two big sisters, his older brothers in the other bed. Lella must have gotten up real early today, because her side was empty and cold. But Caelie was there, warming his back. He listened for the familiar sounds of Ma getting the fire going and stirring up a pot of breakfast gruel and the thwock! thwock! of Da's axe splitting firewood, but there was nothing to hear, everything gone strangely quiet.

He cracked an eyelid. Saw it was in fact morning, though the wan, grey light barely made it in through the cracks in the door. And it was cold. Snuggling deeper under the blankets, he felt rough sacking scrape against his cheek. *Sacking?* He froze in mid-move, last night's events coming back to him all in a rush, fear clutching at his innards with icy claws. He started to sit up but immediately sank back with a groan as violent pain lanced through his head.

There was sudden, quick movement beside him, and the throbbing in his head was joined by another, lesser pain, a sharp pinprick under his chin. Next he knew, he found himself staring up at a pale oval that resolved into a face as his eyes belatedly found their focus. A girl's face. Pretty. Dark hair, dark eyes – green, he thought – a light sprinkling of freckles across the bridge of the nose. Pert nose. Very pretty, actually. Less so the point of the dagger pressing into the soft flesh of his throat. She let out a pent-up breath and withdrew the weapon.

'Sorry. I thought you were someone else.'

A memory of touching something soft and round and exciting flashed before his inner eye, causing him to blush furiously.

'It's… it's all right,' he stammered. 'I understand. And I didn't mean to… whatever you might think… it's just, I thought…'

'It's all right,' the girl muttered, though her expression said different. Then the hard set of her mouth softened a little. She sighed. 'I suppose you're wondering what's going on.'

The story she told was somewhat disjointed, to say the least.

It started with her coolly admitting that it was she who'd hit him over the head last night because she'd thought he was Pace, Pace who was after her, or him, he wasn't quite sure. Finally he asked her if she – Rhea, it turned out her name was – would mind starting at the beginning instead of telling everything backwards, and that was when he began to figure out what she was talking about. It seemed she'd saved his life, or thought she had.

'Thanks, I guess,' he told her when she was done.

'You're too bloody welcome.'

She went silent, not looking happy. Sullen. Angry. Scared, if he wasn't mistaken. Not at all like he imagined a person would look who'd just saved someone's life.

'You're in trouble because of me.' That much he understood without her having to say it.

'Really? You think?' Young as she was, she had the sarcasm down pat.

Patience, he told himself. *She's got every reason to be upset. Me getting angry as well isn't going to help.*

'So what are you going to do now?'

She relented a little, gave a resigned shrug. 'Looks like I'm not done saving you. You need to leave Kingskeep. We both do. Since I know the place inside out, I suppose it's up to me to get us out.

'It won't be easy,' she went on, speaking mostly to herself now. 'But there's ways where with a little luck Pace won't find us. He's the only full Headhunter left in town, and he can't be everywhere at once. Though I reckon he'll use the other apprentices. For the most part they're more bad attitude than brains, but one of them might get lucky all the same. It'll have to be stealth, then.'

She gave him an appraising glance, a horse trader sizing up a lame nag. 'Running's not much of an option, I'd say.' Noticing his expression, she added, 'Sorry. Didn't mean to hurt your feelings. Just trying to figure out how to get us out of here alive.'

Laurin wasn't convinced. Not by a long shot.

'So first you try to kill me, and now you're asking me to trust you, is that it?'

'*I* never tried to kill you,' she flared. 'That was Pace, the evil, murdering whoreson. If you'd paid attention, little man, you would've gotten that much at least. Pace, and the Glassmakers. What are you to them, anyway? What did you do to get them so riled up they'd send a killer after you? Did you steal something? A mirror, maybe? That would be pretty damned stupid. But also kind of neat, come to think of it.'

Laurin almost answered without thinking, but then the oaths kicked in, and his mouth snapped shut just in time.

'What?' Rhea asked. 'It's not like I'm going to rat you out, you know. I'm in at least as much trouble as you are. For saving your little... for saving you. In case you forgot.'

What the hell, he thought. *I don't owe them anything, certainly not after they tried to have me killed. And they'll go on trying, no doubt. For sure they will. Piss on their oaths. Piss on their bloody secrets. I'm not their tame fool anymore.*

'Up until yesterday, I used to be a Waylen,' he said, and watched the girl's eyes go round. Though he'd always avoided using the word, he'd seen the effect it had on others, so he wasn't surprised by her reaction. Saying 'Waylen' of a night in a tavern was like casting a spell that transformed grown men into wide-eyed children, especially when, fueled by drink and superstition, the door to the realm of fantasy already stood open a crack. Many a time he'd sat forgotten in a quiet corner while all the old stories and even the odd new one were shared in hushed voices, further enlarged and embellished with each telling until a bunch of simple mineral-seekers had become a whole nation of supernatural beings who lived in vast, sumptuous cities inside the high mountains and possessed hoards of gold and gems to rival those of the dragons.

'You're shitting me, right?' Rhea said. 'A *Waylen?* Waylen belong in fairytales, like elves and dragons and shit. Now I'm supposed to believe they're for real?'

'Real enough for you to have hit one over the head,' Laurin said, wincing as he touched the egg-sized bump on his forehead. 'That's quite a wallop you pack there.'

'Sorry. Again,' she said. And looked it, too – just for a moment. Then she caught herself, put on her hard-as-nails face again. Laurin reckoned he was starting to believe her, maybe even like her a little bit, though she certainly wasn't making it easy.

Without going into details – no use adding to the danger she was already in by giving her perilous knowledge – he explained why the Guild had hired Pace to get rid of him. After last night, the thought that they'd go to such extremes didn't strike him as all that outlandish anymore. Only made him very, very angry. Left in peace, he'd have never dreamed of betraying their godsdamned secrets. His oath was as good as any man's, after all, dwarf or no. Damned if it wasn't. Twenty years of faithful service, and they still hadn't trusted him half as far as they could spit. So now it was up to them to bear the consequences of their own, twisted thinking.

'That's bloody base,' Rhea said when he'd finished. 'Bottom of the barrel rotten. If I were you, I'd shout out their stupid secrets where everyone can hear, let the whole world know about them.' She snorted. 'Arseholes.'

'You could buy a kingdom or three with those stupid secrets,' Laurin told her, not bothering to hide how angry and bitter he was. 'And they're *dangerous* arseholes. So dangerous they'd hunt a man who betrayed them to the end of the world and beyond. You saw what they tried to do to me, even though they must have been as good as certain I'd never blab. But "as good as" apparently wasn't good enough.'

'All right, then.' He could see her shifting gears, back to the practical stuff. 'Time to move. The gates will be opening soon.'

He was about to nod but thought better of it. His throbbing head felt like it might end up in his lap if he made an ill-considered move. Then he remembered the King Under the Mountain and the bloody sword.

'I can't come with you,' he said. 'I have to go see Avellin. The king.'

With Rhea staring at him as if he'd gone completely mad, he hastened to explain. A little. If he told her the whole story, she *would* think him mad.

'There's something I have to give him. An errand I agreed to run for someone. I'm sorry, but I promised.'

'You really don't have a clue, do you?' she said. 'The king's not

113

here. He's gone to war, up north, to Ardath. Meaning if you want to go see him, you still need to get out of Kingskeep.'

Ardath. Avellin was in Ardath.

Suddenly, what the King Under the Mountain had told Laurin was beginning to make sense. Some of it, at least. He still couldn't see how a king would be keeping company with a sow and her piglets. He wasn't sure whether he should be happy, though. It meant the job wasn't done yet. He sighed. It wasn't like he had anything better to do. Except stay alive. And that looked to be coinciding pretty well with keeping his promise to deliver the sword.

'All right, then,' he said. 'What's the plan?'

*   *   *

9

It wasn't all that different from back home, Macsen decided.

The same four men, the same underhanded scheming, the same jostling for position and a place in the king's good graces. Normally in the field, the captain of the guard would have been there as well. But the post was currently vacant, had been ever since the man who'd held it had ill-advisedly placated a hungry mob in Lowtown with a cartful of bread instead of cutting them down like Edric had ordered him to. The man was out to pasture, back on the farm. Macsen envied him, and thanked the gods he himself was well past the age where he might still be considered for the job.

Otherwise, not so different at all. The door he was standing beside was smaller, the wall-hangings were poorer, and instead of a crackling fire it was a brazier filled with coals that was too far away for comfort. At least the damned thing didn't pull in a draft. He was bloody cold enough as it was.

Why the border lord whose keep Edric had appropriated for the nonce couldn't come up with a decent supply of firewood was a mystery to Macsen. Maybe because every piece of dry wood in the county had gone into burning half a dozen villages down to the ground. Yesterday he'd accompanied the king on an outing to the nearest of them, and seen what Gale's and Pryce's people had accomplished. After a lifetime of soldiering there wasn't much could turn his stomach. But this beat anything he'd ever seen.

On the men, they'd inflicted just about every atrocity a bunch of sick minds given free liscence could come up with: skinned them alive, impaled them, pruned them down piece by little piece, held them head down in the jakes until they drowned in their own and their loved ones' shit, arranged the remains in lewd and disgraceful positions, singly or pairwise. And used the victims' blood to paint Sweeper brooms on the few walls left standing.

But that wasn't the worst of it. The worst was what they'd done to the women and children: herded them into the village inn, nailed shut the doors and windows, and then set fire to the building. For a moment there, he'd thought he could still hear their screams echoing through the charred ruins, the small hairs on his neck rising as if stirred by a cold wind from the other side of death. Ghostly sounds that would likely haunt these places forever.

Edric took it all in without so much as a blink, just gave a short nod as if at a job well done before spurring his horse and riding on to the next killing ground. Almost as if he enjoyed it, or at the least was left entirely cold by the gruesome sight of what men were capable of doing in his name.

It made Macsen sick. Not sick to his stomach so much as sick to his soul. And it put him in serious doubt as to where he stood. It wasn't the first time he'd had this nagging feeling that he might be running on the wrong side of the fence, but it was the first time he

116

couldn't for the life of him manage to tuck the thought away and out of sight by reminding himself of the oaths he'd sworn and telling himself that these were treasonous thoughts.

Though admitting it pained him more than he could say, treason was beginning to look like the honorable thing – if you compared it to what the men warming their hands by the brazier and conversing in low voices were up to.

Gods help me, but I'm lost here. When everything's become lies and deception, it gets hard and harder to tell right from wrong. The Sweepers are misguided fools, and they've done their share of mischief. What Aeron's done to rile Edric so, I couldn't say. But I've a feeling the greater evil by far is in the hearts and on the heads of the men in this room. What in mercy's name's a simple soldier like me supposed to do about it? And would it even make a difference?

*　　*　　*

'My lord king,' Gale said, watching Pryce and Stonebridge head for the door. 'A word, if you please.'

'What is it?' Most men would have quailed under the king's cold gaze and impatient tone. Not Gale.

'I've had a message from Kingskeep. From the new archivar, Master Declan. I've had him going through his predecessor's personal effects. And a good thing too, it turns out. He's found something I thought I should bring to your attention.'

Edric was hardly listening, impatient to be gone. 'Get to the point, then. I've an engagement waiting.'

Gale knew all about that, of course. He'd chosen the girl himself from among Burnt Keep's prettier serving wenches. Had her bathed, coiffed, stuffed into a borrowed dress and whisked up the back stairs to Edric's rooms. She'd be leaving the same way – in a couple of hours if she was lucky, in the morning if she wasn't – and looking decidedly less pretty but a fat purse richer for her troubles, told to say she fallen down the stairs if anyone asked and otherwise keep her mouth shut. Provided she survived.

Edric's trysts had been getting increasingly violent of late, and Gale reckoned it was only a question of time before one ended with the girl being carried out feet first. Not that he minded. One man's dirty secrets were another man's power, after all. Which was why Gale loved nothing better than to collect knowledge of other men's – and women's – missteps. It must have been hard for Edric not to lay hand on his wife while she still lived – but then, who knew what one might have found had one looked under the late queen's long-sleeved, high-collared gowns.

Back to business.

'Declan found a draft of a marriage contract. Hidden away, not accidentally misplaced, seeing as it was tucked between the pages of a ratty old copy of *The Book of Elil*, and the late archivist a stout unbeliever.'

'A marriage contract between whom?' Edric asked, beginning to show a spark of interest. And well he should. The fate of dynasties and kingdoms could hinge on such a piece of parchment.

'Your lord father, may his soul rest in peace. And the Lady Gavrielle Rowan.'

The king was all attention now, and not at all happy about what he was hearing. 'A draft, you say?'

118

'Prepared three months before your lord father's lamentable demise.'

'Are you suggesting he might have actually gone through with it? Married the bitch in secret? Is there another document hidden away somewhere, perhaps the real one?'

If anything, Edric's icy calm appeared to deepen, but Gale's experienced eye told him the king was close to smashing something. Or wringing someone's neck. Fathers and sons. Always a touchy subject. And never more so than with Seorus and Edric.

Not that Edric had loved his mother any better, only hated his father more. And Seorus' mistress Gavrielle most of all. A wonder he hadn't had her killed after Seorus died, instead of ordering her dragged off into exile.

Gale spread his hands wide. 'Impossible to say, your majesty. But – seeing as your lord father and the Lady Rowan are both dead – if anyone knows, it's the witnesses.'

'Witnesses? You know who they are?' There was a glint in Edric's eye that Gale knew all too well, one that usually boded evil for someone.

'Luckily, the old archivist was a meticulous man. The draft he prepared was sufficiently elaborate to have served as the final document, including the apposite spaces where the spouses and witnesses would have signed, with everyone's names neatly lettered in under the dotted lines. The names given for the witnesses were Torvald Tondern and Bowen Threehands.'

'Those two again, damn their meddling souls. But if Gavrielle's dead, then I don't see your point – unless you're worried she might rise up and make demands from the grave.'

'Unfortunately, there's more,' Gale said, inwardly bracing himself. 'It appears she bore a child. A son.'

Seeing Edric's expression, Gale expected the room to start crackling with hoarfrost at any moment, or perhaps surprise him and burst into flames.

'And you tell me about this now.' Of a sudden the steel in the king's voice was cutting sharp. Deadly sharp. 'Something I should have known about years ago. Do you reckon I employ a spymaster so I'll be duly informed every time one of my enemies afield takes a shit, and at the same time remain happily clueless as to what's going on in my own house? At least tell me the boy isn't Seorus' bastard.'

'Alas, I can't be certain.' Gale had an unwelcome image of a headsman's axe falling, and resisted an instinctive urge to pull his neck down into his collar. 'She married a second time. The boy could well be the new husband's. But I'd have to say it's not entirely impossible he's your father's. And, theoretically, if a legally binding document did in fact exist, he wouldn't be a bastard. He'd be legitimate.'

There, he'd said it, and his head was still on his shoulders. 'So I think our best course would be to – '

'I trust you know where to find him,' Edric cut him off. Got a nod from Gale. 'Good. Legitimate or no, I want the boy dead. Forthwith. I want Pryce's people to go after the brat immediately. And after Bowen. Him I should have gotten rid of already years ago.'

'Precisely what I meant to suggest,' Gale said, moving back onto solid ground again. 'Better safe than sorry. But, if I may, I'd counsel against involving Pryce. The less people know about this,

120

the better. In fact, I have just the man for the job. One who won't be deterred by castle walls and closed gates.'

'You mean, your pet priest.' Edric didn't look happy. Gale hadn't expected him to. 'You know I don't like dealing with the black rats.'

'I'm well aware of it, your majesty. But exceptional tasks call for exceptional measures – that's assuming you'll want everyone involved removed. Yes, I thought as much. Pryce might be able to handle the boy. Bowen's another matter, though. I reckon you'd have to send a company or three of Headhunters if you wanted to have any hope of... eliminating him.

'And, in all honesty, I don't see any way at all to get to Tondern by conventional means. He sits in his keep like a badger in his sett, and no way to smoke him out. It's a well-known fact that Dearg Fearna is impregnable. Sadly, it's also one of the few places in all of Dunmark I haven't been able to infiltrate. Shame on me, but there it is. Brother Maynard, on the other hand, has perfected his grasp of the Dark Arts to a point where he can come and go as he pleases, when and wherever he pleases.'

Edric mulled the information over for a moment. 'All right, then,' he said. 'Do it. But leave Tondern to me. He'll have to come out of his hole if he's to help fight Aeron. And then we'll see.' On his way out, he added 'And don't forget the archivist.'

Gale sketched a bow at Edric's retreating back. 'Already taken care of, your majesty.'

Once the king was gone, Gale pulled a kerchief from his sleeve and dabbed the sweat from his brow. How he looked forward to the day when he wouldn't have to deal with the likes of Edric anymore!

Manipulating people was his bread and butter, his true calling, if you liked, but managing Edric was a chore he found increasingly punishing.

Well, tonight's girl might prove a small step forward. He'd told the dumb wench that Edric liked it when a woman showed some spirit, fought back a little. It should be enough to get her beaten to a pulp, if not killed.

Another brick in the wall I've been patiently building over the years, little by little. Shouldn't be much longer, now that the capstone is almost ready for the setting.

*   *   *

Torvald Tondern, Duke of Redfern, rode out of Darg Fearna with twenty men armed to the teeth, on his way to meet with the king. Twenty men, as agreed, plus Wuffles, an old, ratty mongrel who for some reason had attached itself to Torvald and started following him around wherever he went. Time and again, the servants had chased the animal out of the inner keep, but Wuffles persisted, until Torvald had ordered them to let the dog be. Since then, Wuffles slept on an old horse blanket outside the door to the ducal rooms and ate in the kitchens with the other retired old warriors living out their days in comfort. As it should be.

The impending meeting with Edric was the result of a number of messages sent back and forth, beginning with the one in which Torvald had begged off the war on the – admittedly flimsy – grounds that his wife was a cousin of Aeron's. He hadn't chosen such a shaky excuse by accident: he wanted to see Edric's face when he told him the real reason why he was refusing to join in the war against Ardath.

A mile outside Derag Fearna's walls the solitary, colorfully striped tent he'd had set up for the meeting sat waiting in a meadow beside the road leading south. Beyond it Torvald saw Edric approaching with his own contingent of twenty.

He kneed his mount to a trot. Although he was in no hurry at all, etiquette demanded he be there first.

'Your grace,' Edric said once they were settled inside the tent and facing each other across a camp table on which one of the king's men had placed a bottle of wine and two cups. Edric spared Wuffles a distasteful glance as the dog settled beside Torvald's chair. 'I'll have you know I'm disappointed.' No surprise there. Not for Edric to linger over the niceties. 'But I aim to soften you up with a drop of excellent Conaran red.'

It was a poor attempt at bonhomie, but no worse than was to be expected from someone like Edric. Cold as a fish, the man was. Pulling the cork, he splashed heavy wine the color of congealing blood into both cups.

'I'm afraid I'll have to pass, your majesty,' Torvald said easily. 'Healer's orders. Something to do with the liver, they say.'

'Sorry to hear it,' Edric said. 'You don't know what you're missing.' The look he gave Torvald as he set down the bottle was devoid of sympathy. Eyes hard as obsidian, and just as dark. 'To business, then. I've come to remind you of your oaths. In case you've forgotten, you owe me fealty. Dunmark is at war with Ardath. Surely you don't expect a bad liver will excuse you. Nor will your wife's kinships. Am I making myself clear?'

'Perfectly,' Torvald said, leaning back with half-closed eyes as if he were enjoying a peaceful evening by the fireplace. Smoke and mirrors. Knowing what he did, he'd come angry and was getting angrier by the minute. But when it came to deception, he had years of practice under his belt and could play with the best of them. 'If you'll bear with me a moment, I'd like to tell you a story.'

It was only the smallest of twitches gave Edric away.
He was irritated, his attack seemingly deflected, his thread momentarily broken.

'It's about a pair of young lovers,' Torvald went on as if nothing were amiss. 'Let's call them… Birken and Fara, shall we?'

Another twitch, this one more marked. Small wonder. Birken and Fara happened to be the names of two of the destroyed villages.

'So, Birken and Fara. The two are madly in love, wishing fervently to get married. And, I'd wager, even more fervently looking forward to a romp in the conjugal bed. Unfortunately for them, both their parents are strictly against the connection. Generations-old family feud over torn-down fences and escaped livestock, would you believe it? Any road, for the nonce they can only meet in secret, and that's just what they're doing on the evening in question: sneaking out of the village, up to the top of a small rise at the edge of a nearby woods. Not far away. Close enough to hear, should anyone miss them and start hollering. Close enough to see what's going on down there. Yet safely out of sight.'

'Do get on with it,' Edric, impatient as always, his tone approaching a snarl. 'Provided there's a point to this at all.'

'Oh, there is. There is. Almost there, in fact. So, imagine our

124

two lovebirds, hidden in the shadow of the trees. There's a fair bit of canoodling going on, likely some explorative fumbling at each other's smallclothes, when suddenly all hell breaks loose down in the village. Armed men on horseback come galloping in, and in a trice there's steel and smoke and blood in the air. People running and screaming. Birken wants to go down and fight the intruders, though they are many and well-armed and all he's got are his bare fists. But Fara holds him back, clings to him, pleads with him not to throw his life and their shared future away for something it's too late to change anyway.

'In the end, he gives in. They lie low and watch, though it becomes ever harder to look at the horrific carnage being wrought before their eyes. Once, an attacker chasing a runaway villager nearly stumbles upon them, riding past so close either of them could have reached out and touched the horse's fetlocks. And then, what's happening down there gets so very, very bad, Fara takes Birken's hand, pulls him up and away, and they run. Run for their lord's keep, and safety.

'Now what's all this got to do with anything, you'll be asking yourself. I'll tell you. When that man rode by, Birken got a good look at the shield on his arm. It had been painted over, but sloppily. Sometime during the fight, part of the paint had been chipped away. What Birken saw peeking out from underneath was a Lion Rampant, Or on Gules. The Avellin arms.

'So here's the point, your majesty: I know what you've done. And I can assure you I'm not taking it kindly.'

The temperature inside the tent seemed to have plummeted below

125

freezing, though Edric must have been boiling with fury at being caught redhanded. But he was easily as good at the game as Torvald.

'I assume you're offering up this piece of peasant drivel as proven fact,' he said, blithe as you like. 'I must say I took you for a less gullible man. I'd have thought you knew your rabble by now. All those bumpkins need do is set foot in a woods and they'll come back spouting stories of fairies, ogres, dragons and what have you as if it were the gods' own truth. Half of them superstitious fools, the other half likely inventing some tall tale to distract from the fact they were out poaching or stealing wood. Or fornicating. Besides, I heard the Sweepers left their signature in every one of the burnt villages.'

'The Sweepers are mostly simple folk, exactly like the ones who were massacred,' Torvald said. 'Do you really expect me or anyone with half a brain to believe they'd do that to their own? The people they claim to be fighting for? To what end, pray tell? You'll have to do better than that, your majesty. A lot better.'

'Why do you think I'm going after Aeron?' Edric leaned forward, his gaze for once heated. 'How hard do you think it would be for him to have a few shields painted with the Avellin lion? It's him, Torvald. In fact, I wouldn't be surprised to find he's behind the famous Garamon. He's been a thorn in Dunmark's side for years, and now I'm seeing to it that he gets his just deserts.'

'A thorn in *your* side, you meant to say, not in Dunmark's. At least not that I've ever heard. You forget that Ardath and the North are close neighbors. Good neighbors until now, I might add. Aeron has no earthly cause to start a war with us. And he's as likely to be

Garamon as you and I are.'

'You say that because, quite obviously, you're ill-informed.' Edric had the bit now, and wasn't about to give it up. 'My spies tell me – '

'Let's not drag this out,' Torvald cut him off, sitting up straight, matching hard with hard. He was a big man, bigger than the king who was no dwarf, and he knew he could intimidate. Not that it would work very well with Edric. A little, maybe. 'Strip away all the lies and deception, and we both know the truth of the matter. Arguing the fine points of peasant lore is not going to change anything, nor is trying to shift the blame over onto Aeron.

'For whatever reasons, you wanted a war with Ardath, and you went and made yourself one at the expense of nearly three hundred innocent lives. I'm giving you the benefit of the doubt by assuming the whole thing got out of hand, that you didn't plan it that way. Otherwise I'd have come for you at Burnt Keep with every man in the North under arms.

'Now. As far as I'm concerned we're done here. So I suggest you leave. And understand that this ill-considered move of yours has made you no friends here. Blackwood and Whitelake are with me. We're staying out of your quarrel with Aeron, and I strongly suggest you stay out of the North from now on. Have I made myself clear?'

Edric rose to leave. Glowering. Still holding on to his temper, if barely, he gave his parting shot. 'Have a care, Tondern. This business is not over. Far from it. You'll end up sorely regretting this day. You may take that as a promise. One I fully intend to keep if it's the last thing I do.'

Sitting alone in the tent, listening to the fading sounds of Edric and his men riding away, Torvald realized that the king hadn't touched his cup either. Curious – not likely, given the circumstances – but curious. He took his own cup and set it down in front of Wuffles' nose. The old mutt loved his drink, started lapping up as much of the wine as his nimble tongue could reach. Which was not a whole lot, because he soon overturned the cup, the wine seeping into the ground almost instantly. Wuffles gave a few half-hearted licks at the grass. Then, seeing that Torvald still wasn't moving, he settled down for a good scratch. Torvald remained sitting for a while longer, replaying the conversation with Edric and watching with half an eye whether the dog might show any ill effects.

He didn't. Not until they were nearly back to Dearg Fearna, the gates swinging wide to let them in. It was there that Wuffles suddenly keeled over, kicking and scrabbling in the grip of terrible, tendon-ripping, bone-crushing convulsions, foaming at the muzzle and whimpering fit to break Torvald's heart.

Berating himself for having used the poor mutt so badly, he borrowed a crossbow from one of his men and put the animal out of its misery. A pity. He'd grown more than half fond of the old cur. As to Edric, he was surprised that the man should try anything so brazen as poisoning him a mile outside his own keep and with twenty men-at-arms standing by. Made you wonder.

Made you wonder what went on in that overlarge head, and how much of it was still the right side of sane.

*   *   *

Gale couldn't remember ever having seen the king in such a foul mood. Which was saying something, seeing as Edric's basic temperament seemed to be forever fixed at a cold, muted rage. Provided the man had a soul at all, it probably had all the warmth and homeyness of an underground torture chamber.

Gale for once found himself wishing that Pryce and Stonebridge were present to share the brunt of Edric's chill fury but soon changed his mind when he realized that, if he played this right, it was as good a chance as any to place a subtle barb or two in the king's mind.

'Here I'm sitting on bloody Tondern's doorstep with four thousand men,' Edric spat, 'and the brazen beggar has the cheek to accuse me of burning his villages.'

Well now, your majesty, Gale thought but didn't say. *I do believe it was you who gave the order.*

'Once Aeron's taken care of,' Edric went on, 'I'm going to scrape that maggot Tondern out of Dearg Fearna and hang him from his own gatehouse. Gods-cursed duchies are getting above themselves. It's high time someone put them in their place, starting with the North. Insolent, thankless beggars, the lot of them. Bloody Tonderns would still be rooting with the pigs if it weren't for House Avellin having forged their stinking sties into something as viable as a kingdom.'

It was the first time Gale heard the king actually rant, and he didn't deem it wise to comment. In any case, Edric was already on to the next issue. 'I want to know which idiot issued your men and Pryce's with those gods-cursed shields,' he grated. 'I want the imbecile found, and then I want him hanged, drawn and quartered. For starters.'

'Would that be on the grounds of treasonous conduct,' Gale said with a chuckle, 'or mere wanton stupidity?'

A seemingly leadfooted attempt at lightening the mood, it was in truth an elegant step in the dance of deception, a stupid but negligible blunder for Edric to hang his anger on. Something to keep him from looking too closely at Gale's other dealings – for example, how much of the enormous sums the royal treasury was spending on the war had been diverted to accounts secretly controlled by Gale and used for purposes entirely unrelated to the kingdom's business.

Careful now.

'Forgive me, your majesty. A foolish remark, and entirely uncalled for.'

A proper show of remorse instantly makes you appear a smaller target than the fellow standing next in line – which in this case is Pryce. And now for the sowing of doubt.

'With your permission, I can only speak for my own people. But I can assure you they prefer to work in a manner much less... heavy-handed. As a rule they go in light, always on foot, and most definitely without the added encumbrance of a shield.'

There: passed the buck on to Pryce without actually pointing the finger.

Edric favored him with a scowl. 'So you say. I'll have a word with Pryce, then. In the meantime, go find me the idiot who's responsible for this mess. Dismissed.'

Damn it, but it was near impossible to drive a wedge between the king and his pet executioner – not that Gale had expected any different. Whatever else Pryce might be, he was fanatically loyal to Edric, who knew exactly what he'd bought himself by raising the man from ignominious butcher to titled and landed killer.

Murderer by appointment to his majesty, the king.

And Pryce? The man knew as well as anyone that his lordly status meant less than nothing to the trueborn nobility, who would one and all puke at the mere idea of sharing anything of theirs with the Lord Pretentioner, as they called him when safely out of his hearing. But he seemed entirely content with his role as royally appointed icon of threat, disturber of rarified circles, thorn in high-born flesh, shunned but ever-present bogyman, the mere mention of whom drew a whiff of bloodied implements and fly-blown corpses through noble parlors and ballrooms like a trail of noxious rot excreted by a passing specter.

They looked down on him because it was bred into their bones, because it was how they were built, and Gale couldn't really fault them, though in his view they feared Pryce for all the wrong reasons. Or maybe not. Maybe his name did cause them visions of the rack, the block and the noose – which would explain the unflagging persistence with which they sought to cut the idea of him down to a manageable size. Not very successfully, Gale imagined. Pryce was as bad as they came, a natural-born killer, a murderer by calling. A man whom the term 'evil' fit like a pair of breeches tailored to fit like a second skin.

No matter. If he couldn't get to Pryce through Edric, then he'd just have to do it the other way round.

131

Stepping out into Burnt Keep's courtyard, Gale found that it had begun to snow lightly. A bit early for the end of October, but not unheard of in these parts. Still within normal bounds, the locals said. Less so the ten days of bone-breaking frost that had preceded it. Way too cold for the time of year, everyone agreed, himself included. He was getting to an age where winter was no longer something he simply shrugged off as just another slightly uncomfortable season; an age where he'd been around long enough for the cold to have found the chinks in his armor, insidiously creeping past fires and braziers, through blankets and furs, worming its way into his very bones; an age where the mere thought of winter made him shiver.

Two stable boys were waiting for him, one holding his horse – a big brute of a courser, no palfrey for a man with Gale's considerable bulk – the other standing by the mounting block, ready to give him a hand up. The courtyard was a-bustle, scouts and messengers coming and going, servants scurrying along on various errands, horses brought out for care and currying, the smithy fired up for last-minute repairs to weapons and armor.

He had to wait for a wagon loaded high with castle provisions to squeeze in through the gate, then he was out, riding down the hill with the camp spread out before him, a small city unto itself. An orderly city: tents pitched in neat rows, spears racked outside, horses picketed in tidy lines, passages muddy but clear and uncluttered. Four thousand men under arms, at last count. A fine number, though provisioning them was a nightmarish task he was happy to leave to others, one that wouldn't get any easier once they were on the move, especially with winter coming.

132

Foolish of Edric not to wait for spring. He risked losing more men to the cold then to the enemy. But there'd been no dissuading him – not that Gale had tried all that hard. Changing Edric's mind when he'd set it on something was about as promising an undertaking as trying to knock down Dearg Fearna's walls with a lace kerchief. Though Gale did already pity the villagers and farmers west of the border. There were military commanders who frowned on plunder and rape and paid the poor sods for what they took, though the sums involved were usually too piddling to alleviate the months of hunger that inevitably followed in every army's wake. Unfortunately for Ardath, Edric was not one of those commanders.

Gale found Brother Maynard half a mile outside the main camp.
The Black had pulled up his wagon in a small grove a hundred yards off the road. No doubt he'd chosen his spot with care: out of sight and out of earshot of the troops, who wouldn't have tolerated being anywhere near the freight he carried in the sturdy, iron-banded wagon house with the tiny, barred window and feeding slits cut into the door at the back.

As usual, Maynard seemed to have known Gale was coming, was standing by the wagon with his hands shoved up the sleeves of his black robe and no expression at all on his coarse, brutal features, his eyes flat as dark glass, the twisted cross tattooed on his bare pate seeming to twitch with a life of its own.

Gale suppressed a shudder. As he drew near, a low growl issued from the wagon, signaling that Maynard's beasts had caught his scent. It was a hair-raising sound, and though he knew what was coming next and had braced himself beforehand, he still flinched as one of the monstrous things inside crashed against the door with a gut-loosening roar, setting the heavy wagon rocking on its springs.

Knowing from long experience that even the most basic niceties were lost on Maynard, and not being overly eager to stay anywhere near what was in that wagon a moment longer than was absolutely necessary, Gale came right to the point.

'Two people,' he said. 'In Ardath, possibly with Aeron's army at Bentridge. I need them removed. You'll have to make do with the names, seeing as I have neither the means nor the time to get my hands on anything of theirs.' He gave Maynard the names, saw no sign that the man recognized either one. Good. 'Can you do it?'

Maynard repeated them, his voice gravelly from disuse. Small wonder, that. Getting more than two words out of the man was always a task. 'The names will suffice. Consider it done.'

'When?' Gale asked.

'Soon, Amut willing.'

It was the best he would get, Gale knew, and really all he wanted. The details of Maynard's dark doings were not something he felt even the slightest inclination to pry into. Fishing in an inside pocket of his fur-lined cloak, he drew out a fat purse and tossed it to the Black, who caught it with surprising deftness even though he remained standing stock-still, moving only one arm, and that not a fraction farther than was needed.

Economical, forsooth, Gale thought, kneeing his mount around and departing without bidding farewell to the Black, who would likely have considered it a waste of breath in any case. *A wonder the man bothers to breathe at all. And who knows? Maybe he doesn't,*

134

when nobody's around. Now: I wonder when Edric will change his mind about Tondern, and come to me asking to have his grace taken care of. That's when things are apt to get a mite... sticky.

*　　*　　*

10

Six.

The making of six had been foreseen, and six had been made.

Nudd Wiggin was the first, and the most powerful by far. The leader. The boss. Just the way he liked it – because, improbable as it seemed, he was still in there. And pretty much in control. Or so he liked to believe. Not quite the man he'd been before the black stuff remade him, but essentially the same old Nudd Wiggin: sufferer of a thousand wrongs, plenty deserving of redress, brimming with righteous anger, thirsting for revenge. And now finally ready to give the world a painful lesson on the error of its ways. Oh, and: bugger the gods, if they didn't like what was coming.

Perhaps if he'd had a mirror to look into he might have been terrified by what looked back at him. As it was, after the first shock had passed he'd quickly and thoroughly adapted to the new situation. Suddenly he saw possibilities opening up before him in undreamt numbers. Options galore. Now he was ready for action, wound up tight, raring to go. Time for some payback.

Thanks to fate having smiled upon him for once, he finally had the means he'd lacked until now. Though it wasn't quite clear – and lastly unimportant, he reckoned – who was the host and who the passenger in this strangest of unions, himself or the black stuff, it was definitely an alliance forged, if not in heaven, then in a very accommodating version of hell. A melding of purposes that had made him incredibly, gloriously, dizzyingly strong. Unstoppable. And all he had to do in return was factor his ally's agenda into his own plans.

For, just as the stuff had learned and reproduced Nudd's shape, so he had learned its purpose, accepted it, and found that sharing it was a laughably small price to pay for the sheer limitless power it brought to the deal. He learned that it had a name, or rather a designation, the closest word he could think of in Common being 'Scour'. Left behind aeons ago by an ancient race long gone from this world, Scour was essentially a weapon with a clearly defined objective: to seek out and kill its ancient makers' equally ancient enemies. Had Nudd possessed the learning and the words, he'd have called it a sentient artifact. As it was, he saw it as some sort of supernatural ghost-that-lives-in-the-machine. In other words: as pure magic.

Although Nudd and Scour had struck a deal and were working together, there was no doubt as to whose mission took precedence. Nudd had found that much out a while back. He'd been heading straight south with the bit between his teeth and his imagination awash with visions of bloody revenge until there came a point where, following no conscious decision of his own, he'd suddenly veered off in a more easterly direction, his feet at complete odds with the map in his head.

Surprised, he corrected his course.

And after only a few steps began to sense an increasing strangeness to the way he walked, as if he'd turned light as a feather and his feet weren't quite reaching the ground anymore. Suddenly feeling queasy, he stopped.

Looked down at himself.

And saw nothing but empty air, and below that a few tufts of the tough, scraggly grass that was pretty much the only thing growing in these barren wastelands, clinging to the stony ground with a stubbornness that made him unaccountably angry, made him want to kick the damned stuff loose of its roots and leave it to die. Glancing over his shoulder, he realized with a sickening rush of vertigo that he and his body had parted ways and were now heading in different directions, all five of the stupid little snow-wankers still doggedly trotting after his other half.

It took him only a moment between realizing the split to comprehending that he was indeed free to go, if that was what he wanted, though Scour made it clear it was keeping the body. And without it, Nudd was coldly apprised, what was left of him would soon fade away into nothingness, every additional yard opening up between his body and himself another nail in his soul's coffin, so to speak.

With a wrench of gut-freezing terror – funny how he could still feel fear roiling his innards even though they were fast walking away from him – he fled back to safety.

Weird thing that, how Scour got its messages across.

Because it wasn't like it talked to him: no disembodied voice echoing in his mind, no fiery letters appearing before his inner eye – which would have been useless in any case, because he couldn't read for shit – but, somehow, when it wanted him to know something, he just knew.

Like now, when it seemed to have detected a target in Aldland, somewhere close to the mountains. A White, Nudd caught from a trailing tail end of information likely not intended for him. One of the Creator's First Children, as the eternal enemies of Scour's makers, the Bleak, were known to this world's groveling primitives – this last coming across with something approaching a derisive sneer. Rendle, they called this one. A dangerous bitch. One of the worst, because she wasn't above bending the rules that governed her kind if it meant dealing the Bleak a blow. Strange though, that she should be here alone. Usually, where she went...

Nudd lost the rest of it. No matter. None of his business. He just hoped Scour didn't get both of them killed before he got around to his own agenda. Not likely, though. He reckoned the adversary who could stand up to their combined might had yet to be born.

To Aldland it was, then, though it meant a gigantic detour, and put Nudd's own plans on hold for the immediate future. No matter. He had a feeling that, in this new incarnation, he had all the time in the world – just so long as none of the people on his list went and kicked the bucket before he got around to dealing with them. It wouldn't do for any of them to die of natural causes, not with what he had in store for them.

Hundreds of miles later, having crossed a sheer endless stretch of treeless tundra and then more bloody forest than Nudd ever wanted to see again for the rest of his life, their journey came to an abrupt halt in sight of the distant mountains, their snow-covered peaks floating above the midday haze like great white sails over a mist-bound sea.

They were halted on the bank of a small stream. On this side, the trees had already shed most of their leaves, as if they were hastily preparing for an unusually early onset of winter. On the far side, the woods were still green, filled with birdsong and sunlight. The smell of sap, rich loam and things blossoming occasionally carried across the boundary, wafting over on an unseasonably warm breeze that seemed to come straight out of summer.

A white butterfly landed on the back of his hand, probably come from over there. He watched it sitting there for a moment, then he swatted it away. The sight of the far side's calm, almost preternatural beauty awoke Nudd's anger again, stirring up a dark rage deep inside him that might have been his or might have been Scour's. What was definitely his was the infinite longing that washed through him like a warm, gentle wave bearing a promise of peace that was hard to resist.

For a moment, he found himself wishing there was a way he could give in to it, just let everything go and float across the river, a leaf or a feather carried over by the breeze. Then he shook off the feeling like a dog shaking out its fur after a swim in filthy water, thinking, *Gods-damned, fricking goodness! Bloody witchcraft, is what it is.*

Scour concurred, though it didn't seem concerned, as if it had expected something like this: a stream Nudd could have easily waded through without getting more than his shins wet, and yet a

141

barrier that was as insurmountable as it was invisible. He'd tried, and gotten nothing but a bunch of scrapes and bruises for his trouble.

Why'd we come here in the first place, if we can't even get in, that's what I'd like to know, he grumbled to himself. *Gods-bloody waste of time, you ask me.*

Scour communicated nothing more on the subject.

But Nudd had been whiling away the past couple of weeks' endless slog by practicing his eavesdropping on the sly, loitering around the thing's back door and getting better at catching the odd bit of information. Which was why he knew that he was looking at something called a Node, a place where several of the great lines that crisscrossed the earth came together, in this case joined by an enormously powerful one that surfaced from deep within the earth itself, a situation that was pretty much unique: incredible amounts of rare energy woven into an impregnable fortress, a land out of normal time and space. And no way in, at least not for the bad and the ugly.

Somewhere inside that dream of eternal summer, the White bitch was sitting safe and secure, probably laughing up a riot at Nudd's foolish attempts to get across the gods-bloody river.

Patience, Scour let him know. *We will get her.* For, having ascertained how things stand here, we will now proceed to bring untold woe and destruction to these fine lands, from the Nordsmen shores to the Jemmarraa desert, from the high mountains to the deep sea. Sooner or later, she won't have a choice but to come out and fight – if she doesn't want to see everything she's worked so long to preserve brought to ruin, wrecked beyond salvage in what to her

142

kind and mine will amount to no more than the blink of an eye. That's when we'll have her. Now, we depart.

'About time,' Nudd said out loud, sounding like a truculent brat even to himself.

'Move, fishfuckers,' he barked at his five silent companions – completely unnecessarily, seeing as they followed him anyway, wherever he went. But the boring shit Scour had lately put him through was begging for an outlet. 'Move your skinny arses. We're going a-hunting.'

Now, after another long slog that had taken them pretty much back to where they'd started from, Nudd stood on a rise that gave him a good view of the snow-suckers' camp, surveying the savages' comings and goings. Fish-heads, the mariners working the northern routes called them because of all the crap they ate: fish heads, seal guts, whale blubber. Smelled like it, too. Even from where he was standing, he caught the rank odor rising from racks upon racks hung with fish drying in the sun. He saw women kneeling over hides staked out on the ground, scraping off the residual fat and bits of meat left over from the skinning, the hides adding their own special flavor to the stink hovering over the camp. Several small groups of men were busy gutting and skinning caribou carcasses, while dogs yipping and snarling over scraps and a bunch of children playing some sort of game with a ball and sealskin rackets added to the chaos. Smoke was rising from many of the sod-roofed dugouts, muddy hovels the savages lived in until winter came south, or so he'd heard somewhere. Once it snowed, they'd move into those nonsensical ice houses and use the dugouts for storage. Stupid

143

buggers probably *liked* freezing their arses off. There must have been close to a thousand people down there, the camp loosely spread out along nearly half a mile of raised ground overlooking the seashore where scores of their ridiculously flimsy hide boats were pulled up on the pebbly beach.

Weighing the possibilities, Nudd decided there was nothing he wanted down there. For what he had in mind he needed an army, and while these people might make a passable job of hunting down defenseless beasts, as fighters they were next to useless. Too small, too skinny, too peaceful. Too bloody *nice*. But he already knew where to look for his dread battalions: another hundred or so miles due south, he reckoned, and they'd be hitting the first Nordsmen villages. Big, ugly brutes, those Nordsmen. Just what he needed.

*   *   *

Wanderer was alone, stranded on a shrinking island, surrounded by a sea of black. Scour had a firm grip on his body and on the parts of his mind that controlled it, though it only intervened when he openly rebelled – something he'd tried only once, just to test the limits of his freedom. Although he already had a pretty good idea what would happen, a few days into the trip south he broke away from Wiggin and the others. Heading off at right angles, he began to climb up the slope of a gentle rise to the left of their route. Scour let him go a hundred yards. Then it abruptly reined him in, and not too gently. Like a tethered dog, he suddenly reached the end of a chain that had no give at all, coming to a teeth-rattling, bone-jarring halt in less than an eye-blink. Good thing he'd been going slow, he thought as Scour reeled him back in, otherwise he might have ended

144

up seriously damaged.

As for the rest of his mind – after the stuff's initial onslaught, they'd reached a stalemate. In a quick, excruciating flurry of pokes and probes and stabs, Scour had attempted to subdue him entirely, racing through multiple approaches in a mind-boggling blur of ice-cold precision, attacking his very essence from every imaginable angle in less time than it took to think, *No, you can't!*

To Wanderer – defending his island of self, desperately fighting for survival, whirling this way and that, parrying blows that would have crushed him soul and spirit while he shored up defenses that threatened to crumble and collapse under Scour's relentless assault – it felt like the battle lasted an eternity. Without help, he wouldn't have been able to resist.

He called upon the spirits-that-live-in-everything, and they flocked to his need. He summoned the ancestor spirits as well, terrified of Scour though he knew they were, hiding on the verge of Shadows.

You live because you are remembered, he implored them. But if this thing is not stopped, there will be no one left *who remembers. If we die, so will you. The final death. You will fade into Shadows and be gone, along with our whole people. I must try to save them. Please. I beg you. Help me.*

They heard.

And they came, no matter their fear was sheer overwhelming, lending him their strength without which he would have lost the fight even before it was begun.

Another thing Wanderer realized at the cost of nearly losing himself

145

was that he couldn't afford any kind of strong feelings anymore. Not anger, not fear, not sadness, not joy – though he seemed in no danger of ever experiencing the latter again. Allowing emotions meant cracking open the door to his soul – with Scour always out there, ready to come rushing in, to engulf Wanderer's island in a black, evil tide and drown what was left of him. What had taken him the longest to figure out were the origins of the vengeful rage that seemed to constantly boil on a slow flame somewhere deep down in the mix that was Scour and himself. He was shocked and puzzled how such a wealth of all-encompassing hatred could have slumbered unseen in the depths of his self, and him a shaman. Until he realized that the rage wasn't his. Not Scour's either – the thing was incapable of feeling anything at all. Which left only Wiggin. It made sense, in a sick sort of way. And it was something of a relief, though it didn't absolve Wanderer from having to guard not only against his own sentiments but against Wiggin's poisonous under-current as well.

So it was with carefully dampened wonder that he took in the vastness of the forest they traveled through, the immense, ancient trunks rising from the moss-covered forest floor that was like a landscape of soft, green valleys and heights all to itself, the trees' great limbs stretching away into unimaginable heights: soaring pill-ars that seemed made to hold up the sky. Wanderer's defenses held until they reached their journey's destination, a place that almost spelled his doom.

Beholding the Land of Summer nearly undid him. For that was what it was. Standing there staring across the water, he knew with unshakable certainty that he was looking at the secret source of his

146

people's most ancient lore, a collective dream dreamt over and over by countless generations of Snow People, captured and preserved over centuries in the gossamer net of the Summer Song, sung many and many a time during the long, cold months when darkness encroached and fierce winter storms raged for days on end. And now, for him, become real. Suddenly he was breathless, his heart pounding, his inner balance faltering.

Great magic lives here, he thought. *It shines like a bright, clear flame, kindled by a spark come down from the Heart of the All itself. A beacon of goodness and trust. Such beauty! Such peace!*

Gripped by a longing that seemed not of this world, he hardly noticed himself stepping forward, paid no heed to the door in his mind creaking open, nor to the first, black feeler probing the crack, seeking entrance. Then the barrier stopped him.

This was the thing: he could have gone on then.

Easy as breathing, he could have left behind his body and the desecration Scour had wrought on it, drifted off into the beckoning arms of a secure haven where the world's troubles couldn't reach him anymore. He almost did.

It was the sudden, violent collision with the unseen boundary that checked him, the pain serving to remind him of the suffering that surely awaited his people at the hands of Wiggin and his void-spawned passenger, and of the terrible affliction it had already cast on his entire family: Younger Sister, Feather, Raven, and Strongest-of-All, mindlessly following wherever Scour led. And little Rainbow. Gods give that the cold had taken her peacefully before a fox or a wolverine or a bear found her. The message from his bruised knees and chin was clear: stay and fight. He did.

As if his hearing had been lost and returned, he abruptly became aware of the spirits' clamored warnings, slamming the door shut on Scour at the last possible moment.

Now, watching Wiggin study the Seal tribe's winter camp, he had to once again wrestle his mind to a place of indifference, stamping down hard on rage, fear and despair.

He'd already thought the Snow People safe for the time being, passed by and forgotten. But then Wiggin, or Scour, or both of them together, had led them all the way back north for reasons he couldn't begin to fathom. And now this. Sick to the core of his being, he waited for the destruction to begin, hard pressed not to curse the gods for having put his people first in Scour's gruesome path.

But Wiggin turned away. Walked down the hill's near side, turned south.

Still not daring to hope – another feeling he couldn't afford – Wanderer stood rooted to the spot, watched Wiggin gearing up for those long, loping strides that ate up distance faster than a herd of frightened caribou. He didn't move even when the others began to shamble off, following Wiggin like hollow puppets pulled along by invisible strings.

Then his own string suddenly tautened with a palpable twang, nearly jerking him off his feet. For once, he didn't mind. Clamping down on the flood of relief that threatened to upset his precariously balanced defenses, he set off after Wiggin and the others. South again. Towards what – that was a question for another day. For

148

now, at least a part of his people had been spared.

*   *   *

Anuun reckoned he had two days to find food for Snowchild, three at the outside. An impossible task, it seemed. The tribes had long since moved south for the winter, as had the caribou, and with them any chance of finding a suckling female, human or animal, in the time he had left. Still, he had to try. He righted one of the sleighs and stripped it of its remaining cargo, keeping only a few things he thought might come in useful. Then, with the child snug in a pile of furs, he set off at a run, pushing the sleigh over rises and flats, riding the runners where the terrain descended, desperately worried for the small, helpless being that a whimsical, cruel twist of fate had placed in his charge.

Driven by twofold necessity, he ran all through that day, short as it was this time of year, the child so amazingly quiet and uncomplaining, he stopped several of times just to see whether she was still alive. She was, looking back at him with eyes that seemed to contain the patience and wisdom one might expect to see in a person nearing the opposite end of life, certainly not in a babe of, what, a week? It was uncanny. A little unsettling, even. But then, what did he know about humans? Not a whole lot, and less about infants. Were they all like this? Was it normal for them to look as if they stood with one foot in the here and now and the other still in the beyond, continuing to partake in the wisdom of the gods? Somehow, he doubted it.

He continued on through the long night, running in the light of the moon making its slow journey across the vast, star-spangled sky, his steps crunching out a counterpoint rhythm to the runners hissing and bumping over ice and wind-packed snow, the journey testing even his Iceling endurance to the limits. Slowly but surely he was running out of strength, and out of hope. And then, with the winter-weak sun straining to rise over the eastern horizon, its first feeble rays casting soft, golden edges on drifts and seracs, the gods themselves took a hand in the saving of Snowchild.

Rounding a rise, Anuun spied two dark shapes out on the pack ice, maybe a hundred yards from the shore, one large, one small: seals, a female and her young one. They were close to a hole in the ice, the mother nudging the cub with her snout, likely prompting it to follow her into the water before a bear or a fox came along. But, from what Anuun could make out, the little one wasn't reacting. Not moving at all, in fact. Sick, perhaps. Dying, or already dead.

As he stood watching this small episode in the great, ever-recurring cycle of life and death, a snippet of memory drifted into his awareness, one of those seemingly useless things picked up in passing and tucked away somewhere deep out of sight only to surprisingly surface at a time of need. Although he couldn't recall when or where, he remembered hearing that, of all mammals, humans included, it was seals that produced the most wholesome and nourishing milk, a potion ascribed with near magical properties.

Here was an incredible chance presenting itself, but only if he acted quickly, before the seal gave up on the cub and slipped back into the water. Casting about, he found no sign of predators. Snowchild would be safe for a spell. Quick as thought, he took to the ice. Moments later he surfaced behind the seal, reassuming his corporeal aspect and blocking her only route of escape.

She didn't even try to get past him, just looked at him with huge, liquid eyes that seemed to express all the grief and bereavement any mother would feel at the death of a child. Nor did she fight when he gently gathered her into his arms and carried her back to the sleigh. A moment's hesitation, then he laid her down beside Snowchild, ready to intervene if things went badly.

He needn't have worried.

A look of understanding seemed to pass between the two, Snowchild doing that baffling thing with her eyes again. The seal mother cooed. Heaved herself closer to Snowchild, rolled over onto her side and presented her teats. All the little one had to do was turn her head and drink. Anuun helped her find a teat, then he stood back and watched.

With an involuntary shiver he realized that, in all likelihood, he was witnessing the birth of a legend. In his imagination he could already see the Snow People gathered around their fires, the children begging for a tale, an elder giving in and telling them the story of Snowchild: orphaned at the hands of a dread monster sent by the Dark Lord to bring suffering and ruin into the world, rescued by one of the mythical beings known as Icelings, suckled by Verelda herself, the goddess having taken on the form of a seal. No doubt they'd go on to believe that the gods had singled her out, that she was meant to perform great and daring deeds, and no doubt she would end up immortalized in Snow People lore.

Right now, though, she was nothing but a suckling babe, eyes closed, tiny fists balled in contentment, her busy gulping occasionally interrupted by small, blissful sighs.

*   *   *

11

Seeing Aeron again after – what was it, seven, eight years? – Bowen was struck not so much by the similarities between the king and his deceased brother as by the differences. It was as if an un-gifted artist had sketched a slipshod copy of Arnold, rendering him tall but not big, the black mane shrunken to a greying fringe, the vivid, cornflower eyes faded to the washed-out blue of a hazy sky, all of Arnold's vigorous, outgoing personality lost in the translation as well.

Stepping into the inn's low-beamed common room, Bowen saw that it had been turned into a war room: three tables pushed together to accommodate an enormous map, the walls festooned with what looked like lists of anything from fighting units to provisions to the billeting of troops, with half a dozen scribes churning out more of the same while messenger boys scurried in and out. Longshanks was there, and both of the Strongs, old Eilian propped on a cane – likely the old wound from the War of Eight giving him trouble again – his son Iefan sharing the old duke's hawkish features and frank, self-assured manner and still looking trim, wiry and quick, one of the fastest blades in Ardath.

Nodding a greeting to each of them, Bowen got the immediate impression that things weren't as they should be. There was a tension in the air that had nothing to do with the impending war. The room felt divided, Longshanks and the Strongs standing by the smoking fireplace, Aeron bent over the map with a man at his elbow whom Bowen didn't know but would have instantly disliked even if he hadn't been wearing the hooded black habit of a priest of Amut, the god of death. He lacked the shaven head and tattoo, but the twisted cross carved from a massive chunk of onyx and hanging from a silver chain around his neck left no doubt as to which god he followed. With his pale, almost colorless eyes, the dark, three-day stubble and sallow complexion, he looked like a creature who tended to avoid the sun. Bowen could easily imagine him crawling through dark alleys and graveyards at night and spending the daylight hours hanging upside down from the roof of a cave. The Black spared Bowen a superficial glance: unreadable, but certainly not friendly. So the dislike was mutual. What else was new?

'Threehands,' Aeron said, only now becoming aware of Bowen and Bryn's presence. 'Glad you could make it. And the young man would be…'

'Bryn of Bailon, your majesty,' Bryn offered, bending a knee. 'At your service.'

'Good, good,' Aeron said, his eyes already wandering back to the map. 'You've been assigned quarters?'

'We have, your majesty,' Bryn said. 'On the Barrow.'

'Well, then. I trust – '

'If I may, your majesty,' Bowen said, stepping up to the map

154

table before Aeron could finish dismissing them. 'Which way do you reckon Edric will be coming?'

'Why, by the North Road, of course. The scouts have him in Redfern. And as you well know, it's steep, wooded country all along that part of the border, with what low ground there is a tangle of deadwood, thickets, and bogs. No way to get an army through there – at least not in any reasonable amount of time and without losing half his men.'

'What if he doesn't take the North Road?' Bowen asked. 'What if he goes around, leaves us sitting here on our hill while he has a free run all the way to Cullamor?'

'Nonsense,' the Black butted in, giving Bowen a scowl. 'He'll come by the road. There's no other way. Unless he goes all the way round through Harad, which would take him weeks and put his campaign right in the middle of winter. And that's assuming they let him pass without putting up a fight.'

'And you are?' Bowen said.

'Brother Wystan, of Landing.' This time, there was open enmity in the look Bowen received.

'And you're an expert on battle tactics, I take it?' Bowen wasn't about to be fazed by a priest, Black or otherwise.

'Indeed, I am. As you'd know if you'd bothered to read my well-known treatise on Thalios, in which I was able to point out a number of fallacies in his reasoning. Now, I believe his majesty has other – '

'How long has it been this bloody cold up here?' Bowen asked, riding right over him.

'A little over two weeks,' Longshanks offered, stepping up to

155

the table and giving Bowen an almost imperceptible nod. Greyer than he used to be, walking with a slight limp that was probably due to his knees not getting any younger but still a comfortingly solid and dependable presence. 'Long enough for every body of water that isn't an outright rapids to have frozen over.'

Bowen wasn't surprised that Longshanks had seen the same problem he had. 'Here,' he said, tracing a meandering blue line on the map. Originating in the high mountains, it snaked down through the duchies of Whitelake and Redfern, crossing the border into Ardath near a place called Burnt Keep. 'The river Etherelle. Slow-moving, shallow. Frozen through by now, I'd wager. Goat dung to gold that's the way Edric will come.'

'Threehands,' Aeron intervened. 'Not to discount your advice, but we've been through this, and we're agreed there's no way Edric will risk his whole force on the ice. Granted, it may be thick enough by now to carry a small unit or two, but never a whole army. To try would be suicide.'

'We' meaning yourself and your black bootlicker, Bowen thought. *To look at the Strongs and Lyr Longshanks, I'd say they're anything but agreed.*

'By your leave, majesty, I beg to differ. Even if he doesn't trust the river ice, there's a wide strip of open wetlands along most of the southern bank. You couldn't get a single horse through there in warmer weather, but now the ground is likely frozen solid. Not quite as good as a road, maybe, but good enough. I suggest we at least send a scouting party north through Long Valley to assay the situation in the field. In fact, granting your permission, young Bryn and myself would be happy to go.' That got him a nod from Eilian

Strong and relieved looks from his son Iefan and from Longshanks.

'Very well,' Aeron conceded grudgingly. 'Lord Bailon may take what men he's brought and go scout the river. You, I want here on my war council. My brother always valued your opinion, and I'd be a fool to forego what served him well. I expect you back here as soon as you've found your quarters and seen the young man off. Dismissed.'

Damn you, Aeron, Bowen thought as they made their exit.

How am I supposed to look out for the lad if you send him off without me? But I've only myself to blame. Why did I have to go and make that stupid offer instead of leaving the business to Aeron's scouts? Because I don't trust what would come of it, that's why. Still, I should have seen it coming. But what could I have said? Beg pardon, majesty, but the lad's too young and green to go out on his own? Or, so sorry, but I have this irrepressible mothering streak and simply can't bear to let him out of my sight? A lot of good that would have done Bryn's chances of getting ahead in the world. Besides, he would never have forgiven me for making the both of us look like fools. Ah, well. Time to let go, I suppose. Though I doubt I'll rest easy until he's back safe and sound.

Up on the Barrow, they found another of Aeron's lists nailed to the tower door for anyone who could read, billeting Bryn and Bowen in a small, window-less room on the ground floor close to the entrance, a spot Bowen approved of with a nod to himself. Close to the door was never wrong. Chances were, you might have to get out in a hurry. What good was a view when the roof over your head was burning and your only way out was either six sets of stairs swarming with enemies, or a very long jump?

'You could go tomorrow morning, you know,' he told Bryn. 'Nobody's going to begrudge you a night's rest after five days on the road.'

Listen to yourself, old man. Angling for another day's grace as if it made a whit of a difference. Pathetic.

'No. I'm good to go.' The lad was trying hard not to look scared. Which he was, no doubt about it, but he was also clearly determined not to let fear get the better of him. It was all Bowen could ask, all anyone could do. More often than not, the man who thought himself fearless was among the first to die. Look fear in the eye, acknowledge it, use it to your advantage – that was how you stayed alive in times like this.

'There's hours of daylight left,' Bryn was saying. 'Besides, Aeron expects me to leave forthwith, so that's what I'm going to do. I'm taking Daven and Arlie. They're both good in the woods. Any more of us would only make it easier for the enemy to spot us. Even if Edric isn't coming that way, there are bound to be scouts of his about.'

There you go. He knows the stakes, knows what needs to be done, and there's no fault to be found with the way he's going about it. None at all. Wouldn't do anything different myself.

'An hour's rest,' Bryn told Daven and Arlie. 'Ham and Lorin can put up the tent by themselves, give you two a break.'

With going to find provisions for Bryn, Daven and Arlie, and trying hard not to worry too much, the hour seemed to fly by like nothing. Returning to the tower, Bowen found Bryn ready to leave.

158

'Lad,' he said. 'A word.'

'Yes?' Impatient. Always in a hurry. But – and this was new – on time.

'It's your eighteenth nameday tomorrow.'

'Is it?' Bryn said, looking puzzled, no doubt wondering why Bowen was bringing this up now, of all times. 'I'd entirely forgotten.'

'There's something I have to tell you.' Bowen had thought long and hard whether he should tell the lad now, or wait until he got back. He'd decided that, now or later, there was never a good time for something like this, and that he'd already put it off for too long as it was. 'Something I promised your mother I'd tell you when you came of age. Seeing as you'll be gone for a few days, I'm telling you now.'

Seeing as only the gods know what's to come, and whether either of us will still be alive in a few days.

Though he'd rehearsed the speech a thousand times, Bowen suddenly found himself struggling for words, with Bryn looking at him half expectantly, half eager to be gone.

'There's no easy way to say this. But you need to know. Your father... I mean Lord Kendric, he loved you as his son. But... he wasn't your real father. Not by blood, in any case. When your mother and I came to Bailon, she was already carrying you in her womb. I – '

'Enough.' Said in a quiet voice that rang louder than a shout. Bryn was white-faced, hands clenched into fists, staring at Bowen with a wild look in his eyes. Shocked. Hurt. Resentful. 'I'll hear no more of it. Not another word. We're done. I want you gone when I

159

come back. Gone from here, and gone from Bailon Keep.'

Whirling around, he made for the door.

'Bryn, lad, wait up,' Bowen called after him, getting only the sound of boots clattering down the stairs for an answer.

He rushed to the door, shouted down the stairwell. 'I said, wait up, godsdammit! You need to know the rest of it!'

Bowen, you're a bloody idiot, he berated himself, hurrying after Bryn. *You should have reckoned on something like this happening. Should have waited a few more days. Fool, fool, fool.*

The lad was too fast for him.

By the time Bowen got to the ground floor, all he found was a small cloud of dust hanging in the air, and Bryn riding out the gate with Daven and Arlie. For a moment Bowen stood debating whether he should go after them. Hesitated, torn this way and that. Turned away. No. The lad was in shock, which was understandable, and in no fit state to listen to reason. Let him go do his thing, carry out his mission. Give him time to calm down. Try and start over when he was back, hopefully with a cooler head on his shoulders and willing to hear Bowen out. Bloody cockup, though, no matter how you looked at it.

Fool. I should go beat my head against the wall for a spell, if I thought it would do any good.

Fingering the object he'd tucked under his jerkin with the intention of giving it to Bryn, he decided it would be best if he asked someone he could trust to pass it on in case something happened and he couldn't do it himself. Longshanks, perhaps, or Lorin, or Ham. Though he was beginning to wonder whether he'd be doing anyone a favor by it.

*   *   *

Numb with shock, Bryn hardly noticed the winter-grey landscape they were riding through, his two companions no more than vague figures moving at the outermost edge of his awareness. He barely registered the freezing wind, nor did he connect the small, icy stings on his face with the fact it had begun to snow.

Turmoil didn't begin to describe the state he was in. A part of him knew that his reaction to Bowen's confession had been overhasty, childish. Stupid. He'd fled in a cowardly panic instead of hearing Bowen out, and he was already starting to regret it. Not for Bowen's sake but for his own. He *did* need to know. And he would, once he got back.

But then, what was there to know? another part of him argued, aside from the fact that his whole damned life had suddenly turned out to have been one big, bloody lie: his mother, the wise, gentle woman he'd loved and adored, another man's doxy; his father not his father at all, but a cuckold, or at least a trusting fool who'd let himself be slipped someone else's bastard. And Bowen...

Bastard. That's what I am now: a bastard. No other name to call it by. But not half the bastard Bowen is, getting the woman he was charged to protect with child, and then foisting me off on the man who offered them both shelter out of the goodness of his heart. Bowen the coward, shirking his gods-given duty, besmirching everyone's honor, betraying pretty much everything that makes a man's life worth living. His lover. His lord. Me. Probably his king before that – why else would he have been forced to flee Dunmark?

161

How could he? How the hell could he do this to me, his own son?

Snow got in Bryn's face, or maybe it was just the gods-bloody, icy wind stinging his eyes and making them tear. He was damn well not going to cry. Not with Arlie and Daven sneaking furtive, troubled glances at him.

'Everythin' all right, m'lord?' Arlie asked, worry clouding his clear, blue gaze, his massive shoulders hunched as if he were intuitively sharing Bryn's burden. 'You want we should stop and rest?'

'I'm fine,' Bryn said, cursing the hitch in his voice that made him sound like a bairn trying hard not to blubber. He cleared his throat. There. All better. No more thinking about... just, no more thinking, period. They weren't out for a harmless stroll, and he was damned well responsible for these men. Even if they never saw hide nor hair of Edric and his troops, the cold alone could kill them in a trice if they weren't careful. 'Another hour, and then we'll start looking for a place to lie up for the night. It's too bloody cold to sleep out in the open.'

Not thinking turned out to be nearly impossible.

The harder he tried not to, the more insistently the cursed images came knocking. For every time he shied away from the pain and the anger, they hit him all the harder the moment he wasn't looking. *Lies, lies, lies!* they shouted over every defense he threw up. *Bastard, bastard, bastard,* they whispered in time with the horses' thudding hooves until he thought he'd either scream or go mad, or both.

Thinking about the mission didn't help either. Every turn he took, he found himself face to face with Bowen: Bowen who would

162

have said this, Bowen who would have done that. Bowen who would have approved, Bowen who would have cautioned. Bowen who'd taught him pretty much everything he knew. And how much of that could he still take for granted, in the light of what he'd learned?

Stop it! You're driving yourself crazy. Time to find a shelter for the night. A barn. A shed. A bloody cave. Anything. Anything's better than freezing to death in this godsawful cold.

As luck would have it, they did better than a cave. With dusk settling in, they came to a small hamlet, too small even to be marked on their map, a few houses and, lo and behold, a tavern, a hole in the wall in a ramshackle building on what passed for a main street. For a wonder, they had a couple of rooms over the common room, noisy and reeking of ale and smoke, the beds no more than old blankets thrown over piles of straw and probably crawling with assorted vermin. But there was a fire going downstairs, warmth leaking up through the cracks in the floor along with the stink, the jokes and the laughter.

Bryn was wasted. After downing a quick mug of ale and a bowl of beans with a few slivers of stringy meat, he left Arlie and Daven sitting by the fire and went up to his room, where sleep blessedly found him before his mind had a chance to start spinning in circles again.

*   *   *

How heavy, time.
And should the whole mountain come crashing down on top of me...
compared to time, it would weigh lighter than a feather – and hurt

163

far less, I'm sure. So many years, with every hour a new, fresh flavor of pain, every day another ton laid on my breast to crush and steal away what little breath is left in me.

Will it then never end, this sad parody of life, this slow, creeping shadow of true existence, this sufferer's way of darkness, dust, and slow decay? Ah, if only I had known. An oath, an ill-considered word, a promise of sleep, and then eight hundred years of solitude and darkness.

Eight hundred years, give or take. It's been a long time since I stopped counting. Still, I'm not entirely unaware of what goes on outside. Though the odd, unreliable glimpse is all I have – blurry images in a tarnished mirror, shadows flitting along the walls of my prison – I do have all the time in the world to try and make sense of what I see.

How desperate I was! How arrogant!
But such were the times, in the aftermath of Simbalan. I was among the victors in the greatest battle ever fought, yet sentenced to a slow and painful death nonetheless. And to think it was a mere scratch that did me in, and the war as good as over. A nearly bloodless mark, but inscribed by a blade cursed in hell. Just my luck that I should run into one of Malamut's void-spawned monsters wielding steel dipped in sorcery and poison.

What wonder I took the way out they offered me? How could I not, when I'd just finished spitting in Death's milky eye a hundred times over, only to find that, in the end, it had me by the collar after all. A terrible tragedy, they said – so full of sympathy they were, the great mages of the Incantaria: Elwyn of Woodsbury, Orsen

Burnthands, Gisbert the Good. A terrible tragedy, but also a singular chance.

Turn it to the good, they urged. The good of generations yet to come, a provision for the future, protection against someone like Malamut ever threatening the world again. Here is your death that still may serve a purpose. Here is the blade we forged for you, imbued with all our vast knowledge. Here are the words you can choose to say, or not. Speak the oath, and let us do the rest. Speak, and instead of death, the sleep of the just shall be yours, and the world a safer place for it. Sleeping, you will watch over your children and your children's children, guarding against the day when evil might reawaken and the blood of your blood will be called once more to sacred duty.

Such fancy words! Such grandiloquent promises! I should have listened to the young one, Torgrim of Eldinga, who spoke strongly against it, saying it was a thing too close to the dark side's fell machinations. Ah, well! Should, would, could. Now the gate stands open, and the horses are long gone. You might say there's a forest grown, and toppled, and grown again where the corral used to be. But oh, how I longed for the chance to go back and live that day again. To be able to go back and choose death, simple death, no matter how slow and painful. Anything would have been a blessing compared to this. How many centuries since last I slept? How long this endless vigil? How very fragile the sanity of the one who holds it?

Though now, in spite of everything, it seems...

But what is this?

165

What ghoul, what manner of skulking presence dares invade the privacy of my suffering? Show yourself, vermin, and I'll teach you...

Oh! It's you. The boy with the thickest skull this side of the Ard Dromlach. And about time, too. Do you have any idea how many times I've tried to get through to you? And now I find you snooping around in my dreams – or should I say, in your dreams?

Be that as it may. You're finally here, so listen up. Ears cocked and arse cheeks clenched, as my old weapons master used to say. What was his name again? No matter. There's trouble coming your way, lad. Bad trouble, and a hard piece of work. Which is why I've sent you a fitting tool, to help you with the job. Why me? I hear you asking. Because you're of the Blood, is why. Which brings us to a somewhat delicate subject, namely the question of your lineage. Your father, as you may or may not know, was –

No! I don't want to hear it. I don't have a father anymore. I'm a bastard, is all you need to know. Sorry, but you've got the wrong person. You'll have to go looking for your 'Blood' elsewhere.

But –

No, I said! Leave me be! Leave me be leave me be leave me...

Bryn awoke gasping for air, feeling as if he'd been on the verge of drowning. He sat up shivering, bathed in sweat, his heart racing. Still clawing his way out of the nightmarish dream. What the hell had that been about? He'd felt like he was locked inside someone else's head, paralyzed and unable to escape, almost as if he *was* that person.

Gods, but come to think about it, the whole thing did sound a lot like the old fairytale about the King under the Mountain, Cormac

Avellin, founder of the kingdom of Dunmark. Cormac the Great, sleeping away the centuries in a cave somewhere deep under the mountains. When his beard grew so long it reached three times around the stone he was bedded on, so the story went, a great evil would befall the Seven Kingdoms. Then, and only then, would King Cormac ride forth again to save the realm a second time. Kids' stuff, myth, one of the stories his mother used to tell him when he was little.

Bad move, that, thinking of his mother. The memory instantly brought on a fresh wave of anger and hurt. Damn it! Couldn't the godsbloody crap at least leave him alone in his sleep? He needed to get some rest, for mercy's sake, else he'd lead them all into bleary-eyed disaster on the morrow. The only remedy he could think of was something he'd never tried before – and from everything he'd heard, the results might well turn out little better than not sleeping at all.

I don't bloody care. I am not *going to lie awake all night.*

Pulling on his boots, he made for the common room, resolved to drink as many mugs of ale as it took to make the voices and the dreams go away and leave him in peace for what remained of the night.

*   *   *

It was nearly midnight by the time Bowen got to bed.

He'd gone back down to Bentridge, as Aeron had ordered. The village was bustling with the usual collection of camp followers: sutlers, whores, fortune-tellers, card sharps, and most every other shade of lowlife come crawling out of whatever holes they hid in

167

during times of peace, drawn to the impending mayhem like vultures to a carcass.

Walking towards the inn, Bowen saw a pair of scouts come galloping in from the east, their horses winded and a-lather. News from the front, no doubt. He knew what it was even before he heard it from Aeron, the nasty smirk on Wystan's ugly mug telling it all: Edric was on the move, and he was coming down the North Road. Just like the black rat had said he would.

'He'll be here by nightfall,' Aeron proclaimed. 'Tomorrow at the latest. Thanks to the gods and Brother Wystan, we're where we need to be, and ready for him. But I want that no one should blame themselves for having thought differently. Sending someone to scout the river was certainly no mistake.'

No, it wasn't, Bowen thought. *But now Bryn is out there, and will likely find Edric's army sitting square in his way when he tries to get back. Gods give he has the foresight to go around the long way and come in from behind. Though I'm still not convinced we're seeing the whole picture here. Edric is a devious bastard, and he knows his warcraft inside out. I should know, seeing as, to my lasting regret, I was the one who taught him. Going straight for the prize with no feints or shenanigans is not like him. Not like him at all.*

Later, standing atop the tower on the Barrow with Longshanks and Iefan Strong, all three of them wrapped in furs against the bitter cold, watching the Dunmarkan army set up camp a quarter mile out where the forested hills drew back from the wide swath of open, level terrain called Balder's Field, tents going up and fires winking into existence one after the other until the ground below seemed to mirror the star-spangled sky, Bowen had his misgivings confirmed – though he doubted Aeron would pay them any more heed now than he'd done so far.

'How many do you reckon are down there?' Bowen asked, already sure of the answer to within a few score.

'Eleven hundred,' Longshanks said. 'Twelve at the outside.'

'Aye.' Iefan nodded agreement.

'Tell me something,' Bowen said. 'Say your aim was to roll up Ardath and take Cullamor, how many would you field?'

'Three, four thousand?' Longshanks said.

'At least four. More, if you could.' Iefan was suddenly scowling. 'So where's the rest?'

'My thought exactly,' Bowen said. 'Where's the rest?'

'Maybe what's down there is the vanguard, and the others will show up some time tomorrow.' Longshanks didn't sound as if he believed it.

'Right,' Iefan said. 'And maybe Edric intends to drop by for a friendly chat over a cup or two of fennel tea. Mayhap he'll even bring along his needlework.'

'My bets are still on the Etherelle,' Bowen said. 'If I were Edric, I'd deploy enough troops to keep us busy here, and in the meantime I'd sneak past us someplace we aren't looking.'

'Only, thanks to you, we *are* looking,' Iefan said.

'It just might not do us a lot of good.' The longer Bowen thought about the situation, the grimmer it was beginning to look – not least because he had a feeling that nothing short of an earth-quake would persuade Aeron to give up the high ground and risk a

169

counter-move. 'If Edric splits up his second force, he can use half of it to come up from the west and bottle us in, and he'll still have the other half to cause all the mayhem he likes anywhere in Ardath.'

Another thought struck him, no less worrying than the last. 'How is Cullamor manned?'

'The city walls, half strength,' Longshanks answered. 'Same for the keep, though you could hold Cullamor Castle with a couple of blind archers and a serving wench and a half.'

'There you have it,' Bowen said. 'Take the city, and you can hold it hostage against our surrender. Edric doesn't need the keep. But, should he want it regardless, he doesn't necessarily have to take it by force. As we all know, he's a seasoned hand at treachery.'

'Damn,' Iefan said with feeling. 'Arnold would have been the first to see it coming. And *damn* that black rat sitting in Aeron's ear and spouting useless blather. Makes you wonder whose side the bugger is on.'

'Now there's an interesting thought,' Bowen said.

'Forget it.' Longshanks didn't bother to hide his anger. 'All *that* one has to do is wave his godsdamned book on Thalios in Aeron's face, and anything he says will be taken for gospel. Personally I think it's so much horseshit, but as far as the king's concerned it might as well be holy scripture. If we're going to convince him that his pet Black is a bloody fraud, we need facts, not suppositions, well-founded as they may be. So let's hope your lad Bryn brings us something we can work with, preferably before Edric has us bottled up tight. Which is not to say we won't try and convince his majesty anyway, first thing in the morning.'

There wasn't really anything to add, and the meeting broke up

170

shortly, everyone making for their bedrolls and a few short hours of sleep. It was only when he lay down that Bowen realized he'd forgotten to talk to Longshanks concerning the object he wanted Bryn to have. Too late now. First thing, then.

*   *   *

From where he was pulled up half a mile behind the main force, Brother Maynard, as he called himself, still had an excellent view of the two hills. The Bent and the Barrow. Somewhere up there, two lay sleeping whose time had run out. Two who wouldn't live to see another sunrise. Not much longer now.

At midnight exactly, he opened the rear door of the wagon and let out one of the beasts. Once again he marveled at how execrably ugly the things were: the spotted coat a mass of wiry bristles, the back sloping from high withers to a low, hunched croup, the overlarge head with the bulging jaws, a vise that could crush a large bone as if it were a morsel of pastry. Murder on four legs, three hundred pounds of malice slavering with a hunger that had been raised to a frenzy by several days without food.

He'd bought the beast and its sibling from a witch in Enemathea, where people ascribed them all manner of bloody mayhem and black-magical properties. Moordwolves, they called them – but only in frightened whispers, and never after dark. They were the most dangerous creatures that roamed the southern continent, more fearsome even that the huge cats or the water dragons. Still, the ordinary members of the species were harmless compared to these two, each of them carrying a passenger summoned, subdued and implanted by Maynard himself. It was the only means of controlling a moordwolf

171

– providing you knew how to control the demon riding it. Not many left who could – nearly all of those who'd tried having died a quick and terrible death.

Using an obsidian knife, the Black made a cut on the moordwolf's nape. Then he inserted a small bone disk the size of a middling coin into the open wound. It was an occult sigil, prepared beforehand and infused with the power of one of the names he'd been given by Gale. He'd have preferred to have something more tangible, hair or nail clippings, ideally some blood. But the names would do.

People who knew nothing about sorcery erroneously believed themselves safe as long as they took care not to leave such bodily leftovers lying about where they could fall into the wrong hands. They had no idea of the power invested in names. No idea at all. The man who called himself Maynard did – which was why he treated his Truename like a secret more precious than gold and gems.

Once the sigil was in place, he closed the wound: two quick stitches with a bone needle and a length of sinew, and it was done. Ordering the beast's demon mind to give Edric's troops a wide berth, he sent it off. Then he repeated the procedure with the second moordwolf, giving it the other target's name, and sent it after its brother. That was it. Nothing left to do but wait until they returned.

Provided there were no hitches, they should both be back well before first light.

*   *   *

Bowen was a ghost, walking the dark, empty hallways of Kingskeep Castle. He came to a door he'd never seen before yet knew without fail was hers, knew she lay behind it, desperately ill, dying. He longed to see her one last time, to hold her hand, if only for a moment, and tell her that his heart would travel with her no matter where she went. But he knew it couldn't be, and was about to leave when of a sudden he felt eyes on his back. Cold, merciless eyes, watching from a place of impenetrable shadow.

Then he was at another door, still in Kingskeep Castle, this one opening for him as if nudged by an unseen hand – and there was Seorus, sitting at his desk by the light of a single candle, quill flying over a piece of parchment. He was long dead, Bowen knew. And yet, here he was, looking just like the Seorus of old. A bit thinner maybe, but otherwise unchanged by time.

'I can't talk now,' he said without looking up, his voice barely audible, faint from all the years Bowen reckoned it had to cross. Or maybe the king was merely whispering. 'We're being watched.'

Again Bowen felt those terrible eyes staring out of a dark corner, hidden beyond the reach of the candle's flickering light.

'But it's all in here,' Seorus said, rolling up the parchment and sliding it into a slender, silver cylinder. Bowen, gripped by a terrible feeling of foreboding, tried to speak a warning but found he couldn't, the dream allowing him no voice. And so he could only watch in quiet desperation as a dark, smoke-like substance detached itself from the deep shadows and wafted across the room, coming up behind Seorus. Briefly, a black, ill-defined shape seemed to hover over the unsuspecting king's right shoulder, then it wound down his sleeve, momentarily wreathing it in darkness, and slipped

173

into the cylinder along with the rolled-up document.

'My legacy,' Seorus told Bowen, capping and handing him the cylinder. 'You know what to do with it.'

Again Bowen fought to speak, and again he failed. Sickened and distraught, he was about to do the king's bidding and leave, but Seorus held him back with a hand on his arm, pulling him close. 'He killed me, you know,' he whispered in Bowen's ear. 'He killed the both of us.'

Finally, Bowen found his voice.

'I know,' he answered, though he'd only realized the truth of it this very moment. 'It's why you sent her away. It's why I didn't come back. There was nothing I could have done except kill him, and I wasn't sure you'd want that.'

'I didn't,' Seorus said, his face a mask of sorrow. 'I didn't. You did well to stay away.'

Bowen awoke with the feeling of a great weight sitting on his chest. There seemed to be too little air in the room, even though he'd thought to leave the door open, and devil take the cold. The outer door must be open as well.

There was a strip of moonlight draped across the flagstones in the hallway. Troubled by what he'd dreamed, he reached for the weapons belt lying on the floor beside his cot, felt for the familiar shape inside the pouch. Safe. Tomorrow he'd make it safer still, make sure it got to Bryn no matter what.

Somewhere outside, claws scrabbled on stone. One of the camp dogs. Not a single battle he'd fought where the mangy buggers didn't show up, usually even before the rest of the camp-following leeches sniffed out the opportunity. Big mutt though, by the sound of it.

With a weary sigh, he lay back. Was about to close his eyes when he noticed that the moonlight outside was gone, replaced by a shadow.

Someone standing in the outer door, blocking the light? Late for anyone to still be about, other than the sentries, and they were stationed at the curtain wall, not by the tower.

He couldn't have said why – a veteran warrior's instinct, maybe – but suddenly he had a bad, bad feeling.

As if in confirmation, a low growl issued from outside, seeming to set the very walls a-trembling.

Bowen began to rise, reaching for his sword.

It was as far as he got. Then a mountain of bristling, stinking, snarling muscle was upon him, claws and teeth gashing, rending, tearing, ending.

Bryn, he thought as his last breath was ripped from him. *Forgive me, lad.*

*　　*　　*

12

One look at the street outside Daven Bury's cellar and Rhea knew her plans for the day were buggered. She'd already noted with half an ear how the early morning quiet outside had a strange, muffled quality to it. Now she saw the reason for the eerie silence: sometime during the wee hours the rain had turned to snow, blanketing the cobbles with three inches of pristine white, as yet undisturbed by human feet.

Bloody hell, but she did not need this! Two sets of footprints leaving Daven Bury's cellar with none going in would be as good as waving a red flag for Pace and shouting, 'Hey, dickhead! Here we are!'

'Change of plans,' she told the dwarf, who'd found his own crack in the door to peer through. 'We'll have to wait until people are up and about and the snow gets tracked up.'

He nodded, immediately seeing her point. Well, hooray! At least he wasn't stupid. Though otherwise she wouldn't have minded at all if he'd just gone pop! and vanished into thin air. Bloody baggage, was all he was. Baggage that had already cost her dearly, and was like to cost her more. Gods, how could she have been so stupid!

The thought sparked a quick pang of guilt. *You're being totally unfair,* she chided herself. *It's not his fault the Guild sicced the hunters on him, and he's not responsible for the decisions you make either.*

'Listen,' she said. 'I'm going to go get some stuff we'll be needing once we're out of the city. No use leaving if all we're going to do is freeze to death out there.'

'But…'

'Don't worry. I'll be back in a trice. And I won't mess up the pretty snow, either. Meanwhile, do us both a favor and stay put, all right?'

'Just thought you should know,' he said, nodding towards his bulging pack. 'I've got pretty much everything we need right there.'

'Really? Do you have a pair of warm boots and a fur-lined cloak for me in there? No? Didn't think so. How about food? Money? See what I mean? So just sit tight and wait until I get back.'

Like most houses in this part of Kingskeep, Daven Bury's had two tiers of covered wooden balconies front and back, space to hang wash, dry corn, card and spin wool, sit on summer evenings and have a chat with the neighbors across the street, and so on, and so forth. In warmer weather people actually spent more time on their balconies than inside their houses because, owing to the small, horn-paned windows, most of the interiors were so dim you needed a candle even in daylight. Good for keeping out the heat in summer and the cold in winter, bad for doing stuff like reading or mending socks.

Rhea climbed up one of the supporting pillars and over the

178

railing, dropped onto the weathered boards softly as a cat, found an open window. Daven and his fat wife's bedroom, the two of them snoring away to wake up the dead. She shimmied over the sill, came up in a crouch, readying to explain what the hell she was doing here. She needn't have worried. Probably not even an earthquake would rouse these two before the bells tolled half six. She tiptoed past, out into a hallway and to the back, where the house shared a courtyard with three others. Once outside, she went left, over onto the neighbor's balcony, and to the next, and then down and out through the vaulted passage under the building opposite Bury's. No more worrying about leaving tracks, not until she was four houses down from Grandda's. Ducking into a doorway, she spent a long time just looking and listening, feeling for anything out of the ordinary. When she was satisfied no one was watching the place, she took to the galleries again, crossing the remaining distance off the ground. No open windows at Grandda's, but she knew where he hid the key: under the balcony, up where there was small space between a beam and warped floorboard.

Unlocking the door and slipping inside, she half expected to see Macsen sitting by the fire with his pipe and a mug of ale. Silly. It was five in the morning, and besides, he was off to war with the king.

In no time at all she had what she thought she would need gathered in a pile on the kitchen table: boots, cloak (good thing they were still here; another day and she'd likely have fetched them over to her cramped quarters at the Headhunters' barracks); blanket, money – less than she'd hoped for in Grandda's stash, but it would have to do. With Macsen gone, there wasn't any food in the house – wouldn't have been much in any case, seeing as he usually ate up at the keep – aside from some apples she found in the cellar, slightly shriveled but still edible. Trying to think what else she might need, she added a set of throwing knives to the pile. She'd left them here because she didn't like their balance, but they'd serve at a pinch. A pity her good ones were at the barracks. No way she could get to them after last night's disaster. What else? A pack. She found an old one of Grandda's hanging behind the door to his room. One strap was broken, but she could probably mend it. Needles and thread, that's what she'd forgotten.

Sitting down to change her boots, it occurred to her that she might never see this place again. It was her home, the house she'd grown up in, every bit of it infused with memories, some of them bad, most of them precious. It made her want to cry, and she nearly did. But more than that, it made her incredibly angry, brought her rage at the people responsible boiling up afresh. First they'd taken her parents, and now, because of them, she was losing her home. And her Grandda – what were the chances she'd ever see him again? She couldn't let them get away with it. Gods bloody damned, but she was *not* letting this go.

Suddenly – just like that – a plan appeared in her mind, fully formed as if it had been sitting there all along biding its time, waiting for the moment she'd finally see it. Now she did, and it made her swallow once, hard. Riskwise, it was way up there, somewhere between insane and suicidal. But it also felt absolutely *right,* and she knew without a doubt she'd go through with it. Maybe saving the

180

dwarf and getting herself into this mess hadn't been such a bad thing after all. An eye-opener, it was beginning to look like.

Bugger spending gods knew how many years with the Head-hunters, hoping that sooner or later she might somehow wangle the secret of her parents' deaths out of one of them. One thing she should have seen by now was that the bloody bastards were as close-mouthed a lot as you could hope to find anywhere. She'd likely have better luck getting a fence post to talk than one of them.

No, she needed to go straight to the source, and she needed to do it now, while she still had the chance. If the answers were anywhere to be found it was here in Kingskeep, in the records kept at the Lord Executioner's offices.

Why hadn't she thought of this earlier? Well, she *had,* actually. Only not really, because Macsen had made it so emphatically clear that Pryce was untouchable. Besides, *nobody* went in there by choice, not if they could help it. It was like laying your head on the block and hoping you'd have time to withdraw it before the axe came whistling down.

Donning the warm cloak and leaving the rest of the stuff she'd collected where it was – she'd come fetch it later – she set off up the hill. There were a few people up and about by now, opening up shops or running early errands. Wary of running into Pace or one of his apprentices, she made use of every byway and hidden passage she knew, stopping time and again to make sure the way ahead was clear and nobody was following her. By the time she got to Castle Road, Kingskeep's main thoroughfare, winding its way from the west gate up to the keep, the streets were well trafficked, not making it any easier for her to keep an eye out for Pace. But then,

181

the Lord Executioner's offices were pretty much the last place she expected to find him. Arsehole or no, Pace was attached to his head as much as the next man, meaning it was highly unlikely he'd show his face here before he had last night's mess safely tidied away.

An apple-cheeked young clerk was just finishing up sweeping snow off the steps outside the building's entrance. He gave her a quizzical smile when he saw her walking up to the door. A smile! In this place! She almost stepped back to look up and make sure she'd come to the right address. Either it was the fellow's first day on the job, or he was one of those creeps who actually enjoyed being part of maiming and killing other people. Whatever. She needed to get past him.

'Apprentice Headhunter Redbreast,' she said. 'Headhunter Pace sent me to look something up for him.'

'Ah,' the young man said, his smile widening to show admirably white and even teeth. 'You'll want the archives, then. Second floor, turn left at the landing, then it's the third door on your right. Archivist Unham is the man you're looking for. I believe he's already in.' He stepped aside to let her pass. She almost wished he hadn't, had sent her packing instead.

Clench 'em, girl, she told herself. *No backing out now.*

Grandda's whole house could have fit inside the entrance hall. Despite its opulence – marble, dark wainscoting, and gilded stucco wherever you looked – the place had a cold, intimidating air to it, made you feel small and exposed. Probably exactly what it was designed to do. Climbing up the left half of the sweeping double stairs, her footsteps echoing forlornly in the vast, threatening space, Rhea passed under the painted likenesses of Pryce's enforcers, the Judge Executioners, all of them diligent and industrious suppliers of fodder for the noose, the stake, and the block.

She found the archivist in the process of changing into his work attire, a frayed, dirty smock that looked as if it doubled as a dust cloth. Unlike the young man downstairs, Unham had the appearance of someone who belonged here: gaunt, grey, sour-faced. When she opened her mouth to explain why she was here, he merely held up a bony finger, finished buttoning up his smock and went to stand behind a counter that ran the breadth of the room. Behind it were rows upon rows of shelves sagging under the weight of thousands of scrolls and ledgers and scaling off into an impenetrable, dusty gloom.

'Well?' Unham said, eyeing her as if she were something the cat had dragged in.

Suppressing an urge to do something painful to the man, she told him why she was here. Gave him the year and month she was supposed to check for Pace. No names, though, and, thankfully, he didn't ask. No need to know. Wordlessly, he disappeared into the stacks. Was away for what seemed like half the day. Came back with a heavy ledger and plonked it down on the counter, raising a small cloud of dust. Left her to it.

It took her a while to find what she was looking for, longer than she liked. But when she finally got to the right page, it was all there: date of arrest; interrogation notes (they hadn't given the dirty bastards shit, she saw with a surge of fierce pride); crimes committed

183

(disturbing the peace, fomenting rebellion, high treason); sentence imposed ex post facto (death by garrote, carried out in the course of arresting and interrogating the subjects, bodies to be disposed of privily, no notification of relatives). Fighting hard against tears, Rhea came to the names.

Subjects: her ma and her da. Agents commissioned: Charis Carr and Edan Pace. Pace. For a moment, rage nearly blinded her, swamping her vision in a red haze, hammering in her ears like thunder. She wanted to crumple the page, rip it to shreds. Trample on the ledger. Set fire to the whole damned archive.

Struggling for calm, she got a hold of herself. Read on.

Signed off by: Albin Pryce. The Lord Executioner himself. Interesting. Principal: S.I. Who was –

'What's this?' A man's voice. Not Unham's.

Rhea gave a startled jerk.

She'd been so absorbed she hadn't noticed whoever it was come in. Judge Executioner Blaine, she saw when she turned around, Pryce's second-in-command, resplendent in his blood-red robes of office, his bushy, black brows drawn together in a mistrustful frown. Here it was then: the axe, ready to fall. Suddenly her mouth was dry as dust, her heart pounding fit to smash right through her ribcage. To make matters worse, she felt an overwhelming need to pee.

'Apprentice Headhunter Redbreast, my lord,' she managed to get out. 'Looking up something for my tutor, Master Headhunter Pace.'

'Is that so?' Blaine stepped over and glanced at the open ledger. Damn, but she should have thought to close it. Should have heard him coming, too. Fine Headhunter she would have made.

'And what might Master Pace be wanting this information for?' Blaine skimmed the page with a single glance. 'Somewhat outdated, wouldn't you say?'

'I wouldn't know, my lord. Just following orders, doing as I'm told.'

'Hear that, Unham?' Blaine said, suddenly jovial. 'Following orders. We could use a bit more of that around here, wouldn't you say?'

'Absolutely, my lord. Never too much of it, I daresay.' The archivist was suddenly all smarm and solicitude.

'Well then, apprentice, ah... Redbeast. Carry on. And give my regards to Master Pace. Good man, one of our best. Consider yourself lucky to have him as a tutor.'

'Thank you, my lord.' Closing the ledger. *And may you and all your ilk die a slow and painful death, the sooner the better.* 'I'm sure he'll be glad to hear that his work is appreciated.' *Just wait until I get my hands on him, and I'll show him my appreciation in full, no holds barred, no quarter given.* Looking up, she found she was talking to the Judge Executioner's back. A swish of robes, and he was out the door. Gone.

Dear gods, but that had been close! She nearly let out a sigh of relief but remembered just in time that Unham was still there. Forcing herself to thank the slimy bugger, she made her exit as well.

She had what she needed. Pace, and whoever Charis Carr was. Pryce. Untouchable, Macsen had said.

Untouchable? We'll see about that. And then there's still SI. Who the hell is S.I.?

185

*   *   *

Laurin waited.

Waited, and fretted, the longer the more. Rhea had said she'd be back in a trice. And that she wanted to be at the gates as soon as possible – something like that, any road. Now it was going on mid-morning, and still no sign of her. There was no more denying it: something must have happened. Either she'd run into that Pace fellow, or she'd decided that lugging along a dwarf was simply too much of a bother. Either way, he was on his own. No use sitting here any longer, waiting for Pace to find him.

Suddenly it hit him like a fist to the stomach: he wasn't on his own, dammit! He'd completely forgotten Dag. Dag, faithful companion of many years, true and trusted friend.

How could you? he remonstrated with himself. *Is that how you repay friendship? You should be ashamed of yourself. Serves you right if the girl left you in the lurch. Well, you're not leaving Dag behind, that's for sure. But what if Pace is still watching the boarding house on the off chance I might go back there? Nah, I don't think so. The gates is where he'll be. Just take it nice and careful, check things out, don't rush in, and you'll be all right. Making it there without getting busted is likely going to be the bigger problem. And then to the gate, and try to sneak out... Whoa! One thing at a time, laddie. You're getting way ahead of yourself. Go fetch Dag, and then take it from there.*

Just in case, he loosened his long knife in its sheath. Couldn't have it jamming if he needed it in a hurry. On second thought, he rummaged in his pack, got out his hatchet, and tucked it under his belt next to the knife.

186

There. This dwarf is not going down without a fight.

Shouldering the pack, he gave the street outside a careful inspection, then he set out to redeem a shamefully neglected friend – not to mention the only friend he had.

*   *   *

Next thing he knew, shocking cold slapped him in the face, yanking him out of a violently disjointed dream, freezing water clogging his nose and his mouth and running down the inside of his shirt. He spluttered and coughed, caught a breath. Blinking, his eyes slow to focus, he wondered where he was, and how he'd gotten there. No recollection whatsoever, just a splitting headache, twice as bad as the one he'd already had. Some kind of stable, though, by the looks of it. He was sitting on the floor. Looking at a pair of slender, booted feet. Higher up: a girl, holding an empty pail still tipped at an angle. Not Rhea, though she had that same tough, unforgiving look. No, not quite the same. Less tough, and somehow... meaner. And not nearly as pretty.

He tried to get up and found he couldn't. There was something heavy holding him down, lying across his outstretched legs. The gate off one of the stalls, he realized. His wrists were tied to the slats. Good way to keep a person off their feet.

'Back with us?' A tall, dark figure, unfolding itself from a bale of hay it had been sitting on. Pace. Brushing off his trousers, hanging his cloak and weapons belt on a peg beside a row of tack, rolling up his sleeves. Getting ready for something. Surely nothing that was in any way worth looking forward to.

'I have to say, I didn't really think you'd be this stupid. But here

187

you are. Well, then. Time for a chat. As you can imagine, I'd very much like to know where the girl is.'

Laurin thought of several different things he might say, all of them useless. Ended up opting for silence.

Pace sighed. 'You *are* going to tell me, you know – one way or another. Though you should understand that this can go easy for you, or it can be very, very hard. Your choice.'

'You're going to kill me anyway,' Laurin said. 'So you'll forgive me if I'm not inclined to help you out with your problem.'

A pathetic little show of resistance, seeing as he didn't know where Rhea was in any case. Not that saying so would spare him any suffering. Pace wanted an answer, for sure. But more than that, he wanted to hurt someone. Needing a reason didn't really come into it.

Another sigh. 'Wrong answer, little man. Too bad. This could have been quick and painless. Not any more. You're going to end up begging to tell me everything you know, and then begging me to kill you. You can take that as a promise.' Pace held out a hand. 'Gwynne, hand me that hammer, will you? And then go stand watch outside. Oh, and don't forget to close the door after you. This is not something you need to see.'

Sure she does, Laurin thought. *Look at her. A moment ago she was practically salivating, and now she's pissed because she doesn't get to watch the show. Speaking of which, I think I've already wet myself. Never been so bloody scared in my whole life.*

Hunkering down, Pace grabbed Laurin's left hand and forced his fingers flat against the slat his wrists were tied to. He raised the hammer. Brought it down a couple of times, pulling back at the last moment, lightly brushing the nail of Laurin's pinkie. Taking aim. Getting into it. Funny, but it already hurt like hell.

Bang! Laurin jerked, waited for the pain. Nothing. The hammer had hit only wood.

'Oops,' Pace said. 'Missed. Lucky you. Sure there's nothing you want to tell me?'

Laurin remained silent, braced himself. Nothing he said now would convince Pace, he knew. First he had to go through the pain, and then maybe Pace would –

Thunk! Laurin yelled, more from the shock than from the pain. That came a heartbeat later, stealing his breath and bringing tears to his eyes. Right after the pain came a wave of black nausea. Retching, gasping, he tried not to look at his finger, looked anyway, nearly puking at the sight of the bloody mess Pace's hammer had made.

'She's gone,' he panted. Dear gods, but it hurt! 'Left. By now, she's probably halfway to... wherever she's going. Didn't say where that was.'

'Ah-ah, little man.' Pace sounded positively cheerful. Enjoying himself, the bloody arsehole was. 'You don't want to lie to me. Lying will only make things worse.'

Thunk! The hammer came down again. This time it was the ring finger, as far as Laurin was still able to tell, the pain merging into a single, red clump of throbbing agony, enveloping his whole hand and shooting all the way into his shoulder. The tears were streaming freely now, nothing he could do about it.

Suddenly he felt the greatest need to tell Pace everything he knew. Absolutely everything. He'd lay out the story of his entire life, if that was what it took to stop the hammer from coming down one more time. He hated himself for being so weak, but there was simply no more holding back. He'd already had way more than he could take.

'There was this cellar,' he blabbed. 'We were hiding out there. I'm sure I can find it again. I can show you where it is.' No way was he going to lead Pace to Rhea, even if he could find the place again, which he couldn't, not in the state he was in. But if he could get Pace to take him outside, maybe –

Thunk! Laurin heard himself scream like a stuck pig. He didn't know what to do first: puke or faint.

'Where. Is. She.' Pace sounded like he was beginning to get bored with fingers. Like he was ready to move on to bigger things.

Laurin, on the other hand, had reached a state where he was obviously starting to hallucinate, hearing voices that weren't there.

Rhea's voice, to be precise, saying, 'I'm here, Pace. Right behind you.'

Can't be, he thought. *She doesn't even care about me...*

Then he blacked out.

*   *   *

The first thing Rhea thought when she found Daven Bury's cellar empty and the dwarf gone was, *Damn you, little man! Didn't I tell you to stay put?* Then she reconsidered, reckoned it was a good riddance. So much better her chances if she went it alone. Unfortunately, that wasn't the end of it.

I did tell him I'd be back right away. That was this morning early. Now it's almost noon. No wonder he up and left. He must have thought I'd dumped him and wasn't coming back. Damn, but a promise is a promise. My word is pretty much all I've got left. I should have come back here first, told him I'd be gone a while longer. What if he ran into Pace? Shit, shit, shit! Where did he go? Would he have tried the gates alone, and in broad daylight? Maybe, but not likely. Where else could he have gone?

Something nagging at the back of her mind, something about last night...

The smell! She'd caught a whiff just before she smacked him over the head. Wet wool, leather – and horse. Horse. That was it. Suddenly it all came together. He'd smelled of horse. He was some kind of prospector. In that line of work you were out in the wilds for months on end, and you needed some sort of pack animal to carry your supplies and gear, like picks and shovels and stuff. A horse, a mule, a donkey, whatever.

So... the boarding house stables. That's where the dumb shit had gone. And probably run right into Pace, who wasn't stupid, whatever his other shortcomings. Not quite sure who or what was pulling her strings, she took off at a run, part of her wondering what the hell she was doing, and why. She had no answer, not even the beginnings of one, except that Pace had taken one too many thing that wasn't his to take. Having no reasonable answer didn't stop her, though.

With her back pressed up against the wall beside the entrance to the boarding house stables, Rhea snuck a wary peek around the corner. There was Gwynne. The dumb bitch had her eye glued to a crack in the stable door instead of playing lookout like Pace had surely ordered her to. Rhea fought down an urge to take a flying start and kick her in the back of the head. Too noisy: Pace would be warned, her only advantage gone. She had no illusion about what the outcome would be if she lost the element of surprise. She was good, but she was still a long way from beating Pace in a fair fight. He'd make mincemeat of her, was what would happen.

She plucked the garrote from her belt. Holding it loose in one hand, she sidled into the courtyard and around the perimeter so she'd be coming at Gwynne directly from behind. Less chance of being noticed. Then, gripping both handles of the garrote, she took ten light, silent steps forward, flipped the cord over Gwynne's head and pulled it tight, at the same time dragging the girl backwards, away from the door.

Gwynne didn't put up much of a fight, her hands scrabbling uselessly at the cord around her neck. Not long, and she sagged back against Rhea, dead weight. Rhea loosened the cord a fraction, half expecting Gwynne to be playing possum, but the girl was out cold. Good. Rhea didn't like her, but she wasn't about to start killing people just because she found them disagreeable. Looking around, she saw a shed full of junk with a door that bolted on the outside. It was the perfect place to keep Gwynne out of her hair in case she woke up. Rhea didn't want to be watching her back when she went in to deal with Pace.

Inside, someone screamed. Three guesses who that was.

Stowing the garrote, she carefully lifted the latch on the stable door, pushed it open a crack, praying it wouldn't creak. She reached for the small crossbow and inserted a bolt. Holding the bow in one hand and her long-dagger in the other, she used a foot to push the door open just far enough so she could slip in.

Adjusting to the relative dark inside, her eyes found Pace and the dwarf, the former too engrossed in dealing out pain to notice the slight change in the light, the latter looking like he wasn't in a good way, white as a sheet, blue around the lips, his lids half closed. There was a lot of blood on and around his left hand, tied to the slats of a gate from one of the stalls. At the sight of what Pace had done to the little man, Rhea's anger turned cold and hard, like a good piece of steel quenched after the final forging.

Pace said, 'Where. Is. She.' Pronouncing each word separately, like a pissed-off parent who'd run out of patience.

'I'm here, Pace,' she said. 'Right behind you.'

Pace turned around.

Slow, unhurried. As if she posed no threat. As if he were merely curious as to how anyone could be so stupid. Not afraid of her at all, it appeared. Seeing him eye his weapons belt hanging from a peg on the wall, she felt a small thrill of satisfaction. No way he could get to it before her bolt found him. Apparently having come to the same conclusion, he spread his hands in mock defeat.

'Rhea Redbreast. Or should I say, Rhea Branden? Living up to your shitstained heritage, I see. Like mother, like daughter. I told them you weren't to be trusted, but did they listen? Like fuck they did. "She's taken after the old man," they said. "A pillar of the realm, she'll become, just like him, you'll see." Another fucking traitor is what I see. So what is it you want? The dwarf? Please. Be my guest. Take him. Though you'd have to be monumentally stupid

193

to believe you can get away with it.'

'You killed my parents,' Rhea said, fighting to keep her voice even and her bow hand steady. Fighting not to choke on the anger and the fear boiling up inside her.

'Wasn't me,' Pace lied brazenly. 'And no use asking me who did, because I don't know.'

'You and Charis Carr, is who. On Pryce's orders. I *know*, Pace.'

That gave him pause. For the first time Rhea saw a shadow of unease flit across his features, gone in a heartbeat.

'Been into the archives, have we?' he sneered. 'That must have taken some guts, little Redtits. You surprise me. Tell me, did you manage to get in and out without crapping yourself? Or is being here with me the reason why you stink of fear?'

'Stop babbling, Pace. It'll get you nowhere. What I want from you is the name of the principal. Who is S.I.? Tell me that, and maybe I'll let you go.'

Pace barked a laugh. 'S.I.? If you can't figure that one out on your own, you really *are* stupid. Too bloody stupid to let live, in fact.'

The hammer suddenly giving a small jerk in his grasp was all the warning she got. She barely had time to duck before it hit the wooden wall with a deafening bang, missing her head by a hair. She didn't stop moving, feinted left, turned right.

A flick of Pace's wrist, and a throwing knife thunked into the boards where the center of her chest had been less than an eye-blink ago, the only thing saving her the fact that she'd been expecting it. That, and two years of rigorous training. She'd learned from the

194

best, after all. Which was why she knew to dodge the second knife as well, though it grazed her shoulder and nailed a lock of her hair to the wall.

Thinking her sufficiently distracted, Pace went for his weapons belt. Big mistake.

She shot him. Hit him in the thigh, the bolt catching him in mid-stride and taking the leg out from under him. He fell back against the wall, slid slowly to the ground.

But Pace wasn't Master Headhunter for nothing. Even as he sat down heavily beside the unconscious dwarf, his fingers closed around the haft of a rusty old sickle that had lain half hidden under the straw strewn across the floor. The next instant, he had the pitted blade pressed against Laurin's throat.

'Drop the bow,' he said. 'And then your weapons belt. One wrong move, and I'll cut his fucking head off.' He'd gone pale, Rhea saw. Beads of sweat stood on his forehead, and his trouser leg was already soaked with blood. Good. Hopefully he was hurting like hell.

She gave a scornful laugh.

'You think this is about him?' Ignoring the threat, hands trembling, she loaded another bolt. Feigning calm, though in truth she was scared silly for the little man. 'Then it's you who's stupid. Go ahead, kill him if you like. I couldn't care less. Though if I were you, I'd be concentrating on getting out of here alive. So. Last chance. Who is S.I.?'

Pace was already looking worse than just a moment ago, his eyelids drooping like he was about to faint. Maybe she'd hit an artery and he was bleeding out. Or maybe he simply wasn't as good at receiving pain as he was at dealing it out.

'Fuck you, Redtits. Amut piss on your rotten little soul.'

She saw his fingers tighten on the sickle. Knew he was about to cut the little man's throat, determined to go down in a blaze of glory, and to take Laurin with him.

She squeezed the trigger, got lucky with a headshot.

Pace died instantly, before the kill message sitting in his brain had time to travel down his arm to the hand holding the sickle. Not even a weak reflex made it through. He looked surprised, though. As well he might, with a bolt sitting smack between his eyes.

Studying her handiwork, Rhea felt neither satisfaction nor regret. Nothing, was what she felt – or maybe it was all she allowed herself to feel.

That changed the moment she noticed the state the dwarf was in.

*   *   *

For the second time that day, Laurin was rudely awakened by cold water splashing in his face. Instantly, his poor hand began to pulse with agony, every beat of his heart sending the hammer crashing down anew on his already flattened fingertips. He groaned, opened his eyes.

Rhea was on her knees beside him, holding his good hand, her face all scrunched up with worry. Didn't suit her at all. Should he tell her? Maybe not.

Hang on. Was that Pace sitting there beside him with, what, a crossbow bolt sprouting from his forehead? Signs and wonders. Or maybe he was still hallucinating.

196

'Laurin?' Rhea said, patting his cheek. 'Stay with me. I'm going to untie your hands, get this thing off you. Is there anything in your pack I can use to bind up your fingers?'

But he had something more urgent on his mind. 'Never betray you,' he mumbled. He felt woozy, and tired. Forming complete sentences seemed to be momentarily out of his reach.

'Shh. It's all right.'

'No. S'not. Lead him ever'where, 'cept to cellar... you.'

'I know. I'm sorry. I should have come back and let you know I'd be gone so much longer than I'd planned.'

It seemed he'd lost a few moments. Next he knew, she'd somehow managed to free him from the weight on his legs. Then suddenly she was gone.

No, there she was. She'd fetched his pack, was rummaging through it. His eyelids drooped.

Tired. Sleep. Not supposed to. Shock. Don't care.

*   *   *

By the time the little man came round again, Rhea had his hand all bound up. She'd also fetched the pony out of its stall, strapped on the packsaddle, and attached the panniers. She stowed his pack in one of them, grinning to herself. Forget going back to the house to fetch the stuff she'd left behind. With the fat purse she'd found in his pack, the little miser could buy her anything she needed, including a brand-new set of perfectly balanced knives. Though what he wanted with a rusty old sword was a mystery to her. She nearly dumped it, thinking to lighten the pony's load, but decided she'd better not. Who knew but he might get upset if she threw it away.

197

People got attached to the strangest things. Funny though, how it seemed to glow with an inner light for a fleeting moment when she brushed it with her fingers.

Nonsense. She was exhausted. Seeing things.

'We have to leave,' she told him. 'Now. Anyone finds Pace, we're in big trouble. The other apprentices are apt to be somewhere about, probably hanging out by the gates. So you're going to ride in one of the panniers, at least until we're outside the city walls.'

'What about you?' he asked, looking decidedly more alert now.

'Different cloak, different boots. I'll pull up the hood, hope nobody looks too closely. They'll be looking for a dwarf and a girl, not a girl and a pony. I hope.'

Laurin struggled to his feet. She helped him up onto a bale of straw, and from there into the second pannier.

'All right,' she said before she closed the lid on him. 'Fingers crossed.'

Saw him wince at the notion. Oops. One hand only, then.

*   *   *

13

White, white, white, mile after mile after mile of it.

Snow as far as the eye could see, unbroken except by the occasional stand of stunted pines, grotesquely twisted by the winds and thick with ice: crouching, gnomish figures, ice demons lying in wait for the unwary traveler. The sky was a milky, horizon-less haze that made it hard to tell up from down, confounding the senses with false trajectories and sending Nudd stumbling into nonexistent dips or treading air over rises that weren't there.

He was sick of this crap, found crossing these endless, white plains worse than sitting limp-sailed in becalmed seas for weeks on end, sweating like a pig, eating weevils and maggots and drinking stale water rationed down to a sip a day. Unfortunately, what awaited them farther south wasn't any better: bloody trees, millions of them, with no straight path to follow – no fricking path at all, actually. Fricking branches slapping your face, godsdamned roots and brambles tripping you up every other step. Maybe he could get Scour to blast a way through. Blast the whole damned forest to fricking cinders would be even better. Who needed all those bloody trees anyway?

His troubles didn't end there.

They were still out on the frozen, wind-blasted tundra when the other five split off, one after the other, heading east without a gods-damned word. Leaving Nudd by himself.

'Hey,' he asked Scour, 'what's going on?'

Tired of the thing's sparse, wordless communication, he'd taken to talking aloud, furnishing the words to Scour's side of the exchanges himself. It felt less spooky that way – though he did tend to give Scour a few more lines than what it actually said. A lot more, to be truthful, seeing as the bugger hardly ever said anything at all. What else was a man to do? The five snow-pissers were about as talkative as a row of fricking fence posts, their minds wiped clean by Scour, dumb as the driven snow. Probably not much different from how they'd been beforehand. Except the old guy. Something was different with him. For one, his eyes hadn't gone all black and empty like the others'. And then he sometimes had this look, like an innocent man being dragged to the gallows.

Not bloody likely. No one was innocent. Not in the world as Nudd knew it, anyways. Still, the old bugger seemed… desperate. Angry.

Angry, Nudd could relate to. But not desperate. Here they had the Scour-given power to pound anyone and anything that got in their way into the ground unsharpened, so what was there to be desperate about? Fricking jubilant, the old fart ought to be: one moment he was a decrepit bag of bones, the next he'd been turned into an unstoppable force, eating up the endless miles across this blasted wasteland at a rate fit to make even the wind go green with envy. Well, all right: bloody Scour was at the helm. Small price to pay, though, everything considered.

Any road, Nudd got no answer to his question. Hadn't expected one. Bloody Scour would let him know what was going on when it damn well pleased. Fine with him, as long as they were headed in the general direction of Orr and his assorted enemies.

He reckoned he was about twenty miles into the forest and roughly the same distance inland when something stopped him dead in his tracks like he'd run into a brick wall. No, not something: bloody Scour, suddenly taking over the rudder and leaving Nudd a helpless passenger in his own body, or what used to be his body, any rate. Cursing, he caught a whiff of wood-smoke, heard the distant sound of an axe. Shouts, laughter, so faint he might have been imagining them. No, there they were again. He was close to a Nordsmen village, then. Fodder for his army, though as yet he had no idea how he was going to make them do his bidding. Damage a few of them, perhaps, until the others saw the light.

As it turned out, Scour had other plans.

Standing there like his feet had been nailed to the ground, wondering what Scour was up to, Nudd suddenly felt his mouth fill with a thick, acidic fluid, more and more of it streaming together, forcing his teeth apart, stretching his jaws and bulging his cheeks until he thought his face would fly off. Then, with a sudden, explosive 'Pah!' he – or rather, Scour – spit out a fine mist of black droplets. He watched it drift south towards the village, quickly losing sight of it as the breeze took hold of it, spreading it wide and wider.

For the longest time, nothing happened.

Dead quiet, except for the wind whispering through the trees.

Suddenly he heard shouts from the village. They sounded angry, fearful, panicked. Then came the unmistakable clash of weapons, steel ringing on steel. Terrified screams.

Deciding to climb a small rise to his left to get a better view of what was going on, he found he couldn't move. Bloody Scour, keeping him firmly rooted to the spot. He saw no fricking reason for being restrained, got angry, complained, received no answer. Ranted and raved a bit, to no avail. In the end, all he could do was stand there like a dumb piece of gear out of bloody Scour's tool kit, waiting for whatever came next.

'What the fuck is going on?' he asked Scour, and got a mind-bogglingly complicated image of something like countless mechanical thingies, black dots too small for the naked eye to see, drifting into the village. Men, women, children and animals breathing them in. More of them alighting on people's skin and burrowing right through into their bodies. Changing stuff in there. Subtly, but to devastating effect. Like millions of tiny mills capable of devouring matter and spewing it forth as whatever Scour wished it to be. It was too confusing to contemplate for long, and probably nonsense anyway.

By the time Scour released him, it was all over.

Walking towards the village, he saw the thatch on several roofs burning, black smoke boiling up into the sky. Reaching the first houses, low-slung, window-less dwellings built from massive logs with moss stuffed into the cracks, he found bodies strewn on the ground. No clean kills, these. Mainly old people, women, and children, they'd been brutally hacked to pieces, as if a storm of scythes had passed through the village.

He reckoned he was looking at about a quarter of the village's inhabitants. The rest of them were gone, a trail of lost or discarded objects and a couple more dead marking the way they had gone: south.

Slowly, it began to dawn on Nudd what Scour might be up to.

The utter ruthlessness and brutality, the sheer scope of it filled him with awe and admiration. Bugger his idea of trying to persuade or coerce the Nordsmen into doing his bidding. Forget forming them into some sort of organized army. Scour's answer to the problem was beautifully simple and highly efficient: drive them insane with fear and rage. Then sit back and watch them run.

'Next time, I want to watch,' he told Scour. Didn't get an answer this time, either, but at least he'd gotten in the final word.

* * *

Wanderer was the first to split off, and he had the farthest to go. Nearly all the way back to Summerland, in fact, causing him to wonder whether Scour really knew what it was doing. It would have been easier to just leave him there. Easier on him, maybe – he supposed Scour simply didn't care how many miles it chased an old man back and forth.

Sadly though, he didn't get to see Summerland again. Scour stopped him close to a Nordsmen village long before there was any hope of catching a glimpse of distant green. There was nothing he could do to resist Scour when it forced him to spit out a spray of black destruction, only stand and watch as the horror unfolded,

203

trying hard not to feel the villagers' fear and fury and pain as if they were his own. Despairing at the thought that Scour would likely force him to do the same thing over again. And again.

Walking among the dead in the village, he was tempted to end his own life, rob Scour of at least one of its tools. No use trying, he knew. Scour wouldn't let him. On to the next Nordsmen village then, praying for a miracle, hoping that a chasm would open up and the ground swallow him before he got there.

He'd never expected that his prayers would be heard, but, to a degree, they were.

Somewhere along the way, he stopped.

And the surprising thing was: he did it of his own accord, not Scour's. He was stunned. Hardly dared to hope that what he felt was true. Scour was gone.

Not altogether. But, for the moment at least, the black tide constantly battering at the doors of his inner self had receded. If he looked really hard he could still make it out, hanging on a distant horizon like a faraway bank of storm clouds. Scour must be momentarily busy with other things, he guessed, its forces spread too thin to keep all six of them under control.

It was a precious stroke of luck, but one that wouldn't last. No doubt Scour would be back in force once it had sorted out whatever was distracting it. But it gave Wanderer time – time he was determined to make the best possible use of.

The first thing he did was turn around and head back the way he'd come. Because the village back there was already destroyed, and no worse could befall it. But also because he'd seen something along the way, an object that would serve in the plan he'd been hatching over the last few days, even though there'd been no hope of putting it into action.

Now there was.

Not far from the ruined village, he found it again: a scatter of deer bones, stripped clean by scavengers. Bending down with a groan of overworked joints, he picked up a long bone, turned it in his hands. Yes, it would do. Very well, in fact.

What he really wanted was a new Four Winds Drum, but he had neither the resources nor the time to make one. He might have found a piece of hide, some wood and tools in the village, but it wasn't the way. For something like that, you made everything yourself, starting with the cutting flake you needed to make the arrow that would kill the animal that would give you the skin to make the drum with. So he'd come up with an alternative: a Four Winds Whistle. No idea if it would work, but definitely worth a try.

Settling down among the ruins and the dead, a part of him posted as lookout to warn him when Scour came back, he opened the drawstring of his neck pouch and took out an obsidian spearhead, a sacred object passed down through generations of Snow People shamans. He'd never tried to use it, seeing as he'd never dreamed its magic. Now it would serve, but in an entirely mundane function: he would use it as a tool to work the bone and fashion it into a whistle. And – who knew? – perhaps some of the spearhead's magic would rub off in the process.

He hadn't gotten very far when he felt Scour returning.

There was just enough time to slip the spearhead back into the pouch and the bone under his belt, then Scour had him marching south again. He wasn't disheartened. Scour had left once, and it would leave again, in that he believed.

He was right. His next chance came sooner than he'd thought, right after the second village, and this time Scour was absent for several hours. He managed to cut off and smooth one end of the bone while it was gone.

Slowly, bit by bit, the whistle began to take shape. Over the following days he worked on it whenever he could, and doing so he noticed something that filled him first with a glimmer of hope, and then with a mounting excitement: Scour's absences were becoming more frequent, and each time it was gone longer. Almost as if Wanderer's role in its plans were becoming less and less important. As if he were slowly but surely turning into a useless asset. The idea held a certain terror: what would happen once Scour decided it didn't need him anymore? Would it simply abandon him? Or would it kill him off like a dog that had become too old and feeble to keep up with the pack? The latter, he supposed.

And was surprised yet again.

Three villages down, Scour left and didn't come back.

Gone for good, he felt it in his bones. Weak with relief, he sat down on a fallen trunk to rest for a moment. Suddenly his heart began to flutter in his chest like a startled bird. Old, exhausted, abused beyond its natural lifespan. So this was it, then. No. All these years he'd been ready to leave, but now he wasn't. His job wasn't finish-ed. He was... he was...

Darkness enfolded him before he could finish the thought.

*   *   *

The farther Anuun traveled south in the tracks of the sailor and his five companions, the more his steps were weighed down by the ever present fear of cresting a rise and finding another scene of brutal, senseless butchery like the one Snowchild had so miraculously survived.

So it was with infinite relief that he arrived at the Seal clan's winter camping grounds and found them all alive and unharmed. The camp was half deserted, but he spied the rest of its inhabitants gathered down by the sea, everyone pitching in to help a band of hunters drag their spoils, a small narwhale, onto the land-locked ice.

They had a long day's work ahead of them, Anuun knew, breaking up the steaming carcass and carrying it off piece by piece in a race against time as the dead whale's residual body heat slowly melted away the already thin ice it was lying on. Thoroughly absorbed by their task, they hadn't noticed him yet. On his part, he hesitated to approach them, suddenly shy of confronting so many people, for all he'd been so desperate to find shelter and care for Snowchild.

Even among his own kind, where a decade or more might easily pass without one Iceling meeting another, Anuun was considered something of a loner. As to encountering humans – he'd run into a small hunting party once when he hadn't been paying attention. Young and green, he'd been back then. He'd found the experience highly embarrassing, seeing as the moment the humans caught sight of him they all went down on their knees with foreheads pressed into the snow, overcome with awe. Even after he'd persuaded them to get up and face him in a less unsettling manner, they still insisted on treating him like some sort of deity, no matter how many times he told them he was just an ordinary Iceling. It seemed they simply couldn't fit 'ordinary' and 'Iceling' into a single concept. Since then, he'd kept his distance, prepared to intervene if anyone came too close to the Forbidden. Ready to lend a helping hand, should the need arise, but otherwise watching without attracting notice, seeing without being seen.

He was just about decided to simply leave the sleigh with Snowchild and the seal on it standing there where someone was sure to notice it and quietly leave, when suddenly the crowd went silent, all hands stilled, all heads turning his way.

After a few moments, a lone figure detached itself from the crowd, came towards him. An old woman, walking slowly and with the aid of a staff. To his relief, the others made no move to fall to their knees and press their foreheads against the ice. Three steps away, the woman stopped. Leaning on her staff – from up close he saw that it was carved from top to bottom with faces and figures of people and animals – she gave Anuun and the sled a wordless inspection. Although in human terms she was ancient, her gaze felt sharp as a hawk's. Anuun was still searching for words that would allow him to transfer Snowchild into the Seal clan's care, escape this situation, and carry on with his mission as quickly as possible, when the old woman spoke.

'Greetings, Iceling,' she said. 'I am Snow Falling, come to bid

208

you welcome in the camp of the Seal clan. I see a child of the Snow People, and a sleigh that, if I'm not mistaken, once belonged to a man of the Seal clan. I sense a tale worth hearing, so perhaps you'll honor the Seal people by joining us at the council fire and telling us the story of how all this' – she waved a hand, encompassing Anuun, Snowchild, the seal and the sleigh – 'came to be.'

'Thank you, Snow Falling.' Anuun answered, his voice rough from long disuse. 'Much as I'd like to, I can't stay.' A white lie, that. Hurry or no, he wanted nothing more than to get out of there. 'The Forbidden has been breached, and a great evil has escaped. It's the reason why I found the child abandoned in the wild.'

He reckoned it would have been rude to say that sitting him down by a fire with a crowd of curious people gathered round was a good way to torture any Iceling – him more than any other.

Hearing Snow Falling's fearful gasp at his mention of the Forbidden, he hastened to add, 'Not to worry. It has passed you by, and you're safe for now. But I must stay on its trail, meaning I have to travel fast and light. So I was hoping I could, ah, leave the child in your care. It's where she belongs, after all, even if she's from another clan.'

'Why, sure we'll take her in. I suppose you wouldn't know if she's been named yet?'

'No, I don't. I call her Snowchild, because that's where I found her: lying in the snow.' He was getting restless, seeing as he'd already lost precious time over the child and was losing more with the old woman, who didn't seem to be in much of a hurry to let him get on with it. Already she was eyeing Snowchild with the fond, proprietary gaze of a grandmother.

'One last thing,' Anuun said. 'Could you see that the seal gets back into the water, maybe find her a hole in the ice?'

'She shall have the nicest ice hole any seal has ever had,' Snow Falling assured him. 'Needs be we'll keep one open for her all through the winter. And no hunter's spear shall ever touch her. But I can see you're itching to leave. Go then, and thank you.'

'Thank you? For what?' Ever a riddle, these humans.

'For saving this child and bringing her to us. And for giving me the opportunity to do the one thing I had yet to experience in my long and varied life: to meet an honest-to-gods Iceling face to face. We hold your kind in great regard, you know. There are even those who liken you to lesser gods.' She cackled. 'I'll probably become a legend in my own right, just for having spoken with you. And Snowchild? Don't even get me started. I'll probably have my hands full trying to raise her like a halfways normal child. And now, off with you. Whatever it is you're after, it isn't likely to wait on you while an old woman chatters.'

Anuun had bidden Snow Falling farewell and already turned to leave when he felt a sudden tug on his heart. Realized he'd forgotten something important. He should have said good bye to Snowchild. He didn't turn back. Too many eyes on him. Knew he'd regret it but kept on heading south.

The moment he was out of sight of the camp he went into the ice, setting off after his quarry with a burst of speed that made the sea's frozen surface crackle and groan.

It was only a stroke of luck that let him surface in time, otherwise he would have missed the spot where one of the six had split off

210

from the rest, heading east.

So this was the moment of truth. Time to decide whom to follow: the one or the many.

He chose the one – seeing as the place where he hoped to find Greytower lay in that very same direction. And, he reckoned, where the one went, he'd eventually hit upon the others. Whatever they were up to, sooner or later they'd come together again. Probably.

It was a long trek east following the tracks left by his quarry. No way to tell which of the six it was, seeing as all of them ran with those impossibly long leaps, each bound covering ten yards or more.

He was getting close to Greytower's abode when the snow petered out, and with it the tracks he'd been following. Something he should have thought of. But then, he'd never been anywhere there wasn't snow on the ground, so how could he have known? Not used to tracking on moss and dry grass, he lost the trail after less than thirty yards.

Greytower, then. Nothing else he could do.

He found the place easily enough, seeing as it stood on the crown of a grassy hill, a four-storied tower of grey stone over-looking the surrounding forest like a lone sentinel. Feeling a sudden urge to hurry, he hastened his steps. Arrived at the top of the hill out of breath. And found the tower empty. Locked. There was a note nailed to the door that said 'Gone for the winter. Back in spring'. That was it. He'd messed up. Completely.

Weary and defeated, overwhelmed by despair, Anuun headed back west. He didn't hold out much hope of finding the six again, but he had to at least try. Damn, but he should have stuck with the others.

211

Too late now to change what he'd done.

Down the hill, and back into the forest. By Iceling standards, it was warm among the trees. Warmer than the snow-covered plains, in any case. Briefly, he considered going a ways north in the hope of finding a frozen river or creek that might speed up his journey. For some reason he couldn't have named he decided to try the woods for a while. Half an hour later the decision began to pay off in unexpected ways, starting with him finding an ancient man lying beside a fallen tree.

One of the Snow People, unlikely as it seemed to find one of them this far south. Then he remembered that five of the six had been Snow People. What were the odds that this one was here for reasons that had nothing to do with the Forbidden? As close to none as made no difference, Anuun reckoned, kneeling beside the old man and feeling for a pulse. Weak, but there. He was alive, if barely. Wizened, frail, and totally wasted after running hundreds of miles driven by a force that looked to have now deserted him.

Suddenly the old man opened his eyes, clear as virgin meltwater. No sign of black. He smiled at Anuun. 'An Iceling. Didn't expect that would be the first thing I saw on the other side.'

'That's because you're not there yet,' Anuun told him.

'Oh. Well. In that case, I need your help.'

Not again, Anuun thought, despairing. *Another impossible decision. As if the gods themselves were dead set on thwarting me at every turn.*

'That puts me in something of a bind, you know,' he said, hating himself for every word. 'On the one hand I can see that you need help, and simply leaving you here would be a terrible thing to do.

212

On the other hand, the Forbidden's been breached, and – '

'I know,' the old man said. 'That's why I'm asking for your help. I think I know how to trip the bugger up. But I can't do it alone.'

*　　*　　*

Part II – Bloodbound

It will have blood, they say; blood will have blood.

William Shakespeare

14

It was a short walk to the king's tent.

Gale had only to cross the twenty yards of open space between his own quarters and Edric's command post, a bare, closely guarded perimeter left unoccupied to foil any attempt at spying on the king, or worse, to bring harm his person. Glancing up at the two fortified hilltops, barely visible through the falling snow, Gale pondered yet again how Edric aimed to pry the enemy out of his double aerie. In a more clement season, simply sitting there and doing nothing while Aeron's food and water ran out would have done the job nicely enough. Now, with winter apparently determined to settle in for the duration, sustaining a lengthy siege was no longer an option. The cold did not discriminate between friend and foe, would spare the men in the valley no more than those on the hills. Moreover, the Dunmarkan army depended on the northern duchies for supplies. With Edric having thoroughly alienated Redfern, those supplies might be slow in coming – if they came at all. Too much snow, and the supply wagons would stop rolling altogether.

Stonebridge, once he got into position west of the hills, would face the same problems, as would Pryce on his way to Cullamor.

Both of them would be forced to forage without mercy. A large number of Ardath's peasants would be facing starvation this winter.

Another thing that had Gale pondering was how the king expected Pryce to take Cullamor Castle – because that was undoubtedly the prize he was after: the keep, and certain of its denizens. As he was wont to do, Edric was playing his cards close, telling everyone, including Gale, only as much as he judged they needed to know in order to fulfill their part of his grand design. Gale thought it foolish, and not a little frustrating. For all that he had scores of spies at his beck and call, none of them could get him the information locked inside the king's head. It was at times like these that he found himself wearying of the game. Asked himself whether it was worth all the trouble. And whether he was still up to it.

But then, three days past, the fire in him had been rekindled with a vengeance. That was when he'd received the much hoped-for confirmation of his suspicions regarding the Bailon boy. He'd been hard put not to betray the giddy rush of excitement he'd felt when Brother Maynard reported back with the results of his mission.

Though the beast tasked with eliminating the boy had spent many days scouring the countryside between Bentridge and Ardath's eastern border, Maynard said, it had been unable to find the lad. If there existed anyone by the Truename of Bryn Bailon, that person was nowhere in or even near Ardath. Bowen Threehands, on the other hand, had been duly taken care of.

A pity, but inevitable.

No, Gale thought but didn't say. *Bryn Bailon is in Ardath, I'm sure of it. In fact, I'd wager he's not more than two long bowshots away from where we stand right now, sitting on one or the other of those bloody hills and perhaps looking down on us this very moment. Only his Truename isn't Bailon. Which is why that godsawful beast of yours never had a chance of finding him in the first place.*

Sending the beast after the boy had been a huge gamble, but the only means at Gale's disposal of getting down to the truth of the matter. Now that he knew for certain, he could go ahead with his plans – though from here on out the stakes were enormous. It was by far the most dangerous endeavor he'd ever undertaken. Success was a possibility at best. Failure didn't bear thinking on. And yet he reckoned it was worth the risk.

From his encounter with the Black he'd gone straight to his tent, written a terse message, signed and sealed it, and sent it east by messenger. He would have commended himself to the gods' grace then, had he been the least bit devout.

With an inward sigh, he approached the king's tent, the guards outside the entrance saluting him fist over heart. He found Edric seated at his field desk, poring over a sheaf of documents, a single brazier fighting a losing battle against the cold. Redbreast was nowhere in sight, possibly a sign that something was up. Something Edric didn't want the old sergeant privy to. Although it remained to be seen whether the news was good or bad, Gale's pulse inevitably quickened the moment he noted the man's absence.

'Your majesty.' He gave as much of a bow as his girth allowed for. 'You called for me.'

'My lord Gale,' Edric said, leaning back in his chair. Gale didn't much like what he saw in the king's face: the cold stare, the fur-

219

rowed brow, the turned-down corners of the mouth. But then, you'd likely find doomsday come and gone before you received a look from the man that might be called friendly.

'There's been a… deplorable incident.' Edric didn't look as if he deplored anything at all. 'Some of my men took it upon themselves to intercept a messenger heading east. Reckoned he might be a Tondern spy. Turns out he was one of yours. Unfortunately, things got somewhat out of hand. It appears your man didn't survive the questioning.'

Took it upon themselves, my arse, Gale thought, his mind suddenly working at a fevered pace. *You ordered them.* Your *men, as you say so glibly, were doing* my *men's job. Spying on* me. *What in bloody hell is going on? What is it that's suddenly got you all suspicious? You can't* possibly *know what I'm up to, can you?*

'Unfortunate, indeed,' he said, fighting a sudden urge to run for the jakes. 'Seeing as the man was carrying a message to Burnt Keep on your majesty's behalf. After the… mishap with the girl, I thought it expedient to make another attempt at smoothing things over with Lord Hornby.'

The king's latest tryst had ended badly for the girl. Terminally, in fact. She'd probably done no worse than offer a weak bit of resistance, but apparently it had been enough to push Edric over the line. Or free him to finally do what he'd always wanted.

'So you deemed it advisable to offer the man a recompense? For a bloody *serving wench?'*

'I did, your majesty. Burnt Keep is a crucial link in our supply chain, after all.'

'The bitch attacked me, for the love of the gods! Hornby can

220

consider himself lucky I didn't have him hanged from his own gatehouse. You can tell him *that* from me.'

'As you wish, your majesty.' *Damned if I will. I am not going to face starvation just to satisfy your bloody boorishness.* 'Any news from Stonebridge and Pryce?'

'Stonebridge is in position. Pryce has met up with Ensel of Harad, who's agreed to give him a hand in cracking open Cullamor Castle in exchange for a piece of Ardath. Once Cullamor is taken, Pryce will deliver me Aeron's queen and her brats. I doubt I'll have to kill more than one of them to make him see the wisdom in coming down off his hill and surrendering. Everything going according to plan, as you can see. Oh, and I still want the Bailon boy dead. That's what I want you working on. Nothing else. Pox on Hornby and his likes. Find me the boy, and see that he's taken care of.'

He dismissed Gale with a wave, his eyes already back on the documents littering his desk.

Gale emerged into a freezing wind a-swirl with snowflakes, their confused dance perfectly mirroring his state of mind. Edric had taken him by surprise, freely handing out all that information. Not really like him, but then perhaps he'd been trying to make up for the dead messenger. Though that wouldn't be like him either. Still, the picture was a good deal clearer now.

The original plan, as far as Gale had been told it, had been to bull their way past the Bent and the Barrow doing as much damage as they could, and then march on to Cullamor. The marshes along the Etherelle freezing over had been an unexpected stroke of luck, allowing Edric to send two thirds of the army around behind Aer-

221

on's back. From there, it hadn't been hard to figure out that Edric had aimed all along to have someone snatch Aeron's family and use them as hostages.

Ensel, it turned out. Having Pryce and over a thousand men there as well was an unforeseen advantage, as was being able to put Stonebridge at Aeron's rear and box him in. Harad's involvement was news to Gale, though. News with frightening implications. Damn, but he should have known. How the bloody hell had Edric managed to negotiate a pact with Ensel without Gale finding out? And why make it such a big secret?

Because Edric liked nothing better than secrets, that was why. Secrets, and the power that came with owning them. Well, one thing was for sure: fool who trusted any of his promises. Ensel would likely discover as much when he tried to collect his share of the spoils. In fact, Gale wouldn't be surprised if Harad turned out to be next on Edric's list of places to invade and subdue.

His mind circling back to the king and his secrets, Gale experienced a minor revelation of sorts. He'd always wondered why Edric had reserved such a special place in his hating heart for Aeron. Perhaps, he thought, it was because the man knew something about Edric that could be put to damaging use – though more fool him if he'd tried.

The more Gale examined the notion, the more sense it seemed to make. The late queen of Dunmark had been a cousin of Aeron's, after all, and there'd been rumors at the time that he'd had more than just an eye on her before his brother Arnold had given her away to Edric in hopes of forging an alliance. Had she somehow stumbled on one or more of Edric's skeletons? Had she then con-

222

fided in her cousin Aeron, the man who'd once held her affection, and perhaps still did even after she was wed to Edric? Was there any way to get to the bottom of it, short of climbing yonder hill and asking Aeron himself?

Gale roused himself.

Speculation, all of it. Interesting as it might be, there was nothing to be gained from it, at least not in the present. Though at some later stage it might still come in handy, provided one knew where to apply the lever. For now, there were more immediate concerns that needed addressing.

The business with the messenger, for instance. It could have gone badly wrong if Edric's men had been a little more thorough. Which just went to show that one could never be too careful. As it was, it had been a near miss – thank the gods and his own, unerring foresight.

Luckily, smoke, mirrors and false bottoms had long since become second nature to him. Which was why, an hour after the unfortunate messenger had left for Burnt Keep, an empty wagon rolled out of the camp, headed east to fetch more supplies. A mile down the road, the wagoner stopped for a tinker, a ragged, miserable fellow who'd followed the Dunmarkan army to Bentridge. The poor man had obviously had enough of the cold and was set to seek his fortune elsewhere rather than freeze to death for a few extra pennies.

Neither man was what he seemed. They were good at what they did, though, would likely have fooled even Gale, had he not known better. In any case they hadn't aroused the suspicion of Edric's

223

watchers, else Gale would already be a head shorter or dangling from a sturdy limb by now.

Meaning the real message was safely on its way, perhaps even arrived at its destination – a destination that was most definitely *not* Burnt Keep. Nor was Algar bloody Hornby the recipient.

*   *   *

Bryn was in fact where Gale had imagined him: up on the Barrow, returned to camp with Arlie and Daven two days past after a truly harrowing journey. Back at the Etherelle, they'd nearly run straight into the enemy's arms. Coming out of Long Valley, they'd turned east along the river. The snow was falling thick and fast, their hoods pulled low, heads down against the fierce wind blinding them with stinging, icy flakes, shivering so hard it made staying in the saddle a constant chore. Bryn was about ready to turn them around and head for the safety of someplace warm. It was that or a senseless death by freezing, he reckoned.

Neither Arlie nor Daven looked like they'd object. Daven's beard was caked with ice, big, strong Arlie seemed to be shrinking in the cold, and the icy wind was beginning to peel the skin off all their faces. Even the palfreys they were riding – normally tough little buggers that could take a lot of abuse – looked to be close to their limits, snow crusting their rumps and manes and dangling in fat clumps from their fetlocks.

Just as he was about to give the order, Bryn noticed shadowy shapes ghosting through the billowing whiteout up ahead. At first he thought it might be a stand of trees, a place to shelter from the worst of the storm for a few moments and catch their breath before they headed back.

The next instant he realized with a gut-wrenching rush of panic that the shapes were a lot closer than he'd thought – and that they were moving.

'Back!' he hissed. 'Enemy up ahead!'

They got lucky. For once, the brutal weather favored them, just when they needed it most. A particularly violent gust swept a dense cloud of swirling snow between them and the advancing ranks of what had to be the enemy's vanguard, effectively hiding them from sight. Doing a quick about face, they rode south for spell, fast as they dared in the confusing terrain, the going easier now that the wind was coming from behind.

When he was sure they hadn't been noticed and no one was chasing after them, Bryn reined in his mount. Now that they'd found their quarry, there was no more turning back. Daven and Arlie knew it too, he could see it in their eyes. Suddenly the cold felt like the least of their worries, all thoughts of seeking shelter a distant dream.

'We'll circle back,' he told them, 'and shadow them on a parallel course. Make sure we know where they're going before we report back to Bentridge.'

'Aye,' Daven agreed. 'Though it'll not be easy. Open flats by the river ain't wide enough for us to follow 'em an' not be seen. Means we gotta stick to the woods. Tough goin' if we aim to stay caught up.'

'I seem to remember someone sayin' it's the tough stuff what gets the tough guys goin',' Arlie said, cracking a defiant grin. 'Don't know 'bout you two, but I'm feelin' hard for them buggers.'

225

'I believe we can do it,' Bryn said, his frozen face doing strange things with the confident look he tried for. 'If Bowen has it aright, there's bound to be at least fifteen hundred men out there. Moving an army that size is slow business. More so in this kind of weather. Out on the flats, we could probably spend the day riding circles around them. Even going through the woods we should be able to keep up easily enough.'

'I reckon we can, at that, m'lord,' Daven said, clawing ice out of his beard. 'Don't know 'bout easy, though.'

They could, and it wasn't.

The forest was a maze of hills, ravines, and rocky outcrops, some of them too steep to navigate, which meant going around more often than traveling in anything approaching a straight line. Time and again, they had to dismount and lead the horses over difficult passages, slipping and sliding on snow-covered slopes. It took all of Daven's woodsman's skills to find a way through without taking them too far away from the river and their quarry. Every so often, when their path brought them close to the flats, they'd catch a glimpse of the Dunmarkan army through the trees and the driving snow, a long line of grey shades ghosting in and out of the swirling white, the column of men, horses and wagons stretching over two, maybe three miles from vanguard to stragglers.

Thankfully, towards mid-afternoon the Dunmarkans halted, choosing to make camp on the last stretch of river flats before the terrain opened out and the hilly country either side of the Etherelle came to an end. Daven found them shelter deeper in the woods, a cave used by charburners, to judge by the snowcapped piles already

226

prepared but not yet fired. There was no one about, the burners probably waiting out the worst of the weather under a proper roof somewhere not too far away.

The cave was large enough to accommodate the horses, though getting them in through the narrow entrance took some persuading. Inside, they found a plentiful supply of dry wood stacked up against one wall. The discussion over whether they should risk lighting a fire was short and to the point: frozen to the marrow as they already were, they wouldn't survive the night without one. Besides, they were far into the woods, and it seemed unlikely that even the most hard-bitten of Dunmarkan scouts would come crawling through knee-deep snow in the middle of a blizzard.

The next hour rolled past Bryn in a blur of exhaustion. Get a fire started. Rub down the horses and fill their nosebags with oats. A meal of hardtack and jerky, washed down with cup after cup of hot tea brewed with melted snow. Getting warmer ever so slowly. Bedroll. Sleep.

He woke once during the night, startled out of a confused dream by the slap and sizzle of a lump of muddy snow falling into the fire, dislodged from the edge of the smoke hole up in the cave roof by the heat rising up from the fire. Arlie threw on a few more logs, they all went outside for a piss, and that was it. Bryn, who hadn't made it past half-awake in any case, was asleep almost before he was back in his bedroll.

Sometime during the early hours the storm blew itself out, and dawn came with a promise of clear skies. Bryn woke to find Daven gone. Outside, he saw a set of tracks leading north, towards the edge of

227

the forest and the river. He reckoned Daven must have gone to find out what the Dunmarkans were up to, wishing he had half the man's courage. He roused Arlie, still snoring beside the cooling embers, and they set to packing their bedrolls and saddling the horses. Bryn wanted to be ready to leave the moment Daven got back. They'd just led the beasts outside when the hunter returned, breathing hard after a long wade through knee-deep snow.

'Them Dunmarkans is early risers,' he said. 'And there's a whole bloody lot of 'em. A lot more'n fifteen hundred, I reckon. They was startin' to move out when I left. And it looks like they're splittin' up. Half of 'em's goin' on westward, the other half's turnin' south. We should get a move on, if we aim to stay ahead 'em.'

'Just like Bowen predicted,' Bryn said, his heart giving a sharp, painful twist at the thought of the unfinished business that awaited him on the Barrow. 'The ones going west are headed for Cullamor, and the rest are likely going to try and box us in at Bentridge.'

'Ain't gonna have to try all that hard,' Daven offered. 'Unless Aeron comes down off them hills an' gives 'em a fight for their money, that is.'

'Then let's go help his majesty find his thumb so he can stop sittin' on it,' Arlie said, grinning.

Irreverent lout, Bryn thought, suppressing a smile. *But he's right. Someone probably needs to light a fire under Aeron's arse. Bowen, if anyone can do it.*

They rode south, staying inside the treeline.

On this side the hills ran out into the flatlands in gentle slopes, and the going was easy, no comparison to what they'd been through the

228

day before. Bryn marveled at how Daven seemed to always find a break in the trees, until he realized the hunter was following a trail that lay hidden under the snow, perhaps the one the charburners used to get to their piles.

It was approaching noon and they were well ahead of the Dunmarkan army when Daven, riding point, suddenly stopped them with a raised fist. As he turned his mount around and came back to join them, Bryn saw him nock an arrow to the bow he'd kept strung all morning.

'There's tracks up ahead,' Daven said, keeping his voice down. 'Man wearin' snowshoes, came in from out on the plains at a nor'westerly angle. Might be an enemy scout.'

The forest ahead of them was a confusing jumble of light and dark, patches of sunlit snow blinding the eye to the shadows and making it near impossible to see what might be hiding among the trees.

There could be fifty men out there, and you'd never see them, unless –

He never finished the thought.

There was a sudden hiss, immediately followed by the meaty thunk of an arrow finding its mark. Close. He turned and there was Arlie, eyes wide with shock and disbelief, looking as if he wanted to say something, though no sound came from his half open mouth. Couldn't, with an arrow lodged in his throat. Swaying in the saddle, he tried to draw a gurgling breath. Then he toppled over sideways and fell into the snow.

'Down!' Daven hissed, slipping out of the saddle and shielding behind his mount, his bow already half drawn as he searched for a target.

Bryn paid the warning no heed.

His fear forgotten, lifted out of himself by a blinding rage that left room only for a single, bloody purpose, he drew his sword and kneed his mount forward.

Vaguely, he heard Daven say, 'No, m'lord!'

Then another arrow came sizzling, hit something.

Not him. Close, though.

Moments later he felt the horse falter under him. Next he knew he was tumbling through the air, his fall cushioned by the snow. Found he'd lost his sword. Saw the hilt sticking out of the snow three feet away. Grabbed it, got up and ran on, following the tracks.

Of a sudden he felt light as a feather, practically flying over the ground. He saw movement up ahead: a man, half hidden by a tree, pulling for another shot, loosing. The arrow hissed by, grazed Bryn's left cheek and sliced through his ear. He felt no pain.

Then he was on the man. Crouched behind the tree was not a murderous monster but an ordinary-looking fellow who took one look at Bryn's face, dropped his bow and fumbled out a long-dagger. Coming to his senses, Bryn hesitated. Part of him, the angry part, still badly wanted to kill this man for what he'd done to Arlie. The rest of him didn't want to kill this man, or any other man, for that matter.

The decision was taken out of his hands. The Dunmarkan lunged. Bryn had the longer reach, and could have ended it then and there. Instead, he caught the dagger on his blade and turned it away, brought the tip of his sword to within a few inches of the man's

230

throat, pointing at the exact same spot where Arlie had taken it. Panicking, the Dunmarkan swiped at the sword with his dagger. It was an unconsidered, hasty move, and he'd obviously forgotten that he was wearing snowshoes. Overbalancing, he couldn't correct because he was standing with one racket caught under the other. He fell right onto Bryn's blade, impaling himself, all of it happening so quickly Bryn had no time to pull back.

The Dunmarkan took a little longer to die than Arlie had, but not much. A few extra heartbeats, was all.

Afterwards, to his surprise, Bryn felt very little.

He'd killed his first man. Not something to feel proud or satisfied about. Not an accomplishment to wear on his sleeve or notch up on his scabbard like some men did. Beyond that, he could see no wrong in what he'd done. Not a whole lot of right either. It was as it was. War changed the rules, even your own.

His anger gave way to pity, now that the man was dead, though it was no more than a slight twinge compared to the grief he felt over losing Arlie.

Two years older than Bryn, he'd been a big brother of sorts all through Bryn's childhood, forever ready with a joke and a laugh, a song or a lesson in peasant lore, always game to go along on some stupid adventure and afterwards shoulder his share of the blame if they got caught. Time and the difference of birth had changed the rules of their relationship, but not the fondness Bryn felt for Arlie.

Seeing him lying there now, Bryn wept, not caring whether Daven was watching, though he found when he was done that the hunter had moved off a ways, giving him space to grieve in private.

Swiping a sleeve across his eyes, Bryn beckoned him over.

'I hate doing this,' he said. 'Nan and Hurn will never forgive me. But we don't have a choice, Daven. We have to leave him here.'

'Aye,' Daven said heavily. 'Only two horses left, and time's a-wastin'. But I ain't leavin' him like this. There's a dry creek bed over yonder. I reckon we can spare the time to cover him up so's the wolves don't get to him.'

It wasn't easy with the rocks all frozen together, but they did manage to build a secure cairn for Arlie. Before they covered him over, Daven closed his eyes with two flat pebbles, as was the custom. 'May the living close the eyes of the dead,' he said, speaking words that were probably as old as the human experience of death.

'And may the dead open the eyes of the living,' Bryn gave the due answer. He took a gold from his pouch and placed it on Arlie's chest, thinking that, if the burners found him, the coin might persuade them to give him a proper burial once the ground was no longer frozen.

When the cairn was built, Daven laid Arlie's axe down on top of it. Then, leaving the Dunmarkan scout and Bryn's dead horse in each other's silent company, they resumed their journey south.

Somewhere down the road, it all caught up with him.

Of a sudden his body revolted, trembling so hard he had to stop and dismount. For the longest time he just stood there, bent over, hands on knees, fighting for breath.

'Sorry,' he told Daven when he could speak again.

'Don't be,' Daven said. 'First kill, you're doin' good, consider-in'. These things don't go easy on any man. Takes time. Meanin' you gotta give it time.'

After a while, Bryn started walking, just taking one step after another, leading his mount by the reins. It helped. Slowly, the trembling lessened, his breathing slowed, the panic and despair faded. Became something else. An immense, wearying emptiness.

Feeling it take hold of him, Bryn realized he'd lost more than a friend. He'd lost a part of himself. Something clean and precious, an edge he'd always taken for granted. The thrill of the hunt was gone, as was the pride in being part of something bigger than himself, a kingdom, a cause, a war. Right now, he just felt old, and tired, and very alone.

All the more reason to get back to Bentridge and patch things up with Bowen, he told himself. After what had happened this day, it was beginning to look like he might find it in himself to forgive the old man after all.

*   *   *

Coming into Bentridge, Bryn saw grave faces everywhere he looked. He put the somber mood down to the cold and the impending battle, wishing he could go right on to the Barrow instead of first having to climb up the Bent and report to Aeron, who'd moved his headquarters out of the village and up onto the bigger of the two hills while they'd been gone.

He was relieved to find only the king and his pet Black in the command tent, padded out with rugs and tapestries and heated by a couple of braziers. He wanted to meet Bowen in private, not with all sorts of eyes looking on.

Aeron listened to his report in silence, waving down Wystan

233

when the Black opened his mouth to comment.

'So it turns out Threehands was right after all,' the king said when Bryn had finished. Suddenly Aeron seemed lost for words. Cleared his throat. Gripped the pommel of his sword as if he needed it for a prop.

'My lord Bailon. I have grievous news for you. There's been a terrible misfortune. Threehands was killed the other night. By some sort of beast, it appears. Wystan here swears there was magic involved. Demons, or some such.'

'Demons,' Wystan confirmed with a look Bryn didn't care to interpret, else he'd have felt compelled to kill a second time. 'And slaughtered would be a more apt description. Torn to pieces, virtually. They had to scrape parts of him – '

'That will do, Wystan,' Aeron said, looking ill. 'I'm very sorry, lad. You have my heartfelt condolences. And my thanks for bringing us such vital knowledge. The Strongs are preparing for the Rites of Parting over on the Barrow as we speak, and I imagine you'll want to join them. You have leave to do so. I'd attend myself, but after what you've just told me, I have much to think on.'

Nodding stupidly, too numb for words, Bryn made his way out to where Daven was waiting with the horses.

'Bowen's dead,' he said, and found he had hardly enough air to get out the words.

'I'm sorry, m'lord. Truly, I'm sorry.' Daven looked as if he were fighting back tears.

'Yes. They're holding the Rites. Over on the Barrow. I need to be there.' Bryn barely had enough strength left to make it into the saddle. When Daven handed him the reins, he sat there for long moments wondering what he was supposed to do with them.

'Let's go, m'lord,' Daven said softly, setting Bryn's mount in motion with a pat on the rump.

'Thank you, Daven,' Bryn said across what felt like a bottomless abyss. 'I loved him like a father, you know.'

They got there in time for Bryn to light the pyre.

No chance of digging a grave on this stony hilltop, even if the ground hadn't been frozen solid. Bowen wouldn't have minded, Bryn thought. It was a fitting way for a warrior to go. Better than lying in the cold ground, in any case.

When it was over, the fire burned down to a heap of glowing embers and the Strongs gone after offering him their sympathy and support, Ham and Little Tom stepped up to press his hand, both of them visibly downhearted. Over Arlie's death as much as Bowen's, he reckoned. It was beyond cruel. Already two out of their company of six were dead, and the war not even properly begun. If this was how it was going to go, not a one of them was apt to see Bailon Keep again. How was it possible that the happiness he'd known there and the grief was experiencing here could exist in one and the same world?

'M'lord.' Ham's voice brought him back to the present. 'We found this amongst his things an' reckoned you'd want to have it.'

Bowen's weapons belt, minus the sword. Bryn had seen the broken halves lying on top of the shroud when he lit the pyre. He thanked them for keeping it safe, and put it with the rest of his things, moved to another room – the one Bowen had died in had been bricked up on Eilian Strong's orders – and soon to be taken

235

over to the Bent. Aeron had asked that Bryn, the Strongs, and a few of the other nobles quartered on the Barrow move over there, seeing as traveling back and forth between hills might soon become impossible.

It wasn't until much later that evening that Bryn picked up the weapons belt again. Going through the pouch, he found a silver cylinder, thick as his thumb and twice as long. Twisting off the cap, he saw that there was something inside: tightly rolled-up parchments, it looked like. A document and two letters, both addressed to him. The first was from his mother, he saw, and started to read.

Halfway through the first page, what was left of his world collapsed in a pile of rubble, most everything he'd ever thought he knew crumbling to dust and blowing away on a cold, merciless wind of ill fortune.

*   *   *

15

They made it out of Kingskeep alive and in one piece, though afterwards Rhea claimed that there'd been at least three of Pace's apprentices watching the gate.

'Pimply buggers are too dumb to find their own peckers in the dark,' she said disdainfully, once they were safely away. Laurin wasn't fooled. She was as shaken and relieved as he was, no matter she was trying to come across all hard-boiled and unflappable.

'I suppose this would be the third time you saved my life,' he said. 'So in case I haven't said it already: thank you.'

'You're welcome.' She seemed irritated rather than pleased by his show of gratitude. 'And just in case you're wondering: no – I *don't* plan to make a habit of it.'

'Though I guess we're even on at least one count,' he went on, unfazed, 'seeing as you started out trying to kill me.'

'I didn't – ' The scowl she gave him was impressive. 'I never... Oh, fuck you very much, *dwarf*.'

'If you insist. You did bang me over the head, though. Just a tad harder, and I might have been dead. So that should count for at least half a life, wouldn't you say?'

237

Briefly, it looked like she was going to grab something and bang him over the head a second time. But she merely threw up her hands, said, 'Whatever', and stalked off ahead.

'Just joking,' he called after her. 'Thought we could both use some lightening up.'

From the way she hunched her shoulders and didn't answer, he reckoned he was only making things worse. Then he remembered she was a woman, a fact one tended to forget over all the tough-girl, martial-arts, better-than-those-pimply-buggers attitude. He might have to rethink his approach. Especially where the humor was concerned.

Serious didn't work all that much better, though.

Like when he asked her how she felt about killing Pace. They hadn't found an inn that night, and were camped inside the walls of a roofless ruin, bedded down either side of a fire he intended to keep going full tilt all through the night, it was so damned cold. Watching her across the flames, her face softened by the firelight, he could see she was troubled, chewing on something that wouldn't and wouldn't go down. He reckoned it must be Pace – seeing as she didn't strike him as someone who shot a person in the head and strolled away afterwards like nothing had happened.

'None of your business,' she told him when he asked.

'I know it's not,' he said patiently. 'But that's not the point. There are things it's better to talk about than sit on them until they eat you up. I'm guessing that killing someone is right up there. Just wanted to let you know there's somebody here who's willing to listen.'

'He murdered my parents,' she relented. A little. Still trying to come across all cold and matter-of-fact. Which he didn't buy for a moment, not with her lower lip starting to tremble and her eyes tearing up. 'Pace and his boss, Albin bloody Pryce. He's next on my list.'

'Did it help?' he asked.

'Did what help?'

'Killing Pace, did it make you feel better?'

'You know what?' she said, rolling over so she was facing away from him. 'Let's not talk about this anymore.'

Some time later – he was almost asleep – he was roused by strange, muffled sounds he couldn't place at first, until he realized it was Rhea making them. She was crying, probably with her face buried in her blanket so he wouldn't hear. His heart went rushing out to her, and he felt a nearly overwhelming wish to comfort her, if not by taking her in his arms and holding her, then at least with words.

He didn't, knowing full well that neither would be welcome.

Traveling north, they saw more and more snow.

And lots of crows. Always a murder of them, never less. A day or two might pass without them showing up, but then they'd be back, sitting in a tree by the road, circling overhead, or accompanying them for a stretch. Whether they were always the same ones or there was a changing of the guard, so to speak, Laurin couldn't say. But he knew they were there for a reason. For him.

If Rhea noticed anything, she didn't say. Didn't say much at all.

Did a lot of spending, though, and Laurin watched his nest egg dwindle at an alarming rate. But there was simply no stopping her. The first thing she did when they reached a town of some size was buy a couple of sturdy palfreys, arguing they'd never get anywhere if they continued on foot. Adding a muttered something about 'short legs' that he pretended not to have heard. He could go along with buying horses, thought it a dear but sensible purchase. The same went for fur-lined mittens and caps for both of them. Less for the set of mind-numbingly expensive throwing knives she acquired at a shop that looked to be the sort of place catering to people who ate whole villages for breakfast and shat on gilded commodes – not dwarves who'd just been done out of their life savings by a murderous ex-employer. She also insisted on staying the nights in inns whenever possible, which again made sense, seeing as it was colder than witches' tits. But did it always have to be the best one in town? The kind with sheets on the beds, very few bugs, and a hot bath before dinner? Apparently yes.

At least it meant he could properly care for his poor fingers, a good soak in hot water seeming to be the best way to lessen the pain. They were healing, if slowly, but he doubted they'd ever be the same as before. And there were fine chamber pots for him to piss in, much needed with the King under the Mountain repeatedly inveigling himself into his dreams, waking him up in a sweat and with exhortations to 'Hurry! Hurry! Hurry!' ringing in his ears. His increasingly disgruntled observations that he was doing his best and that the living needed their undisturbed rest went entirely unheeded.

Neither of them was an easy traveling companion.

Rhea remained sullen and uncommunicative. Still chewing away on her inner conflict, he reckoned, but refusing to talk about it. He had to admit he wasn't much better, unused to human company as he was after twenty years of going it alone. If she'd been just another bloke it might have been easier. As it was, it seemed he could hardly open his mouth without putting his foot there.

Two weeks into their journey – the map said they were close to a place called Burnt Keep – things came to a head. They were sitting side by side in front of a crackling campfire with their backs to a shed full of fragrant hay that promised a reasonably warm, if itchy, night, when it occurred to Laurin that he'd never really thought this whole crazy undertaking through to the end. Much less talked it over with Rhea. Which led him to the realization that he had no idea what exactly her plans were. They'd just sort of fallen in together after Kingskeep, with no thought as to when and where their ways would part again.

'You don't have to go on with me, you know,' he said. 'There's really no reason for you to put yourself in any more danger on my behalf. There's apt to be Headhunters about where I'm going.'

'You think I don't know that?' Tetchy, tetchy. 'And I'm not going *with* you. I just happen to be going in the same direction you are. Besides, I'll "put myself in danger" whenever it damn well pleases me. If you're fed up with my company, just say so.'

Suddenly Laurin's patience snapped.

'Now listen here, missy. I – '

'Don't you "missy" me, *stubby*,' she hissed.

'And don't you "stubby" me!' he shouted. 'I've just about had it with your bloody moods and big-people attitudes!'

241

'So fuck you,' she said, got up and stomped off into the night.

'In your dreams,' he yelled after her. Gods, could the woman ever be aggravating!

Half an hour later, he gave up waiting for her to come back and apologize, and went to bed. He'd barely gotten comfortable when he heard her worm her way into the hay at the far end of the shed. Probably been freezing her stubborn arse off out there. Served her right.

It took him forever to go to sleep. To judge by the persistent rustling of hay at the other end of the shed, Rhea wasn't doing much better.

When he woke up the next morning, she was gone, bedroll, pack, horse and all.

'So it's just us three now,' he told Dag and Lil, as he'd named his palfrey. 'Her loss, not ours. We'll do just fine without her, you'll see.'

He didn't believe a word of what he was saying. Nor did Dag and Lil, by the looks of them.

He found her waiting at the crossroads outside Burnt Keep.

Unsure what this was about, he reined in Lil a few yards away. Long moments went by with Rhea just sitting there staring at the ground. Then she surprised him by looking up and saying, 'I'm sorry. I've been a right bitch these past few days.'

Days? he thought. *Days, she says? Weeks, is more like it.* But he decided – wisely, he felt – not to argue the point.

'I'm sorry too,' he said instead. 'I guess we've both been under a lot of strain lately. And I'm not used to being around people.

242

Makes me tend to blather.'

'Blather? You? If you say five words a day, it's a lot. You're worse than I am.'

'Really? I thought… no matter. Shall we start over, then?' He gave her his best grin. 'Hello, my name's Laurin. As you can see, I'm a dwarf and – '

'All right, already.' Was that a smile? *Dimples?* Of a sudden he was overcome by a sense of longing so strong it… *Stow it, dwarf!* He told himself sternly. *There's nothing but grief waiting for you down that road.*

'Just because I've forgiven you doesn't mean you have to go all chatty on me,' she went on, unaware of his brief inner struggle.

Chatty? And she's *forgiven* me? *How did* that *come about? Oh well. Gift horse, and all that.*

'So we're good?' he asked. 'Friends?'

'I guess.' He could see her shifting gears, clearly uncomfortable with the subject. 'So. While you were still rubbing the sleep out of your eyes, I've been talking to the gate guards up at the keep. They say Edric is twenty miles west of here, at a place called Bentridge. No Headhunters, apparently. Pryce and his bunch seem to have headed off elsewhere. Still, we need to start thinking about how we're going to handle this. Tell me about that sword again. And this time I want the whole story.'

So he did – dream, King under the Mountain, crows and all. Expected her to laugh him down. Call him a fool. Ride off and never look back.

She didn't. Instead, she asked if she could see the sword again. So he got down off Lil and went to fetch it from Dag's pannier.

243

Handed it to her.

What happened next left him dumbfounded, speechless.

She'd taken off her mittens, and the moment her bare hands touched the sword, he saw a faint glow run through the battered scrollwork on the scabbard, like fireflies darting along spirals and runes half hidden under all the rust and patina. There and gone so quickly it left him wondering whether he hadn't imagined the whole thing.

'Weird, huh?' she said, handing back the sword and rubbing her hands on her cloak before stuffing them back into her gloves.

'You can say that again.' He was still reeling. 'Never happened when I touched it. What do you suppose it means?'

'It means I believe you. Otherwise, I've no idea. But I'm beginning to think this rusty old sticker might be a lot more important than it looks. There's one thing that bothers me, though. The bloke you described, the one with the pigs? Young, blond, farm boy sort of type?'

'What about him?'

'That's not at all what Edric looks like. Not one little bit.'

'Oh. Well.' It was a piece of news he could have done without. Sent his whole plan down the jakes, in fact. 'Looks like I have a problem, then. Big one. Like, what the bloody hell am I supposed to do with the damned thing now? Lug it every which way across Ardath with a war going on, hope I'll get lucky and find the right keep before I catch a stray arrow or a spear in the gut?'

'Not a good idea.' She considered for a moment. 'How about we go find my grandda. Might be he has some helpful ideas.'

Laurin doubted it. But, with no better plan coming to mind, he supposed they might as well go and see Grandda.

The road west snaked through steep, wooded hills, a narrow, winding strip of white crowded by dark, silent pines that only rarely drew back to make room for short stretches of open land, meadows or bogs hidden under a foot or more of snow. The road was well traveled, the snow packed down by wagons and teams ferrying supplies to Edric's army or rolling back empty to pick up more, and less than four hours saw them to the outskirts of the Dunmarkan encampment. Passing through a haphazard jumble of battered wagons and ratty tents where whores, fortune-tellers, card sharps and assorted craftsmen had set up shop, Laurin saw painted signs depicting everything from foaming mugs to a hammer and anvil to halfnaked women in suggestive poses. There were a few catcalls and explicit offers, the same sordid stuff you could hear in the sleazier quarters of any city in Aldara, but the callers shut up right smartly under a hard stare from Rhea. The girl seemed to have a way with intimidating people.

On the edge of the camp proper they were stopped by a couple of grim-faced sentries. Not for long, though: it was surprising how quickly their miens went from forbidding to friendly when Rhea explained that she was Macsen Redbreast's granddaughter. One of them went to fetch the First Sergeant, and shortly a crusty old warrior came stomping up, not looking happy at all.

He gave them both a piercing glance, first Rhea, then Laurin. Said, 'Come with me', turned on his heel and went stomping back the way he'd come, the two of them following behind like sheep to the shearing – at least that was how it felt to Laurin.

245

The old man held the tent flap open while they tied the horses to a hitching rail outside. He seemed impatient to get them inside and out of sight.

'Bring the sword,' Rhea whispered. 'We're going to need it.'

'I'm not sure this is such a good idea,' Laurin whispered back. On the way here from Burnt Keep he'd been assailed by all sorts of doubts. Was it really wise to come here? Could Rhea's grandda be trusted? What if he went straight to the king? The old man was Kingsguard, after all.

'Trust me,' was all Rhea said, and then it was too late.

'What in the name of all gods are you doing here, girl?' was the first thing Macsen said as soon as he'd dropped the flap behind them. 'This is a war, in case you hadn't noticed, not a sightseeing jaunt. No place for either of you to come gallivanting.'

'Good to see you too, Macsen,' Rhea said, seemingly unfazed by the gruff reception. 'This is Laurin, by the way. And we're bloody well not sightseeing. You should know me well enough to realize I wouldn't be here without a damned good reason.'

'Listen to the girl,' Macsen told Laurin, throwing up his hands in defeat and settling heavily into a rickety camp chair. 'Has a mouth on her like soldier, for all I spent years trying to teach her some manners. So what is it that brings you two here?'

'Long story,' Rhea said. 'And you're not going to like it.'

Here we go, Laurin thought. *Gods, but I hope she's right about the old man.*

Macsen listened, mostly in silence, while Rhea told him her part of the story – though he did make a few choking sounds, and once

246

even banged his fist on the arm of his chair when she described what she'd found in the Judge Executioner's archives, and what had subsequently happened with Pace.

Then it was Laurin's turn. *Too late for half measures,* he thought, and left nothing out. Only once did Macsen interrupt him, and that was when he mentioned the Bailon boy.

'An Avellin, you say? In Ardath? But how is that...' He banged the chair again. 'Of course! Gavrielle Rowan. But in that case he'd be a bastard, unless...'

Macsen fell silent. Laurin waited a few beats, and then continued his story. When he was done, Macsen sat looking at them for the longest time.

'You two are totally insane,' he finally said. 'In fact I should – '

'Give me the sword,' Rhea said to Laurin, taking off her gloves.

What else could he do? He gave it to her.

Fireflies again; in the half-dark tent, the effect was even more startling.

'Still think we're nuts?' Rhea asked Macsen, who looked even more dumbfounded than Laurin had been. Watching the old man's mien, Laurin saw disbelief give way to wonder.

'Well, I'll be,' Macsen finally said. 'Legends and myth come alive. Looks like there's some truth to the old stories after all.'

'What stories?' Rhea asked.

'Cormac Avellin. The King under the Mountain. They say he fought at Simbalan, turned the whole battle around practically single-handed, with a sword made by the mages of the Incantaria. Then he got stuck by one of the baddies with a poisoned dagger. Made

247

some kind of deal with the mages so he wouldn't have to die. They used magic to put him to sleep, somehow keeping him in the In-between.

'Story goes, he'll come back and save Dunmark in a time of great need. Doesn't look like he's going to make it himself though, seeing as he sent you with the sword. But one thing I'll swear to: it's not Edric who's supposed to have it. There may be Avellin blood running in his veins, but there's not a shred of goodness in the man.'

Macsen sat brooding for a moment. Then he gave Rhea a sharp look.

'Another story comes to mind, one my grandda used to tell. Claimed there was an Avellin bastard somewhere in our family's bloodline, way back when. I always thought he was just bragging. But, seeing what I just saw, I'm inclined to – '

He broke off in mid-sentence, his gaze riveted on the entrance.

With a rustle of stiff canvas the flap was pushed aside and a man stepped into the tent. A big man, nearly as wide as he was tall and wearing the sort of clothes that shouted 'noble'. Smiling benignly but with a roguish twinkle as if he had an amusing remark or a naughty joke on the tip of his tongue.

Bloke makes you want to like him, Laurin thought. *Like everybody's favorite uncle.*

'My lord Gale,' Macsen said, heaving himself out of his chair and standing to attention. 'What can I do for you? As you see, we were just having a small family reunion. My granddaughter Rhea. And a friend.'

Too much the soldier to come right out and tell the man to bugger off. Still, the fellow would have to be blind not to see he isn't welcome.

'Yes,' Gale said, jolly as you like. 'I noticed. And a very interesting reunion it is. I'll come right out and admit I've been shamelessly eavesdropping on you good folks. I do hope you'll forgive the intrusion, but I simply couldn't resist. Far too fetching a subject. Very enlightening as well. Is that the famous sword? May I see it?'

Rhea, protectively hugging the sword to her breast, looked as if she were a mere breath away from doing something rash and irreversible. But Macsen gave her a slight shake of the head, and then nodded towards Gale. After a tense moment, she handed it over.

Thank gods she'd put her gloves back on. No fireflies. But Laurin's relief quickly faded. How long had Gale been listening? He might have already heard all there was to know.

'Thank you, lass,' Gale said, giving her a winning smile. 'I appreciate the trust. And rest assured, I'm not here to steal it. Just wanted to have a look. Rusty old thing, though, isn't it? I daresay I can tell you – '

Another high-and-mighty-looking bloke came barging in through the flap without knocking. Behind him Laurin caught a glimpse of two men-at-arms taking up station outside. It was beginning to get pretty cramped in the small tent. Mighty strange, how all these people were suddenly showing up. Was it possible they were somehow being attracted to the sword, like flies to fresh dung?

'Your majesty,' Gale said smoothly. 'What a surprise.'

So this was the King of Dunmark.

Grim-looking fellow. Rhea had been right: this was definitely the wrong Avellin. Dark. Built like a barrel. A presence like hoarfrost.

'What's going on here?' Edric asked, impatiently slapping his gloves against his thigh. 'Who are these people?'

'My granddaughter, your majesty,' Macsen said. 'And a friend. Come to pay me a visit.'

'Have they, now?' Edric said. 'Bloody stupid of them. They'd better make it short, then. We're attacking tomorrow. Gale, I... what's that you have there?'

'Just an old sword, majesty,' Macsen offered. 'Master Laurin here found it somewhere in the mountains, asked me to have a look at it. See if it might be worth something. As you can see, it's not.'

'Obviously,' Edric said, touching a bare finger to the scabbard and jerking back his hand when the sword suddenly began to crawl with light, many times brighter than when Rhea had held it.

'Well, well.' he reached out again, his fingers closing around the sword and prying it from Gale's grasp. 'I think I'll take that. Where did you say you found it?' he asked, looking at Laurin for the first time. Suddenly there was light in those cold eyes. Not the benign kind, though.

'In the Caerrocks,' Laurin said, belatedly adding 'Your majesty.'

The king gave him another searching look. Scary as hell. He suppressed a shiver.

'Well,' Edric said, slipping the sword under his cloak. 'I suppose we can leave that for another day. Purdy!'

One of the soldiers stuck his head inside. 'Yes, your majesty?'

'See that a guard is posted outside. We don't want anything

untoward happening to these good people during the night. You never know what the rabble over yonder will get up to. Cutthroats, the lot of them. Sell their mothers for a copper. Sergeant, you're free for the night, to report in the morning. Gale, with me.'

'Shit, shit, shit,' Rhea whispered when it was just the three of them again.

'Damn right,' Laurin said. 'The King under the Mountain said that – '

Macsen stopped him with a warningly raised finger. 'Not here. Let's go buy us a drink over in Sleazetown.'

'Will they let us go?' Rhea asked, nodding at the entrance, where two men had already taken up station.

'Only one way to find out,' the old warrior said, strapping on his weapons belt, looking like he wouldn't mind bloodying a few noses.

The men standing guard outside let them pass but followed them at a distance. Their boots crunching over the frozen snow, Macsen led Rhea and Laurin past long rows of tents and dozens of cook fires surrounded by freezing, hungry soldiers. Once past the sentries he steered them to a large tent pitched on the edge of Sleazetown. This time of evening, the place was crammed with soldiers and the various lowlife parasites that made a living off them. The noise was deafening, and the stink of smoke, spilled ale, and unwashed bodies hanging under the tent roof was thick enough to cut with a knife.

A round of soldiers made room for them at their table consisting of a couple of rough planks laid over trestles, with benches to match. Laurin reckoned that chances were high they'd all end up pulling splinters out of their bottoms later that night.

'So,' Macsen said after he'd exchanged a few words with the soldiers and they'd been served watery ale in mugs that likely hadn't been washed in a fortnight and were at best three quarters full. They'd put their heads together so they could keep their voices down, wary of eavesdroppers. 'Bloody cockup, that. I've no idea what that bloody sword is capable of besides making pretty little lights. But I have to say that the idea of Edric having it makes me damned uncomfortable.'

'Me too,' Laurin agreed. 'And the King under the Mountain said that if the sword falls into the wrong hands, the kingdoms are probably done for. But what can we do?'

'Get it back,' Rhea said, as if only a simpleton could ask such a stupid question.

'And how do you propose we do that, young missy?' Macsen said. Laurin noted that Rhea didn't protest when her grandda 'missied' her. 'The perimeter around Edric's tent is tight as a gnat's... er, tight.'

'Not *we*,' she said. '*Me*. I've spent two years learning this sort of thing. Trust me, I can do it.'

'Out of the question,' Macsen said, starting to bang the flat of his hand on the table and thinking better of it. 'Much too dangerous. I won't allow it.'

'I'm not asking you,' Rhea flared. 'I'm telling you. There's no other way.'

Laurin could see that Macsen was about to explode, with Rhea not far behind. 'Friends, friends,' he said. 'Let's all keep our tempers. Maybe there's another way.'

'Just so we're clear,' Macsen said. 'No matter how it's done, I won't have the king harmed. Not on my watch. Like it or not, I've sworn an oath to protect him, and I aim to keep it. I can stretch that oath to include saving him from a dangerous object that's unfortunately come into his possession. But I can't go along with any plan that's a threat to his person.'

For over an hour they studied the problem, turning it this way and that and trying to come up with an alternative solution. It all came back down to Rhea being their best – and only – bet. Though he feared for her, Laurin supported her plan. Finally the two of them together got Macsen to grudgingly agree, though it was plain to see what it cost him.

And then something happened that put paid to their whole flimsy scheme.

Laurin, getting up to go for a piss, suddenly found himself face to face with a pair of enormous breasts threatening to pop out of a dangerously low-cut bodice. Traveling upwards, his gaze met a sharp pair of eyes that seemed entirely out of place among all the powder, rouge, and kohl. Not enough of it to cover up the crowsfeet and the hard lines around the mouth, though.

'Hello there, sweetling,' the whore said – because that's what she was, no doubt about it. 'Lonely, are we? How about comin' over to my place, let Tilly make you comfy, show you a good time?' Provocatively swaying hips that were running to fat.

'I'm, ah, sorry,' he stammered, taken completely by surprise. 'I'm with friends. Another time, maybe.'

'Too bad,' she said, reaching out a hand and cupping his cheek. 'And here I was fixin' to offer you a bargain. Half price, honey.

Sure you ain't up for it?' She gave him a leer with everything but her eyes. 'Never had me a dwarf before.'

'As I said, sorry.' Pulling away from her soft, pudgy fingers trailing down the side of his neck, he felt something being slipped down inside his collar. Next moment she was gone.

Mystified, he had the presence of mind to wait until he was outside and no one was passing by before he fished the object out from under his shirt. A piece of parchment, very thin, and folded several times. Curiouser and curiouser. Going around the side of the tent, he found a spot where there was just enough light falling through the canvas to read by.

The person you seek is with Aeron. Look to the Bent or the Barrow. Ask for Bailon. If all goes well, three hours past midnight tonight a guide will come to your tent and take you through the cordon. The guide will also return the missing object to you. Godspeed. A friend.

Laurin was decidedly wary of the offer.

As were Rhea and Macsen, when he told them about the note. It sounded too good to be true, and whoever was behind it must be capable of working magic, seeing how quickly it had been set up. The whole thing smelled of a trap – though if it was, it seemed overly elaborate, the point of the exercise being hard to see. Edric already had the sword, and if he wanted to have them killed, he didn't need to go looking for a reason. He was the king, after all. Maybe Gale was preparing to steal it, and needed them as scape-goats. Although, should they be caught making off with the sword, it would go right back to Edric, not Gale. Made no sense. Was there a third party involved, then? But who? And why? It was a mystery.

In the end they decided to wait until the appointed hour and see what would happen. Take it one step at a time. If they didn't like how things developed, they could always stay put, say they had no idea what their late-night visitor had wanted if anyone asked. Not if they went along with whoever came to fetch them, though. Once they left Macsen's tent and headed for the forward cordon, they'd be committed, for better or worse.

Probably worse, Laurin thought, if things continued to go as they'd been doing lately.

*   *   *

One hell of a bloody mess, Macsen thought on the way back to camp. *Crazy. Crazy as bedbugs.*

Rhea being in the middle of it worried him silly. At least the little man seemed to have a level head on his shoulders, though Macsen doubted he'd be much good if it came to a fight. Thinking of which gave him an idea, causing him to change course in mid-stride and head for the quartermaster's tent. Jakken Sykes was a good friend of his, and a man who knew how to keep his mouth shut. They found Jakken still up, mending a broken strap on a piece of armor by the light of a candle, sweat shining on his bald pate despite the cold.

'Redbreast,' Jakken said. 'Come to keep a lonely man company? Lucky I happen to know the lass is your granddaughter, otherwise I'd a thought you was tryin' to lead an old man into temptation. Hope you brought your own drinks, though, 'cause I'm pretty much run dry here.'

'Sorry, Jakken,' Macsen said. 'It's business tonight. I need these two outfitted as best you can.'

'You're in luck then,' Jakken said, eying Laurin like he was measuring him up. 'Some dunderhead back in Kingskeep packed half a dozen boy's gambesons and hauberks in with all the other stuff. Mayhap the idiot thought we was goin' to a nameday picnic instead of a war. Any road, I got 'em lyin' around here somewheres. Just give me half a jiff.'

It was a large tent, packed to the ceiling with weapons and supplies, and Jakken's half a jiff ended up being closer to a quarter hour. Macsen could hear him huffing and cursing back in the stacks, until eventually he came back laden down with what looked like half the armory, dumping the whole lot on the makeshift counter.

'Here you go, then,' he said, fingering mail that ran through his hand like liquid silver. 'Good stuff, this. Made for some of the Avellin lads when they was little, I'd wager. Here, try 'em on.' He handed Rhea and Laurin each a thickly padded shirt. 'First the gambeson, then the mail. There we go. Fits like it was made for 'em. Reckoned the lass would do better with a large boy's size than with a small men's, an' I was right. Let's see what else we got.'

Helms, bucklers, a short sword for Rhea and a small war axe for Laurin. Jakken knew his work, Macsen thought with a touch of pride. A quartermaster who loved a job well done saved lives in the field.

Laurin hefted the axe, looking pleased. The helm was made for a bigger head than his, but it was the smallest Jakken had. Better than nothing, though. Stuff it with some with extra padding, and it should do the job. Rhea rejected the sword and the buckler, said she had all the weapons she needed and a shield would only cramp her style. Asked if Jakken had a swordbreaker, though. Which he did.

'Thanks, Jakken,' Macsen said in parting. 'And in case anybody asks: we were never here.'

'Who was never here?' Jakken said. 'Ain't seen nobody all evenin'.'

Back in his own tent, the waiting seemed to drag on forever.

Finally, there was a scratch at the flap and a hooded figure slipped inside. A woman, Macsen saw when she pushed back her hood. He thought he'd seen her before but couldn't figure out when or where. Not around Edric, that was for sure. She wasn't the type, and besides, Edric's women never showed up a second time.

'Ready?' she asked.

'Have you got the sword?' Laurin shot back.

'Yes.' She drew back her cloak, revealing the rusty old blade stuck in her belt beside a whole array of new and very sharp-looking relatives. Prepared for trouble, then. 'I was told to give it to you once we've crossed the cordon. Safer for you if we're stopped.'

Made sense. 'I'd best come with you,' Macsen said. 'Make sure you get through.'

'No. I have very clear orders on that. You come with us all the way, or not at all. If you decide not to come, I'm to tell you it might be a good idea if you went east instead. Soon. Tonight.'

For long moments, Macsen was torn between duty and love. In the end, duty won. He wasn't going to defect to the enemy. Not him. Not ever. Better to stay and face the music than become a turncoat. He wanted to be able to look himself in the eye without shame when he died. Whenever that was. Probably sooner than later, by the look of things.

'All right, then,' he said, giving Rhea a fierce hug. 'Take care.'

'You too, Grandda.' Were those tears in her eyes?

He clapped the little man on the shoulder. 'Watch out for her, Master Laurin. She's the most precious thing I've got in this world.' The only precious thing, actually, apart from his soldier's honor, which seemed to pale in comparison.

He saw Rhea give the guide a level look. 'Anything I don't like happens,' she told the woman, 'you're the first one I'll kill. Just so we're clear.' Said matter-of-factly, but Macsen never doubted her.

Nor did the guide, by the look she gave Rhea. 'Fair enough,' was all she said.

My little girl, he thought. *Where did she go? Who is this hard, fearsome woman? Must have happened while I wasn't looking. Man doesn't watch out, life will go right on by and leave him sitting by the edge of the road. Never catch up, once that happens.*

'Take care,' he told them, and then they were off, the tent flap giving a last whisper as it fell back over the entrance. Leaving him alone with the silence and the uncertainty. Damn, it just wasn't fair.

But then, when was it ever?

He spent the next hour or so sitting in his chair, anxious, brooding, listening for any sign that things had gone wrong. Nothing. And still nothing. They'd made it.

All of a sudden he reached a decision. Got up and packed a few things. Put on his armor, buckled on his sword. Went to fetch his horse from the picket line, divided up an apple between Rhea and

Laurin's palfreys and the little man's pony. They'd be well taken care of, no matter what crimes their owners would be charged with on the morrow. Then he heaved himself into the saddle and rode east, taking the advice passed on to him by the woman. Gale's emissary. That was where he'd seen her before: talking to the Lord Treasurer in a secluded corner of the camp. Making a report, most likely, or receiving orders. It cast a whole different light on the man. Still a puzzle, though.

He rode past the sentries with a wave, keeping the horse to a walk. They had no reason to stop him. He was the First Sergeant, after all, could go where he wanted, whenever he wanted. First Sergeant tonight, still.

Tomorrow, not anymore. Didn't matter. Not where he was going. If his honor didn't allow him to join the enemy, it said nothing about joining friends, not when chances were high he'd not survive the coming day if he stayed until morning.

With Sleazetown behind him, he kneed the horse to a canter, feeling a great weight lift off his shoulders. Feeling younger than he had in a decade. Decided it was a fine night for riding.

*　　*　　*

16

Bryn, dearest,

In the event that this letter reaches you on your eighteenth nameday, it means I will not be there to feast the occasion with you. But trust that I will be watching over you all the same, from wherever it is we must all go when our time here has come to an end.

My sweet boy – how strange, to think that you'll be a man grown when you read this – what I have to tell you is grave. If I hesitated to do so sooner, it was because I wished you to grow up as carefree and unburdened as could be, knowing full well that the responsibilities and worries of adulthood would overtake you soon enough.

Would that these secrets could stay buried forever. But yours is a dangerous legacy, too dangerous to risk leaving you in the dark. Others may find out, and their intentions towards you may well be of a less than friendly nature. Much as I'd like to spare you this knowledge, I cannot leave without knowing you armed and fore-warned. That the only weapon I have to give you is a hard and painful truth, I deeply regret. But such is life: we seek to do the best we can with what we are given.

As you can see from the enclosed documents, Kendric Bailon was neither the first man I wed, nor was he your real father. But you should know that I took him as my husband for no other reason than love, and that his affection for you was as deep and true as any father's for a child of his own blood. You were lucky to have him, and the same goes for Bowen, a true and trusted friend if ever there was one. I rest easier for knowing him at your side.

Your father –

He couldn't read on, and not just because his vision was suddenly blurring. It hurt so damned much. Bowen. Dear faithful, stern, wise, exacting, gruffly affectionate Bowen. Bowen, whom he'd done such a great and unforgivable injustice. Because he'd hastily jumped to all the wrong conclusions, thoroughly misunderstood the implications of what Bowen had been trying to tell him. How he hated fate and the gods for having saddled him with such cruel and intractable circumstances. But most of all he hated himself, for having been such a faithless, untrusting fool. Childish. Inept. Blind to the obvious. How then was he supposed to deal with what he'd learned from the documents? How...

Listen to yourself. Yammering like a little girl who found a fly in her sweetmeats. Yes, you made a mistake, and there's no fixing it now Bowen is gone. But his death was not your fault. He was your liegeman, lived and died as such, and you paid him due farewell at his parting rites. If you want to honor his memory, then face the challenge set before you like a man. In order to do that, you must become hard. Cunning. Merciless. Because the enemy you face is all of those things, and more. Either you match him strength for

262

strength, blow for blow, or you die. It's that simple.

He took up the letter again.

Your father – Seorus Avellin, that is – was a good man as well. True, he was not always a faithful husband to Helise, but then who among us can say that he is entirely without fail? As king, he was everything the people of Dunmark could have hoped for: just, wise, merciful.

How such a man could have fathered a son like Edric will always remain a mystery to me. And Helise, Edric's mother, was a woman of unsurpassed grace and gentleness who should have made a perfect mother, yet she couldn't bring herself to love the child. Perhaps it had to do with the fact that Edric's birth was such a long and hard one, a three-day travail that nearly killed her. Bowen, who as weapons master was tasked with training Edric, tried his best with the lad, and failed. It was almost as if by some evil slight of hand a changeling had been slipped into the cradle, and whispered rumors to that end abounded once Edric reached an age where his true nature began to emerge.

Much of this I only know from what Seorus and Bowen told me, but I have no reason to doubt their word: Edric, it seems, was a difficult child from the very beginning, stubborn and intractable, prone to fits of temper. Nurses and servants learned to fear him at an early age, seeing as he repaid even the mildest rebuke with the most cruel and insidious devilries. For instance, dead animals began to show up around the keep, in beds, drawers, shoes, what have you: cats, lap dogs, birds, all manner of pets that had been horribly mutilated. Edric was never proven the guilty party, but among those affected there was little doubt as to the authorship of these atro-cities. It was obvious, after all, that the boy was up to no good: for-ever sneaking up on people, lurking in dark corners, spying and eavesdropping on all and sundry.

When Edric was sixteen, first a stable boy and some weeks later a serving girl were found beaten to within an inch of their lives. Both refused to say what had happened. Whether they'd been pro-mised a fat purse if they remained silent or cruel retribution if they didn't, I cannot say. Fact is, it was the same year Helise died of a strange wasting sickness that left the physicians puzzled and help-less. Some time after her death, a laboratory of sorts was found in one of the deepest cellars. Someone had used it to dabble in alche-my, it was surmised. If so, it was an amateur adept with an odd penchant for exotic poisons.

Again, no blame was traced to Edric. Bowen had the place watched for weeks, but whoever had used it never showed up again.

Through all of this Seorus never gave up on his son, refusing to see the extent of the evil in the boy, hoping against hope that some miracle would occur and Edric would yet come around. It was only after the alchemist's den had been discovered that Seorus began to seriously doubt Edric's intentions. Though he didn't admit it, I could see that he was very worried. We were secretly wed – secret-ly, so as not to upset Edric, absurd as the idea seems in hindsight – and neither of us ventured anywhere without a complement of guards.

And then came the day when I was certain I was with child. Not an hour after I told Seorus, the master of horse came running to report that a three-day-old foal by the mare Seorus had given me for our wedding had been brutally butchered. The king and I looked at each other, and in his eyes I saw that he knew, had finally admitted to himself what manner of monster he'd raised. And still he didn't draw the final consequence, a mistake that would cost him his life.

That evening he summoned Edric, told him in no uncertain terms that he was disinherited, barred from the succession, and that if one more untoward incident should occur he'd have Edric clapped in irons and locked away for the rest of his life. Seorus told me afterwards that Edric never tried to argue or protest his innocence. He didn't say anything at all, in fact, merely listened in silence, studying his father in a manner that made Seorus' blood run cold.

That very same night Seorus sent me away, ordered Bowen to take me to a safe place, insisting that not even he be told where we went. Later, Edric tried to make it look as if he'd generously offered us pardon and exile, even insinuating we might have had something to do with the king's death.

Because Seorus didn't survive the night. Again, nothing was proven, not even the true cause of his death. A poor heart, the physicians hastily determined, no doubt because it was what Edric told them to say. Bowen brought me to Bailon Keep, where the lord was an old friend of his. The rest you know.

So now you've been shown the nature of the beast you'll be faced with, should you choose to confront it and thereby honor your father's last will. As a mother whose first and foremost wish for her child is that he may be granted a life of peace and happiness, I make no such claim on you. The decision is yours – though bitter experience has taught me that fate has a way of taking the choices we make and throwing them back in our face as something entirely different.

Whatever you do, know that my love will accompany you always.

His father's last will, laid out with a few, terse sentences in the second letter. Should he tell Aeron, ask for his help, suggest an alliance? No. Not yet, in any case. Even if the King of Ardath didn't laugh him off immediately, Bryn had nothing to offer except a few scraps of parchment and three disheartened men.

He knew it was going to be a lot harder than that. So close to impossible as made no difference. Madness, actually. But he'd be damned if he went back to Bailon Keep with his tail between his legs and spent the rest of his days looking over his shoulder, waiting for the axe to fall. He would try. If not to the living, he owed it to the dead.

He must have nodded off. Some time later, he startled awake with the words *Beware! Beware!* ringing in his ears. Old Cormac again, fretting away in his cave.

No idea what the hour was. Still dark, in any case, Daven and Little Tom snoring a duet.

There was a scratch at the tent flap, and Ham stuck his head in. He was on gate duty tonight. 'M'lord, there's visitors for you. Girl and a dwarf. Say they've got somethin' to give you. Won't let anyone else touch it, whatever it is. They was pretty damned insistent, so I made 'em give up their weapons an' brought 'em right over. Should I let 'em in?'

Bryn was baffled, but too exhausted to give it a lot of thought.

266

He gave a tired wave. 'Show them in. And thank you, Ham.'

'No trouble 't all, m'lord.' He lowered his voice. 'Gotta say, the lass ain't hard on the eye. But if y' ask me, I'd say beware.'

Beware! Beware!

Suddenly wide awake, Bryn studied the young woman stepping in past Ham, who was holding the flap for her. By the way Ham's eyes followed her, he'd already forgotten his own advice. Not a beauty in the conventional sense, Bryn thought. A little too hard for that. Unkempt. Road-worn. But definitely not hard on the eye. Put her beside Meris Conlin in a silken gown, she'd look like a tramp. And still carry the day, colors flying. Even just standing there, she appeared lithe and graceful, like a dancer at rest, or a warrior poised in readiness.

Checking himself, he considered her companion. A dwarf, indeed. First one he'd ever seen. Small, but definitely no child. Looked... weathered, as if he spent most of his time outdoors. Favored his left hand, Bryn noticed.

'Are you Bailon?' the girl asked without ceremony.

'Who's asking?' he shot back.

'Rhea Redbreast. This is Laurin Semson. So, are you?'

'I am.'

She and the dwarf nodded at each other. Then the dwarf brought something out from under his cloak. A rusty old sword, Bryn saw. Very optimistic, these two, if they planned to assassinate him with that. But the little man stepped forward, held the thing out to Bryn, who hesitated a moment, then took it. Almost dropped it when it suddenly began to crawl with tiny lights, like scores of fireflies flitting along its whole length.

'It's him, all right,' he heard the girl breathe.

'With regards from his majesty, the King under the Mountain,' the dwarf said.

Morning wasn't far off by the time Master Semson had finished telling the tale of how he'd come into possession of the sword. It was a fascinating story, and seemed to confirm Bryn's own dream experiences with the ghost of Cormac Avellin. Trying to draw the blade, though, he had no more luck than the dwarf. It wouldn't budge, not even a hair, rusted fast inside the scabbard.

'Well,' he said. 'Thank you, I guess. Though I'm not really sure what I'm supposed to do with it.'

'You'll find out,' the girl – Rhea – said with utter conviction.

'I'm afraid I have no idea how,' Bryn sighed. 'I haven't got a shred of talent for magic. And that seems to be what this is about, Mistress Redbreast.'

'Don't call me that.' She looked annoyed. 'I'm nobody's mistress. Rhea will do.'

'Fine. In that case, don't call me my lord. Bryn will do.'

'Wasn't planning to,' she grumbled. Proud as a Tanuri. Touchy.

He was still searching for a fitting retort when he was suddenly distracted by a strange noise that seemed to come from somewhere near the eastern ramparts. Whup-whup-whup, it went, like huge wings beating the air. Rhea and Laurin looked as puzzled as he was. Two heartbeats later, there was a mighty crash of splintering wood. Men shouting.

Daven and Little Tom were out of their bedrolls and going for their weapons before they noticed the visitors.

'What was that?' the dwarf asked.

'Catapult,' Daven said. 'Looks like the war's finally started.'

*　　*　　*

Edric was in the foulest of tempers.

'Here I'm surrounded by a dozen guards, and you're telling me the girl just walked in and took the sword?' He nearly shouted the last words. 'And what about the guard I had posted outside Redbreast's tent? I'll have their heads if it turns out they were slacking.'

'I can have their heads brought to you right now, if you like,' Gale said. 'I'm sure they won't mind, seeing as they're already dead. Strangled, both of them. As for the girl, it turns out she's an apprentice Headhunter. Best they've had in a long time, apparently. Killed her mentor before she left Kingskeep. Man by the name of Pace. Fearsome bloke, I hear – or used to be.'

'Why are you telling me this *now*, Gale?' Edric was pacing, more agitated than Gale had ever seen him. Not his usual, wintry self at all this morning. 'Why not a week ago? Have they run out of birds in Kingskeep?'

'The weather, your majesty. Couple of birds never made it through. Must have gotten turned around by the storm and frozen to death somewhere along the way.' Gale shrugged. 'Vexing, but it happens. Occupational hazard. So what is it you would have me do?'

'About the girl and the dwarf, nothing. We'll be seeing them again soon enough. Nowhere they can go from where they are now.' Edric paused, gave Gale a sharp look. 'You're sure they're on the Bent?'

'No doubt at all, your majesty. My people found their tracks leading out through the cordon and then straight up the hill.'

'Redbreast, then.' The cold was back, frostier than ever. 'Find him for me, Gale. No matter the cost. I want to see the craven traitor hang. I want *everybody* to see him hang. Oh, and I want the catapults to start shooting without delay. Enough sitting around twiddling our thumbs. Stonebridge has had all the time in the world to get into position. Tell them to chuck over the dead guards while they're at it. A little something to let the murdering thief know we're aware of her whereabouts. And don't forget to signal Stonebridge. I want those bloody hills taken under fire from both sides, understood?'

'Perfectly, your majesty. I'll get right on it.'

'One more thing.' Edric stopped pacing. 'Who's next in command of the Kingsguard after Redbreast?'

'I believe that would be Purdy, majesty.'

'Purdy it is, then. Last night, the Guard failed me. Miserably. For that, I shall have Purdy flogged, discharged from the Guard, and chased off in disgrace. Tarred and feathered, perhaps. The entire Guard made to watch while he receives his punishment. Actually, I should have all of them flogged.'

'Are you sure, majesty?'

'Are you questioning my judgment, my lord?' He gave Gale a dark look.

'Never, your majesty. Just suggesting it might be in your majesty's best interest to weigh retribution against the Guard's continued loyalty. Mayhap making an example of Purdy will suffice to get the others' attention.'

'Very well. We shall make a memorable example, then. Flog

Purdy. Thirty lashes. Then sit him in the bucket of a mangonel and send him on over to Aeron. That should get everyone's attention right smartly, don't you think? Well? What are you waiting for? Get to it. Oh, and nice touch that, firing the catapults in the wee hours. I'd wager Aeron and his rabble aren't all that well rested today.'

He's slipping closer to the edge, Gale thought as he went to carry out Edric's orders. *Three whores dead in as many days, and the rest of them refusing to service him, no matter how fat a purse they are offered. The sword snatched away when he'd barely gotten his hands on it. He knows his history well enough to have an idea what it might represent. Betrayed and deserted by Macsen. Now that was a strange relationship if ever I've seen one. Almost as if Edric need-ed Macsen to stand in for what he can't find in himself. Someone to hold place for things like trust, honor, decency. Goodness, in a word. Macsen turning his back on him is like knocking the last prop out from under a stage where appearances still count. Opening a sluice gate. Freeing the worst in Edric to do as it likes, because Macsen's desertion has given him proof that goodness is only an-other lie among many.*

Still, he must be handled with the utmost care, now more than ever. Ever so delicately nudged in the desired direction. Never pushed. Try that, and you'll find yourself back at the bottom of the ladder, hurting very badly – and that's if you're lucky.

Speaking of lucky: Edric's order to move the catapults into position last night had been a godsend. The perfect cover for spiriting the girl and the dwarf past the sentries. With all the coming and going, the cordon had been leaky as a sieve for half the night.

271

And what should have been the trickiest part had gone smooth as you like. While the men of the Kingsguard had been diligently watching out for anything suspicious, they'd been duped by the obvious: the theft had been carried out more or less in plain sight, and by one of their own.

It pays to employ only the best, Gale thought, congratulating himself, *and to have them in the right place at the right time. If you knew how good I really am at what I do, Edric bloody majesty, you'd have had me removed already a long time ago.*

Shortly, the camp was awakened by the two-fold melody of Purdy's screams and the whang! thwock! whump! of the ballistae and mangonels delivering their deadly loads to Aeron and his bunch. Unfortunately, Gale wasn't able to appreciate any of it, worrying himself sick over the lad sitting up on the hill. If anything happened to him, the whole elegant plan would come crashing down around his ears and bury him alive. Nothing he could do, though. Hands of the gods.

Understandably Purdy, his back a bloody ruin from the flogging, didn't relish being fired into enemy territory by catapult. They had to truss the screaming man up like a feast-day turkey before they could get him to stay in the bucket, but from there on everything went smoothly. Gale reckoned that the jolt of the release would already suffice to kill the man – the human body simply wasn't made for this sort of thing. And if by some miracle it didn't, the impact surely would. In the meantime Purdy would get to see what it felt like to fly like a bird, albeit without wings to cushion the landing.

Lastly, for appearances' sake Gale sent a couple of his people after Macsen, making sure they understood that they were not to lay a finger on the man.

'Take your time,' he told them. 'Admire the landscape, enjoy the scenery. And don't forget it's often the little things that hold the greatest wonders. It pays to stop for a closer look once in a while. In fact, regard this trip as leave time, a sign of my appreciation for services rendered. Should you happen to catch up with Macsen, say hello to him from me, and make sure he gets safely to wherever he's going.'

Gale knew exactly where that was but saw no reason to make things too easy for the two. A bit of work mixed in with the leisure would do them no harm.

*   *   *

The Dunmarkans resumed shooting at the crack of dawn, though the morning's first payload landed on the eastern rampart with a wettish thud instead of a crash and a splinter. And there, hanging skewered on the stakes, was a naked man, his back shredded by a cat o' nine tails. For a wonder, he was still alive, if just barely. From what Bryn heard later, the crew of the nearest mangonel watched him squirm for a while before they scraped him off the stakes, loaded him in their bucket, and shot him back down to the Dunmarkans. Apparently his carcass made several more trips back and forth, until the crews on both sides wearied of the game. By then, there wasn't much left of him in any case.

Now, with death raining down from the sky as Dunmark's giant catapults heaved load after load of boulders and scattershot onto the Bent, Bryn labored alongside Longshanks and Flatside, helping to

273

move two of their own mangonels across the hilltop. Struggling to plug the huge hole in Ardath's defenses that had become obvious when the besiegers in the west began firing as well: though there were war engines on the hills – six ballistae and four mangonels on the Bent, five trebuchets on the Barrow – they were all on the eastern side. There would have been time enough to move a few of them during the last few days, as the Strongs had repeatedly urged the king to do. But Wystan the Black had argued against it. Even if marching an army along the river had turned out to be feasible, he insisted, transporting heavy equipment across roadless country was most certainly not. Though he'd already been proven wrong once, that didn't prevent Aeron from taking his advice over the Strongs'. Meaning that now they had to risk their lives in a hailstorm of flying rocks to do what could have been safely accomplished a day or two earlier.

'Heave... ho!'
Cursing the Black, Bryn dug in his heels and pushed with the others. That Wystan had promised Aeron a powerful new weapon he claimed to be working on didn't reassure him one bit. In Bryn's view, anything that thrice-damned follower of Amut came up with could only spell more trouble. Provided he delivered at all, and wasn't just blowing hot air.

'Move that bloody tent, you lazy oafs, or we'll roll right over it!' Bois Terengil, a cousin of Aeron's, had been put in command of Ardath's artillery. He was stomping ahead, shouting and cursing, his bald boulder of a head bobbing in and out of sight as he moved along the tent rows, clearing a way through the camp. Though it had been set up in an orderly fashion, with lanes left clear between the neatly squared-off tents, none of them were wide enough for a behemoth the size of a mangonel to pass through. Another oversight, one among many.

'Heave... ho!'

Slipping and sliding, straining and swearing, they forced the big machine forward inch by inch, until once again it got hung up on the rocky terrain and Little Tom was called in to break up the obstacle with his big hammer.

'Bloody mess,' Bryn heard Flatside mutter under his breath as another large missile thudded into the western ramparts.

'Aye,' Catch, who'd joined them a moment ago, agreed. 'An' bugger all men in black who think they know better'n the rest of us.'

'Watch that mouth, Catch,' Flatside warned. 'Gonna get you in trouble.'

'What?' Catch said. 'Ain't but the truth.'

'Aye, but there's some who don't place much value on truth,' Longshanks observed, wiping sweat from his brow. 'Especially when it concerns their own selves. Man wears a lie for a face, he'll fight that much harder not to lose it.'

'Right,' Flatside said. 'An' them's the sort who take it amiss if a fellow comes along an' points out their shortcomin's.'

'Ain't pointin' out nothin' what ain't already in plain sight,' Catch grumbled. 'Just sayin', is all.'

'Well, now you're done sayin', you can save yer breath an' use it for helpin' us move this fucker.'

Another volley of scattershot came whistling and all of them ducked low – for what little it was worth. If you happened to be standing in the wrong place at the wrong time, you'd get hit no matter how small you tried to make yourself.

One stone bounced off the mangonel's crossbeam and then tore through the side of an unoccupied tent. The rest flew past and struck somewhere up ahead.

Getting up and wiping the dirt from his hands, Bryn saw Bois standing motionless in the middle of the lane maybe thirty yards away. Something looked off. It took him a moment to figure out what it was: half of the man's head was missing. Dumbfounded, Bryn watched the rest of Bois topple over.

'Right,' Flatside said. 'Whistler, Chuckles, go move his lordship out of the way. The longer we stand here, the likelier someone else is gonna get whacked.'

Longshanks moved up to take over where Bois had left off, a whip cracked over the rumps of the team of six hitched to the front of the machine, and the rest of them set to pushing again. Meanwhile Whistler and Chuckles dragged Bois' body off towards the south wall, where the dead, stacked in mounting numbers like sides of frozen beef, were least likely to get in the way if – when – Edric tried to storm the hill. No more pyres now, not with firewood having become such a precious commodity after they'd been cut off from resupply in the west.

When Bryn got back to the eastern rampart, he found Aeron and Wystan in a huddle with one of the catapult crews. Turned out the Black was instructing them in the use of something he called a slow match, a piece of cord with one end lit and smoldering. There were also three clay balls the size of large melons lined up on the ground near the bucket, wicks sticking out of nozzle-shaped protrusions on their tops. Wystan called them fusibles, and the balls bursters.

He picked one up and gently placed it in the mangonel's bucket. 'You want to handle these carefully,' he told the crew. 'Never light the fusible unless the burster is already lying in the bucket and you're all set to throw it. No time for fumbling around once the fusible is lit. One mistake is all you'll ever make with one of these. Is this thing aimed and ready? All right then, let's fire away.'

Bryn suddenly had a very bad feeling about where this was headed.

Must be Almorican fire in those bursters. Bowen told me about it once, said it was one of the worst things man had ever invented. Gooey, clinging stuff that burns everything it touches, flesh, wood, steel, whatever. It even burns underwater, Bowen said. Try washing it off, and you'll only spread it around. It hasn't been seen in Aldara since the Battle of Simbalan eight hundred years ago, and the past is where it should have stayed. How the hell did Wystan get his hands on it?

Wystan lit the burster's fusible and quickly stepped back, signaling the crew to release. With a mighty thump! the machine sent the burster hurtling towards the enemy lines, where it hit the ground and rolled to a stop scant yards from a Dunmarkan catapult. For a few moments, nothing happened.

'Damn,' one of the men said, 'missed by – '

Suddenly there was an earth-shaking WHUMP! and a huge ball of fire engulfed the Dunmarkan engine and crew. Splintered beams and body parts were flung high into the air. Raining back down, they were swallowed up in a quickly spreading cloud of billowing smoke. Watching it slowly drift away, Bryn saw with a shudder that all that was left of a crew of six and their catapult was a patch of blackened ground with irregular, sooty streaks running away from it like the spokes of a broken wheel. Not Almorican fire after all. Something else, but no better. Worse, actually.

Aeron looked ill.

Like maybe he was just beginning to realize that he was getting more than he'd bargained for. Wystan, on the other hand, appeared to be hard put not to dance a jig. Very pleased with himself.

'Fusible was a bit too long,' he told the king. 'Ideally, they should burst ten to fifteen feet off the ground. My calculations say they cause the most damage at that height. Shall we try another one, majesty?'

'Ah, yes, I suppose.' The king sounded shaken.

'Good. Let's see if we can hit the camp. The load should be light enough.'

While Wystan shortened the next ball's fusible by a quarter of an inch, the crew realigned their engine. It was a long shot, Bryn knew, at the limit of the big catapult's range. He found himself hoping for a hit, even though this weapon of Wystan's was the most dishonorable thing he'd ever witnessed and made him feel sicker even than Aeron looked.

But they'd killed Bowen and Arlie. Bois and two score others. They should be made to pay for that. They *would* pay. Most of all Edric, who had his own special set of crimes to answer for. Under no circumstances could that monster be allowed to remain on the

278

throne of Dunmark. If Wystan's abomination was what it took to unseat him, then so be it. War was an ugly beast, Bowen had said. What he'd neglected to tell Bryn was that he himself would become a part of that ugliness, that he'd wake up one morning and find the beast living right there inside him.

He didn't wait to see the results of the second shot. It would likely be the last one of the day in any case. The light was fading fast. Heading off for his quarters, he flinched when he heard the explosion but kept on walking.

Back at the tent, he found only Laurin.

The little man had been busy, he saw. There were tools spread out on his bedroll, a small hammer and chisel, a file, a pen knife, oil, wads of oakum. *Altingal* was lying across his knees.

'I hope you don't mind,' Laurin said, getting up and offering him the sword. It looked quite different from when Bryn had last seen it. Clean. Less of a ruin, more of a sword. 'It just seemed like something that needed doing.'

The rust and dirt were gone, the scrollwork on the scabbard gleaming brightly in the light of the lamp Laurin had been working by. He'd cleaned and oiled the cross-guard and pommel, still scarred and pitted by centuries of rust but looking a lot more... solid now. He'd also wrapped the hilt with strips of leather. Very neatly. Not that they'd do any good on a sword that was useless. Looked nice, though.

'Thank you,' Bryn said. 'Looks almost as good as new.'

'That isn't all,' Laurin said, obviously proud of what he'd accomplished. 'Try drawing it.'

279

Not really expecting anything, Bryn gripped the scabbard in one hand and the hilt in the other, and pulled.

The sword came out smoothly, with the melodic ring of excellent steel.

The blade looked as if it had been forged yesterday. Edges sharp enough to cleave downy feathers with. Perfectly balanced. Glowing with a soft, amber light.

'How did you...'

'I reckoned it might be just the cross-guard stuck to the rim of the scabbard,' the little man said. Gave it a few taps with the hammer and chisel. A lot of taps, actually. But it worked.' Being modest about it, but not quite managing to hide how pleased he was.

'I don't know what to say. You've worked a miracle. Maybe the most important thing anyone's done so far in this bloody war, except for you finding the sword in the first place and bringing it here. Thank you, again. If we get through this alive, I reckon there's a place in the songs waiting for you. Laurin Swordfinder, how does that sound?' Seeing Laurin blush, he hurried on. 'Well, then. I guess now it's my turn to do something worth mentioning with it.'

'I trust you will. It would be a shame if I'd gone to all the trouble for nothing, wouldn't it?' A shy smile, gone in a moment. 'Speaking of trouble. Have you seen Rhea, by any chance?'

'She was over on the western ramparts a while back. Staring down at the enemy camp as if she wanted to jump down there and kill the whole bunch of them single-handed. Rocks flying everywhere, and not once did I see her duck. Fearsome woman, that.'

'Oh dear,' Laurin said. 'I hope she hasn't gone and done something stupid.'

'No, she hasn't,' Rhea said, stepping into the tent. 'But I'm thinking about going down there tonight. I need to find out whether Pryce is there. They've hoisted Stonebridge's banner, and where he is, Pryce usually isn't far.'

Bryn and Laurin both started to tell her she was totally insane when suddenly they heard men shouting somewhere outside. Sounding agitated. Shocked. Moments later Little Tom burst into the tent.

'M'lord,' he panted, white as a sheet. 'Come quick. The king's been hit.'

*   *   *

17

Macsen never made it past Burnt Keep.

Reaching the crossroads a little after first light, he found his way blocked by an army in the throes of striking camp and assembling on the road. By the looks of it, they were planning to march west into Ardath. Not good.

His heart sank further when he recognized three men standing together by the side of the road, grooms holding their horses ready a few yards off: Torvald Tondern, Duke of Redfern; Gair Kildown, Duke of Blackwood; and Bhorric Varna, Duke of Whitelake. Also called the Colors.

The entire North, marching to Edric's aid. So they'd changed their minds after all. No hope for Aeron, and no hope for the boy. No hope for Macsen, either. This was it, then. The end of the road.

He rode on, stopped a few paces away. Dismounted and took a knee before Tondern. The Duke of Redfern was as big as Macsen remembered him, his black hair and beard in need of a comb, his gaze as direct and unrelenting as ever. And yet his blue eyes hadn't lost the humorous twinkle that made it seem as if he were always on the verge of laughing over a good joke, as if he might find something amusing even in a situation as grim as this.

'Redbreast,' Torvald said. 'What is this? Since when does the Kingsguard bend the knee to anyone but the king?'

'I'm no longer Kingsguard, your grace. Not to beat around the bush, I've deserted. It was either that or go over to the enemy. Or wait until his majesty picked a suitable tree to hang me from. But now it seems that I've nowhere left to run to. Any road, running doesn't seem to agree with me. So I reckon it's best if I surrender to your grace's judgment and mercy.'

For long moments, Torvald stood looking at Macsen, his expression unreadable.

'Well, now,' he finally said, hitching up his sword belt. 'I can hardly pass judgment without knowing the whole story, can I? Happens we're still waiting for this sorry lot call themselves soldiers to finish rubbing the sleep out of their eyes. Time enough to hear why a man whom I've always counted a pillar of the realm saw no choice but to leave his post.'

'Thank you, your grace. That's generous of you.'

Bloody pickle, this, Macsen thought. *What do I tell him? Nothing about the Bailon boy, that's for sure. No use making something up, either. It'll all come out the moment he hands me over to Edric. Half the truth, then.*

'Well?' Torvald said. 'I'm listening.'

Come on, Macsen, gather your wits.

'It's to do with my granddaughter, your grace.

'She and a friend brought me a sword to look at, rusty old thing her friend found in the Caerrocks. His majesty saw it and wanted it for

284

himself, though I can't think why. Took it, actually. And then the stupid girl went and stole it from him, and I helped her escape. It was wrong, but what could I do? She's blood of my blood, all the family I have left. Doesn't change the fact that I broke my oath, though. Treason's what it was, like it or not.'

'What oath would that be?' Bhorric Varna asked. A man like a chunk of grey iron. Had a reputation to go with it. Probably won more jousts than he could count.

'The oath to protect his majesty from harm, your grace. Including thieves.'

'Aye,' Varna said. 'But you could make a point of asking who stole first. And whether taking back what's been stolen can be called thievery at all.'

Strange, that. Varna's not a man known for bothering overmuch with the finer points of law, or of anything else. Could he be looking for a way to spare me? But why the devil should he care?

'Still doesn't excuse me for helping her get away. All the more because she's with Aeron now.'

'Aeron, eh?' young Gair Kildown said, thrusting out his chin and squaring his broad shoulders as if he couldn't wait to see the enemy from up close. 'Still sitting up on those hills, is he? Tough piece of work for Edric, if he aims to pry him out of there.'

'Be that as it may,' Torvald said. 'I've a feeling there are still things the good sergeant hasn't told us yet. And right he is, seeing where we're headed. Only one possible reason for us to be riding west, am I right, sergeant?'

'I reckon so, your grace. And begging your pardon for saying so, but I can't say it makes me any happier. There's going to be enough

285

bloodshed as it is without the North taking a hand in it as well.'

Macsen watched the three of them exchange looks, Kildown and Varna each giving a nod.

Torvald heaved a sigh. 'I agree with you wholeheartedly, Macsen. Even after I found out it was Edric who burned my villages and killed my people, I was still prepared to sit this war out. No use throwing lives after lives with nothing to gain. But now something's come up that's changed everything. I'm prepared to tell you about it, but it means you'll have to make a choice. And I'm warning you: it won't be an easy one. So if you like, you can leave now. I don't care what truck Edric has with you, and I'm not making it my business. I won't stop you from going wherever you want, as long as it's not back west. So what will it be?'

'I'd hear what you have to say, your grace.'

'Very well, then. Here's a bit of real treason for you: we of the North have long been agreed that Edric has become a liability to Dunmark. Not to mince words, the man is a monster. But I doubt you need me to tell you that. We would have moved against him, if not for the fact that doing so would have been more of a disaster for the kingdom than leaving him where he is. With Edric gone, in no time at all we'd have had a dozen or more factions fighting over the succession, a dozen petty wars that could have dragged on for gods know how long. Stonebridge alone would have seen to that.

'But we've recently received information that changes all that. Seorus Avellin sired another child. A boy.'

'A bastard.'

'No. Seorus wed the boy's mother three months before his

286

death. I happen to know this for a certainty because I was there. Signed the document myself. Gavrielle Rowan was Seorus' lawful wife and queen of Dunmark when she birthed the boy.'

Macsen's heart gave a sudden leap when he saw where this might be headed. *Might* be. Too early to say for sure. 'I'm afraid I still don't understand, your grace.'

'Oh, I think you understand all right, Macsen Redbreast. We've found us the next king of Dunmark. Edric's days are numbered. Now, we can finally replace him. Presenting a true-blooded Avellin will shut up even the likes of Stonebridge.'

'So you're not going west to help Edric against Aeron,' Macsen said, filled with wonder at this unexpected turn of events but not yet sure whether it was cause for rejoicing. 'You're moving against him, and you're looking to find the boy.'

'Exactly,' Torvald said. 'And now comes your choice. After what I've just told you, you'll understand that I can't allow you to simply be on your merry way. So this is what it comes down to: either I have you put in irons and send you back to Darg Fearna, there to await the outcome of the war and the judgment of whoever wins it. Or you swear fealty to me.'

That was an easy one for Macsen to decide.

'It'll have to be the irons then,' he said. 'I'm sorry, your grace, and no offense, but I can't. I may have broken my oath to the king when I deserted him, but I'm not going to compound the misdeed by swearing another to you.'

To Macsen's astonishment, Torvald clapped him on the shoulder. 'Good man. That's exactly what I wanted to hear. Don't look so

287

surprised. Did you honestly believe I'd welcome an oath-breaker into my ranks? No, I hold with Bhorric's view: Edric was the thief. And it was Edric who broke the compact between lord and liege-man, not you. Because an oath that doesn't go both ways isn't worth the breath used to speak it. So come, First Sergeant, I'll have your hand on a propitious encounter.' He grinned. 'Provided you tell us the rest of your story. A gold for a gilder, as we say in the North.'

'Ha,' Bhorric snorted. 'His grace is pussyfooting. "You've got to sweet-talk her before you get to fondle her teats," is what we really say in the North.'

It wasn't until much later that Macsen realized he'd never thought to ask how Torvald had found out about the boy.

*   *   *

'Yes? What is it now?' Edric looked up from the map he'd been studying.

'Worrisome news, I'm afraid, your...' Gale paused as another one of those infernal missiles exploded not far away, shaking the ground. After a devastating hit last night that had cost nearly three score lives, they'd moved the camp back fifty yards where it was out of the Ardathian catapults' range. Their own engines remained sitting ducks, though, with the enemy's aim getting ever more accurate. So far, Edric had refused to pull them back, with the result that a second crew had already been blown to bloody bits, and the day hardly started. But with a bit of luck poor visibility would take care of the problem, for a while at least. It was starting to snow again, fat, lazy flakes that looked to be working up to a heavy fall.

'Worrisome news, your majesty. I've been keeping a watch on

288

our supply lines as you ordered, and I've just had a scout in from Burnt Keep. It appears that the Colors are on the march, headed our way. Nearly two thousand strong, by a rough count.'

'Has Tondern changed his mind? Are they coming to help us with Aeron?' Edric asked, looking suspicious. As well he might.

'That's the big question, isn't it? Though I have to say I rather doubt that they're coming here to hold our hands. From what I know of Tondern, he's not a man who forgives easily. At the very least he'll ask a stiff price for his help. Very stiff. Bit of a predicament, however one looks at it. Which is why I'm here. What would you have me do?'

'Stonebridge, obviously.' Edric seemed surprisingly unperturbed. Invigorated, actually, as if he relished the thought of bloodshed on an even grander scale. 'I need him this side of those bloody hills as fast as he can get here.'

'I see a problem with that, majesty.'

And not just with that. Problems everywhere I look. Which is fine with me. Though I'm beginning to wonder whether I haven't perhaps left my farewells a bit late.

'If Stonebridge goes the roundabout way, it'll take him at least a day to get through the hills either side of the Bent and the Barrow. Nothing but trees, rocks, and slopes too steep to stand on.'

'What about Long Valley?'

'No good. He'd have to go nearly all the way back to the Etherelle, then double back. It would take him two days, maybe three. Which leaves the road. I have reports that both the hillsides facing it are riddled with nasty surprises. They've got trunks and boulders piled up, ready to roll down and crush whoever sets foot between

289

the two hills. They've got arbalests trained on the road. Archery positions dug out every fifty yards. Roadblocks. Pitfalls, no doubt. Gods know what else. And in there, they hardly need catapults. They can practically drop their bloody exploding devices right on our heads. That defile is a death trap, your majesty. You'd be lucky if a tenth of Stonebridge's men made it through.'

'Then we'll clear the way for him.' Edric was standing now, eager, tensed for action. 'Spring as many of those traps as we can. Round up the camp followers. For once, I can see a good use for the poxy rabble.'

The idea was a bit rich even for Gale's hardened stomach.

Not that he harbored any sympathies for the residents of Sleaze-town. But sending a bunch of noncombatants to their certain deaths when the achievable gains were doubtful at best seemed like a very good way to ruin one's reputation. But then Edric didn't have much left to lose on that account, and neither did he. Still, the whole thing didn't sit well with him. Not well at all.

'But will the enemy fall for it?' he said. 'They're not blind, you know. And I doubt they'll feel very much threatened by a bunch of terrified cardsharps and half-naked whores scampering down the road.'

'So dress them up. See what Sykes has in store, give them a few helms and spears, and I'll wager Aeron will see what he's expecting to see: a company of Dunmarkan soldiers trying to break through. And while he's busy cutting them down, our main force will be storming the Bent. How long to get a message to Stonebridge?'

'Using the signals chain, not long, your majesty. Though we'll probably expose our man up on the Bent. He's stationed about half a mile south of the fort, with a direct line of sight on us as well as on Stonebridge. He'll have to get out of there fast once he's noticed, meaning we'll lose that particular edge. But if it's the Bent you want, then I'd say it's worth it. We should do it soon, though. If the weather gets any worse, poor visibility might break the chain.'

'Very good. Let Stonebridge know he should be ready to join us. Then go and assemble our road-clearing crew. I'll handle preparations for the main thrust myself. This day is going to be ours, Gale, I can feel it. Once we have the Bent, it won't matter any longer what the Colors are up to. They can sit here and rot, for all I care, but they won't be going anywhere except back where they came from.'

Sleazetown's inhabitants didn't go willingly.

Gale hadn't expected them to. But soldiers driving them out of their hovels at sword-point were an argument even the most vicious bruisers among them couldn't resist. With the help of the props supplied by Jakken Sykes and putting the more believable characters out in front, Gale assembled them into something that might just fool the men up on the hills. Surveying the ragged ranks, he couldn't help but notice some of their faces. What he saw there wasn't pretty, nor was it apt to make his sleep any more peaceful: eyes filled with rage, sullenness, bare hatred, or hopeless surrender; mouths twisted and features crumpled in desperate weeping; rotten teeth bared in snarling curses, hands raised in useless entreaty.

Worst of all were the ones who looked back at him with a level, knowing contempt – because they mirrored so faithfully what he felt for himself.

291

He'd thought beforehand of giving a little speech and telling them that Stonebridge's army had requested their services. That the soldiers were there to escort them to their new place of work. But for once, his usually well-oiled sarcasm deserted him. Watching them move off with a company of spears prodding their backs, he found himself hoping that the enemy would see through the ruse, and that Edric's disgusting plan would fail.

It didn't look that way, though.

Edric was displaying a worrisome amount of clarity and shrewdness in a situation that was anything but clear. Something of a predicament, in fact. If he stayed where he was, he risked getting caught between Aeron on the hills and the possibly hostile Colors. If he moved out and joined Stonebridge on the other side of the hills, there'd be nothing left to keep Ardath and the North from uniting their forces against him. Taking the Bent would put him in a strong position, though bringing Stonebridge's force over would open a way of escape for Aeron, who might well head for Cullamor and make trouble for Ensel and Pryce. But leaving Stonebridge where he was when it wasn't at all certain that an attack on the Bent would succeed wasn't an option either. In the end, it all came down to choosing the lesser evil. Exactly what Edric had done, quickly and decisively, before Gale had even begun to think through the problem properly.

All in all, it wasn't encouraging.

*   *   *

By mid-morning the snow was falling thick and fast, with Bentridge all but hidden from sight. And it was cold. So cold you risked losing skin if you touched steel barehanded. Bryn hadn't stopped shivering in days, felt like he'd never be warm again. Standing on the western rampart with Eilian Strong, Longshanks, and Flatside, he stared into the swirling flakes, trying to make out what was going on down there.

Half an hour earlier, lookouts had spotted a lone enemy signalman farther south on the Bent, waving a pair of pennons. Flatside had sent a squad to roust the fellow. But, as was to be expected, the man was long gone by the time they got there. Whatever message he'd passed along seemed to have gotten through, though, prompting an unusual amount of activity in the Dunmarkan camp down by the village.

'They're packing up,' Eilian said. 'Looks like they're getting ready to move out.' Peering over the stakes, he looked more hawkish than ever, as if the cane he was leaning on were merely a modish accessory while it was the well-used sword at his side that said what he was really about. Probably did, Bryn thought.

'Don't seem likely, though,' Flatside objected. 'First they go t' all that trouble an' box us in, an' then they just trundle off? Not hardly. Y'ask me, yer grace, they're fixin' to pay us a visit up here.'

'Aye,' Longshanks agreed, scratching his beard. 'Seems like the only thing that would make sense. But why take down their whole camp? If they're aiming to storm the Bent, they must feel very sure about the outcome.'

'I don't know,' Bryn said. 'I have a feeling we're missing part of the picture. And not just because of the snow.'

'You could well be right, young Bryn,' Eilian said. 'We're

293

dealing with Edric Avellin, after all. A more underhanded bastard has yet to be born.' The old duke gripped the hilt of his sword as if to reassure himself it was ready to hand. 'Best get back to your station, lad. I've a feeling things are warming up, if not the weather. And I'd thank you to pass by Iefan's and let him know what's going on this side.'

With the king down, Bryn had been seconded to Darin Cullan, another cousin of Aeron's, who commanded the wall overlooking the defile. Iefan had the east with Elwyn Griswold as second, and Eilian the west with Longshanks. Olin Trant was left with the south, where the attack would likely be lightest. He wasn't happy about it. Owain Cullan, Darin's brother, was in charge of the Barrow – though the hill and what had happened there seemed very far away just now. Seen through the driving snow, the Barrow's tower appeared to be slowly drifting by, a strange ship come unmoored, lost and floundering in a sea of grey and white.

They all still got their orders from the king. Which didn't inspire much confidence in any of them, seeing as Aeron was drugged to the gills. And worse, he'd chosen Wystan to convey his messages. Or maybe the Black had appointed himself – it was hard to tell.

Last night, Bryn had found the Strongs outside the king's tent. Longshanks, Darin Cullan, Elwyn Griswold and Olin Trant were just arrived as well, the lot of them making for as grim-faced a gathering as Bryn had ever seen.

'He's in a bad way,' Longshanks told them, keeping his voice low. 'Piece of scattershot hit him in the foot. Physician says the ankle's too smashed up to fix. If it goes to rot – which most likely it will, seeing as it's an open wound – the foot will have to come off. Wystan, on the other hand, seems to think he can save it.'

A low moan came from inside the tent, freighted with a wealth of agony that made Bryn shiver. 'Can he? Save it?'

Old Eilian snorted, jabbing his cane at the frozen ground. 'Not unless he's got magic. But he's given Aeron enough milk of the poppy to put a draft horse out of its misery. State the king's in, he'll believe anything. More so if it's something he very much wants to be true in any case. One can only hope that – '

The flaps parted, and a servant looked out. 'Your grace, my lords, captain. His majesty asks if you'll all step in for a moment.'

Aeron was sitting in a field chair, his wounded leg propped up on a stool. He looked terrible: pale, sweating, his face drawn in agony notwithstanding the drugs he'd been given. But he'd had his maps and charts pinned to the walls of the tent, and a couple of scribes were busy keeping them up to date.

'My lords,' he greeted them, his voice hoarse with pain. 'As you can see, I've had a bit of a mishap. Damned stone obviously hadn't been told it wasn't supposed to hit any kings. In any case, it looks as if I won't be moving around much in the near future. Meaning, I'll be relying on you even more than I already have been. Wystan tells me tomorrow might well be the day Edric decides to make his move. True or not, we must be prepared. Iefan, I'd have you take the east with Griswold. If they do come, it will likely be from both sides.'

'Let them try, your majesty,' Iefan said. 'Bloody noses is all they'll get for their trouble.'

Aeron nodded. 'Eilian, the west, with Longshanks. Trant, the south. And young Bryn has shown a good eye and a level head, so he'll help Darin keep an eye on the road, make sure Edric doesn't try to break through. Wystan here will see to coordinating our efforts and keeping everyone up to speed. That will be all for now. Good luck to all of us.'

'Aye,' Eilian murmured as they filed out of the tent. 'Luck is something we'll be needing a lot of these coming days. Especially seeing who all has their fingers in the pie.'

'He's holding up well, though,' Griswold observed. He reminded Bryn of a walking boulder, with a face and character to match. 'First time I've heard the man try for a jest.'

'That was the poppy juice talking,' Trant said. Another itinerant rock, this one, only craggier still and with a voice that could shake the bricks out of a wall or set off an avalanche. 'And as to holding up: for how long still, is the question.'

There was even less to see on the eastern side.

The Dunmarkan camp was no more than a slightly darker smudge in a haze of white. The only things still recognizable were Edric's remaining catapults, and even those were becoming harder to make out with the snow piling up on every level surface.

'Aye,' Iefan said when Bryn told him about the activity down in Bentridge. 'It was the same here, as long as there was still anything to see. They're up to something, no doubt about it. Question is, will they let this bloody weather stop them? Or will they reckon they can use it to their advantage? Hard to see what for, though. Climbing the damned hill is hard enough without having to fight your way blind through a foot and a half of snow. I'd say...'

He broke off, peering into the whiteout as if he could penetrate it by sheer willpower alone. 'Here they come. Aiming for the defile, it looks like. Bloody Edric, using his men as bait to spring our traps.'

Bryn had seen it too: a column of men making straight for the gap between the two hills. Not in much of a hurry, though. They seemed hesitant, as if their hearts weren't really in it. Small wonder, seeing where they were going.

Then more men appeared out of the driving snow. Not a column, this time, but a broad front aimed at the Bent itself like a dark stain seeping out of the white and quickly spreading towards the foot of the hill. For long moments, Bryn stood transfixed. The scene seemed entirely unreal – not at all like the hordes of fired-up men he'd imagined, roaring and beating their shields as they charged into battle. Instead there was an eerie silence, the snow swallowing up any sound of the enemy's advance.

'Steady, now,' Iefan told his men. 'No use wasting arrows on long shots in this crud. Archers, let them come up to thirty yards. Crossbows, fifteen paces.'

His voice brought Bryn out of his fugue. He had a job to do. Turning on his heel, he set out for his post at a run.

The northern rampart was fully manned and prepared for battle. Darin was doing what everyone seemed to be doing of late: staring into the swirling snow. Rhea was there. Catch, and the three remaining men from Bailon. Unfortunately, so was Wystan. He'd brought more of his infernal bursters. Smaller ones this time, no larger than Bryn's fist. And a toy-sized catapult. Which was probably all he'd need to cause bloody mayhem down on the road.

Seeing him there infuriated Bryn. He despised the man. Hated the disgusting new weapons. And this was Darin Cullan's command, not Wystan's. He would have liked nothing better than to tell the odious fellow to get lost but doubted that even Cullan had the authority to do so, though he seemed less than happy with the Black's presence. In his banged-up armor and threadbare cloak, the spare, squint-eyed lord from southern Ardath didn't look all that impressive. But, from what Bryn had heard, Cullan was regarded as one of the meanest blades in the kingdom.

'Bailon. What news?' Not one to waste words, was Darin Cullan.

'It's started,' Bryn reported, still out of breath from running. 'In the east, the main body is coming up the hill. A column of maybe two, three hundred is headed our way. We should see them any moment now. And on Eilian's side they're striking camp, though it's not quite clear yet what they're aiming to do.'

Cullan nodded. 'Catch. Everyone's to hold fire until the whole column is well inside the gap. See that word is passed on to the men down on the slope. Master Wystan, I'll thank you to hold as well.'

Wystan nodded, though the look he gave Cullan was anything but friendly.

'And they should keep an ear out for the order to cease fire,' Cullan added. 'No use dumping everything we've got on a diversion, if that's what this turns out to be.'

'If I may, my lord,' Bryn said. 'It might also be that the main attack is the diversion, and their real aim is to clear the road.'

'There's that.' Cullan gave him an appreciative nod. 'All the more reason to keep something in reserve.'

298

Driven by a feeling of restlessness – and not least to get away from the Black – Bryn walked east along the line. Across the defile, the Barrow was all but invisible, only the tower's dark shadow emerging every so often between one flurry and the next. Down in the valley, the column had rounded the first bend and was steadily advancing, though for all Bryn could see, it might as well have been an oversized grey worm crawling up the road. Its rear end was just passing into the defile. Soon. Any moment now.

He was about to head back to center position when one of Wystan's bursters suddenly exploded behind the last Dunmarkans, mowing down at least a dozen of their rearguard. Panicked, the rest of them broke into a run, any semblance of order gone in a heartbeat. At least they were going forward, and not back the way they'd come.

As if Wystan's missile had been the signal for everyone to start shooting, a volley of arrows descended on the men in the valley, the column already beginning to pull apart and scatter. Bryn heard the muted double thwock! of hatchets hacking through the ropes holding back one of the log piles, and then distant screams as the huge trunks rumbled and banged down the slope and onto the road, crushing everything in their path.

Curse the black bastard! he thought, breaking into a run himself. *He's not even bothering with countermanding Cullan's orders. He's just godsdamned bloody ignoring them and doing exactly as he likes.*

By the time he rejoined Cullan, the battle was in full spate.

If you could call it a battle. A turkey shoot, was more like it.

Slaughter, plain and simple. More logs and boulders went rolling and bouncing away, mad, completely unpredictable missiles that changed course with every leap and bound as they careened down the steep hillside.

Over on the Barrow, they were lighting up man-high, spherical wicker cages packed with oil-soaked straw and sending them down the slope, huge balls of fire that burst open when they hit the road. Soon dozens of Dunmarkan soldiers were burning, ghosting through the whiteout like stray will-o'-the-wisps. On both sides of the defile, arbalests were whanging away and archers were picking off the surviving enemies one by one.

'Master Wystan.' Cullan looked furious. 'I recall asking you to hold fire like everyone else. Would you care to – '

'Sorry, my lord,' Wystan interrupted, not looking sorry at all. 'A slip of the hand. Nerves, no doubt. Entirely unintended.' As if to underline the blatant lie, he let his hand brush the small catapult's trigger, obviously set to a hair, and fired off another shot.

Bryn saw it land in the middle of a group of stragglers. Saw it clearly, suddenly realizing there was a break in the snowfall and he could see the butchery they were committing down there in fine detail. It wasn't all he saw.

'My lord,' he said, shocked, appalled, angry. 'Those aren't soldiers down there. They're ordinary people.'

Cullan squinted down at the carnage below.
Cursed. Yelled, 'Hold your fire! Hold, godsdammit! Catch! On the double!'

A dozen more died as word was passed on and the attack came

300

to a stuttering halt. Over on the Barrow, Cullan's brother Owain had obviously reached the same conclusion, his men standing down as well.

But for most of the poor souls down there it was already too late.

A group of maybe two score ragged, terrified survivors hurried on towards the defile's far end, dragging along a few wounded. The rest, five or six times that number, were strewn across the valley floor, leavings of a sad and gruesome mowing, innocents sent running straight into the reaper's scythe by Edric. Sent into Bryn's scythe, among others.

Suddenly his anger at the man flared into full-blown hatred, so intense it nearly took his breath away. Because of bloody Edric, he'd just helped kill a few hundred ordinary people, commoners who had little or nothing to do with this war, except that they'd been in the wrong place at the wrong time. Not enough that Edric had to be his half brother. Now he'd made Bryn an accomplice to murder, two-fold bound in blood.

And here, finally, was the bare, hard truth: like as not, it would take more blood to break those ties. A lot more, perhaps. But, whatever the price, Edric Avellin needed killing.

A fleeting image of himself holding company with Em and her piglets crossed his mind. He quickly pushed it away. That wasn't him, not anymore, if it ever had been.

Bowstrings twanged on the eastern rampart as the defenders loosed their first volley. Moments later the first Dunmarkans were swarming over the stakes.

'Bailon, go give Iefan a hand,' Cullan ordered. 'Take the whole

301

right wing. Catch, have the left wing move up and fill their positions.'

'You heard his lordship.' Bryn told the first man on the right, his heart suddenly beating double time. 'All of you, with me.' Making to draw his sword – his own, not *Altingal* – he found it was already in his hand. Nor did he remember picking up his shield.

This is it, he thought, setting off at a run. *My first battle. May the good gods give that it won't be my last.*

Fleetingly, he tried to think of a battle cry, something to rally the men behind him, but nothing came to mind. Perhaps because it was a day too cold and grim for words.

Then the battle was joined, the air suddenly bright with steel and blood, the ancient hilltop fortress resounding once again with the clash of weapons and the shouts and screams of men going about the age-old business of killing and dying.

*   *   *

18

Apart from the king and his scribes, servants and guards, Laurin was probably the only person on the Bent not manning one of the defensive works. He wasn't welshing, though. At the first sign of push coming to shove he intended to be up and fighting like everybody else, for all the good a dwarf would do in a big people's battle. In the meantime, he'd decided to do some exploring.

It was sitting on a hill surrounded by enemies that had first given him the idea. That, and what the trip west from Burnt Keep had shown him of the nature of these hills, setting all his Waylen senses twitching.

There was a large rock outcropping in the center of camp called the Hump, a weathered, riven chunk of light grey limestone that resembled a crouching beast, a truncated tower, or a lopsided toad-stool, depending on which side you were looking from. More interesting than the formation's shape was a deep cleft in the rock's south face, not least because at some time in the past someone had seen fit to close it off with a dry-stone wall. It was the kind of thing people put up to keep children or livestock from falling into deep holes. It was also exactly the sort of wall Waylen miners would build to seal an abandoned heading.

Seen from up close, the wall looked like it had been there for a long time. Just how long, Laurin found out when he discovered a row of Waylen signs chiseled into the side of the cleft, down low in a place where no casual observer would think to look.

Eighty years since the mine had been closed down, the signs told him. They'd found cobalt here, the mineral used in making precious blue glass. Some gold as well, but that had probably been incidental. The deposits had been cleaned out, exhausted. Nothing left that would have made it worth the miners' while to hide the entrance. For someone who knew how to read the signs, it was an interesting piece of Waylen history. But it was the last pair of glyphs that really grabbed his attention, causing him a thrill of excitement.

He was about to remove a few stones so he could get a peek and a sniff of the mine itself, when of a sudden he heard shouting and bow-strings twanging on the eastern rampart, the side facing Edric's camp. Hurriedly abandoning his investigation, he rounded the outcropping just in time to see the first Dunmarkans climbing over the stakes. Moments later they were swarming over the rampart like a colony of ants. And there was Bryn, running straight into the thick of it, followed by Rhea and half the north wall's complement.

The thick of it was the very last place Laurin wanted to be. Any halfway sane dwarf knew to stay out of a fight between big people.

He cursed. Set his borrowed helm straight. Hitched up his belt. Took a deep breath. Then, gripping his axe in trembling, sweaty fingers, he set out after his friends.

Supposing he didn't get himself killed right away, this might be his chance to repay at least part of the debt he owed Rhea. Cover her back, maybe. Somehow.

To his surprise, he was largely ignored.

Apart from a few more or less accidental swings that he managed to fend off with his buckler, nobody bothered with him. Friend and foe alike were obviously far too busy hacking away at people their own size to take notice of anything closer to the ground. Like dwarves, for instance.

He wasn't about to complain. Instead, he wended his way into the surging mass of iron-shod boots, jabbing spears and flailing swords. Sizing up the situation, he reckoned his best bet would be to deal with enemy legs – preferably from behind, seeing as most of the Dunmarkans wore greaves.

Unfortunately, none of them seemed prepared to hold still for Laurin's axe. And then, when he did find one who was locked in a stalemate and not going anywhere, his stupid arms went and deserted him. Simply refused to swing the axe at living flesh. Wouldn't do it.

Bloody wimp, he told himself. *Get a grip. This might well be the man who goes on to kill one of your friends. Rhea, for example. Is that what you want? For her to die because you chickened out?*

It helped. So did thinking of the men who'd taken him away from his home and family all those years ago. Men just like these: hard, uncaring, never more than a breath away from violence. Forever ready to rape, maim, and kill. Or steal little boys. If only the pay was right and the arsehole in charge wanted it so.

That did it. He swung. Winced when he felt the axe bite.

Watched the man go down. Didn't stick around to finish the job, though. Someone else could do that. Bad enough that he had to go around hurting people. He still wasn't ready to kill anybody unless he absolutely had to.

Finally he caught sight of Rhea. Unlike him, she seemed to be in her element, whirling this way and that like a maddened demoness, long daggers flashing as she ducked and flowed around enemy blades. A flick and a jab, and a Dunmarkan who had his sword raised high and was about to split her down the middle fell to his knees. She laid him out flat with a kick to the throat. While Laurin was making his way over to her, she downed another one. And already she was facing her next opponent.

Only this one was different.

The size of him made Laurin want to yell at her to hurry up and get out of there. A noble, by his fancy armor, and one who looked like he could break a man in two with his bare hands. Straining against a barrier of weapons and legs, Laurin thought he saw a flicker of uncertainty cross Rhea's face. Might have been his imagination, though. Because she didn't give an inch, just spun out of the way when the Dunmarkan's huge two-hander came whistling at her midriff. In the blink of an eye, she'd tucked one of her daggers under her belt and was holding one of those over-priced knives in her hand. Throwing it, she slipped on a patch of hard-packed, blood-drenched snow. And missed. Then the last man she'd taken down suddenly stirred back to life, reached out a bloody hand, and grab-bed her by the ankle.

Desperately, Laurin fought to get past a last knot of combatants barring his way. Up went the big Dunmarkan's sword.

Laurin's view was momentarily blocked by a flailing shield, its lower rim smacking into the side of his face and nearly knocking his teeth out. Head ringing, eyes watering, it took him a moment to get his bearings.

The Dunmarkan was done winding up. And there was Rhea, hacking at the wounded man's arm. The stupid bugger wouldn't let go, seemed to have her in a death grip. Laurin had a terrifying vision of the two-hander coming down and slicing her in half, an image that was an eye-blink away from becoming reality.

Finally he got through. Too late, he saw: the big man's shoulders were already bunching for the downstroke. Swinging his little axe anyway, Laurin was surprised to feel it bite deep into flesh and bone – and to see Rhea still standing. Then somebody bumped into his back, nearly sending him sprawling. The place was getting crowded.

Unfortunately, the giant didn't go down.

With an ugly growl, he pivoted on his good leg. Planted his feet wide, the injured knee buckling slightly but holding up, the huge sword already beginning its downward arc.

With no room to retreat, Laurin could think of only one thing to do. He took a running start, straight into the two-hander's path. In the same motion, he dove between the big man's legs.

Made it through. Rolled. Came up.

Swung his axe at the giant's good knee so hard it stuck fast in the bone.

This time, the big bastard did go down. Not all the way, though. Letting go of the axe, Laurin stepped back, still wary of the Dunmarkan's sword. And not a moment too soon. Not even taking the time to look behind him, the kneeling man swung the blade one-handed, a great, sweeping arc that would have surely cut Laurin in two if he hadn't already moved.

Then Rhea was there, finally free of the dying man's grip. While the giant was shuffling around on ruined knees and winding up for another strike, she stepped in, light-footed as a Tanuri temple dancer. Using the pommel of her long-dagger, she struck him a hard blow on the back of the neck. She must have broken it, for he flopped down like a sack of lard, dead as a man could get.

For a couple of heartbeats, they stood looking at each other.
She was out of breath, her hair a mess, her face streaked with sweat and blood. There was a light in her eyes he hadn't seen there before, a grim sort of satisfaction that made him feel unaccountably sad, as if he'd just lost a dear friend. If he'd expected her to thank him for saving her life, he was disappointed.

'You trying to get yourself killed, Stumpy?' she said. Making light, but looking worried. Possibly for him. Which made it hard to be angry with her for calling him 'Stumpy'.

So he gave her the best grin he could manage with his battered face. 'Nah. Just trying out my new axe, Missy.'

That was it for pleasantries. Suddenly fighting men were crowding into the small space that had momentarily opened up around the dead giant.

Somebody bumped into Laurin, sent him reeling into someone else, and then he was down, rolling this way and that and doing his best to avoid getting trampled. By the time he made it back onto his feet, Rhea was nowhere in sight, caught up and swept away in the mass of struggling bodies. So he went back to doing what he did best, namely damaging enemy knees.

He never saw the killing blow coming. One moment he was sizing up a Dunmarkan leg, the next he was hurtling into darkness as if he'd been shot from a sling, thinking, *Thank the gods that's over and done with*. And then it *was* over.

*   *   *

It had stopped snowing, but the sky wasn't getting any lighter.

It must be past mid-afternoon, Bryn realized. Had they really been fighting all this time? It seemed like the battle had begun only a short while ago. He remembered very little of it, as if someone else had done the fighting for him, repeating the same few bloody moves over and over again until it seemed pointless to watch that person any longer. His numbed mind and weary body told a different story, as did his battered shield and bloodied sword.

He was standing with Iefan Strong, both of them still breathing hard after the fight. Still standing. They'd done it. They'd fended off the attack. Survived. Many hadn't, though. The eastern rampart and the ground below were strewn with bodies, the air ripe with the stench of torn flesh and voided bowels, the eerie silence that had descended on the hill in the aftermath of battle broken only by the occasional screams, groans, or mumbles of the wounded and the dying. It seemed that, for the time being at least, those still standing had lost the capacity for words.

Already a murder of crows had settled on the big rock in the middle of camp, black heads bobbing this way and that as they eyed the feast laid out for them, diners eager to proceed to table but wary of the fact that parts of the meal were still moving. They too were silent. Bryn watched the first one flap down from its perch, hopping closer to the bloody banquet in cautious fits and starts.

'Godsdamned vermin,' a man close by said, nocking an arrow.

'No,' Iefan told him. 'Leave them be. It's us who made this mess, not them. They've only come to clean up after us.'

Movement caught Bryn's eye.

The exhausted men thronging the foot of the rampart were parting to let Eilian Strong and Flatside through. Right behind them came Longshanks, Cullan, and Griswold. All of them looked less happy than they should have. The old duke gave his son's shoulder a short squeeze, a gesture freighted with a father's relief over finding his child still alive and unharmed.

How I wish Bowen were here, Bryn thought, struck by a fresh pang of grief. *If only I'd listened to him, maybe things would have gone differently.*

'We sent the bastards packing,' Iefan said. 'For now.'

'Aye,' Eilian said. 'But at a price. We've yet to count our dead. And Stonebridge got through. He's with Edric now.'

'And with nary a scratch,' Cullan grated. 'Buggers were well prepared. Double shield rows flanking the baggage train either side, archers on the wagons, drivers shielded. Even had armor for their ruddy horses. And us just having thrown most everything we had at a bunch of whores.'

'Whores?' Iefan raised an eyebrow.

'Aye, whores.' Cullan looked thoroughly disgusted. 'Camp

followers. Stands to reason that's who he used. You could probably search for a year and not round up three peasants in these ruddy hills.'

'But why would Stonebridge want to join Edric?' Iefan wondered. 'Here they had us in a perfect pincer, and now they've gone and left us a way out? It doesn't make sense.'

'According to Bowen, there's still at least a third of Edric's army unaccounted for,' the old duke pointed out. 'Could be he's just setting up another snare for us. He offers us a clear run to Cullamor, waits until he has us out in the open, and then bang! He springs the trap.'

'Something else comes to mind,' Cullan said. 'Right before Stonebridge left, he received company. A coach and some forty horse. Came out of the west. Went with him. But whoever it was couldn't have been the reason for the move. Stonebridge was already set to go hours before they arrived.'

Another puzzle, Bryn thought. Nothing about this war was going as expected. But then, that was how Bowen had said it would be. *War is an ugly beast. Fool who thinks he can tame it.*

He noticed Wystan making his way towards them.

Interestingly, the men didn't make room for him like they'd done for Eilian and Cullan. Made him push his way through. He had half a dozen of Aeron's guards in tow.

'His majesty wants the enemy wounded taken care of,' the Black said once he'd reached them.

'They will be,' Eilian said. 'Once the healers have looked after our own men. Then we'll see to the Dunmarkans, load them on a

311

couple of wagons, send them back to Edric.'

'That's not what his majesty meant,' Wystan said. 'He wants them put down.'

Bryn stared at the man, aghast. He wasn't the only one – though he noticed that Griswold and Trant didn't seem all that disturbed by the prospect.

Iefan made to speak, looking outraged. The old duke silenced him with a hand on his arm.

'You must have misheard, Master Wystan,' he said evenly. 'I can't see his majesty standing for such a disgrace. We're not beasts here, after all, to kill defenseless men out of hand. Besides, they'll be a greater problem for Edric alive and wounded than dead. I'll go and talk to his majesty myself in a moment.' He made to move off.

'Halt,' Wystan ordered the old duke. Eilian gave him a hard stare, not bothering to hide his contempt. The black bastard on the other hand seemed to be relishing the confrontation. 'Are you refusing his majesty's orders?'

'You're getting above yourself, priest.' Eilian growled, visibly annoyed now. 'And you'd do well to listen. I said I'd talk to him.'

'It's you who'd do well to listen, since it's I who speak for his majesty.' This was going exactly where Wystan wanted, Bryn realized. 'Disregarding an order in wartime is a serious business... your *grace*.' The last was added with a sneer.

There was no telling where the dispute would have ended if Rhea hadn't chosen that moment to come pushing her way into the middle of it, seemingly heedless of the fact that fresh violence hung in the air like a bad smell.

'Has anyone seen Laurin?' she asked. 'The dwarf? I can't find him anywhere. Oh, and there's another army coming out of Dunmark.' She made a show of pointing east, as if they were all dullards who needed to be shown which way Dunmark was. 'I'd have thought someone would have noticed by now. But you all seem to have more important things on your minds than the fact that Edric's army just tripled in size.'

That got everybody's attention right smartly. Aeron's guardsmen rushed to the stakes along with the rest of them, leaving Wystan standing alone, his cause forgotten. Bryn saw him stare murder at Eilian's back before slinking off towards the royal tent. To foment more discord, no doubt.

Iefan, who had the sharpest eye, recognized the newcomers' banners. The Colors, he said, Dunmark's northern duchies. So now they were facing nearly three times their numbers. Meaning, they'd need more than just a simple miracle if they were to survive the next attack. And even if they did, Edric wouldn't stop there. But those were tomorrow's cares, Bryn decided. Right now, it was the dwarf gone missing that had him worried. In the short time he'd known him, he'd already come to like and respect the little man.

'Come,' he told Rhea. 'Let's go find Laurin.'

'He's probably somewhere about camp,' Bryn said. 'Waiting out the battle.'

'That's just it,' Rhea said, looking miserable. 'The little idiot got it in his head to play the hero. He actually saved my life during the battle. I'd never forgive myself if he... if something happened to him. Because of me.'

She was seriously worried, he saw. *So the iron maiden has feelings after all. Could it be that she fancies the little man? Stranger things have happened, old Andras would say.*

The thought that Rhea might have tender feelings for Laurin came with a surprising pang of jealousy.

Stupid, he told himself. She just happens to be the only nice-looking female around, that's all. And anyway, you can't afford her. All love does is make you vulnerable. Look what's happened to everyone else you loved.

'We'll find him,' he told her. In light of the carnage spread out along the rampart, going on to claim that the dwarf would be all right would have been utterly preposterous.

He saw the king's physician and the healers at work, pitifully few for so many wounded. Catch and a squad of men from the north wall had started sorting through the dead, a job Bryn didn't envy them.

This is what's left after the rush of battle is over. And I'm responsible for some of it. I think I even enjoyed it while it lasted. Maybe I'm not as different from my dear half brother as I'd like to think. He quickly stamped down on the thought. *No. This is Edric's fault. All of it.*

But in his secret heart, he knew it was never one man alone who was to blame for this kind of thing.

Time seemed to slow down to a crawl as he picked his way among the dead and the dying. Some of them appeared strangely peaceful, as if death had relieved them of all their fears and worries. Others merely looked like what they were: dead. Empty shells of flesh, bone, and gristle not so different from what hung from hooks in the back room of a butcher shop. And yet the stuff of nightmares. More so the ones still on their way out. The reaching hands, the beseeching eyes that said, 'Please don't let me die alone'. It took all he had not to kneel and offer comfort to each and every one of them. But there were far too many, and he'd come to find Laurin, not play the healer or the priest.

And still he nearly missed the helm, only noticed it because he stumbled over it. It looked familiar. Picking it up, he turned it in his hands. One side was so badly dented the man wearing it couldn't possibly have survived. Yes, it was familiar. He was about to discreetly discard it in the stupid hope of sparing Rhea the terrible truth for a little while longer, when he saw her on her knees, shoving at a dead body.

'He's here,' she said. 'Help me get this guy off him.'

They had to move not one but three dead men – two Dunmarkans and one of their own – before they got to Laurin. The dwarf was not a pretty sight. There was a deep cut on his cheek, but his head wasn't the bloody mess Bryn had expected after having seen the shape the little man's helm was in.

'He's alive,' Rhea said, feeling for a pulse. She shouted 'Healer! Over here!'

But the healers, all of them busy, weren't to be hurried. So they sat there and waited, Rhea cradling Laurin's head in her lap, Bryn holding one small hand and patting it as if that would make him all better. Once, their eyes met and held for the longest time, but he found her expression entirely unreadable. Unsettling. He looked away first.

315

Finally, after what seemed like hours, a healer came over, a frail, white-haired man who looked like he needed a healer himself. 'What's wrong with him?' he asked.

'That's what you're supposed to tell me,' Rhea snapped at the man.

'He got hit over the head,' Bryn added, trying to keep things calm.

'Let's have a look, then,' the healer said, kneeling beside Laurin and peeling off the padded cap the dwarf had worn under his helm. It had been stuffed with a bunch of straw, Bryn saw, and underneath that was another cap. And another.

When he'd removed the last layer and palpated the lump on Laurin's head, the healer looked up and grinned at Rhea. 'Cautious little fellow, your friend, isn't he? He'll probably be out for a while still, and he'll definitely have a mean headache, but otherwise there's nothing wrong with him.' Bryn could hear the man's joints pop as he rose.

'Can't you do something to wake him up?' Rhea asked.

'Try rubbing some snow on the back of his neck. If that doesn't do the trick, you can take him to the infirmary. They've got some truly vile smelling salts there, bad enough to wake a dead horse. And now excuse me, I've got wounded to see to.'

Snow didn't work, so Bryn carried Laurin to the infirmary and left him there with Rhea, judging it was time he returned to his duties, whatever those might be. On the way back, he saw Eilian Strong climbing up to where the other nobles still stood atop the rampart. Back from seeing Aeron. There was anger in the set of the old man's shoulders and in the way he stabbed his cane at the frozen

316

ground with every other step. With a sinking feeling, Bryn went to join them.

'… seems Wystan forgot to pass on half of Aeron's orders,' Eilian was saying.

'It's only the hopeless cases he wants released from suffering. An act of mercy. With so many of our own dead, he says, we have tents and bedrolls to spare, meaning we should give the ones who stand a chance some shelter for the night and send them down in the morning. And then, seeing as the way is open, we move out.'

'We're running,' Cullan said, not bothering to hide his disappointment.

Trant growled a curse. Griswold looked ready to go and shake some sense into the king.

'Aye,' Eilian said. 'A tactical retreat, he calls it. Back to Cullamor. Although in my opinion, there's nothing tactical about it. We're legging it, pure and simple. But I have to say I agree with him. If not for the Colors, we could have stayed and played a waiting game, hoping Edric would run out of supplies or freeze off his privates before we did. Now he's got all the men he needs to simply overrun us, and fool who thinks he'll count the cost. There's nothing left for us to do here but die.'

'There are better ways to go out than as cravens who turn tail as soon as things get dicey,' Griswold grumbled.

'Stay, then,' Eilian said. 'Make a last stand, go down in a blaze of glory, with nothing gained for anyone but Edric. Me, I'll trade that dubious honor for another day and a chance to take another crack at the bastard.'

Bryn agreed wholeheartedly with the old duke. As did the others, after further discussion and a sober look at their remaining options.

*　　*　　*

'Bloody fool! Watch where you're going!'

Gale was nearly unseated when his courser reared of a sudden, unsettled by a careless duchy man crossing the road in front of him as if he owned the right of way. Looked like the same idiot who'd already gotten underfoot as Gale was mounting up to leave. Not the animal's fault, even if it was a warhorse trained to stand fast against anything short of a rampaging mammoth. Under a rider as preoccupied as Gale, though, the beast had a right to be skittish.

He was on his way back from parleying with the Colors, and though he'd known beforehand what the outcome would be, he had a feeling the message he bore for Edric might well be that famous piece of bad news that proved one too many. Messengers had died for bringing the king less unpleasant tidings.

He should probably have taken the opportunity and defected – and would have, if not for the fact that he was the only one who might serve as a line of communication between the Colors and the Bent. He wasn't usually wont to put himself at so much risk. But he'd come too far not to see this through to the end, whatever the cost. Still, it would be nice if someone else was made to pay, not him. Gentling his mount, he rode on, wishing Edric were a month's ride away instead of a couple hundred yards.

The attack on the Bent had failed, that much he'd caught from where he sat negotiating with the Colors under a hastily erected canopy while the rest of their camp was still going up around them. Gods give that at least Stonebridge had made it through, else Edric would surely be in a killing mood.

To Gale's profound relief, neither the defeat on the Bent nor the Colors' invitation to surrender seemed to overly disturb the king. On the contrary. He was wearing that eager look again. And Stonebridge was there, gloating as if he'd carried the day with his dash through the defile.

Gale was still wondering why everyone seemed so unaccountably happy when the flap was pushed aside and Pryce came strutting in, four of his Headhunters pushing a woman and three children in after him. Gale bit back a curse. Though he'd never seen any of Edric's guests before, he knew immediately who they were.

'Your majesty,' Pryce said in that annoyingly offhand way of his. 'You wished to meet Ardath's royal family. These here were all I could find, but I daresay the only one missing is the king himself. I'd have gone and fetched him for you as well, if our friend Stonebridge hadn't been in such a bleeding hurry.'

Queen Merys looked to be half Aeron's age. Gale put her daughter Valda at close to twelve, the boys, Adair and Alain, at six and eight or thereabouts. All of them plump, blond, and fair-skinned, all of them terrified. As well they should be.

Damn, damn, and damn again! Gale thought. *This is the* one *thing that was not supposed to happen. How the devil did Pryce manage to pry them out of Cullamor and get them here so fast?*

'Your majesty, your highnesses,' Edric said. 'How good of you to come.'

'We didn't "come," sir, as you so dishonestly put it,' the queen of Ardath said. She was passably pretty, if a bit on the heavy side and marred by a slightly receding chin. It took neither the quaver in her voice nor the trembling lower lip to prove that her show of courage was nothing but that: a show. 'We were brought here by treachery and main force, as you well know. I demand we be set free and allowed to join my husband immediately.'

'Why, certainly,' Edric told her in a solicitous tone so obviously false he might as well have slapped her in the face. 'Though immediately is perhaps a bit faster than can be managed. But we'll see you all reunited soon enough. In the meantime, I've had quarters prepared for you, the best we have to offer under the circumstances. Stonebridge, if you'd be so good and see that her majesty and her family are settled in.'

Seeing Stonebridge deflate like a stuck bladder as he was reduced from savior of the day to errand boy was almost enough to lift Gale's spirits.

'That was fast,' Edric addressed Pryce when everyone else had left. 'A miracle, I'd say if I didn't know better.'

'No miracle, majesty. Since you said speed was of the essence, I decided to go with a scaled-down approach. Always time to sic Ensel and his lot on Cullamor later if it didn't work out. So I left the army to plod along on their own, and rode ahead with twenty of my people and a change of horses. Sent them into town in ones and twos, and your man inside the keep was kind enough to let them in. That done, I asked for a private audience with her majesty, which the dumb bitch granted immediately.'

Pryce gave an ugly chuckle. The man had all the charm of a knife in the gut. 'Must have somehow gotten the false impression that I had a peace offering in my baggage.

'Be that as it may, we had her and the pups out of there in no time and without anyone the wiser – at least anyone who was still in a state to make a fuss about it. Went a bit slower on the way back, with the coach and all, but here we are. Goods delivered.'

A man inside Cullamor castle! Gale was shocked. *That's the second time in a few days I find bastard Edric's been maneuvering behind my back. What else has he been up to that I don't know about? This is bad. Oh, this is very bad.*

'Excellent, Pryce.' The king was as close to not scowling as Gale had ever seen him. 'In truth, you couldn't have come at a better time. As of two hours ago, we've got the Colors sniffing at our backside. Came to throw in their lot with Aeron. Think they can bugger us from behind. Now we'll show them different.

'Gale, I want you to pay our friends on the Bent a visit, explain to Aeron why he should come down and surrender. Tomorrow morning, this end of the defile. Should he object to the arrangement, say I'll be glad to send him a little present that will help him come around. A couple of fingers off his lovely daughter, for instance, nicely wrapped and tied with a pretty bow.

'Pryce, you have the honor of informing the Colors that they're dealing with a fresh set of circumstances. I want them out of here by tomorrow morning. Tell them for every hour they linger past first light, one of Aeron's dearest will suffer.'

Gale went with twenty men.

321

Not to make an impression but because he wanted the light of twenty torches to leave no doubt that he was approaching the Bent under a flag of truce. Seeing as he was coming as the envoy of the most underhanded bastard in the seven kingdoms, he could hardly fault the men on the hill if they shot first and asked questions later.

He chose the roundabout way, the road through the defile and then the bridle path leading up the hill from Bentridge. Damned if he was going to struggle up the bloody thing on foot.

Whether they could actually see the white flag from up there or simply couldn't be bothered to shoot at so small a company, he didn't know. He made it up in one piece, was all that counted. After a bit of shouting and messages being carried back and forth between the gate guards and whoever was in command at this hour, he was admitted into the hill fort, though not his men. As the gate swung shut behind him, he was still racking his brain for at least the beginnings of an idea how he might salvage something from the wreckage Edric had made of his plans. Nothing came to mind. Nothing to leaven the news he bore. Not a glimmer of hope to sweeten the bitter facts.

*   *   *

19

Laurin steadfastly refused to wake up.

Though there was nothing she could do for him, Rhea stayed with him well past nightfall, growing ever more worried as the hours went by without the little man stirring back to life. It was the smell from a nearby cook fire that finally drew her away. Between the fighting and the unrelenting cold, her reserves had become dangerously depleted. In these conditions, she knew, it was eat or die. Or perhaps it was eat and then die anyway. If so, better to go out on a full stomach.

The healer at the infirmary, Makin, seemed bent on wrecking any hope she might hold out for the little man. He'd seen men similarly afflicted go on living for weeks, he said, even months. One or two might have woken up eventually, he conceded, but they sure didn't come right again, no siree. Drooling idiots who couldn't take a piss without someone holding their dicks for them. He only shut up when she showed him her dagger and told him she'd cut out his tongue if the only use he could find for it was bringing people down.

The damage was already done, though. Makin had gotten to her.

Next time she ran into someone like him she should choke them right off, ram their noxious drivel back down their throat before they even got started. Gods, but it seemed she was always angry these days. Ever since she'd met the little fool... but no, that wasn't true. And totally unfair. She'd been angry much longer than that, and it wouldn't stop until the people responsible were made to pay. And they would be, if it was the last thing she did.

The bowl of stew they handed her hardly deserved the name. A few bits of carrot and potato swimming in a watery broth, was all it was. She was too hungry to care, wolfed it down like it was the last food she'd ever see. And then she nearly choked on a lone scrap of gristly meat when she saw Corwin Gale ride past on what must have been the biggest horse in the Seven Kingdoms. Finishing up the food without tasting any of it, she watched him head for the center of camp. Going to see the king, no doubt. Not long after, Cullan and the Strongs came hurrying by, with Bryn in their wake. Nobody invited her along, but she joined them anyway. She wanted to know what was going on. If she got lucky, Gale might even drop a hint as to Pryce's whereabouts.

With Griswold, Trant, Wystan and Longshanks already there, and even the other Cullan brother come over from the Barrow, the king's tent was crammed. So it was easy to slip in behind Bryn without anyone noticing. Aeron looked terrible, pale as winter, with dark rings under his eyes and clearly in a lot of pain. But he bore up.

'My lord Gale. Forgive me for not rising. As you can see, I'm somewhat incapacitated. But do tell me, to what do I owe the honor?'

'Your majesty.' Gale gave as deep a bow as his girth allowed. 'Let me say how shocked I am to find you hurt. My deepest regrets. It should never have happened. None of this should. But alas, the message I bear will make things no better. I come on an errand that I can't but call shameful. I can only beg you to believe me when I say it is none of my doing and that I deeply deplore having to bring you such ghastly tidings. Painful as they are, you might prefer to hear them with... less of an audience.'

'Wystan,' Aeron ordered, 'a chair for his lordship.' The Black looked fit to strangle someone, but complied. 'There. And now, out with it. Things may be different where you come from, my lord, but here I trust my bannermen to stand by their king for better or worse. So they'll stay and hear what you have to say.'

'Your majesty.' Rhea saw Gale take a deep breath, looking as if he truly disliked what he was about to say. Meaning it was probably something really, really bad. 'Edric has your family. He's holding them hostage against your unconditional surrender.'

No burster of Wystan's could have had a more shocking effect.
Gale's words were followed by a profound silence. Looking for Aeron's reaction, Rhea saw him shrink, his very flesh seeming to deflate and fall in on itself as he went from wounded to fatally stricken, from middle-aged to ancient in the space of a few heart-beats.

Then suddenly everyone was talking at once, giving vent to anger and outrage, cursing Edric to hell and back and promising him a slow and painful death.

Men, she thought. *Always the need to bluster before they start*

325

using their heads. If they get around to using them at all, that is.

With a visible effort, Aeron pulled himself together, raised a hand for silence. 'So he's asking me to choose between saving my family and saving Ardath.' Spoken in a quiet voice. 'What would you do in my place, Gale? Can you tell me that?'

'I can't, your majesty. All I can say is, it's a choice no man should be faced with. But, if you will, I have more to tell you.'

Aeron gave a tired nod.

'The rest of it is better news,' Gale went on. 'Though I can't yet see how it might help you give Edric the slip.'

Aeron's head came up with a jerk. 'Whose side are you on, my lord?' he asked with surprising sharpness.

He hasn't given up yet.

'By your leave, majesty, I'll answer that question in a moment. First let me assure you that the Colors are most definitely not on Edric's side. They asked him to surrender, in fact. Until Pryce brought him your wife and children, it looked very much as if he was beaten.'

Pryce! I knew it! I should –

'But why would the Colors go against Edric?' Aeron asked.

'Two reasons,' Gale said. 'One, because Torvald found out who burned his villages. It was Edric, making himself an excuse to invade Ardath. More precisely, to come after you, majesty. Which begs the question why. What has he got against you?'

'Gods!' Aeron groaned. 'Can a man really be so mean of spirit? But yes, it must be so. I can think of no other explanation for this madness.' He buried his face in his hands for a moment.

Rhea pitied him. *He's overwhelmed. And who wouldn't be?*

326

Even a king has his limits.

'A year ago, I received a letter from Edric's daughter, Wilda,' Aeron recounted. 'The missive was quite confused, full of the wildest accusations against her father. She said she had proof that he'd killed both her grandparents. That he'd killed her mother as well, because she'd discovered he was violating his own daughter and was threatening to expose him. The girl begged my help, said her life was in danger. "He knows that I know," she wrote. "And he wearies of me. My days are numbered."

'Now – young Wilda is a trifle moonstruck, from what one hears. Meaning, I took her claims with a very large grain of salt. But she's also my niece, and I felt sorry for her, so the least I could do was offer her harborage in hopes that a change of surroundings might do her some good. I wrote to Edric, suggesting he send her to Cullamor for a spell. Let her get to know that part of her family, and so on. That was all. I never received an answer.'

'Ah,' Gale said. 'But you did now, majesty.'

'But it seems so unlikely,' Aeron objected. 'I mentioned none of Wilda's allegations in my letter to Edric. It was a harmless invitation, nothing more.'

'With Edric, nothing is harmless,' Gale said heavily. 'If half of what the girl says is true, he may have more of a hold over her than she realized when she wrote to you. Perhaps she had second thoughts, confessed what she'd done. Or was made to confess. Edric has an uncanny knack for sensing betrayal. It's as if he can smell it when a person is hiding something from him. Moreover, he's all about control, and insanely jealous over what he regards as his.

Quite possibly he knows nothing of her letter, and it was the mere fact of your reaching out to his daughter that set him off.'

'The man is insane!' Aeron said.

'Yes,' Gale agreed. 'He is. But his is a very dangerous breed of insanity: cold, clear-sighted, calculating. And most often murderously to the point.'

'You said there were two reasons why the Colors have set themselves against Edric,' Aeron reminded him.

'Ah, yes.' Gale looked around, his gaze briefly catching on Rhea and then coming to rest on Bryn. 'They want Edric gone, have wanted him gone for quite some time. Now they've found a replacement for him. One that everyone in Dunmark will have to accept, whether they like it or not.'

Rhea felt Bryn stir beside her, saw him darting a glance at the tent flaps.

'Don't,' she whispered, surprising herself by grabbing his hand, just in case he decided to make a run for it.

His eyes fixed on Gale, he squeezed her hand in acknowledgement. Warm and strong. A sudden tingly feeling made her quickly snatch it back. She felt herself blushing for no good reason.

'And who might that be?' Aeron looked more than doubtful.

'My lord Bailon,' Gale said. 'Or should I say, my lord Avellin: would you be so kind as to step forward?'

Rhea gave Bryn a small push. 'Go.'

'Your majesty,' Gale said, 'I give you Bryn Avellin, son of Seorus Avellin and Gavrielle Rowan. Born in wedlock, and legitimate heir to the throne of Dunmark.'

There was a moment of stunned silence.

Then everyone started talking at once, until Aeron raised a hand for silence. 'I suppose you have some sort of proof?'

'A copy of the marriage contract has been found in Kingskeep,' Gale said.

Eilian snorted. 'You might want to do better than that. If all the documents in the Kingskeep archives were genuine, you'd likely have hundreds of "legitimate" heirs cropping up all over Dunmark next time the throne stands vacant.'

'I do have more,' Gale said, unperturbed. 'I have the word of Torvald Tondern, who signed as a witness. As did Bowen Three-hands. I'm sure he'll tell you the same as Tondern if you ask him. As a matter of fact, I wouldn't be surprised if he were in a position to produce the original document. Where is he, by the way?'

'He's dead.' Bryn sounded strained, hoarse. He didn't elaborate. 'But he left me the document. You can see it if you like. It's true.'

'Well,' Aeron said. 'This does come as quite a surprise. You and your family certainly did a good job of keeping it a secret all these years. But I suppose you had your reasons.'

'I suppose they did,' Bryn said. 'As for myself, I didn't know until very recently. And to be honest, I'm still not sure what to do with it. As Lord Gale said: I can't see how it might help you against Edric.'

Bryn had said 'you', not 'us', Rhea noted. Suddenly he looked very alone, no matter he was surrounded by men who doubtless bore him nothing but goodwill. He must *feel* alone, with the burden that had been dropped in his lap. She felt an urge to reach out a comforting hand – and quickly slapped it down. What was she thinking? She wasn't his nanny. And in any case he didn't need one: he seemed to be getting harder by the hour, like clay left out in the sun.

Or a pail of water in this dreadful cold, she thought with a shiver that intensified when she noticed Wystan studying Bryn. The man's murderous glower had given way to something even scarier, sharp, hungry, avid.

Aeron gave a sigh that turned into a groan as he shifted his wounded leg. 'Neither can I. And if by tomorrow morning I still can't see a way, it will be either Ardath or my family that has to suffer for it.' He pulled himself up in his chair, wincing. 'My lord Gale. You still owe me an answer to my question: whose side are you on? After – what? – fifteen years of loyal service to Edric, the sudden change of heart seems a bit late, not to say contrived.'

'I'm glad you asked, your majesty. I could claim that I'm on your side now, or on young Bryn's, and it wouldn't be a lie. But neither would it be the whole truth. Because first and foremost I am on Dunmark's side, and always have been. My service and my loyalty I've given to the kingdom, and tried to work with Edric as best I could. Which turned out something of a mess, I'll grant you. Still, I may be deceiving myself, but I like to believe that without me things might have been worse. In any case, there's been no change of heart. I still serve Dunmark. And I believe it deserves a better king that Edric Avellin.'

Aeron nodded. 'Well spoken, my lord. I'll take it as the truth. What now, then? If you seek refuge with us, I'd say there are better choices.'

'Not refuge, your majesty. But should you have a message for the Colors, I'd be glad to pass it on. With your permission, I'll withdraw, and leave you and your bannermen to deliberate. I reckon I can tarry another hour or so without raising suspicion, but then I'll have to go back.'

'Very well,' Aeron said. 'We shall see you off in an hour, with or without a message. You may leave us now.' He looked around, nodded at Rhea. 'You, the young lady. You'll be forgiven for sneaking into this gathering uninvited, provided you look after his lordship and see that he's made comfortable while he waits.'

Caught out, Rhea felt herself blush. But she didn't mind being sent off with Gale at all. On the contrary. It was exactly what she wanted. The Lord Treasurer looked to be in a generous mood tonight. Maybe she could get him to give her Pryce.

*   *   *

Making his way back to the Dunmarkan camp, Gale felt like screaming out his frustration. So close. He'd been a hair's breadth away from seeing fifteen years' work come to fruition, only to have Albin bloody Pryce snatch victory out from under his nose at the very last moment. Now he was left with a deadly dilemma, and no solution in sight.

As he'd feared, Aeron had come up with the idea of sacrificing himself. The man was far too good for this dirty business. He wanted to give himself up, feign surrender, and then have his and the Colors' forces attack regardless, in hopes that Edric would take it out on him and spare his family.

Gale had had a hell of a time convincing him that the plan was pure folly. Because doubtless Edric intended to kill Aeron, no matter what. But first, he'd make the king of Ardath watch while he mutilated and killed his wife and children one by one until Aeron gave in and called off the ill-considered attack, with nothing gained for anyone except Edric. What Gale didn't mention was that Edric would likely kill Aeron's family anyway, if only to make sure there was no one left who might harbor thoughts of revenge and come after him at some point in the future.

The upshot of it was that Gale had departed with a message from Aeron asking the Colors to 'Stand by and be prepared for the worst'. Which was about as helpful as a case of piles. But, alas, everything hinged on Aeron's decision whether to sacrifice his kingdom or his family, and thus far he hadn't been able to make up his mind which it was to be. Not that Gale could fault him. It was the worst sort of quandary he could imagine a man finding himself in, and he doubted he himself would have found the choice any easier. As things stood, all their fates would hang suspended until tomorrow morning, when they'd find out one way or another what Aeron had decided.

And then there was the girl.

Much as he admired her courage and determination, she couldn't be allowed to go after Pryce just yet. If she did and was caught, she'd be put to the question. He refused to even think about the damage that would cause. He'd done his best to dissuade her, pointing out that, competent as she might be, taking on the seasoned Headhunters guarding Pryce at any given time was not apt to go well for her.

Unfortunately, he was far from sure she'd seen reason, seeing as she went on to ask him if he happened to know who 'S.I.' was. For a moment, when he realized what she was talking about, he was tempted to tell her. It might have solved a lot of problems. 'Might have' being the operative phrase.

Ordering his escort to wait outside the king's tent, Gale went in to deliver an accounting. An entirely fabricated one, of course. He found the usual suspects gathered inside. Pryce was there, accompanied by two Headhunter bodyguards, and Stonebridge, his usual, fawning self, sidling up to Edric and no doubt whispering important nonsense in his ear.

The other two men present he wouldn't have expected to see there: a nondescript-looking fellow in civilian garb, obviously a commoner. And one of Pryce's henchmen – Egan, if he remembered correctly. Though Egan looked like anyone's harmless, friendly neighbor, he was reputedly one of Pryce's best when it came to putting people to the question.

Gale hoped the man's presence didn't mean Edric was about to start working on Ardath's royal family regardless of the period of grace he'd accorded Aeron. It would be just like him, though. Fool who even considered trusting Edric's word

Gale never got to make his report.

When Pryce saw him come in, he motioned to his two bruisers to leave – or so Gale thought, letting them pass. Then suddenly his arms were gripped from behind, and with a rush of chilling clarity he saw what was coming, though the how of it still escaped him. Pryce's sardonic smile told him he was about to find out, as did the expectant look on Stonebridge's face.

'Gale,' Edric said. 'I have to say you disappoint me. Stupid of you to come back here. You should have stayed on the Bent, or with your friends from the North.'

If Edric expected a reaction, he didn't get one.

Gale knew that anything he said would be useless. Though he reckoned he could talk his way out of almost any situation, this wasn't one of them. Better to concentrate on not shitting himself. Better to save his breath for when Egan had him all to himself. No doubt screaming took a lot of it.

'Carver here' – Edric indicated the nondescript civilian – 'is very good at getting into places he's not supposed to be. He's also blessed with an excellent memory. Which is why he was able to give a word-by-word account of your conversation with the Colors.'

Suddenly Gale remembered where he'd seen the fellow: getting underfoot as he was mounting up to leave the Colors' camp, and then again cutting across in front of him on the way back, causing his horse to shy. Bold move, that, using the in-your-face obvious as a disguise.

Fellow had me fooled, and that's saying something. Takes balls to make something like that work. Cocky bastard would have made a good spy. Which he is, actually, only Edric's, not mine, and more's the pity.

'As you can imagine,' Edric went on, 'it's made me curious to hear the whole story. And I mean every last bit of it. Which is why Egan here is going to have you as his guest for however long it takes to scour that conniving, traitorous mind of yours until it's empty as a newborn's. He's supposed to be very good at what he does. So I trust you can look forward to an interesting and highly edifying experience. Egan, you may take his lordship away. He's all yours.'

Hustled outside by Pryce's bruisers, Gale saw no trace of his twenty men.

No surprise there. Edric probably had them all arrested the moment I turned my back on them. Thinking he'd get his hands on twenty of my people in a single scoop. If that's the case, he's in for a disappointment. Not a one of them was mine. So up yours, Edric bloody majesty.

Now, stripped naked and bound to a chair in a tent he couldn't place because they'd pulled a hood over his head before leading him here, Gale prayed to all the gods that his message had gotten through.

The only one of his people who'd been even marginally involved in the trip to the Bent was a guard on the Dunmarkan perimeter, stationed there with aforethought. Coming back, Gale had exchanged a few entirely innocuous words with the man, a jest to do with standing guard all night in the freezing cold and what it would do to a man's private parts. A code that, funnily enough, represented exactly the same message Aeron had sent to the Colors: stand by, and prepare for the worst. Just a bad feeling he'd had but, as it turned out, right on the spot.

Gale fervently hoped his people would come through for him – and be quick about it. Egan was already busy laying out the instruments of his trade on a folding table. The way he lovingly lingered over a two-foot iron bar was enough to make Gale shame himself by losing control over his bladder.

*   *   *

20

Sometime during the wee hours the weather changed.

Dawn came with scudding clouds and a warm, damp wind blowing out of the southwest, the snow already turning to slush. On Balder's Field, the two opposing armies were just beginning to stir. Between them Sleazetown lay deserted, those few of its inhabitants who'd escaped the previous morning's roundup having made off during the night, stealing through the Colors' camp like frightened shades.

Up on the Bent, Bryn stood with the other nobles in the first, grey light, silently watching Longshanks and Flatside carry Aeron out of his tent and set his chair down beside his waiting horse. They'd offered to cobble together a litter for him, but he'd refused. He would ride, no matter the pain. It was his only concession to pride of appearance. He wore no armor, was unarmed except for a dagger on his belt. Dressed in somber grey and wearing a simple woolen cloak instead of furs, he looked wasted, reduced to a pale ghost of his former self by another long night of pain and despair.

More like a penitent than a king, Bryn thought.

And in fact, Aeron wasn't king anymore.

337

He'd found an answer of sorts to his dilemma, and abdicated, appointing Darin Cullan as regent. Aeron's plan was to surrender only his person. If Edric wanted more than that, he'd have to take the matter up with Cullan. Bryn reckoned the whole thing wouldn't amount to more than a defiant gesture, but if Aeron felt better doing it that way, why not?

The problem is, he shouldn't be surrendering at all. But it's his crown, his family, his choice. No one else can make it for him.

Longshanks and Flatside were still debating how best to get Aeron onto his horse when Cullan stepped forward, motioning them to stand down.

'Your majesty,' he said. 'This has gone far enough. It grieves me to go against your wishes, but I simply can't allow it. I've sworn an oath to protect you as well as the kingdom, and neither will survive if we give in to Edric now. Which is why, for your own good and for Ardath's, I'm placing you under protective custody.'

The hurt and disappointment in Aeron's face were almost too much to bear. 'Darin, please. Don't do this, I beg you. You'll kill them.'

'No,' Cullan said. 'I won't. Edric will. And he'll do it regardless of whether you surrender or not. I can't let him have you as well. I'm sorry.'

Crushed, desperate, Aeron looked to Eilian Strong for support.

With a look of infinite sadness, the old duke shook his head. 'I'm sorry, majesty. He's right. You can't – '

Whatever else he'd meant to say was drowned out by the sudden, deep moan of a warhorn blown on the western rampart. Moments later, a messenger boy came running.

'Yer majesty, m'lords,' he panted. 'Come quick. There's somethin' comin' outta the north, an' it's huge.'

'Who in all the gods' name…' Cullan looked stunned, as did they all. 'Flatside, see that his majesty gets back to his tent.'

'No,' Aeron said, surprising them all. He sounded grim, determined. 'I'll see this for myself.'

'As you wish, your majesty.' Relief written plain on his face, Cullan stepped back to let Aeron's chair pass – and just like that, the king looked to be back and in charge again.

The sight that awaited them was chilling.

As far as the eye could see, the plain west of the hills had developed a rash of black dots. Moving dots, headed their way. Thousands of them. Where a farm or a hamlet stood in the way, parts of the dark stream momentarily slowed and massed around it like ants swarming over something dead or dying while the rest streamed by on either side. Not long, and the clumps dissolved again, flowing back into the larger tide and leaving behind columns of dark smoke that rose wavering towards the deep-hanging clouds until the wind took them and bent them into something resembling spidery fingers, crooked as if to say, 'Come hither! Come see what we've done!'

'Who the devil are they?' Aeron asked of no one in particular.

'Not Edric's.' Iefan had sharp eyes.

Bryn's were sharper. Perhaps half a mile away, the nearest dots closing in on Bentridge were beginning to resolve into running human shapes. He saw bared steel reflecting the slowly lightening sky. Hulking figures swathed in pelts. Round shields much larger than ordinary bucklers. Rimless, horned helms.

339

'They're Nordsmen,' he said, once he was sure.

'Aye,' Iefan said a moment later. 'Nordsmen. Gods help us.'

'Bloody hell!' By his angry looks, Griswold was taking the Nordsmen's appearance as a personal affront. 'Godsdamned buggers couldn't have picked a worse moment to show their ugly faces. Twenty years they haven't come this far south, and now of all times...'

'This changes everything,' Aeron said. 'We need to renegotiate with Edric. None of us can stand against such numbers alone. And we should try to warn the Colors.'

'Looks like that won't be necessary,' Cullan said, nodding towards another messenger approaching at a run from the eastern rampart. Simultaneously, they heard the distant moan of horns being sounded down on Balder's Field. 'I've a feeling they already know.'

'Nordsmen,' the messenger boy gasped. 'Lots of 'em. Comin' outta Long Valley. An' down the road from Burnt Keep.'

'Longshanks.'

Suddenly there was steel in Aeron's voice, as if the last few days had forged him into something new and harder. 'A message to Edric. Truce and an alliance until this is over. I want an answer within the quarter hour. And I want every man who can hold a weapon on the ramparts, now. Oh, and I'll need that horse. Can't very well fight sitting in a chair.'

As if he'd foreseen that something like this would happen, Longshanks gave Flatside a nod, and the sergeant produced the king's sword from under his cloak, handing it to Aeron.

'Thank you, Flatside.' Aeron cleared his throat. 'Right, then.

340

Owain, back to the Barrow, fast as you can, before they reach the road and cut you off. And you, my lords, pray take up your stations, same as before. May the gods be with you, and with us all. Highness, a word if you will.'

It took Bryn a moment to realize that Aeron meant him. 'Yes, your majesty?'

'I wanted to say you have free passage to go wherever you wish, provided you can find a way out of this sorry mess.' He waved a gesture that encompassed the Bent and everything around it. 'This is not your fight.'

'You're wrong,' Bryn said. 'It's my fight as much as anyone else's. I'm not abandoning my friends in their hour of need. I owe Ardath eighteen years of peace and safety. I'm staying, and I'm fighting.'

He didn't mention his other reason for staying: Edric. Friendship and loyalty paled in comparison to the hatred he fostered for his brother. Just thinking of him, he felt it running in his veins like hot, dark poison.

'Well,' Aeron said, and Bryn thought he saw a touch of moisture in the king's eyes. 'Good hunting, then, I suppose.'

'And to you, majesty.'

*   *   *

'What's going on?' The King under the Mountain sounded irritated. 'Why is that young fool using an ordinary sword instead of *Altingal*? I gave it to him for a reason, you know.'

'How should I know?' Laurin was feeling a mite vexed himself, not least because the old king was keeping him from concentrating

341

on staying safely under. No doubt the distant pounding he sensed on the horizon was the mother of all headaches, waiting to pounce the moment he woke up. 'Why don't you ask him?'

Cormac gave an exasperated groan. 'Because he's awake, dwarf. And even if he wasn't, getting through to him is bloody hard work. Can you imagine what it's like having to wade through miles of sticky tar every time you want to talk to someone?'

'Not really,' Laurin said, although it did remind him of Rhea when she was in a really bad mood.

'There you go, then,' Cormac said, as if he'd gotten an affirmative. 'So kindly tell him he damn well needs to use it. There's a very large amount of particularly ugly magic headed your way, and *Altingal*'s the only defense you lot have got against that sort of thing. So do us all a favor and stop skulking. It's time to wake up.'

Very much against his will, Laurin felt himself stirring.

'About time. You nearly made me miss breakfast.'

Rhea. Seemed everyone was annoyed with him today, even though he was pretty sure he'd done nothing to deserve it. But when he cracked an eyelid, the mixture of worry and relief on her face put the lie to her gruff tone. And the way she was sitting cross-legged beside him playing with one of her knives suggested she'd been there for quite some time. He fought the urge to close his eyes. The light from the lantern hanging from the tent's center pole was far too bright, and things looked blurry, every object including Rhea trailing a disconcerting aureole. As far as he could make out, it was still mostly dark outside.

He groaned, his stomach heaving in unison with the pounding in

342

his head. 'Please don't talk to me about food. Not unless you fancy me throwing up in your lap. My head feels like someone took an axe to it.'

'Duh.'

'You're saying that's what happened.' Gingerly, he pushed himself up and back until he was resting half prone against his pack.

She grinned, though without much humor. 'Except you got lucky. With your helm stuffed like a feast-day roast, your noggin hardly took a dent.'

'If you say so.' He was having trouble seeing straight. Willing his eyes to uncross, he found them immediately wandering back to focus on a point just beyond the tip of his nose. So he gave up and closed them. 'Why is everybody up so early?'

'Long story. It can wait. First, I'm going to get us both some kaf. You need to wake up some more.'

He'd have much preferred something that put him back to sleep for, oh, say, a week or so. Instead, he made the mistake of nodding dutifully, which immediately set his stomach climbing up his throat again.

'Be right back,' Rhea said, vanishing the knife. Rising with astonishing grace, she slipped away before he could make good on his earlier threat and puke on her boots.

She returned with a whole pot of kaf, and made him drink three cups of it. To his surprise, the bitter, black brew did make him feel better. His stomach settled. His head stopped swimming, the pounding lessened. His eyes gave up trying to cross and agreed on both looking in the same direction, though Rhea was still wearing a faint halo.

'So, what's up?' he asked, bracing himself for bad news. Which he got, listening in disbelief and then in growing anger as she told him of Edric's disgusting sleight of hand and Aeron's decision to surrender, if only himself.

'What a low-down shit,' he said when she was done. 'I'm not usually for killing people. But in Edric's case, I'm willing to make an exception. I reckon it's high time someone went and cooked that bastard's goose.'

'My thought exactly. I wish – '

Suddenly a horn blared somewhere close by.

'Shit,' Rhea said. 'That can't be anything good.'

'Not likely,' Laurin agreed.

'Stay here.' She was on her feet. 'I'll go see what it's about.'

'Wait.' He reached for *Altingal*, lying on Bryn's bedroll beside his own. 'Take this. Give it to Bryn. Tell him old Cormac says he's supposed to use it.'

'All right. But I'm not going to go looking for him all over the place. I need to find out what's happening out there.'

So do I, he wanted to say, but Rhea was already gone. He tried to get up but collapsed before he'd made it onto his hands and knees, dizzy and entirely out of breath. It was no good. He'd just have to wait until someone came by and told him what was going on. He doubted it would be Rhea, if things were really getting ugly. Somehow, ugly seemed to draw her in like a moth to the flame.

He poured himself another cup of kaf, spilling half of it because his hands wouldn't stop shaking. Then he settled back against his pack, sipping cold kaf and going in search of the reserves he was sure he must still have tucked away somewhere.

*   *   *

The first horn had sounded from the western rampart.

Rhea was about to go that way when she heard another long, mournful blast, this time from the opposite side of camp. For a moment she wavered, then she went west, simply because it was closer. On the way there, a wide-eyed messenger boy overtook her, running as if Amut's hounds were after him. She saw Bryn and the other nobles gathered in a knot atop the rampart. As she climbed the last steps, the gathering dispersed and the men hurried off in different directions, revealing Aeron sitting in his chair and Bryn standing beside him. With his greatsword lying bare across his knees, the king looked determined to stop whatever was coming single-handed, if need be.

She managed to get a hold of Bryn before he rushed off after the others.

'What the hell is going on?' she asked. The whole plain down below seemed to have come alive, as if it had been infested by a gigantic swarm of locusts. Only they weren't locusts. They were men. And women. Even a few children, if she wasn't mistaken. She saw pelts and painted faces, horned helms and muscular arms festooned with rings of gold and silver. And everywhere, weapons, glinting with a cold, grey light.

Something felt wrong, though.

Something about the way the Nordsmen moved. Like those huge swarms of migratory birds you could see over the marshes south of

345

Kingskeep in spring and autumn, hundreds, sometimes thousands of them dipping, rising and flowing as one great creature, the individual parts completely given over to the whole. With birds, it was a thing of beauty; translated to people, it became a chilling thought. She suppressed a shudder.

'Nordsmen,' Bryn said. 'I have to go.'

Nordsmen or no, it pained her to see what this stupid war was doing to him. He was beginning to look like the rest of them, like Griswold or Trant. Or one of Pryce's henchmen. Heartless. Ugly. Vulgar. She caught his arm. 'I can see what they are. What are they doing here?' She caught his arm. 'I can see what they are. What are they doing here?'

'You'll have to ask them. I have no idea.'

'All right then. So nobody knows anything. That's all I wanted to hear. Oh, and I'm supposed to give you this. Seems your many-times-great-grandda insists you use it. Here, let me help you.'

With Bryn fidgeting impatiently, she replaced the sword on his weapons belt with *Altingal*. To her surprise, when she was done he didn't hurry off immediately. Instead, he stood looking at her for a moment, his expression softening.

'Be safe,' he said. 'I'd feel a lot better about all of this if I knew I'd be seeing you again when it's over.'

Her first impulse was to ask him if he really believed any of them were going to survive what was coming. Her second was to stand on tiptoes and plant a kiss on his cheek – only he turned his head a fraction and she ended up coming dangerously close to kissing him on the mouth.

'Go,' she told him, her face burning with embarrassment. 'You be safe too. See you afterwards. I'm holding you to it.'

Gods! she thought when he was gone. *That couldn't have been me just now. I'd never do something so... soppy. Now he probably thinks I fancy him. Which I don't. Definitely not.* Her face still felt hot, though.

Meanwhile, the Nordsmen hordes had reached Bentridge. The village hardly gave them pause, just long enough to set it alight. Then they were coming up the Bent. Suddenly she remembered Laurin.

Can't leave him in the lurch, not again. Got to get him somewhere safe. But where? Nowhere to hide on this bloody hill.

*   *   *

21

Always an early riser, Macsen was awake, armored up and halfway through his second cup of kaf when the horns sounded. Meaning he was as ready as he'd ever be after a mostly sleepless night plagued by aching joints and endless worries over Rhea.

Hobbling outside, he found Varna and Kildown striding towards Tondern's tent, pursued by a gaggle of squires and servants carrying their masters' shields and helms or trying to finish buckling up breast-plates and vambraces on the fly. Tondern came out to meet them, trailing a retinue of his own and already calling for the horses to be brought around.

'What's that gods-cursed whoreson Edric up to now?' he asked, his black beard seeming to bristle with anger. 'I thought he wanted us to clear out. If he thinks pushing us will help, he's bloody well mistaken.'

'Might not be Edric,' Macsen said. 'Seems to me the commotion's on the other side.'

As if to confirm his words, shouts rang out on the eastern side of camp, followed by the din of swords and spears being beaten against shields.

'Could it be the sneaky bugger's kept another army hidden away somewhere behind us?' Varna wondered. He got his answer a moment later when a messenger came running.

If the news matches the look on the fellow's face, Macsen thought, *I'm sure I don't want to hear it.*

'Yer graces,' the man said, obviously terrified but pulling himself together and standing to attention, the effort earning him points with Macsen. 'We got Nordsmen attackin' our rear. Hard to say how many, seein' as they're still comin' down the road. Seems to be a big lot, though.'

What I thought. We just got dropped in it all the way up to our necks.

'What the devil...' Kildown looked ready to chew iron. 'If this is Edric's doing, the conniving swine's gone completely mad. Does he think those vermin will stay out of Dunmark and the other kingdoms, once they've come this far? We'll be lucky if there's more than a stone and a half left standing when they're done with us. Where's that bloody horse? I'll kill the bastard.'

'If Edric's behind this, we can expect him to attack us from his side as well,' Tondern said.

'And if not,' Varna added, 'he might still attack. I reckon it's a chance the dishonorable rat will find too good to pass up.'

'Right,' Tondern said. 'Bhorric, Gair, I suggest you see to the east. I'll take the west. I expect nothing fancy from the Nordsmen, but Edric will likely try and roll us up from the flanks, so have a care. Sergeant, with me. I'll not have you fighting against your own if it can be helped.'

Now there's a man who knows his warcraft. For all the good it'll do us. Hard place and a rock is nothing compared to this. Just wish I could see my little girl one more time, say good bye properly. Doesn't look like that's going to happen, though.

Mounting up, Macsen got a view of what was going on in the east. Big lot indeed. Already they were spread five and six deep halfway across Balder's Field, with more still pouring forth where the road left the woods. Turning west, he saw Edric's camp a-bustle, soldiers hustling, a first line of attack forming up just the other side of Sleazetown.

Nope. Definitely not going to happen.

Wheeling his horse around, he followed Tondern east.

Reckon this is the last time you'll be doing this, Macsen old boy. So see that you make a good job of it, one that's worthy of a few lines in a song, even if it doesn't look like there'll be anyone left to tell the tale of what happened here today.

*   *   *

Camped in a small clearing off Balder's Field where he and his cargo were well out of sight of prying eyes, Brother Maynard had just decided that, in light of recent developments, this looked like a good time to leave. It didn't take a soothsayer to see that the king of Dunmark's ill-considered campaign was fast turning into an unmitigated disaster. But that was only the half of it.

There was something disquieting in the air, had been for several days, an as yet undefined threat that raised his hackles and had him looking over his shoulder with increasing frequency. Truth be told, it scared him. He hadn't felt this exposed since the day of his initiation into the Order some thirty years ago, when unseen hands had

351

thrust him naked and blindfolded into the warren of crypts under the Great Temple of Amut in Orr, there to face the god's trials and either be judged worthy or die in some forgotten corner of the vast subterranean labyrinth.

Even the beasts were unusually restive, the moordwolves growling and whining like frightened pups who'd scented a large predator prowling outside their lair, the horses snorting and sidling nervously as if a pack of slavering hounds were snapping at their heels.

He'd wrestled one of the horses into the traces and was about to fetch the other when the woods around him sprang to life and a score of dark, hulking figures stepped out into the clearing. Taken completely by surprise, he experienced a brief lapse during which he took them for bears walking upright.

No, not bears, he realized a moment later. Men swathed in furs. Armed to the teeth. But it wasn't the weapons that scared him. With sudden, terrifying clarity he knew that the thing he'd felt approaching had arrived together with these men – though he still couldn't say what it was. Not magic, at least not any kind he'd ever encountered before. No. Something worse. Something even his extensive knowledge of the Dark Arts was no defense against.

It wasn't so much a conscious decision as desperate instinct that propelled him towards the rear of the wagon and the door of the moordwolves' cage. He got as far as reaching up to unbolt the door, then several arrows smacked into him with shocking force, all in the space of half a heartbeat. One of them burrowed through his stomach, the razorsharp broadhead finding the gap between two vertebrae and severing his spinal cord before the point came out the other

352

side.

Falling, he reached out for his magic, but it eluded him, slipping out of his grasp when he tried to take a hold of it. The last thing he saw was the glinting edge of an axe approaching his face at what seemed like a snail's pace, until the gleaming arc of steel filled his entire field of vision and then plunged him into darkness in a last, violent concussion.

What ensued was a scene of mindless destruction.

Perhaps if the Northmen had been following their own good sense instead of dancing to Scour's ruinous design, they might have seen their danger and not started rocking the wagon until it tipped over and crashed onto its side, the door springing open as the wagon house collapsed under its own weight. In a trice, the moordwolves shot out of their cage like twin bolts of fanged lightning, tearing the first Nordsmen limb from limb and head from shoulders even before their paws connected with the ground.

The residual part of the Nordsmen's consciousness not occupied by Scour would have sent them fleeing in primal terror – if not for Scour keeping them firmly rooted to the spot. Removing its makers' ancient enemy was Scour's remit, death and destruction the means of drawing that enemy out. Who got killed in the process was of no concern to it. On the contrary. The more the better, no matter which side they served.

In less time than it would have taken the Nordsmen to reach the sheltering trees, the moordwolves created a scene of carnage no battlefield could have hoped to match – though a score of Wystan's largest bursters detonated in the small clearing might perhaps have come close. Their appetite whetted, the beasts and their demon passengers exulting in their newfound freedom and the prospect of more blood, the unholy creatures moved on in the direction of Balder's Field.

*   *   *

It was the longest night of Gale's life.

Once Egan had finished laying out his tools – no doubt in an order that to him was satisfyingly logical – he stood back to admire his handiwork, rubbing his hands together in what Gale reckoned was anticipation.

This is it, he thought, his bowels beginning to loosen. He felt an overwhelming urge to start babbling, tell Egan everything he wanted to know – or almost everything. Some things he was prepared to take to his grave no matter the cost. But it wasn't to be that easy in any case.

'That's me off to dinner, then,' Egan said with the air of an ordinary bloke packing it in after a long day's work of laying bricks or milking cows. A convincing performance, if Gale hadn't known better. But then, maybe the man was just that: an ordinary bloke, only one with an empty space where most people kept a conscience. Before he left, he laid a blanket around Gale's shoulders, tucking in the corners like a caring mother so it wouldn't slip off. 'Don't want you catching a cold now, do we?'

Then he was gone, leaving Gale alone with the horrors that were to come.

It wasn't until the early hours that Egan returned.

The intervening time crawled by with excruciating slowness, and still it went much too fast. Whenever Gale heard, or thought he heard, a sound outside, his heart leaped in hopes that here, finally, were his people come to rescue him. Time and again, he was disappointed. Only when he grasped that the muted sounds he was hearing came from a sizeable group of stationary men did he understand that no one would be coming to his aid. There must be two score guards or more stationed around the tent, he realized. Probably half of them Headhunters. An insurmountable barrier even for the most loyal and determined of his people.

And so the hours dragged on, and still no sign of Egan. In the meantime, robbed of his last and only hope, Gale nearly went insane with dread. Being made to wait for the pain with no idea when it would begin was worse than the thing itself – or so it seemed at the time. Of course he knew that this was the whole point of the exercise. To soften him up. To turn him into a malleable, garrulous heap of blubbering goodwill and compliance. To drive him to a point where he was ready to welcome whatever instrument Egan chose as if it were a good friend come to redeem him.

Of course he knew. And of course it made no difference. Sooner or later the pain would come, and in the end that was the only bit of knowledge that counted.

Perverse as it seemed, Gale was relieved when Egan finally returned. 'Right,' the questioner said, already perusing his choice of implements with half an eye. 'Let's get rid of that blanket, and then we'll get you started.' He sounded like a physician reassuring a nervous patient, though on Gale it had the reverse effect.

It was beyond absurd. And terrifyingly real.

'What is it you want to know?' Gale asked, aware of how vain his attempt to stave off the inevitable was. Egan would get answers his way, not Gale's.

'Now, now, your lordship,' Egan said. 'Let's not get ahead of ourselves. Everything in its own good time. And, if you don't mind, I'll be the one asking the questions.'

He selected a harmless-looking two-foot length of wood – hazel, if Gale wasn't mistaken – not much thicker than Gale's thumb. Pulling up a camp stool, he sat down opposite Gale. Then, without warning, he gave Gale's knee a smart, precise rap, right on the upper edge of the kneecap.

The pain was excruciating, and for a moment Gale was on the verge of blacking out. Nauseous, sweating hot and cold, he found himself trembling uncontrollably. It was shocking: only a tap, and already he felt like he'd reached the limit of what he could bear.

When the first wave had passed, he opened his mouth to speak, but Egan shushed him.

'Not yet, your lordship. It's all about getting you into the right mood. And trust me, you're not there yet. Not by a long shot.'

He struck again, in the very same spot. Gale was hard put not to howl.

I am *ready!* he wanted to shout. *Can't you see? I'll never be more ready than right this moment, no matter what you do to me.*

Instead, he surprised himself by saying, 'Pox on you, you sorry excuse for human being. And pox on the whore who birthed such a pathetic monster.'

'Really, your lordship.' Egan looked genuinely hurt. 'And you a highborn lord. I'd have expected better of you.'

Gale was still searching for a scathing riposte when suddenly a horn moaned not far away, followed by shouts and the sound of running feet.

Strangely, the noise seemed to be coming from both sides, from their own camp as well as from the Colors'. Feeling that something momentous was up, he silently thanked the gods. Surely Egan would want to go and see for himself what the commotion was about.

Which meant he'd stop hurting Gale, maybe for good. Maybe they were under attack. Maybe Egan would go out and get himself killed, and never come back.

Apparently unperturbed, Egan showed no sign of leaving off. Seeing him calmly exchange the stick for the iron bar, Gale was yanked out of his fevered hopes and back into the real world, where his tormentor wasn't going anywhere and his walk through hell was just beginning.

Taking careful aim, Egan swung the bar at Gale's kneecap head on. This time, Gale felt the bone crunch and shatter under the impact. Then the pain hit him like nothing he'd have ever believed possible.

It was too much.

Beyond too much. His heart stuttering through a series of missed beats, he fought to breathe and couldn't. The tent went dark, with Egan no more than a vague, blurry shape that Gale could hardly make out as his tormentor took aim and swung again.

357

Mercifully, he passed out before the bar connected with his other knee. Which was why he failed to see Egan pull the punch. No use wasting pain on a man who couldn't feel it anymore.

*   *   *

22

By the time the massed Nordsmen reached the ramparts, Bryn had passed through fear, resignation, acceptance, gone back to fear again, and from there to a cold, all-encompassing anger that was sharp as a good knife.

For want of anything better, he held on to it. There were so many of them, far too many to leave any room for hope. But the anger would do well enough to replace it. Already scores of Nordsmen lay dead on the slope, felled by archers drawing and shooting as fast as they could. It made no difference. They simply kept on coming, not even bothering to raise their shields over their heads, tramping over their dead and dying as if they were just another feature of the hillside.

Which fit with the sense of wrongness he'd felt ever since he'd first seen them down on the plain. The way they were acting, they didn't seem to care whether they lived or died. And when the first of them were close enough to make out individual features, he found nothing human there. Instead he saw rabid beasts, faces like pale death masks, smeared with crumbling white clay and twisted into horrifying grimaces of insane fury and ravening bloodlust, eyes that were as black and as empty as the sky on an overcast night. They looked like they'd as readily use claws and teeth instead of weapons, he thought with a cold shiver.

Men under a spell, ridden by some unspeakably cruel and dark magic, if such a thing was possible. But then, perhaps this was what *Altingal* was meant for. The thought almost made him laugh. To stem what was coming up the Bent, what was climbing the Barrow and streaming through the defile between the two hills, a thousand men wielding a thousand *Altingal*s wouldn't have sufficed, magic or no.

'Gods be good,' Flatside said. 'Them blighters look like they was raised from the grave.'

'Scary buggers,' Little Tom agreed, his brow furrowed as if he were studying a particularly tricky piece of work in the smithy. Ham beside him didn't say anything at all. Just spit and hefted his axe.

'Damned if they ain't,' Daven said. 'But I don't reckon they're walkin' deaders. Though whatever's wrong with 'em's probably worse.'

'You think at least it'll make 'em easier to kill?' Catch said on Bryn's other side.

'We're about to find out,' Flatside grunted, raising his spear and ramming it into the first Nordsman climbing over the stakes. Even with Flatside's spear stuck in his gut, the Nordsman didn't seem of a mind to give up. Hissing and spitting, he hacked at the shaft with his sword until Flatside gave a mighty shove and sent him crashing into the ones coming up behind him. 'Nope,' he said. 'Not easier. Harder, I'd say. Phew! But those pelts them buggers wear sure stink somethin' fierce.'

'Damn,' Catch complained, loosing a last arrow point-blank into the face of another Nordsman before he discarded the bow and drew his sword. 'We should be gettin' double pay for this. Betcha we won't, though.'

That was it for banter.

From then on, it was desperate, bloody work that saw their line on the verge of faltering almost from the start. Bryn did his fair share of it. Its faint glow unnoticeable in daylight, *Altingal* seemed to be behaving like any other sword, not like something imbued with the power to stop magic. All the same, it was an excellent blade, perfectly balanced and sharp enough to cut through boiled leather. From the moment he drew it, Bryn felt as if he and it were made for each other. Pity it would likely end up in the hands of some hulking, foul-smelling Nordsmen revenant.

Not in this one's, though, he thought, cutting an assailant open from chest to groin, *Altingal* slicing through cheap mail like a hot knife through butter. The next face coming up belonged to a woman, though the only tell were two long braids sprouting from under her helm – that, and the missing beard. Gripped by the same, murderous madness that seemed to be driving the whole lot of them. Thin as a rake, quick as a weasel, she was over the stakes in the blink of an eye. Unsettled, Bryn let her get past his guard, nearly losing an eye for it. Against his every instinct, he cut her down, wishing all kinds of hell on whoever had brought her here.

And it got worse. Cursing for all he was worth, Catch swatted a peculiarly small Nordsman off the stakes with the flat of his sword. A boy, Bryn saw, no older than twelve. Moments later the kid was there again, heaved over the stakes by the men behind him and raising a crossbow bigger than himself. This time Catch had no choice in the matter. It wasn't the last child Bryn saw die that day.

'M'lord!' A man came running up the line.

'What is it?'

'It's Lord Cullan, m'lord. He's dead. Took an arrow through the eye. Meanin' you're in command this side now. It don't look like the right's gonna hold much longer, an' the middle ain't far behind. What do you want we should do?'

Bryn looked down the line, saw it was about to give way in several places. Too many defenders fallen, too few left to shore up the gaps. In the east, Iefan and Griswold didn't seem to be faring much better. Looking west, he saw Aeron, high ahorse and killing Nordsmen with the same meticulous precision he applied to other, less violent tasks. Behind him, Eilian and Longshanks were slowly falling back, the men of Ardath ceding ground but exacting a price for every inch lost.

'Find Iefan Strong,' Bryn told the messenger. 'Tell him we'll be falling back on his position. Say I suggest we try and join forces with the Colors, that I believe it's our only chance. There's no way we can hold the Bent for much longer. Then find Trant and tell him the same.'

He was about to order his left flank to fall back along with Eilian and Longshanks' line but saw they were already doing so. Not long, and he was forced to call a retreat, abandoning the rampart. With the Nordsmen pressing in from all sides, they were soon fighting in among the tents, being pushed ever farther south instead of east where they wanted to go. For a wonder, the man he'd sent to Iefan found him again amidst the chaos, but the message he brought was a crushing blow to Bryn's hopes of reaching the Colors: Iefan was retreating as well.

Except there was no place left to retreat to. They were surrounded on all sides by an overwhelming force, herded like cattle into an ever-diminishing space.

Suddenly Rhea was there beside him, shouting over the din of the battle. 'All of you, you need to come to the Hump! Laurin's found us a way out.'

*   *   *

Almost back at the tent, Rhea realized she wasn't far from the Hump. Seeing the big rock sitting in the middle of camp like a sleeping giant, she figured she'd be able to get an overview of the entire situation from up there, something no one else on the Bent seemed to have thought of doing. Laurin would just have to wait a little while longer.

Getting to the top wasn't as easy as she'd thought but feasible, though the sight that greeted her when she stood up there and looked around almost made her wish she hadn't come. There were Nordsmen everywhere.

One thing's for sure, she thought, trying to come to terms with the enormity of what she was seeing. *No way this is merely a bigger-than-usual raid. There must be tens of thousands of them. Can't be a single Nordsman left up north. It's like the whole lot of them, men, women and children, just pulled up stakes and headed south, leaving their homes and pretty much everything they owned behind. What in all the gods' name would make them do such a thing?*

The slopes of the Bent were so thick with them, it looked as if a forest of strange, pelt-bearing trees had grown from naught to man-high in less than an hour. Same on the Barrow. They had come through Long Valley and down the road from Burnt Keep as well, she saw. For the time being, Edric seemed to have them contained at the valley's narrow outlet, where numbers didn't count for much and fifty or a hundred men could hold them up for a time, if not forever.

The road was another story.

Probably because they'd been taken completely by surprise, the Colors hadn't been able to keep the enemy from flooding the open ground and spreading out, and there was already a fierce battle raging across the whole width of Balder's Field. And they were being attacked from the other side as well, a second front cutting through the tattered, trampled remains of Sleazetown.

Damn that madman Edric! The only sane thing would have been to put all differences aside and ally with the Colors. Instead, he's risking all of our lives, including his own, just to get back at Tondern for not going along with his stupid war against Aeron.

But Edric was in for a nasty surprise, she saw. Suddenly a horde of Nordsmen come through from the plain swept out of the defile between the Bent and the Barrow, overrunning what little defenses Edric had seen fit to place there like an avalanche flattening a few, sparse blades of grass. Now Edric was caught between two fronts as well, and it wasn't long before she saw a flag of truce go up on the western edge of Sleazetown. The man was absolutely disgusting.

In the west, Aeron on his horse was laying about with his great-sword. Cut off from the retreating line and surrounded by Nordsmen, his chances didn't look good. As if he'd realized his predicament at the same time she did, he turned his charger and gave it the spurs, trying to break free. But he'd left it far too late. Helpless, Rhea stood watching as a huge warrior wielding an axe chopped at the horse's neck. The beast went down, and Aeron with it. The last she saw of him was his greatsword, raised high in triumph by the big Nordsman.

Back at the tent, she found Laurin standing upright.

He was clinging to the tent pole like a seasick sailor to the mast of a sinking ship, looking as if he were about to either faint or throw up but back on his feet nonetheless. Which was where she needed him. She'd figured out where to hide him, but she didn't fancy having to carry him there.

'Good, you're up,' she said. 'Think you can walk?'

'Where to?'

'The Hump. There's a good place to – '

'Damn!' He made to smack his forehead but thought better of it. Wisely, she reckoned. The state his head was currently in, he'd have probably knocked himself out again. 'I completely forgot.'

'Forgot what?'

'Come on,' he said, nearly falling on his face when he bent over to pick up his pack. 'I'll show you.'

She grabbed his pack, and her own. Seeing him reach for the lantern, she wondered if the crack on the head had messed with his thinking. No matter. She had to get him to the Hump. She'd found a shallow dip on the top where she could see only sky. Meaning nobody could see her from down on the Bent, and the climb was difficult enough so no one would try it without a very good reason. It was the perfect place to hide Laurin – and herself, she was beginning to think.

Her doubts as to the little man's state of mind redoubled as he kept stopping to collect more lanterns from tents along the way. What on earth could he want with so many of the things? She decided to save the question for later. A discussion now would only slow them down further.

Finally, he directed her to the side opposite the one she'd climbed up. There was a deep cleft in the rock here, sheltered by an overhang and closed off in back by a dry-stone wall. They weren't alone, though. Someone neither of them had expected to find here was crouched in the shadows near the back of the crevice, studying some sort of squiggles chiseled into the rock.

It was Wystan. A bulging shoulder bag rested on the ground beside him. Judging by the shape of the bulges, he was either lugging around several dozen apples, or the thing was crammed with fist-sized bursters. Which made her wonder why the slimy fellow wasn't out there helping defend the walls. With those infernal devices of his, he could have actually made a difference. Well, a bit of one, in any case.

Noticing them, he rose – and did a double take when he saw Laurin. It was the first time she could remember him paying any attention at all to the dwarf. Now, though, his weird, colorless eyes fastening on Laurin like a pair of pale leeches, he inspected the little man as if Laurin were the most interesting thing he'd come across in a long time.

'Master Laurin,' he said. 'Just the man. I was wondering if by any chance you might be capable of interpreting Waylen signs.'

'No idea what you're talking about,' Laurin said, scowling. Clearly, he didn't like the Black any better than she did.

'Ah. Do you mind if I ask what brought you here, then? Because just now it looked very much as if you'd come with a purpose, and not merely by chance.'

'He's hurt,' Rhea butted in. 'I was looking for a place to keep him safe. And what about you? Have you "by any chance" noticed there's a battle going on outside? Has it occurred to you they could maybe use your help?'

'I'm not in the habit of wasting precious time prolonging the inevitable,' the Black waved away her question. 'And I don't believe for a moment that you're stupid enough to think your friend would be safe here for very long. No, I reckon Master Laurin's been here before, and I also think he knows more than he's letting on, seeing as he even thought to bring lanterns.'

Rhea was ready with an angry retort, but Laurin stopped her.
'Forget it. He's not going to go away. So yes, I've been here before,' he told Wystan. 'If you stand close to that wall in the back, you can feel a draft coming out through the cracks. Which means there's a cave back there. And seeing as these hills are honey-combed with caves, it's possible there's another way out. Maybe on

367

one of the slopes, maybe down at the foot of the Bent, or maybe on the next hill over. And maybe not. Maybe it's a dead end. But I'd say it's worth taking a look.'

Without further ado, Laurin approached the dry-stone wall, climbed onto a knee-high shelf jutting out of the adjoining rock wall and began pulling stones from the uppermost row.

'I *know* there's a way out,' he whispered when Rhea joined him. 'The signs say so, and Waylen marks never lie. We should let the others out there know about it, though.'

'You're right,' Rhea said, turning to address the Black. 'Brother Wystan. How about if you go and give our people a heads-up, tell them there's a way out, and to fall back on this place.'

'So you and the dwarf can take off and leave the rest of us to get lost down there? Not hardly. Why don't *you* go, if you're so concerned about your friends?' The arsehole was sneering.

'You really are all about saving your own neck and not giving a fig for anyone else's, aren't you?' she said. 'Fine. I'll go. But you could at least help Laurin take down the wall while I'm gone.'

Wystan gave a sour grunt but rolled up his sleeves and stepped forward. Rhea didn't like the idea of leaving Laurin alone with him one bit. She could easily see the black bastard doing exactly what he'd accused her of having in mind, forcing Laurin to lead him to safety without waiting for the rest of them. But there was no helping it. She had to go.

*   *   *

It didn't take long for the retreat through the camp proper to turn into a complete shambles. In among the tents, the line's cohesion

368

was lost in a matter of moments, men splitting up into smaller groups and fighting shoulder to shoulder and back to back as they tried to make their way towards the Hump and Laurin's promise of escape.

With scores of tent rows restricting lines of sight and offering countless back passages to both sides, Bryn's forces were soon so intermingled with bands of Nordsmen that it became impossible to keep track of who was where.

Getting to the Hump became an odyssey of twists and turns, avenues opening up only to be blocked a moment later by more Nordsmen than Bryn and the three men with him – Daven, Little Tom, and Flatside – could fight their way through. Somewhere along the way they'd gotten separated from Catch, Ham, and half a dozen others they'd started out with. Time and again they seemed close to reaching their goal, and time and again they had to turn around and find another route.

In spite of it all, Bryn managed to keep them headed in the general direction of the big rock – it helped that the damned thing stood tall enough so he could see it over all but the biggest tents – and slowly, ever so slowly, they got to a point where only three more rows of tents separated them from the open space around the Hump.

Then another band of Nordsmen spilled into what a moment ago had looked like a clear avenue to safety. It was the largest group they'd encountered since the fighting had moved into the camp, and taking them on was out of the question.

Bryn was about to turn back and go looking for another way when he heard someone off to their right utter a high-pitched, ululating cry.

The Nordsmen froze.

Watching in disbelief, he saw a minuscule woman come walking into their midst, looking like a doll even beside the shortest of her companions. She had jet-black hair, almond-shaped eyes, and was dressed in outlandish garb of a kind he'd only ever seen in drawings in a book – Eamon Darbin's *Northern Voyage,* it came to him unbidden, an entirely useless piece of information under the circumstances.

The woman would have looked ridiculously misplaced and entirely harmless if not for the almost palpable aura of violence hanging about her like a dark fug. Her eyes passing over Bryn and discarding him and his men as a threat were entirely black, so cold and soulless he suddenly found himself shivering despite the heat of the battle. Distantly, he realized that he and his men were standing there mesmerized, when they should have been long gone.

This is it, he thought sluggishly. Bloody stupid way for it to end. *Pretty little Snow woman is going to kill us all.*

But it seemed she'd found bigger fish to fry. Pointing farther along the row she'd come down, she directed her force onward, likely at what she judged a more worthwhile target. She didn't spare Bryn and his men a second glance.

'Gods above,' Little Tom breathed. 'I swear I just looked evil in the eye.'

'That was nothin',' Flatside said. 'You should see my old lady some time.' The joke was somewhat spoiled by the tremor in his voice.

'Let's go,' Bryn said, shaking himself loose from the strangeness. 'The way's clear, but it's not going to stay like this forever.'

As if his words had lifted a spell, they all burst into a run.

*   *   *

23

Another crossroads.

This time, there were three passages to choose from. Holding the lantern high, Laurin searched the tunnel wall for a sign that would point him in the right direction. Despite what he'd told Rhea about Waylen markings, he was beginning to have his doubts. The place was a veritable labyrinth. He reckoned they'd been wandering through the maze of chambers and passages for several hours.

Turning to inspect the opposite wall, he heard fearful mutterings behind him. To the people following him, he knew, it must feel like they'd been stumbling through the dark for days. If you weren't used to this kind of thing, being deep underground for any stretch of time could mess with your senses pretty badly. Even he wasn't altogether immune against the unpleasant knowledge that a million tons of rock were relentlessly pressing down on the fragile, little space they were in, a space the unversed couldn't help but think might collapse and bury them at any moment.

Though this here was mostly solid stuff, it wouldn't matter a whit if he took a wrong turn and got them lost. He had no idea how many people were behind him, but getting them all turned around and backed up to the last junction – or the one before that – would be a nightmare he didn't even want to think about. Even discounting the Nordsmen, there was no going back to where they'd started out from. Some time after entering the initial passage, he'd heard the distant crump! of the burster Wystan had given Bryn going off, sealing the entrance against the enemy after the last survivors of the battle had made it inside. He hoped Bryn was among them. Staying out there until the very last moment was an insanely risky business.

Laurin simply couldn't afford to make a mistake. Having Rhea right behind him was no help at all. Though she was doing her best not to show it, she was scared witless, fear coming off her like a once-pleasant perfume gone stale. So Mistress Tougher-than-thou had finally found her match in the Deep. Entirely understandable. Even if she'd so far managed not to voice it, he knew exactly which question was foremost on her mind, and on the mind of every single person following him blindly, hoping that trusting him to lead them to safety hadn't been the biggest mistake of their lives.

Gods be thanked, there it was, hidden in the shadow of a small ridge and appearing like a heaven-sent gift when he moved the light a fraction to the right: the next mark, indicating the branch they need- ed to take. The middle one, as he'd already guessed from the faint current of air coming out of it.

'There,' he told Rhea. 'We're right on track.'

'How far do you think it still is?' she asked.

'I've no idea. The marks tell you what's where, not how long it takes to get there. But I reckon we've already got a good part of the way behind us.' Only a guess, but the best he could give her.

374

'You'd better be right, dwarf,' Wystan, hard on Rhea's heels, muttered darkly. It was the first time he'd spoken since they'd entered the underground warren.

He's scared even worse than Rhea, Laurin realized, gaining not a little satisfaction from the thought. *I just hope he doesn't lose it. He's got enough bursters in that bag of his to blow the whole Bent to high heaven.*

'Or what?' Laurin couldn't help saying. 'You'll do something nasty to me, and then find your own way out of here?'

He immediately regretted needling the Black; things were tense enough as it was. But Wystan only grunted, as if saying anything more meant too much of an exertion. Not surprising, that. Despite the feeble current, the air was close, and every step down here seemed to take twice the effort it did on the surface.

Two branchings on, the Waylen marks ran out.

Try as he might, Laurin couldn't find any trace of one. To make matters worse, there was a slight draft coming out of both of the two passages on offer. It might mean they reconnected somewhere farther on, but unfortunately it said nothing about which of them was passable and which might narrow down to the size of a rat hole farther an, or lead them to a chasm they couldn't cross.

Which way to choose? Behind him, he heard Rhea's breathing becoming steadily more labored, slowly accelerating towards full panic.

This is taking too long. But if I rush it and end up picking the wrong one... Easy, now. Take your time. Let's see, then. The larger passage looks promising, but something's pulling me towards the other one. A Waylen's instinct? Or just my imagination picking the worst possible moment to interfere?

'Laurin?' Rhea's voice was decidedly shaky. 'Can you shine your light on those pieces of rubble over there for a moment?'

Doing as she asked, it suddenly hit him. How could he have missed it? Rubble on the floor, and over it a lighter spot on the tunnel wall from where it had broken off. Kneeling, he sifted through the pieces of fallen rock. When he turned over one of the larger fragments, there it was. The Waylen mark. Left, it said. The larger passage. Stupid of the miners, to place the mark on a flawed stretch of wall. But then, pointing a bunch of desperate fugitives towards safety probably hadn't been a big priority back then.

'Good thinking,' he told Rhea, not mentioning how close he'd come to leading them all into disaster.

Roughly another hour went by before he was finally able to confirm what the steadily freshening breeze had been telling him for a while already. A first, faint glimmer in the distance said they were nearing the end of their journey. Not much longer, and they stepped out onto the edge of a forest glade that was surrounded on all sides by steep, wooded hills.

Laurin was so relieved he could have burst into tears or danced a jig. He did neither. Instead, he stood by the tunnel mouth, watching and counting as a procession of pale, hollow-eyed fugitives came tottering out into the open. Big, strong men, fighters all of them, but the Deep had taken its toll on every single one. Wystan was number sixty-one, having fallen back quite a ways for some reason or other. Behind him came another thirty-two, and then Little Tom, Daven,

Flatside, and Iefan Strong.

The final tally was devastating. Where he'd expected a few hundred and hoped for more, he'd counted only to ninety-eight when the last one was out: Trant, grimmer than ever. But even he had that slightly crazed look of someone who'd just spent many hours staring his worst fears in the face.

In truth, Laurin felt pretty much the same. Beside him, Rhea made a sound halfway between a gasp and a growl.

'Where's Bryn?' she asked Trant.

'He was right behind me after we blew up the entrance,' Trant said. 'He can't be far. Give me a lantern, and I'll go find him.'

'I'm coming too,' Rhea said.

'No,' Laurin told them both. 'Too easy to lose your way in there. I'll go.'

*   *   *

Bryn reckoned he was lost.

It had been a mad rush to get away from the burster before it blew up, and still the blast had ripped him off his feet and sent him tumbling down the tunnel, maybe because he hadn't run fast enough, or maybe because Wystan had given him a big one, insisting a smaller one wouldn't do the job.

He and Trant had been the last ones defending the entrance, holding out as long as they could in hopes that more of their own would somehow manage to fight their way through. When it was clear that no one else was coming, Bryn lit the fusible, yelled at Trant to run, and lobbed the burster into the knot of Nordsmen pushing into the crevice.

His head ringing from the explosion, he felt around for the lantern he'd used to light the fusible. He found it, but it was smash-ed, useless. By then the others had already gone far enough so all he could see were tiny figures trailing huge, jumping shadows as the last lantern rounded a bend in the tunnel some distance away. Scrambling to catch up, he reached that same bend only to see them disappearing around the next one.

And so it went. Where those ahead of him had lanterns, most of the time he was forced to stumble along dark passages with nothing to guide him except the weak reflection of faraway lights occasion-ally raising a slick, intestinal sheen off wet patches of wall, never losing the others altogether but never quite managing to catch up either.

And then, after what felt like hours, he did lose them.
No more lights up ahead, not the faintest glimmer. No more echoing voices. Nothing. Only pitch-black, smothering darkness, and unre-lieved silence.

You are not *going to panic,* he told himself, his heart beating furiously, his breath coming much too short. *You're going to go on, and you're going to find a way out. Unless you take a wrong turn, or fall into a hole, or knock yourself out running into a wall. Which isn't going to happen. Because you're going to take your time and be really, really careful.*

Unbidden, an image of old Cormac popped into his mind. He batted it away. One Avellin imprisoned forever deep under a moun-tain was enough.

It was probably the worst quarter-hour of his life. Had it lasted any longer, he might have eventually sat down and never gotten up again, despite the brave little speech he'd given himself earlier. As it was, his heart did a relieved caper when he saw a faint sheen reflected on the tunnel wall ahead, and then a bobbing light appearing in the distance.

'Hoy! Bryn? Anybody there?' It was Laurin, come back to look for him.

'I'm here!' Bryn had liked the dwarf from the outset, but right now he positively loved the little man, was hard put not to sweep him up in a crushing hug.

'Oh, am I ever glad I found you,' Laurin said, slightly out of breath. 'Rhea would have had my – '

Suddenly there was a flash of light somewhere farther down the passage, immediately followed by the muffled thump of an explosion.

'What was – ' Bryn started to say but broke off, silenced by a cracking, ripping noise that seemed to be traveling their way. Fast.

'Cave-in!' Laurin shouted, pulling Bryn hard against the tunnel wall. 'Ceiling's coming down!'

Bryn came to with the distinct impression that someone had been shouting at him. Not Laurin. There was no answer when he tried calling the little man's name, and the attempt brought on a violent coughing fit. Every bit of air seemed to have been replaced by dust. His nose was clogged with it, his mouth and eyes gritty. But those were the least of his problems. Though the dust didn't help, what made breathing really difficult was the great weight pressing down on him from above, sharp edges digging into his back right through his mail and gambeson. Another hard lump – *Altingal*'s hilt, probably – was caught under his hip.

Weird, he thought abstractedly. *I should probably be panicking right about now. Maybe when things have gone so far beyond hopeless, some part of you knows it's no use being afraid any longer, so you're not.*

He lay there for an indefinite stretch of time, inspecting the thought. And came to the conclusion that, no matter how unpromising the situation looked, he didn't feel ready to give up and die. Not quite yet, anyway.

'Laurin? Can you hear me? Are you there?'

A cough. 'No. I got blown all the way back to the Bent, and now I'm busy beating those Nordsmen arseholes to pulp single-handed.' More coughing. 'Sure I'm here. And honestly? It doesn't look like I'll be going anywhere soon. Feels like half the mountain just sat down on me.'

'Sorry. Stupid question. Maybe this one is too: do you reckon there's another way out of here?'

'Might be. Though the part where we get up, relight the lantern that miraculously didn't get squashed under a rock and go sauntering off into the sunset might be a bit of a problem.'

'Right. Let me think about it.'

But Bryn's mind didn't seem inclined to consider the issue. Instead, it chose an entirely different direction to go wandering off in.

*   *   *

This is totally ridiculous, Laurin thought after Bryn had gone silent. *Twenty years of crawling through the bowels of the earth, with*

380

never a cave-in. And then, the moment I quit the job, this happens. If the gods have anything to do with what goes on in the world of men, they're either cruel bastards or entirely irresponsible brats playing stupid games.

'Laurin?' Bryn's breathing sounded even more labored than his own. 'There's something I've been meaning to ask you. Not to pry, but are you and Rhea... you know, close?'

'Nah. We're just friends. When she's not mad at me, that is.'

Wish it could have been more, though. Maybe if I grew another three feet, turned into the most fearsome warrior in all of Aldara...

'So you don't... fancy her?'

'If she were two feet shorter and about a mile gentler, I might consider it. She's not exactly... approachable, you know. Not the cuddly type at all. I reckon anyone who tries getting closer than an arm's length stands a good chance of ending up with a bloody nose or missing a couple of teeth.'

I'm babbling. And why are we talking about this now? Oh. Probably because that's what people do when there's nothing else left. Talk. Better than thinking.

'So you wouldn't mind if it turned out she, ah... liked someone else, maybe?'

Oh. 'No. Not at all.'

Idiot! This is the place where you should be saying yes, I would mind. Because, deny it all you like... Oh, don't be ridiculous. She's way beyond your reach, and always will be. And besides, neither of us is ever going to see her again in any case, so what does it matter?

'Right. It's probably nothing, anyway.'

381

Laurin didn't ask what that 'nothing' was. 'So have you figured out how to get us out of here?'

'Oh. No. Give me a moment.'

Bryn went silent for what seemed like a very long time. Laurin waited patiently. Wasn't much else he could do. He was able to move his right hand, but not even far enough to scratch the itch on his nose. Better if the cave-in had killed them outright, he thought. This way, if nothing more came down and their air didn't run out, it would likely be thirst that did them in. Not a nice way to go, from what he'd heard.

*   *   *

24

Bryn still wasn't pondering their predicament.

Instead, he'd drifted off and fallen asleep. Hadn't even noticed it happening. A couple of battles and two days with hardly any sleep had worn him out – not to mention being buried under tons of rock.

'I don't believe it,' a voice said somewhere close to his ear, giving him a fright. 'The fate of Aldara is hanging in the balance, and all you can think of is lying down for a snooze.' Cormac, putting in his two coppers' worth.

'I'm stuck down here, in case you hadn't noticed. Probably going to die here, too.'

'Poppycock! What have you got *Altingal* for? All you have to do is use it.'

'Use it how? I can't move. And even if I could reach it, magic or no I don't really see it cutting through tons of rock, do you?'

'I didn't mean use it like that, numbskull. The thing's got power. What you need to do is connect to that power. Do that, and you can make things happen, make them go your way. So stop lollygagging and wake the hell up, laddie. Time's a-wasting.'

Bryn woke to the unpleasant sensation of a cramp starting up in his left calf. Instinctively trying to shift his leg, he found to his surprise that he could. From the knee down, it was unencumbered. So was the other one.

Which meant they might have been lucky and gotten caught on the edge of the rockfall. The notion was enough to ignite a first, faint glimmer of hope. Maybe there was a way out of this after all.

Experimentally, he tried rounding his back, pushing upward. It hurt, the supple mail of his hauberk affording him less protection than he'd hoped. But he also felt the stuff lying on top of him give a slight wobble. A big rock, it felt like. Not wedged tight, else it wouldn't have moved at all. Hope gleamed a little brighter. Now for the hard part.

He'd been caught with one arm under him and the other cocked at right angles above his head. Getting his hands to where he could use them to lever himself up was slow and painful work, pushing, pulling, wriggling and shifting an inch at a time with rocks digging into his arms and lacerating the unprotected skin of his hands. But, every time he thought he was good and stuck, something gave, allowing him another little bit of space.

Finally, when he had both hands positioned where he wanted them, braced against the floor close to his shoulders, he took a deep breath, wincing as sharp corners and edges dug deeper into his back.

Ignoring the pain, he gave a mighty heave, pushing upward. Felt the weight over him move an inch or two before it fetched up against something else and wouldn't budge any further.

Twice more he tried, giving it everything he had, straining and heaving until he thought his ribs would crack. It was no good. The thing was just too damned big and heavy. Lying there, winded from the effort as much as from the violent coughing fit that had followed it, he remembered what Cormac had said about using *Altingal*. He doubted it would work, had no idea how he was supposed to 'connect' to a sword. On the other hand, it wasn't as if he had a lot of other options left. Might as well give it a try.

It turned out to be astonishingly, almost disappointingly easy.

All he had to do was think, *Sword, I could use some help here.* That was it. No idea how it worked, or why, but *Altingal* responded to his need like a faithful hound eagerly waiting on a word from its master. It wasn't a big thing, either. No rush of superhuman strength, no magical abilities tingling through his veins, nor did the weight pressing down on him miraculously disappear.

Something shifted, something so small he couldn't even have said whether it happened in or around him. It felt encouraging, though, like he should give it another go.

Bracing himself for another heave, he heard a small rock fall, perhaps dislodged by the tiny shift of his tightening muscles. Buoyed by a sudden certainty, he reared up, and, like a great unweaving of an intricate puzzle, rocks large and small began to slip and slide and tip and tumble this way and that, grinding, rasping, clattering, thumping. No longer held back by whatever had been blocking it, the big rock wobbled once and then rolled off his back. He was free.

'Bryn?' Laurin said. 'What the hell was that?'

'That,' Bryn said, 'was the sound of freedom. Hang on, I'm going to dig you out.'

'This had better not be a joke, because I'm not in the mood.'

'It's not. I just need to figure out where – '

'Ouch! I've got enough stuff lying on top of me without you adding your weight to it.'

'Sorry. I wish I had some… Oh. Idiot.'

'Who, me?'

'No, me. I should have thought of this earlier. There.'

'Hey, where's the light coming from?'

'*Altingal.* Not quite as good as a lantern, but I think I can see somebody's foot poking out of a big heap of rubble. Reckon it might be yours?'

'Ha bloody ha. So dig me out, already.'

'That burster could only have been Wystan's doing,' Bryn said.
He and Laurin were sitting with their backs to the tunnel wall not far from the rubble blocking the passage. Covered from head to toe in light grey rock dust, in *Altingal*'s mild, amber light they looked like two tired ghosts taking a break from haunting.

'It was,' Laurin said. 'He was right behind Rhea and myself for most of the way, and then he fell back. I remember noticing a deep niche down where the explosion was, deep enough for someone to hide in and not be seen by the others passing by. That's probably where he left the burster.'

'Yes. Though I reckon he must have gotten lucky with the fusible. A little longer, and I'd have been past the spot. A little shorter, and he'd have blown up gods only know how many other people.'

'Luck – or something darker. Don't forget he has magic. Or says he does. And I don't think he's the kind who loses sleep over blowing up a few extra people. That man isn't just a slimy creep, he's

386

downright evil.

'Which still doesn't explain why he wants you out of the way so badly he'd run that much of a risk. There are nearly a hundred people out on that clearing, none of whom are too stupid to figure out what that burster going off meant. And none of them are apt to take kindly to Wystan trying to kill you. If I were him, just knowing Rhea was out there would have made me think twice.'

'He probably thinks he can handle her, maybe even all of them, if it comes to it. As you said: he's got magic. Not to mention a bagful of bursters. And as to why he wants me gone – I'd say it's pretty clear by now whom he's been working for all along: Edric.'

Laurin shook his head slowly, obviously not convinced. 'Either that, or Edric's not the only one who wants to get rid of you.'

Bryn groaned. 'As if things weren't already messy enough.' It was a chilling thought, though. Suddenly he was very afraid for Rhea.

'You ready to lead us out of here?' he asked.

'Ready as I'll ever be,' Laurin said. 'Just don't get your hopes up too high. This is not going to be easy. If it works at all, that is.'

*   *   *

Laurin led them back to the junction where he'd nearly missed the fallen Waylen mark. The draft coming out of the smaller, right-hand passage seemed stronger than before, as if it had been joined by the airflow cut off by the cave-in. He took it for a good sign.

It was hard going, though. The tunnel twisted and turned like a borehole made by a mad woodworm, with enough ups and downs and lefts and rights to make a person dizzy. Might have just been his head, though: after the knocks he'd taken, it still felt like it was sitting slightly askew.

There were steep inclines to navigate, and stretches so narrow they had to crawl on all fours. Twice they came upon floorless chambers, huge, gaping holes that looked to have no bottom. Getting around them with nothing but tiny ledges and fragile handholds to cling to was right up there with Laurin's scariest adventures ever. And it must have been worse for Bryn. Unlike Laurin, he wasn't used to crawling around the insides of mountains. After they'd rounded the second abyss, he looked ready to puke. But he held up.

Some time later, there was another hole in the floor, though this one was smaller, and easy to circumnavigate. A few yards past it, Laurin suddenly stopped.

'What?' Bryn said.

'The draft. It's gone.'

'How can it just disappear? It's not like somebody could have cut it off by closing a door somewhere.'

'No. We've gone too far. It must have been coming up through that hole we just passed.'

This might turn out to be very bad news, Laurin thought, his heart feeling like it had already gone on ahead and plummeted down that very hole. We might have to go all the way back to the junction we started out from.

Only there had been a couple of steep, water-slicked drops along the way he wasn't sure they could get back up. And even if they made it past those, he had no idea where to go from there. But maybe… 'Let's go back and take a look.'

The hole looked as dark and deep as the other ones. But when Bryn stuck *Altingal* down into it, the sword's mild light revealed a flat, scuff-marked surface maybe fifteen feet below.

'That's it,' Laurin said. 'That's our way out.'

But getting down there was going to be a problem. It was quite a drop for a man, though someone strong and supple enough might make it down unharmed. For a dwarf, it looked like a sure-fire bone-breaker. Bryn had seen it too.

'This is what we're going to do,' he told Laurin. 'There are some good handholds right here on the edge. So I'm going to climb down until I'm hanging from them, and then you use me as a ladder. Once you reach my feet, you let go. Shouldn't be much of a drop from there.'

That was how they did it, and it worked. Climbing down Bryn's back with not a whole lot to hold on to made for a few nervous moments, but the remaining drop was less than four feet. Bryn landed a bit harder, but undamaged.

'Thanks,' Laurin said. 'I'd have never made it down in one piece without you.'

'And I wouldn't have made it this far at all without you, so I reckon we're even. Come on, I've had just about as much of this underground stuff as I can take.'

So had Laurin, truth be told.

It was late afternoon when they stepped out onto the clearing.

In no time at all they were surrounded by a crowd of people... no, not just people. Friends. Smiling, clapping him and Bryn on the shoulders, congratulating them no matter they were all run ragged

389

and the near future looked anything but promising. For now, everyone was relieved and glad to see them both alive and well – everyone who was still around to be relieved and glad, that was. The gaps where the missing should have been were glaringly obvious: Aeron wasn't there. Neither was Eilian Strong; the sorrow etched on Iefan's face would have said as much all by itself. Longshanks was dead, killed in a last, futile attempt to reach and save his king. Griswold hadn't made it, and Ham. Catch, Darin Cullan, and close to seven hundred men from all over Ardath come to help defend the kingdom against blackguard Edric. Brave men, all of them, though they surely hadn't expected ten or fifteen thousand Nordsmen to come rolling over them in an avalanche of steel and death. What had become of Darin's brother Owain and the men on the Barrow, no one knew. Overrun, probably, just like the Bent.

Wystan wasn't anywhere to be seen. Neither was Rhea.

'Where is she?' Bryn asked Iefan. More than ever, he looked like a ghost, his face caked with a mixture of sweat and whitish rock dust. Only he no longer resembled a lost and lonely wraith but a grim, vengeful revenant risen from some subterranean crypt.

'Gone,' Iefan said. 'After the explosion, she rushed back into the passage. Stayed in there for over an hour, calling both your names, digging and shifting rocks until her hands were bleeding. We helped as best we could, but there was simply no getting through. Rocks big as houses pressing down from above, and no way to move them except maybe with the black rat's bursters. Only he was gone, snuck off right after he came out. Then more of the ceiling started coming down, and we had to drag her out, else she would have died in there. By then, we'd given you up for dead.'

'She went after Wystan,' Laurin said, sure as he'd ever been of anything.

'Aye,' Iefan said. 'I sat her down outside and tried to get her a drink of water, but by the time I found someone who still had a few drops in their field flask she was up and away, gone before anyone could think to stop her.'

'I'm going to find her,' Bryn said.

Seeing his expression, Laurin pitied anyone who got in his way. 'I'm coming too,' he said.

'We're all going,' Iefan said. 'We were about to move out in any case. No use hiding out here with no water, food, or shelter.' He pointed east. 'Best I can tell, Long Valley's that way.'

Laurin saw a steep-sided gorge leading off the clearing, its narrow floor gouged by a rocky streambed, dry except for a small trickle from the melting snow. Just a run-off, then, since Iefan had said there was no water in this place.

'All right,' Bryn told Iefan. 'But I'm not waiting for anyone.'

'You don't have to,' Iefan said. 'Everybody's ready to go.'

'Looks like maybe they should be ready to fight, too,' Laurin said. 'There's somebody coming the other way.'

Nordsmen, he saw as the incoming men drew closer in the waning light. A lot of them. But it was the fellow out front who gave him the jitters. Dressed like a sailor, he would have looked ordinary enough aboard a ship or trawling the sleazier sort of waterfront dives. Here, he seemed decidedly out of place. But that wasn't it. What made him stand out was the hair-raising dread that preceded him like a foul wind – that, and the fact that every inch of the fellow

391

was entirely black. Black as the devil's arsehole on a moonless night.

*   *   *

Part III – Unbound

Death is not the greatest loss in life.
The greatest loss is what dies inside us while we live.
Norman Cousins

25

Nudd was becoming increasingly frustrated, not to say angry.

Here he had a long list of people whom he justly aimed to cause considerable grief, all of them in and around Orr, and instead he was going in the opposite direction, the gulf between himself and his well-deserved revenge widening mile after gods-cursed mile.

The reason was – what else could it be? – gods-buggering Scour, pushing Nudd and the Nordsmen ever farther east. Why? Because there were several bloody wide rivers to cross on the way south, and apparently none of the arse-fricking Nordsholes knew how to swim. Neither did Nudd, but he reckoned that a bit of water was hardly going to put a crimp in Wiggin the Weapon's style.

But did Scour make the buggers build rafts, like Nudd had so reasonably suggested? Or simply find a ford and chase them over, and to hell with it if a few of them drowned? No, they had to go all the way east where it was bloody, fricking cold and the rivers were frozen, just so the precious Nordsladies didn't get their delicate little feet wet. To Nudd's great satisfaction, a couple dozen drowned anyway when they broke through a patch of thin ice, giving him a fine reason to gloat.

'Told you so,' he needled Scour, though in truth he'd never said anything of the sort.

Scour didn't answer, so Nudd did, speaking for the damned thing. 'Oh, my dear Nudd. I'm so, *so* sorry. I know I should have listened to you, should have bowed to your vast experience and superior wisdom. Sadly, I haven't had my head on straight these past few weeks. In fact, I'm beginning to see how right you were when you said we should go to Orr instead of – '

Communicating something very much like annoyance, Scour cut him off, snapping his mouth shut so violently he nearly bit his tongue off. Could have easily chipped a tooth there as well. Not that it mattered when everything inside you was more or less liquid.

Pissed him off all the same.

Nudd had long since lost count of the days he'd been forced to tramp through endless forests in freezing weather, though he deeply resented every minute of it. It wasn't that he felt either fatigue or the cold, not since Scour had transformed him. Physical discomfort was a thing of the past. No, it was a question of principles. Scour wanted something, Scour should damn well give something back. Like letting him march at the head of the army, not make him tag along behind as if he were a mangy camp dog instead of Scour's chosen general. What made it so much more humiliating was that the blasted snow-buggers were somewhere up front, possibly even in the vanguard. He chewed on that one for days, until he remembered having heard somewhere that the greatest generals usually preferred to command from the rear.

And there was another thing that gave him no small measure of consolation: as the days and the miles dragged by, he increasingly got a sense of preoccupation from Scour, as if the damned thing were actually worried about something. Unfortunately, Nudd's glee lasted only until whatever was bothering Scour started to affect him as well. Eventually he began to experience moments of sudden disorientation, almost as if Scour were leaving the helm unmanned for short periods of time, too busy with something else and unable to stretch its hitherto inexhaustible resources far enough to control everyone at once. It was disturbing, to say the least.

In time, it began to happen more often.

At first Nudd was thrilled, already envisioning the moment when Scour would falter and then lose its shit altogether, already seeing himself taking command and leading his forces where he wanted them to go. The fact that he was losing color and slowly but surely turning a uniform, shiny black didn't bother him at all. On the contrary, he felt it only added a certain cachet to his overall appearance, made him even more awe-inspiring than he already was. Then one day – Scour was in the middle of one of its lapses – Nudd's left leg suddenly wobbled and shed a large gob of its own substance, throwing him completely off balance.

Kneeling there, looking back at the splotch of black that had until recently been a part of him and was now marring the pristine snow, he was suddenly gripped by a terrifying certainty that he was about to melt. Shocked to his liquid core, he was fast approaching a screaming panic when Scour came rushing back. Instantly firming him up, it made him shuffle back and scrape up what he'd lost. For once, he didn't mind being moved about like a minor game piece.

The thing was – Scour's reentry had been so precipitate that Nudd had been able to catch a glimpse of what it had been doing: cutting out and abandoning one of the snow-fuckers. The old man, it looked like. Interesting. And worrying. What if Scour decided to leave *him* in the lurch like that? But no. He was Number One. And they had a deal, didn't they? Didn't they? Fricking Scour had bloody well better honor it, or else…

There were a few more similar incidents along the way, but to Nudd's disappointment Scour somehow managed to regroup each time. So he waited, biding his time, prepared to jump in and take control when his moment came. Then bloody Scour led them to a pair of hills with a whole fricking army sitting on top of them.

Nudd was outraged. 'This is *not* what I signed up for!' he yelled at Scour. 'Here there were scores of towns and villages to choose from, full of dumb civilians who can't tell their arse from a fricking pitchfork, and you lead us right into the teeth of a gods-buggering army? Are you stupid, or what?'

But the Nordsmen were already tramping up the hills, oblivious to the arrows raining down on them.

'I am *not* going up there,' Nudd told Scour.

He needn't have worried – at least not about the men on the hills. Instead, resist as he might, Scour marched him into a narrow defile between the two hills and out the other side. Where another, even bigger army was waiting.

'You're crazy!' Nudd raged. 'You're going to get us all killed! You're going to get *me* killed! This was *so* not the deal!'

400

Already the first enemies were upon him.

I'm going to die! he thought, desperately struggling against Scour's compulsion. An arrow hit him square in the chest. Strangely, he didn't feel a thing. Looking down, he found nothing where he'd expected to see the shaft and fletching sticking out of his chest. Damned thing must have gone right through. Someone rammed a spear into his thigh. Someone else hacked at his neck with a sword. His shoulder. None of it hurt. Then he got it.

I'm fricking, bloody invincible! Stupid buggers can't hurt me. But I can hurt them. And oh, am I ever going to.

Lacking any sort of weapon, he grabbed the closest enemy by the front of his tabard. Lifted him off his feet, high up into the air. Allowed himself a moment to savor the look of utter terror on the man's face. Took a hold of an arm with his other hand and gave it a yank. It came of with a wet, sucking sound. Nudd used the arm to batter another man in the face, the power of the blow such that the arm came apart and the other fellow didn't have much of a face left afterwards. Shifting his grip, he ripped the man he was holding in two at the waist and threw the parts after his mates, who by now had turned and were running for their lives as if death itself were after them. Which was pretty much the case. Nudd caught up easily.

Look at me now, you no-good, double-dealing gods! See what I've become? Would you like to come down and try me? No? Didn't think so. All high and mighty as long as you can badger a helpless man from afar, but when he's not so helpless anymore, turns out you're just a bunch of overblown, pissant cowards. And oh, Master Brychan! Are you and your no-good slut of a daughter ever in for a surprise. Soon as I'm done here, I'll be coming your way.

Making his way into the heart of the fray, Nudd disassembled a few more enemy soldiers. But after the first, gratifying rush he soon lost the taste for this kind of work. Not that he minded killing the buggers. It was just so... messy. Disgusting, really, coming into touch with other people's assorted body fluids like that. Not his thing at all.

Scour was busy elsewhere for the moment, so he contented himself with batting aside the ones who got in his face, marching on without really knowing what he was supposed to be doing here. Until he noticed a disturbance on the far side of the enemy camp, something bad enough to stick out even in the midst of a full-fledged battle. Whatever it was seemed to be headed his way, driving fleeing men ahead of it like a bow wave of terrified, screaming flesh, the odd tent standing in its path going down in a welter of ripped canvas and flying accoutrements. Next, a man – or rather several parts of a man – came flying by in an arcing spray of blood and other stuff.

Nudd barely had time to wonder whether there was someone else like him fighting for the other side – which would have been very bad news indeed – before two huge, frickingly ugly beasts vaguely resembling hunchbacked dogs with spiky, mottled fur came hurtling towards him.

No time to run. No time to even think. Instead, he watched in surprise as his hands shot out and plucked both beasts out of the air in mid-bound. A shake, a twirl, a rip, and the ugly fuckers were writhing on the ground with their throats torn out.

I really am *invincible,* he thought as he stood watching the things die, oblivious to the fighting going on around him. The beasts

402

were the ugliest things he'd ever seen, and they stank to make the trees shed their leaves if they'd had any this time of year.

What happened next was weird, frightening, and totally unexpected. Clearly alarmed, Scour came rushing back.

It arrived just a fraction of a second too late to keep the two passengers who'd been riding the beasts from taking up residence in Nudd.

Scour had been vested by its makers with a degree of intelligence and autonomy that brought it close to sentience. But only close. It was still just an artifact, and as such should have been entirely immune to magic as well as demons. But more than ten thousand years of lying dormant in Arctic temperatures hadn't exactly enhanced its abilities.

And then there was the butterfly – the white one that had fluttered over Summerland's unseen boundary to alight on the back of Nudd's hand and perch there for a few moments before he swatted it away. Time enough to unfurl its proboscis and deposit a miniscule package, the contents of which proceeded to permeate his skin – or should one say, his outer shell – swiftly, quietly, and completely unnoticed even by Scour.

The reagent had been busy inside Nudd ever since, working an infinitely subtle form of sabotage on a level that wasn't part of Scour's memory and so remained outside its awareness. As it happened, it was the very same level on which magic operated. And it was here that the butterfly's payload quietly opened a few doors Scour's makers had never intended to be tampered with.

There was a short but violent battle between Scour and the stowaways. Clueless as to what was going on, Nudd suddenly found himself flat on the ground with no idea how he'd gotten there. Feeling as if a giant butter knife had descended from the heavens and smeared him across the trampled, muddy snow. Helpless, he lay there spasming, his body cratering and bulging as it was buffeted by the forces warring inside him. When it was over, the two demons were firmly if not comfortably ensconced in Nudd, though they yet had to wrest control from Scour.

And Scour was far from beaten, he was given to understand. It still had resources and, what with the changes wrought by the butterfly and the information gathered while fighting the demons, it now had a pretty good idea where to find more. In fact, it was already computing a course of action that would render it stronger and more resilient than ever before.

Jerking Nudd back onto his feet and setting him in motion, it headed north into Long Valley, leaving what it now regarded as the secondary battlefield behind. Blood would be spilled here with or without it, its four remaining lieutenants more than capable of creating a staggering amount of mayhem. Meanwhile, it had something more important to do – something to find, actually.

*   *   *

26

Catching sight of the sailor, Bryn instinctively understood two things. One: if he wanted to go on living, then now was the time to turn and run as fast and as far as his legs would carry him; and two: he wasn't going to.

This is what I'm here for, he realized. *This is why Cormac gave me Altingal. If I run now, everyone I care for is going to die. And I'll never get a chance to see Rhea again, never find out if that scary, wonderful feeling I keep getting when I'm around her is really what I think it is.*

He wasn't sure he could do this, but he had to at least try.

As if it were only the two of them there on the clearing, the sailor came straight for Bryn, ignoring the weapons raised against him by a few very brave or very foolish men. A spear pierced the black man's side. A sword cut at his back. He batted aside a man who stood directly in his path, taking another hit in the process. None of it seemed to have the slightest effect on him. None of it slowed him down.

Then he and Bryn stood facing each other.

No taunts were exchanged, no insults bandied, no threats made.

No words were needed.

Instead, Bryn chose and executed a form Owen used to jokingly call 'Shortening the Odds' and had recommended he use only for dicing vegetables. Dangerous or no, under the circumstances it seemed like the fitting choice. Feinting low and right and then stepping left, he whirled around in a tight circle and swung high, *Altingal* taking the sailor's head off with a single blow.

At least it should have done. Bryn had perfectly executed the form. He'd felt and seen the blade bite through the man's neck – though his steel had met less resistance than he'd expected. But then, *Altingal* had one hell of an edge. Any moment now, the man's head should part company with his body and come tumbling down.

Only it didn't. The fellow didn't even flinch. Instead, in one fluid move so lighting fast it made Bryn's attack look desperately sluggish, he plucked *Altingal* out of Bryn's grasp and swatted him away as if he were made of straw. Flying head over heels, Bryn saw the fat, grey trunk of an ancient, winter-bare beech rushing towards him and then, for a good long while, nothing.

When he opened his eyes some indefinite time later, he was looking down at himself. His body, lying motionless at the foot of the ancient tree, looked small and broken, like a toy soldier carelessly discarded by a boy who'd outgrown games of pretend.

He raised his gaze and, with the surreal logic of dreams, found himself instantly transported to another place. Someone was already there, waiting for him.

It would have taken neither the resplendent but centuries-out-dated attire nor the gold circlet on his brow to leave no doubt that the old man facing him was a king – or had been. His white beard wasn't nearly as long as the fairytales would have it, but it did reach almost to his gem-studded belt. Nor did Bryn need the lions rampant embroidered in gold all over the old man's deep-red cloak to tell him that this was his ancestor, Cormac Avellin, the mythical King Under the Mountain.

They were in some kind of arbor, Bryn saw, an airy, latticed affair fronting lush, paradisian gardens, the air sweet and heavy with the mingled scents of a thousand things blossoming. Despite the pleasant surroundings, Cormac didn't look happy.

'What happened, boy? What the blazes have you done?'

The old man's gaze had all the mildness of an executioner's axe, but Bryn wasn't about to be intimidated.

'It didn't work. Your fabulous sword didn't do what it was supposed to.'

'Oh, my.' Cormac suddenly looked crestfallen, all the sharpness fled from his iceblue stare. 'Oh, my,' he said again. 'I'm sorry, lad. I have to admit this is *very* disappointing. Not to say grievous. Puzzling, as well. Only thing I can think of is, whatever you were facing must have not been magic after all. Though I'll be damned if I can see what else it might have been. Are you sure? Maybe if you tried – '

'It's gone, Cormac. He took it from me. He took *Altingal*. And it looks like I'm done trying anything. Far as I can see, I'm dead – or so close as makes no difference. Look around. Doesn't it make you wonder why we're here in this place, and not in that dark old cave inside whatever mountain it is you usually spend your time under?'

407

'Oh, that.' Cormac waved Bryn's concerns away. 'Not to worry, my boy. You're not the reason we're here. I am. I've a feeling I've finally been allowed to move on, and I reckon this is some sort of halfway station on the road to wherever it is I'm headed. Which means nothing is lost, don't you see? There's still reason to hope, maybe now more than ever. Why else would they let me go, if not because this mess they've kept me waiting around for is about to be resolved? So take heart, lad. It's not over. And by the way: you're not dead. Take it from me, I should know. You're just out cold. In fact, I think you're about to wake up.'

*   *   *

Crouched low in the bed of an empty Dunmarkan supply wagon, Rhea watched the battle raging not fifty yards away. It had taken her well over an hour to get this far, time that had served her well. The state she'd been in after they dragged her out of the tunnel, she'd have probably never made it this far. She'd gone after Wystan with grief and rage threatening to tear her apart, more likely to get herself killed than catch up with the Black.

Moaning like a woman deranged, she'd stumbled along the dry creek bed leading away from the clearing until, blinded by tears, she nearly ran into a tree. A larch, soft, golden needles still clinging to branches spread wide as if offering sympathy and support. Leaning her forehead against the rough bark, she heaved a single, great sob, one that came from the very bottom of her soul, where the loss of the only two people aside from her grandda she'd allowed close to her heart in a very long time now lay alongside the death of her parents like something huge and heavy and unbearably painful.

It hurts, it hurts, it hurts, a small voice inside her wailed. *Please, dear gods, make it stop, make it go away.* She quickly quashed it.

Listen to you, whimpering like a whipped puppy. You're who I used to be, a very long time ago, a little girl who still had a ma and da. Me, I'm done trusting in the gods. All they ever did was take people away from me. But not anymore. From now on, I'm *going to be the one doing the taking. And I'm not letting anyone close anymore. Not ever again. Done, finished.*

A few moments still she remained leaning against the tree, battling with the grief. Then, forcing several deep, trembling breaths past the suffocating knot in her chest, she took the pain and made it into a sharp, angry edge – something she could use to make Wystan suffer until he begged her for the mercy of a swift ending. Then, forcing a few deep, trembling breaths past the suffocating knot in her chest, she took that pain and made it into a sharp edge – something she could use to make Wystan suffer until he begged her for the mercy of a swift ending.

So far, the Black had eluded her.

He had an hour's head start, and he obviously hadn't tarried along the way. But there was no doubt in her mind that he had come this way. It was the only thing that made sense. Apart from lobbing a few bursters at the Dunmarkans, he'd done more harm than good to Aeron's cause. And he'd killed Bryn, whom Edric had surely seen as even more of a threat than Aeron. His mission completed, there was only one place Wystan would go. Back to his master. Back to gods-bloody Edric. Where she intended to go, only there was a battle in her way: Nordsmen ten and more deep, and then gods only

409

knew how many Dunmarkan soldiers on the other side.

And there was another obstacle blocking her path, a short, black-haired man dressed in sealskins and furs, standing motionless behind the Nordsmen line and looking as out of place as a priest in a whore-house. Despite his looks and the fact that he seemed to be doing nothing besides watching the fight, the sight of him sent shivers down Rhea's spine. There was something hair-raisingly scary about the fellow, as if whatever twisted evil was driving the Nordsmen were concentrated in him like a rabidly contagious disease.

Twice, he'd looked her way, seeming to stare right at her. He couldn't have seen her, she reassured herself. She was well hidden and too far away to even make out his eyes. And yet she felt exposed, threatened, as if he not only knew exactly where she was but also who she was and what she was thinking. She tried to shake off the feeling, only to see something even worse coming her way: another man who looked like he belonged anywhere but here, wearing an Orrian sailor's garb and ordinary-looking as you liked – except for the fact that he was entirely black.

Here was the eye of the storm, the epicenter of evil, no doubt about it. Frozen with dread, she cowered behind the wagon's siding, everything in her screaming to run yet unable to avert her gaze as the black man strode purposefully straight for her hiding place.

Though she neither saw nor heard it, there must have been some sort of exchange between the two men. The short one suddenly uttered a piercing, ululating cry, whereupon at least a hundred Nordsmen abandoned the fight and turned to follow the black man, others moving up to fill in the gap.

She might have made a dash for it then, if not for the sailor

410

walking past her with impossibly long strides, so close she could have reached out and touched him, the men following him already breaking into a full-out run just to keep up. He was headed into Long Valley, she realized, and hoped it wasn't the last survivors from the Bent he was after.

If so, there was nothing she could do about it, no way she could warn them, not unless she suddenly grew wings. By the time he was gone, the Nordsmen ranks had closed again and it was too late to try and get through. So she settled down to more waiting while daylight slowly began to fade.

Some time later, it started to rain.

The battle showed no signs of letting up, or of going one way or the other. So far, the Dunmarkan soldiers' experience and better weapons made up for the Nordsmen's greater numbers – still. Though the Dunmarkans were resisting bravely, there was no way this could end well for them.

It was getting dark when she ran out of patience and decided to go looking for a better spot to cross the lines. She was about to slip off the wagon when suddenly the air was rent by a high-pitched, keening whistle, a terrifying sound like a thousand banshees screaming at once. Coming from somewhere the other side of the Dunmarkan camp, it was still loud and piercing enough to make her cry out in pain and clap her hands over her ears.

She saw the short man freeze as if he'd been struck by palsy or turned to stone. For long moments he stood there like a statue with the plinth pulled out from under it. Then he collapsed and lay motionless, a darkish lump blending in with the slush and wet earth

411

already churned into an ankle-deep morass by hundreds of tramp-
ling feet.

He'd barely hit the ground when the Nordsmen line began to
falter. Of a sudden they seemed unsure, bewildered, aimless, a
bunch of over-sized puppets whose strings had been cut. By the
looks of them, they'd just awakened into a nightmare, clueless as to
where they were and how they'd gotten here. Slowly, still fighting
but with their hearts clearly no longer in it, they began to fall back.
And Rhea saw her chance coming up.

Lying low, she let them get past her, and then the Dunmarkans
pursuing them. When the way was clear, she took one last look at
what lay before her, fixing the position of the large, striped tent
flying the Avellin lion in the center of the camp firmly in her mind.
Then she slipped down off the wagon and into the darkness that was
fast gathering among the long, orderly rows of Dunmarkan tents.

*   *   *

Never before had Anuun felt so utterly exhausted.
Storming down the road from Burnt Keep and out onto the battlefield with Wanderer riding piggyback, it was only sheer will that
kept his legs from giving out and sending the two of them down in a
sprawling heap.

It shouldn't have been like this. The old man was a lightweight,
little more than skin and bones. Besides, it hadn't been all that far
from Summerland to Balder's Field, at least not for someone used to
traveling the vastness of the Ice Wastes. Back home, Anuun could
have carried Wanderer from seaboard to seaboard and back again
and hardly felt the strain. He was an Iceling, for the gods' sake,

412

twice as strong as any human and with the stamina to match. But herein also lay the rub, he was beginning to suspect: he was too far and too long gone from his natural element, from the land that was as much a part of him as he was part of it. And from the ice. Gods, how he missed the ice!

These past few weeks, he'd seen enough tangled greenery to last him a lifetime, not to mention the fact that the southern climate was beginning to get to him. To the people living here it might have felt freezing cold this time of year; Anuun found it almost unbearably warm. Hopefully, all of this would be over soon. He needed to go home. Badly.

And then there were these crazy humans, thousands of them, hurting, maiming, and killing each other as if it were the most natural thing in the world, just another pastime to while away the day. Gods only knew what was wrong with them, to make them act this way.

Granted, there was the sailor and what he'd carried out of the Forbidden taking a hand in this horrible, senseless butchery. But Anuun strongly suspected that these people were perfectly capable of behaving like they did even without the additional incentive.

Not like the Snow People at all, he thought, suddenly feeling a deep affection for the hardy, snowbound people he'd spent so much of his time avoiding.

Coming up behind the Nordsmen ranks, he felt Wanderer's right hand let go of his shoulder. Getting ready to put his secret weapon to the test, Anuun assumed. With a clear purpose to keep him going, Wanderer had found some hidden reserves and rallied to a surprising extent, seeing as he'd been nearly dead when Anuun found him. But it was a respite, no more. Having been in such close contact with him these past few days, Anuun knew well enough that the old man was on his way out, that the task he'd set himself was the last, fragile thread connecting him to life. A long life, by human standards, though still pitifully short when measured against an Iceling's span.

Slowing down, Anuun spied a young man in Snow People garb on the battle's fringe not far away – directing the Nordsmen attack, it appeared. One of Wanderer's relatives, no doubt.

Wanderer had seen him as well. 'That's my grandson, Raven,' he said, waving the bone whistle he'd made in front of Anuun's face. 'You might want to put me down now. If this thing works like it's supposed to, you'll want both your hands free to cover your ears.'

'It's all right,' Anuun told him. 'Go ahead.'

The old man seemed to have momentarily forgotten that he didn't have the strength left to stand on his own. Meaning, Anuun would only have to prop him up. Meaning, he might as well stay where he was.

Moments later, when Wanderer went ahead and blew the Four Winds Whistle, Anuun wished he'd done as the old man had said. The sound was excruciating, a painful screech that seemed to drill straight into his brain as if someone were trying to shatter his teeth by way of shoving a couple of barbed awls down through his ears.

It worked, though, even if Anuun wasn't sure the effect was what Wanderer had intended. Raven collapsed like a rotten serac, gave a last twitch, and then lay still as death. Wanderer didn't seem

414

worried.

'Yes!' he shouted, waving the whistle with one hand and pounding Anuun's shoulder with the other. 'Bonk me a bear, but it worked!'

Maybe not so close to death after all, the old sticker. He was jiggling up and down like an excited child, forcing Anuun to lean hard forward to keep his passenger from falling off.

'Let's go check on Raven,' Wanderer said. 'And then we have to find the others.'

For the longest time after Anuun had gently set him down beside his grandson Raven, Wanderer just sat there, head bowed, eyes closed, praying, or perhaps just resting. Eventually he raised the whistle to his lips and blew a series of soft, staccato notes that sounded for all the world like someone saying, 'Wake up! Wake up!'

Anuun didn't see it working. To him, Raven looked like he was dead and gone, not the slightest movement of his chest betraying that he was still breathing. Sad, to see the old man's hopes so cruelly shattered.

His own legs finally giving out, Anuun sat down as well, heedless of the wet, muddy ground. Now that the chase was over, he was beyond exhausted, too tired even to pay much attention to the Nordsmen streaming by on either side, heading east towards Burnt Keep, away from Balder's Field. They looked dazed, disoriented, as if they'd just now realized they'd been fighting a battle instead of lying at home in bed, tossing and turning through a terrifying dream. Thankfully, all the fight seemed to have gone out of them. Had they decided to attack, Anuun wouldn't have known where to find the strength to protect Wanderer, Raven, and himself. All he wanted was to lie down and sleep. Couldn't, though. Not yet.

Of a sudden he saw Raven's eyelids flutter.

Wanderer lowered the whistle. Raven took a huge, gulping breath and opened his eyes. His expression was the same as the Nordsmen's: lost, confused, deeply shocked. But the eyes were a clear brown, not black like Wanderer had said they'd gone after the sailor had taken him and the others.

'Grandfather,' Raven said, still sounding like a dreamwalker. 'You're here.'

'Yes, Raven my boy, I'm here. And it's time to wake up. We need to go and find the rest of our family.'

'Rainbow?' Raven asked. 'Is she – '

'She's fine,' Wanderer said. 'Thanks to Anuun here, without whom we'd probably all be dead.'

Raven's eyes went wide when he became aware of Anuun's presence. 'Is he…'

'An Iceling, yes,' the old man said. 'Maybe now you'll understand why I always insisted you should treat his kind with the greatest respect.' He gave Anuun a wink. 'Not everyone would have come all this way just to save your lazy young behind. So, if you're all done resting, now would be a good time to get up and show him he hasn't gone to so much trouble for nothing.'

Raven struggled to his feet. Looked around in confusion. 'Where are we, Grandfather?'

'We're in the Southlands.'

'What… how did we…'

'Later, my boy. Right now, our loved ones need us.'

'Do you think they're still alive? Feather, Younger Sister, Strong-est-of-All?'

'You are,' Wanderer said. 'So why shouldn't they be? Don't worry, we'll find them. And then all of you are going home.'

'Will... he be going with us?' Raven cast a shy glance at Anuun.

'Not just yet,' Wanderer said, suddenly looking sad. 'Anuun and I still have something to take care of here.'

'But then you'll come?'

'Anuun will. I won't. My time is up, Raven. The ancestors are calling me. I have one more thing to see to, and then I'm done. The best I can hope for is that the gods will give me a few more days to see it through. My spirit will be coming home, but not my body.'

*   *   *

27

Nudd knew the sword was trouble the moment he laid eyes on it and realized that this was what Scour was after. It wasn't the young fellow holding it that had him worried. The bloke looked pretty grim and competent, but no way was he a match for Nudd. No, it was the bloody weapon that frightened him, the blade glowing in the near dark as if it were crawling with scores of fireflies. He'd never seen anything like it, and yet there was no doubt in his mind as to what he was looking at. Fricking magic.

'This is *not* a good idea,' he told Scour, who ignored him as usual.

Though he knew it was useless, he fought with every ounce of rebelliousness he could muster to keep his hands by his side, to turn around and walk away from this sure-fire disaster. Nothing doing. Scour wouldn't budge. Terrified, Nudd watched the young soldier raise the sword and feint and whirl, saw a quick flash of steel before the godsdamned blade bit right through his neck. Hell, did it bloody *hurt!* And godsdamned son-of-a-bitch Scour wouldn't even let him scream.

Helpless, he watched it use his right hand to reach out and

wrench the sword from the fellow's grasp, batting the man away with the other and sending him flying into a tree.

And then all hell broke loose.

Taking hold of the blasted sword was like grabbing a bolt of lightning. Suddenly the palm of his hand was sizzling, a blast of pure agony shooting up his arm and straight into his head where it nearly made his eyeballs pop out. A heartbeat later, Scour made him drop the damned thing. Not quick enough, though. The damage was done. The pain kept on coming, but it was nothing compared to the other stuff going on inside Nudd. Now, for the first time, he became aware of the passengers he was carrying, the shock almost blowing him off his feet. Gods-bloody, fricking demons! Two of them! It was like the gods-buggered sword had just woken them up, and now they were getting ready to do something unspeakably *horrible* to him! And fricking Scour was bloody well *losing* it, all its stupid little machines gone haywire because they'd been totally fucked up by the sword's magic.

Get your fricking shit together! Nudd silently yelled at Scour. *Do something!* You *got us into this mess. Now* you *get us the hell out of it. I* told *you this was a fricking stupid idea.*

But whatever working parts Scour still possessed were busy fighting the demons, who if Nudd wasn't mistaken were a hair's breadth away from taking over. Which left him to find his feet, shuffle them around, and persuade them to carry him, Scour, and the demons away from this accursed place. With everything else going on, Nudd hardly noticed the Nordsmen take off like they'd suddenly remembered they urgently needed to be somewhere else. Not his

420

fricking problem.

It was the demons going for each other that momentarily turned the tables. Not that it gave Nudd much of a respite. It felt as if a couple of screeching-mad tomcats were having it out inside him – only a hundred times worse. For a while there, he thought the damned things were going to rip him clean in two, the way they were tearing around in there. Staggering this way and that, throwing bulges like a bagful of pissed-off fire eels, he had a hell of a time just staying on his feet, never mind sticking to his course. After what seemed like ages, one of the fuckers finally gained the upper hand, gobbling up its rival like a fricking cannibal.

Bloody disgusting, but at least it's over, Nudd thought with an imaginary sigh. Only it wasn't. Just when he thought he could allow himself a breather, he was plunged headlong into the next horror.

Instead of two demons getting in each other's way, suddenly he was dealing with a single one that, having incorporated its companion, was now twice as strong. The first thing it did was turn on Scour, who as far as Nudd could see was still a limping wreck after the ill-fated encounter with the fricking sword. Compared to what happened next, the fight between the two demons had been a stroll in the meadows.

Never in his whole life had Nudd been so fricking terrified.

There was nothing he could do except bolt for the remotest corner of his mind and cower there among the dust and the cobwebs in abject dread, desperately hoping he wouldn't be noticed – not while the battle was raging, and hopefully not when it was over, either.

421

Not ever again, if at all possible.

The outcome, when it happened, was as unexpected as it was devastating – devastating for Nudd, that was.

The demon didn't win. Neither did Scour. Instead, what was left after the dust had settled was a double-headed monster the likes of which Nudd couldn't have come up with even in his worst nightmares.

Scour and the demon had merged into a single entity. Apparently, so had the machines and the magic. The result was something so utterly terrifying, merely suspecting that such a thing might exist somewhere far, far away would have kept Nudd awake nights for the rest of his life. And here he was, sitting right inside the damned beast – *and he couldn't even fricking run.* Going screaming mad seemed like a pretty desirable option right about now, but even that looked to be out of his reach. Making himself as small as possible, hardly daring to peek, he felt the body that was no longer his set itself in motion again. From now on, his first and only priority was to stay well out of sight, seeing as the pitifully small remainder of his original self was now nothing but a helpless prisoner, a passenger along for a ride he'd never have signed up for if he'd had any idea where this was going.

Some time later, he heard alarmed shouts, and then terrified screams. Curiosity getting the better of him, he risked a peek. They were in Long Valley, heading back towards Balder's Field. And there were the Nordsmen, hundreds upon hundreds of them, coming the other way. It took him a moment to understand what he was seeing: the buggers were hightailing it! Scour's whole, godsdamned army was fricking deserting!

Serves the bastard right, he thought, until he remembered that the old Scour was gone, and that from now on he'd better do his thinking real quiet-like. *If DemonScour catches me at it, things are not likely to go well for me. Best shut it down and get back to my hidey-hole.*

Against his better judgment, he kept watching. Saw Demon-Scour kill a few score deserters in passing, but not like it was seriously trying to stop them. No, it seemed to have some entirely different objective in mind, as became clear when it went through the Dunmarkan soldiers chasing the Nordsmen without so much as a hitch in its stride, merely tossing aside the ones that were unlucky enough to get in its way. With bodies flying left and right, Demon-Scour made straight for the center of camp, where a huge, red-and-yellow striped tent stood all by itself on a stretch of open ground.

The soldiers guarding the entrance made a brave show of pointing their spears at Nudd, though he would have bet the mailed-up pussies were shaking in their boots. Then they went the way of their comrades before them, only without any neighboring tents to cushion their fall. Next, Nudd was looking at the inside of the big tent, and at a stocky, barrel-chested man who he reckoned must be the fricking King of Dunmark.

Ugly fellow, Nudd thought. *Cold customer, too. Didn't even flinch when he saw us come in. Way I read him, he'd probably make a fricking great white look like your cuddly best playmate. Fuck does Scour want with this guy?*

The king – if that's what he was – didn't bother drawing his sword.

Instead, a look passed between him and DemonScour that made Nudd's skin crawl – figuratively, since currently his skin was no more his to command than the rest of him.

Well, fuck me crosswise, if this ain't a fricking meeting of kindred fricking spirits.

'So,' the king said, all easy like he'd been expecting them. 'Finally you show yourself. Have you come to offer your services to me, now that your army seems to have deserted you? If so, I have work aplenty for you, and all of it exactly the sort that appears to be your specialty.'

Instead of answering, DemonScour stepped right up to the fellow. Took him by the shoulders in what started out looking like a friendly embrace but quickly turned into something entirely different.

Ugh! Don't tell me DemonScour is actually kissing the bugger. And on the mouth, to boot. Like gods-bloody fricking faggots. Let me out of here! I don't want to see this.

The next moment, Nudd realized that what was happening was actually much, much worse. Worse even than if they'd started buggering each other right then and there. Far from it. Bloody Scour and the demon were pouring themselves into the fricking king. Leaving Nudd.

Bloody hell! They can't do this to me! Good riddance to the fricking demon, I say, but what's going to happen to me, once Scour is gone? I've got to stop this!

Giving up any further attempt at hiding, Nudd grabbed whatever parts of Scour he could still reach. Held on in desperation, a drowning man clinging to the only spar in sight. Watched in horror as piece after piece slipped through his fingers, DemonScour brushing him off like a pesky fly. Eyes squeezed shut, hanging on for dear life, for the first time ever Nudd found himself wishing he had someone or something he could pray to for help. He'd have laughed at the idea if he hadn't been so godsdamned busy.

Then Scour and the demon were gone, and Nudd was left clutching a double handful of Scour's stupid little machines, none of which seemed to be working properly anymore. Dumb with shock, he stared at the king. Who looked completely calm, as if he'd just downed a cup of tea instead of the worst pair of monsters that had likely ever walked the earth. The only thing different were the man's eyes: where before they'd been merely dark, now they were entirely black. Black as the devil's arsehole on a moonless night.

As if nothing had happened, he threw a cloak over his shoulders and strode out of the tent without sparing Nudd so much as a glance.

*   *   *

Gasping for air like a man surfacing from deep water, Bryn came to. 'Easy now, lad. Give it a moment before you try to move.' Gradually, the pale, blurry oval hovering over him resolved into the face of someone he thought he should recognize. Eventually it came to him: Makin, the healer who'd taken care of Laurin.

'What happened?' Bryn asked, pain beginning to seep into his awareness, together with the realization that it was dark and drizzling. A fire burned close by; he could feel the warmth of it, hear the occasional larger drops sizzle as they landed on the embers. His whole front hurt as if he'd run into a brick wall. His face seemed to have gotten the worst of it. Felt like someone had split it with an axe.

'You took wing, flew smack into a tree,' Makin said. 'Though I'd wager no bird ever made such a messy landing. You're a lucky sod. Only thing that seems to be broken is your nose, and that'll heal in time. It's already set. Thought I'd spare you the experience and do it while you were still out cold.'

'Thanks,' Bryn said, sounding like he had a bad cold.

'Your grace!' the healer called out, rising to make room. 'Patient's awake.'

Bryn was momentarily confused to see Iefan squat down beside him. Hearing Makin say 'your grace', he'd expected it to be old Eilian. Then he remembered: Eilian was dead, making Iefan head of House Strong.

'Bryn. Good to have you back.' Iefan looked like he'd aged ten years since this morning. They probably all did.

'Iefan. What happened? How come we're still alive?'

'They're gone. Turned around and left almost as soon as they got here. The moment that black monster had your sword, he turned around and walked back the way he'd come, and the Nordsmen with him. Gods be thanked, we didn't lose a single man.'

Altingal! In the hands of the enemy! Bryn reared up, the sudden movement sending pain slicing through his face, fierce enough to make his eyes water.

'The sword,' he said. 'I have to get it back. He can't be allowed to keep it.'

'Steady, my friend. He doesn't have it. It's right here.'

Following Iefan's nod, Bryn saw Laurin sitting nearby. The

426

dwarf had *Altingal* across his lap and was doing something with the hilt. He gave Bryn a weary grin. 'Almost done. There was some sort of black goo smeared all over the hilt, so I'm re-wrapping it. Didn't reckon you'd want to touch that stuff. Probably not healthy.'

'What... how...'

'Black bastard got all of twenty paces with your sword,' Iefan said. 'Then he dropped it like a hot stone. Looked as if your trusty blade didn't agree with him at all. He seemed a bit unsteady on his feet after that, but he just kept on going like he suddenly couldn't get out of there fast enough.' Iefan gave Bryn a curious look. 'Strange thing, that, wouldn't you say?'

'Strange, yes.' Bryn didn't elaborate, because suddenly he remembered the most important thing of all, fear and worry catching up with him in a hot rush. 'Rhea. Has she come back?'

Iefan shook his head. 'I'm sorry, lad. But we're ready to go look for her, soon as it gets light. Shouldn't be long now. Provided you're up to it, that is.'

'I *am* up to it,' Bryn said, shocked at how much time had passed since he'd been knocked unconscious. Anything could have happened to her in the meantime, and damned if he was going to wait until morning. Wincing, he struggled to his feet, his whole body feeling like one big bruise. Might have cracked a rib or two. Wasn't going to let that stop him, though.

They navigated the gorge in darkness, afraid the lanterns would give them away. They needn't have worried. Arriving on the edge of Long Valley in the first, grey light of dawn, they found it deserted. It wasn't until they were close to the valley's end that they came upon the first Nordsmen: dark, furry humps strewn across the dirty snow like sleeping wolves or bears – only these weren't going to wake up ever again.

Out on Balder's Field, the ground was thick with bodies, Dunmarkans and Nordsmen thrown together in a welter of pale faces and outflung limbs, the dead seeming to reach out to each other with offerings of peace and consolation, brothers now, all their differences laid to rest by the Great Leveler.

Hunkered down alongside the dead, Bryn studied the Dunmarkan camp, unable to detect any sign of life. The place looked deserted. His apprehension redoubling, regretting every moment wasted, he fretted through the quarter-hour it took two of Iefan's men to do a quick-and-dirty reconnoiter.

'Nothin', yer grace,' they reported back. 'Place is empty, far's can be said without checkin' every single tent. That's gonna take a while, though, seein' as there's at least a couple hundred of 'em.'

'Don't bother,' Bryn said, informed by a cold, dread certainty. 'She's not here.'

To his surprise, Iefan agreed. 'Aye. But we're still not going to rush in there. I'm not doing Edric the favor of blundering into another one of his sly traps. I want – '

'Hist!' A warning from the rearguard. 'Someone comin'.'

Turning, Bryn saw a group of maybe fifty men making their way down the Barrow's steep eastern slope. Another eight were coming down the Bent.

'Gods help me, they're ours,' Iefan said. 'That's Owain Cullan. No mistaking that ugly pot of a helm. And the other ones…'

'Ham,' Bryn said. Immensely gladdened by the sight of the butcher's stocky figure, he rose along with Iefan and Flatside and went to meet the newcomers. 'And Catch. They made it.'

'Ham,' Bryn said, clasping the man's hand in both of his, unashamed of the wetness in his eyes. 'Gods, but it's good to see you.'

'An' you, m'lord. Wouldn'a never dared go back home an' face the music if I'd lost yer.'

'Me neither,' Bryn said, knowing full well whom Ham meant by 'the music'. Facing Nan and telling her Arlie and Bowen were dead was going to be hard enough as it was.

'Tough little bugger, ain't you,' Flatside was saying to Catch, boxing him on the shoulder. 'An' here I was fixin' to get worried.'

'Pah,' Catch answered. 'Ain't lettin' a couple'a smelly Nordsmen spoil my day. Found us a nice little hidin' place on top o' that big old rock. Had us a smoke an' a chat while we waited for the stinkers to get bored an' leave.'

Owain and his men, it turned out, had barricaded themselves inside the tower after they'd been forced to abandon the curtain wall. It had been a close call even so, with the door broken down and the Nordsmen threatening to overrun the entrance by force of sheer numbers. And then, as on the Bent – as everywhere, it seemed – the attack had suddenly slacked off. Looking bewildered as if they'd just that moment come to their senses, the Nordsmen had retreated from both the Barrow and the Bent, turning north as soon as they hit the plains. Like sleepwalkers dumped out of a dream, Owain said, Ham and Catch nodding their agreement. Why they'd left was a mystery, but not one they'd solve by standing around talking. As far as Bryn was concerned, nothing had changed. Nothing mattered more than finding Rhea – and finding her fast, before some harm befell her that was beyond his or anyone else's ability to mend.

Turning back towards the Dunmarkan camp, he paused, a patch of brightness catching his eye. It was a figure in white: a woman, if he wasn't mistaken, though she was too far away to say for sure. Captivated, he stood watching for a moment. Saw her bend over, perhaps offering a dying man words of consolation. But no – now she was reaching out a hand, helping someone to their feet. Not a man dying, then. More likely a soldier wounded in battle, in all likelihood not too severely, else he wouldn't have risen so easily.

The fellow didn't stay on his feet for long, though. Surprised, Bryn watched him take a knee before the woman, even bending down to kiss the hem of her dress as if she were a queen or a holy person.

Of a sudden he felt the weirdest urge to do the same, to go over there and give himself up into the care of this strange woman from whom an offer of peace and succor seemed to emanate like a warm summer breeze carrying a promise of better things to come. As if he only needed to ask and she'd take away his pain, fix everything that was wrong with him.

There was no telling what might have come of such an encounter, had he given in to the impulse. But his course was set, and nothing, not even the promise of salvation, had the power to turn him from the call of duty.

In the aftermath of the Battle of Three, as it came to be called, wondrous tales would arise: tales of men grievously wounded, visited in what they'd believed to be their last moments by an apparition in white. To some she came as a young girl, to others as a woman in her prime, to others still as a crone, but all of them – and there were hundreds – agreed that she'd turned them away from death's doorstep and left them healed and whole of body and mind. It was doubtless a miracle, though the dead did stay dead, perhaps because raising them was beyond even her. But not a one who still had a breath in him was left to suffer and die, or so the men swore – Dunmarkans, Ardathians, and Nordsmen alike. And when all of them left the field and went their separate ways, they did so with no wish whatsoever to cause their erstwhile enemies further harm.

And so it was that the Battle of Three gave rise to a new deity, a protectress of warriors revered and worshiped by the soldiers of several disparate nations. Rendle, they called her, Rendle the White, for that was surely who she was: the only one of Elil's First Children believed to still reside among men.

The Dunmarkan camp gave every appearance of being deserted. Which didn't mean there were no surprises. Less than thirty paces in, they were assaulted by a stench so breath-takingly rank it had them gagging and breathing into their cupped hands like novices at a tanner's yard. The stink came from a pair of huge, hideously ugly cadavers lying a few steps off the lane atop the torn and bloodied canvas of a ruined tent as if they'd been flung there by a giant hand. The same hand must have torn their throats out. Still Bryn found himself clutching *Altingal* with whitened knuckles. Even dead, the beasts were by far the most terrifying thing he'd ever seen, the stuff of a madman's screaming nightmares. As was the swath of destruction they'd left behind, a blood-spattered trail of flattened tents and dismembered bodies that cut through the camp from the southeast and ended where they lay.

'Gods!' someone breathed behind him – Flatside, he thought. 'Now there's a sight to rob a man of his sleep for good an' all.'

'And a stink to ruin his appetite forever,' Catch said. 'Though I did come across this whore over in Landing once who – '

'Stow it, Catch,' Flatside said. 'This ain't no time for dirty jokes.'

'This is what killed Bowen,' Bryn said, the sudden realization as sickening as it was undeniable. No man deserved to die from something like this. Least of all Bowen.

'Aye,' Iefan agreed. 'I'd wager it was. Curse the man who'd stoop to using such monsters to do his dirty work.'

'And thank the gods they're dead,' Trant added, though Bryn thought he sounded more disappointed than relieved, as if he wouldn't have minded taking these abominations on himself. Better this way, though. It seemed highly unlikely that even a mountain of a man like Trant would have stood a chance of surviving the ordeal. Which begged the question who or what had killed them. But now wasn't the time. He had to find Rhea, not stand here trying to figure out the how and why of things that had already happened. Find Rhea, and then kill Edric.

With the rain falling steadily now, they headed farther into the Dunmarkan camp.

*   *   *

28

Macsen was devastated. And furious.

Not long after the Nordsmen's unlikely retreat, Edric had shown up under a flag of parley and with Stonebridge, Pryce, and fifty men-at-arms in tow. To announce that he was leaving, and would the Colors kindly make way for him and his army. Seeing him again made Macsen's flesh crawl. Something about the man was different than he remembered. Darker, if that was even possible. In the flickering torch-light, he couldn't say what exactly it was that had his hackles raised, but one thing was for sure: whatever the change, it definitely hadn't been for the better.

To emphasize his demand, Edric had Merys and her children brought forward so everyone could see them. Physically, they seemed unharmed, as far as Macsen could tell. But the queen had that dull-eyed, broken look of someone who'd given up on hope entirely, and the bairns weren't far behind. Edric had many ways of destroying people.

'We can do this two ways,' Edric told Torvald, who was speaking for the Colors. 'You either get out of my way, and these good people get to live another day. Or you make things difficult for me, in which case they die and I leave all the same. Your choice. But you should know that, either way, you haven't a hope in hell of stopping me. So what will it be?'

'Staying true to form, are we?' Torvald didn't bother to hide his contempt. 'What's to say you won't kill them anyway, once we've let you pass?'

'Nothing.' Edric gave a nasty smile devoid of any trace of humor. 'Or would you perhaps like my word on it?'

'I think not.' Torvald looked like he was chewing on something vile. 'But rest assured we'll be coming after you, if just to see that nothing happens to them. Anything does, you have *my* word that I'll personally cut you open and feed your guts to the hogs. Have I made myself clear?'

'Big words, Tondern,' Edric sneered. 'Pity they're so much bigger than the man using them. Oh, and I almost forgot: you're welcome to tag along, but you'll be giving me a head start. Twenty-four hours. I'm leaving some men behind who will make sure you don't cheat. You won't see them, but they *will* be there, and they'll be watching you closely. Any premature move on your part, I'll know about it posthaste. With unpleasant consequences for her majesty and the younglings. And another thing: just in case it turns out they're less dear to you than I thought, here's something else to help keep you in line. Pryce, have the prisoner brought forward.'

Pryce gave a languid wave, looking as if he'd never been so bored in his life. Shortly, two of his Headhunters dragged a slender, hooded figure into the light. A woman, wearing the same black leathers her gaolers did. Gripped by a terrible premonition, his guts suddenly

434

shrunken to a painful knot, Macsen waited for the hood to come off.

When he saw who it was, he nearly lost it. Did lose it, actually, for a moment there. If Kildown and Varna hadn't held him back, he'd have killed Edric on the spot – or at least tried to, and damn the consequences. The bloody fiend had his little girl. Edric had Rhea. She looked a mess, her face all bruised and bloody, one eye swollen shut.

'Recognize her, do you? Edric said, looking at Macsen for the first time, who found himself staring into twin black voids colder than the empty spaces between the stars. 'I'd say that this is what you get for being a craven and a traitor, except she brought this down on herself without any help from you. Chip off the old block, isn't she? Rotten through and through, just like you.'

Macsen was too shocked and angry for words. Torvald threw him a questioning glance.

'She's my granddaughter, your grace,' Macsen told him. 'Only family I've got left.'

The hard lines around Torvald's mouth went harder still as he turned back to Edric. 'There really is no bottom to you, is there? Very well. Go. And may the gods have mercy on you, because I surely won't.'

Turning on his heel, Torvald strode away, pulling Macsen along with him. 'We'll get her back,' he said. 'I'll see her and the others out of this alive and hale, if it's the last thing I do. But you have to promise me you'll wait with the rest of us, not go haring off on your own.'

'I will, your grace,' Macsen said, though he wasn't sure it was a promise he'd be able to keep.

They say Amut's Realm of Shades has a special place reserved for people like Edric. It's called hell, and it's supposed to be the coldest spot in all the realms, so cold it makes the Ice Wastes feel like blooming meadows in comparison. That's where I'm going to put the bastard, if it's the last thing I do. Though given his disposition, I wonder if I won't be doing him a favor.

Two hours later, Edric and his surviving men were gone. Macsen tried to catch a glimpse of Rhea as the Dunmarkans marched through the gap the Colors had made for them, the road lined by a double row of torch-bearing men-at-arms and a company of archers, just in case Edric had something nasty up his sleeve. But either he missed her, or they'd stuck her in one of the wagons or the coach with the Ardathian royals – in any case he saw neither hide nor hair of her. Which did nothing to lessen his fear for her.

The remainder of the night carried a sense of heaviness, an intangible burden of loss and defeat. When dawn finally came, it revealed a muddy field littered with the remains of wrecked tents and dead bodies where Sleazetown had been. Beyond it, most of the Dunmarkan camp was still standing. Edric must have lost a lot of men over on his western flank, seeing as at least half of the tents had been left behind, including his own, striped monstrosity.

Daybreak also brought visitors. Standing alone on the western edge of camp, Macsen watched the crows arrive: first in ones and twos, then by the murder, and eventually in numbers like you only ever saw in the field after a bloody battle. This one had been plenty bloody, no doubt about it.

Next, a rag-tag band made up of a few soldiers, a wagoner, and what looked like leftover camp followers came trudging out of the Dunmarken camp, four of them laboring under a makeshift litter cobbled together out of tent poles and a chair. It was Gale they were carrying, Macsen saw as they drew close. The Lord Treasurer looked as if he'd had a very bad night. Draped in a blanket, he appeared drawn and deathly pale, obviously in some serious pain. And yet he managed a smile for Macsen.

'Time for a breather, lads,' he told his bearers. 'I think I'll have a word with Sergeant Redbreast here before we move on.'

As they set him down gently, the blanket shifted, revealing a leg that was splinted and heavily bandaged from mid-calf to mid-thigh.

'Sergeant. Good to see you alive and well.' Gale's brow was lined with beads of sweat.

'And you, my lord. Though I can't say you look all that well.'

'Long story, that.' Gale winced as he tried to find a better position for his injured leg. 'So, Edric's gone, I take it. I'm assuming he used the queen and her little ones to blackmail the Colors into letting him go.'

'And my granddaughter, my lord. I don't know how he did it, but he's got her as well.'

'Oh.' Gale looked genuinely stricken. 'I'm so very sorry, Macsen. I met her again up on the Bent. Even had time for a chat, seeing as Aeron kept me waiting. She's a good girl, if a bit headstrong. Well then, we'll have to do our very best to get her back, won't we? I'm surprised you lot haven't gone after Edric already.'

'We can't. He made giving him a day's head start part of the deal. Said he'd kill them all if we didn't abide by it. Has people watching us to make sure we stay put.'

437

'Ah, the underhanded bastard! Knowing him, there's probably nobody out there, but he's got you in a fix all the same. Damn him and his backstabbing schemes. Why luck should lower itself to favoring such a monster, I'll never understand. Speaking of which – have you any idea what made the Nordsmen suddenly up and run?'

'None, my lord. Only thing I know is, there was this strange sound last night, like somebody blowing the biggest, meanest whistle the world's ever heard. Shrill as all hell. Busted more than a few eardrums, I'd wager. That was pretty much around the time the smelly buggers gave up and legged it, though whether the one had anything to do with the other, I couldn't say.'

'Ah. Yes, I heard it too. Quite impressive, and something of a riddle. Well. I suppose I should go have a word with Torvald and the other two, see where we go from here. Care to join me?'

'In a moment, my lord. You go on ahead, and I'll catch up with you. Just need a couple more moments.'

Why do I still not trust the man? Macsen thought when Gale had left. *Back when I mentioned Rhea, I swear he looked more than just sorry, he looked... guilty. Take me for a fool, but I'd bet my left nut there's something he could have told me and didn't. Something important.*

Macsen was about to follow Gale when there was fresh movement out on the field. The two people coming towards him surely made for the strangest pair he'd ever seen. One was squat and looked powerful enough to break a tree trunk over his knee. He also looked kind of... silvery, like he'd been dipped in hoarfrost or in very fine, powdery snow. The other one, riding on the squat one's back, was dressed in furs and sealskins. White-haired and frail, his face a mess of wrinkles deep enough to break a leg in, he looked older by far than anyone had a right to be. It was when Macsen noticed the bone whistle the old man was clutching in one hand that he had a first inkling of who he might be dealing with.

'Greetings, good sir,' the squat one said, stopping in front of Macsen. 'I am Anuun, and this is Wanderer of the Seal clan. We were wondering if you might have seen a man dressed like an Orrian sailor – '

'Sorry to interrupt,' Macsen said. 'But you'd best move along smartly. Looks like things might turn unpleasant here in a moment. Go on into camp and ask for his grace, Lord Tondern. He'll see you right, if anyone can.'

The fellow called himself Anuun nodded and did as asked. In passing, the old man gave Macsen a radiant smile that made him think there was still some good in the world after all. Not a likely threat, these two, but the men coming out of Edric's camp might well be. There were well over a hundred of them, he reckoned.

'Look sharp, there!' he cautioned the sentries nearby. 'We've got company coming.'

Not a threat after all, it turned out.

Friends. Ardathians. When he saw how few of them were left, Macsen's heart went out to them, and he gave them the warmest welcome he could manage under the circumstances. Recognized Master Laurin, who clasped his hand and told him how sorry he was about Rhea. And that was before Macsen told him Edric had her. Lest they both get weepy, he clapped the little man on the back and sent him

439

on with the others. Ordered the closest sentry to take them in to see the Colors. Stayed behind to give the field one more sweeping check, then he turned and followed them. Couldn't say how, but he knew without a doubt that no one else was going to show up. This was it.

There would be a lot of things to talk about during the coming day. Problems to sort out, agreements to reach, plans to lay. Then, when all that needed saying and doing was said and done, Macsen and whoever else was going after Edric would move out. An hour before midnight, Edric's period of grace would be over. Less than fifteen hours to go.

*   *   *

Sitting down to a war council with Iefan, Owain, Gale, Macsen, and the Colors, Bryn was prepared for a long day, and at first it looked as if that was exactly how it was going to turn out. Everyone was in a bind of some sort, with no easy way out. Listening to Iefan spell out Ardath's dilemma, Bryn reckoned their chances of resolving this whole mess were bad going on worse. If they even had a chance at all.

'On Ardath's part,' Iefan began, 'we have two urgent matters to address, and a hundred and fifty men to do it with, where ten times as many would still be too few. We have to rescue our royal family, but we also have Ensel of Harad and around a thousand of Edric's men running loose in western Ardath.'

'The Colors are willing to lend you a hand,' Torvald said. 'But we also have Edric to deal with. Meaning, as much as we'd like to give you everything we've got, we can't. We have sixteen hundred

440

men under arms, and could probably double that number if we had the time for another muster. Which we don't. And even if we did, it would still leave us about seven thousand short, if we were to have any hope at all of prying Edric out of Kingskeep.'

'My lords.' Gale had kept mostly quiet until now. 'If I may, I'd like to make a few remarks concerning both Ardath's and Dunmark's situation. Firstly, it's winter, and even if we had the manpower, to my knowledge Kingskeep Castle has never been taken by force. So I think we can all agree that a siege is out of the question.'

That got him nods all around.

'And secondly, though freeing the hostages in a timely fashion is paramount, we mustn't lose sight of our other, equally important objective. Which is to remove Edric from the throne and put his highness here on it. As I see it, whoever has the castle has Kingskeep, and whoever has Kingskeep has Dunmark. Meaning, it's a race between us and Edric. If he gets there first, we've as good as lost.'

More nods. Bryn thought he was beginning to see where Gale was headed.

'As far as I can tell,' the Lord Treasurer continued, 'our only chance lies in stealth and speed. Overtake Edric and his army, sneak into Kingskeep, and secure the castle before he gets there. A task for which a small force is much better suited, in my opinion. I'd say fifty men, no more. Which brings us to Ardath's plight. If I'm not mistaken, sending fifty men to Kingskeep would leave you lords of the North with over fifteen hundred you could let Iefan Strong borrow for a time.'

'Sounds good,' Iefan said. 'Except it won't be me going to

relieve Cullamor, it will be Owain. And I reckon he'll be able to find more help along the way. The muster Aeron held was by no means comprehensive. Given the situation, I believe the men of Ardath will be more than happy to come to the defense of the realm. As for myself, I'm going to Kingskeep with Bryn.'

'As am I,' Torvald said. 'I think Gair and Bhorric here will do a very fine job helping Owain kick Ensel out of Cullamor without me getting in their way.'

'Aye,' Bhorric growled. 'Kick the bastard so hard he flies right past Harad.'

'I'd expect no less of you, Bhorric,' Torvald chuckled. 'I won't be joining Bryn, though. And instead of fifty I'm taking three hundred men – sorry, Owain. We're going to catch up with Edric and stick to his heels like fleas to a dog. Firstly because that should keep Edric's attention focused on me, and hopefully make it easier for Bryn and Iefan to slip by him. And secondly, I'm sure none of you will disagree with me when I say that we're all dancing on the knife's edge here. So having some backup at Kingskeep in case it's needed seems like a pretty good idea to me.'

'Very astute, your grace,' Gale said. 'Sound tactical reasoning. Wish I'd thought of it myself. So who's going with Bryn and Iefan, then?'

'I am,' Macsen said, his expression daring anyone to contradict him. Nobody did.

'I'll take Daven and Ham, if they'll come,' Bryn said. 'I'm sending Little Tom home to Bailon with news. Mostly bad news, but it's time they heard. And he might be able to rustle up some more Bailon men for Owain. Oh, and I reckon Laurin will want to come too.'

'Catch and Flatside will be accompanying me,' Iefan said.

'Seven,' Torvald said. 'Sounds like a good number.'

Bryn saw the Lord Treasurer shake his head.

'A good number indeed,' Gale said. 'And yet, I'd like to suggest adding another two to your party.' He looked at Bryn. 'Because, highness – '

'Bryn will do,' Bryn grumbled. Being called 'highness' made him uncomfortable. Just didn't feel right. Not when the whole idea of becoming king still seemed like hardly more than a pipe dream. Not while Edric was still alive.

'All right, then. Bryn.' Gale's smile reminded Bryn of an indulgent uncle. 'I reckon we'll all be calling you "your majesty" soon enough. As I was about to say, we haven't addressed one important aspect of this venture yet, namely how you'll get into the city, and from there into the keep. Unfortunately, Edric's not stupid. I'm willing to bet my other kneecap that he's thought of this possibility and will send someone on ahead to alert the gate guards, make sure they keep an eye out for you. So you'll need someone who knows how to get around the guards. Hart and Mullin are two of my best, and they know more ways in and out of Kingskeep than all the city's rats and pigeons put together. I'd rest much easier if I knew you had those two along.'

Bryn gave it some thought. Of course Gale was right – none of them except Macsen had even been to Kingskeep, and he'd been responsible for guarding the king, not the city walls. But how far were Gale and his men to be trusted? In Bryn's eyes, Gale still had a whole lot of explaining to do, only now was neither the time nor the place.

'All right,' he finally said. 'I'll take them. There's one more thing, though. You've all met our friends from the far north.' He nodded towards Anuun and Wanderer. They'd been sitting quietly ever since the council began, the Iceling obviously uncomfortable and trying hard not to fidget, the old man seeming to have fallen asleep.

'And you've all heard their amazing story, which has shed a very different light on recent events. I guess what I'm getting at is this: over everything that's going on here, we shouldn't forget that we're not just faced with Edric and a bunch of armed men. Like it or not, we're also dealing with magic.'

He noticed miens darken all around at the mention of magic. Only Wanderer looked unperturbed, even gave him a smile. As for the others, it was not a subject anyone liked to discuss. But there was no helping it. It needed to be addressed. So he forged on.

'That sailor Wanderer and Anuun told us about. He's still out there somewhere. In fact, he was last seen heading into Edric's camp. Gods know in what ways Edric would use such a man, should he find him. Not to forget Wystan, who's gone missing as well.'

'We hear you,' Torvald said. 'But I'm afraid there's not much we can do about either of them, seeing as none of us are mages. The best we can hope for is that those two have well and truly gotten lost. If Edric has them – well, I'd rather not think about it.'

Briefly, Bryn considered telling them about *Altingal* but thought better of it. If he and the sword performed anything like they'd done

444

back there in the hills, he'd only be setting himself up for a fool. Not to mention giving them false hope and a promise he was in no way sure he could fulfill. To his surprise, Wanderer spoke up.

'I think Anuun might be able to help with that, honored sirs,' he said. 'The Four Winds Whistle seems to have worked quite well, though sadly not against the sailor. Therefore, Anuun will endeavor to dream the Spirit Spear tonight. If he is successful, the dream will give us another powerful weapon. In any case, he will also accompany you to Kingskeep.'

The old man's announcement was met with polite nods, no more. Probably because no one had any idea what a Spirit Spear was, only that it sounded suspiciously like magic. Anuun's presence alone was enough to have them all on edge. An honest-to-gods Iceling, a myth come to life in their midst. It was already far more magic than they cared for. Given that, they were handling the situation quite well, Bryn thought. He didn't comment on the spear either, but he did notice Wanderer looking at *Altingal* and then raising his eyes to give Bryn a meaningful stare. And another smile.

Thinking of the coming night and of the hours that still lay ahead until Edric's deadline expired, Bryn came to a sudden decision.

'Anuun is welcome to join us,' he told the old man. 'But he'll have to do his dreaming on the road. I intend to leave as soon as we're done here.'

'What if Edric does have watchers out there?' Iefan asked. 'Are you willing to take that risk?'

'No,' Bryn said. 'But I know how we can outsmart them. This is what we'll do: they're going to see two small groups of men, one in

445

the north and one on the south, riding along the edge of Balder's Field at an easy pace, checking the perimeter. An entirely natural precaution under the circumstances, and nothing to worry about, seeing as everybody else will be staying put. We pace ourselves so we meet up at the road, and then we make a dash for it. By the time they realize what's happening, we'll already be past them. Then *they* will have to get past *us* if they want to reach Edric.'

'Oh, that's clever.' Torvald grinned. 'They won't be able get around you because there's no other way but the road. First chance they might give you the slip is a trail branches off fifteen miles past Burnt Keep, and by then Edric's twenty-four hours should be up in any case. I'm for it.'

'All right, then,' Iefan said. 'Anuun, have you ever ridden a horse?'

'No, I haven't.' The Iceling looked alarmed. 'But I am a fast runner. I believe I will be able to keep up, unless you intend to gallop all the way to Kingskeep.'

'No.' Iefan smiled. 'Only until we're past the watchers, if there even are any. Half a mile at most.'

'Then I would greatly prefer to use my feet,' Anuun said.

Through all of this, Rhea remained first and foremost on Bryn's mind. Rhea, and Edric. One to save, one to kill. Right now, he didn't give a quarter copper for his father's legacy or Gale and the Colors' plans to put him on Dunmark's throne – not until he found Rhea and made sure she was safe and sound. And until Edric was dead. He did realize this wasn't exactly kingly thinking he was indulging in, putting the welfare of a single person he cared about –

cared very much about, if he was honest – before the welfare of the kingdom.

But then, if you couldn't keep one person safe, how were you going to look out for thousands? Besides, as far as he was concerned Dunmark wasn't really his problem yet – not until he was actually king, and that was still a long way off. If it ever happened. If he even *wanted* it to happen. Wasn't sure he did. Sure about Rhea, though. A little frightening, that. From what he'd seen, she was pretty good at rejecting people, even the ones who had saved her life.

An hour later, they set out.

Leaving Balder's Field, they saw no trace of any watchers. Halfway to Burnt Keep, they crested a rise from where they could see several miles of the road behind them. It didn't look as if anyone were following them, but Bryn saw a pall of dark smoke hanging over the distant hills. Pyres. They'd started burning the dead back there. A task he didn't envy them, though he doubted any of them would have been overly keen to exchange places with him.

*   *   *

The war council was over.

Everyone except Anuun had departed to see to their various tasks. Wanderer was very, very tired, but in a good way. His job was done, and now he was allowed to be as tired as he wanted. Only one more thing to do.

He took out the Spirit Spear and handed it to Anuun, the beautifully worked obsidian spearpoint's edges gleaming against the soft leather wrapping with a sharpness even the finest steel couldn't match.

'Here. You'll need to make a shaft for it, something light and strong. Ash would be good, if you can find any. But don't join the haft to the point until you've dreamed it.'

'What if I fail?' The Iceling looked worried.

Wanderer wasn't. Not anymore. It was other people's turn to worry now. 'You won't,' he said, sure as he'd ever been of anthing. 'Already the Spirits are gathering around you, both Iceling and Snow, and more of them than I've ever seen in one place. They will guide you, and give you the strength you need to dream the Spear and then to use it.'

'I will do my best,' Anuun said, 'and hope that it's enough. But what will become of you, my friend? I am not at all happy to leave you behind. Your kin are gone. Soon everyone else will depart this place as well. Will you go on to Cullamor with the Colors, or do you intend to stay here all alone?'

'I'm staying, but not alone. Rainbow, my wife, is coming to fetch me. Already I can feel her, just a small step away. So go, my friend, and godspeed. I will be in good hands. As a matter of fact, I'll just sit in this comfortable chair for a little while longer. I believe I could do with a nap.'

When Anuun had left, Wanderer closed his eyes, only for a moment. And there she was: Rainbow, looking exactly the way she had on that long-ago day when they'd spoken the words and joined their lives together for better or worse. Looking back, there had been a lot of better, and very little worse.

Now, feeling her small, strong hand in his, it seemed like they'd never really been parted, as if the past sixteen years had been but a dream. Perhaps because that was what life was: a long and sometimes arduous dream that ended not in death but in awakening.

Very distantly, he felt the part of himself that had completed its service and was no longer needed exhale a last, soft breath. Then, filled to overflowing with a wondrous sensation far beyond anything words could describe, he stepped with Rainbow over onto the other side.

* * *

29

There was one good thing to be said about Rhea's current situation: she wasn't cold. Riding in the queen's coach with five other warm bodies and a wealth of furs and blankets saw to that. Otherwise, her prospects were looking pretty bleak.

You've got no one but yourself to blame, dimwit, she told herself. *Had to go and get yourself nabbed like a bloody beginner.*

Last night, she'd snuck undetected through half the Dunmarkan camp. Made it all the way to the last row of tents circling the open ground around Edric's fancy pavilion. Found Pryce and four of his Headhunters conferring outside it. Something about going back to Kingskeep.

Well, good luck with that, fellows, she thought, crouching in the shadows and slotting a bolt into her crossbow. *You seem to have forgotten there's still the Colors standing in your way.*

Pryce was less than twenty yards away, a range she felt confident she and the little bow could handle. Made to Headhunter specifications, it was a lot more accurate than the big, unwieldy weapons the soldiers used. A couple of torches burning outside Edric's tent gave her all the light she needed. Only problem was, she couldn't get a clear shot because one of the Headhunters was standing in front of Pryce, blocking her line of sight.

I need to get on the other side of this tent, find a better angle. And quick, before they're done talking and Pryce walks away.

She slipped in between the tents, careful to avoid the guy ropes. Rounding the far corner, she froze. One of Pryce's men had turned around and was walking towards her. Didn't look as if he'd spotted her, though.

Slowly, so as not to draw his attention, she hunkered down in the shadows, making herself as small as possible. To her horror, he kept right on coming, stepping in between the tents where she was hiding, already fumbling with his codpiece. Damn! This was obviously one stupid shit who was too lazy to go use the jakes. It looked like the arsehole was actually going to piss on her.

Problem was, she was wearing black leathers. Huddled up against light grey canvas. And there was still some snow on the ground. No other way it could have gone: he saw her.

'Hey! What the fuck – '

She shot him. Nothing else she could do. Just her bad luck that he came crashing down right on top of her. Struggling to get out from under him, she got tangled up in the damned guy ropes. And then the other three were all over her.

When they realized she'd killed their mate, things got ugly real quick. By the time Pryce stepped in, she was already hurting all over, and one of them had his dagger out, ready to start cutting pieces off her.

'Hold!' Pryce said. 'Bring her out into the light and let's see

452

what we've got here.'

So they dragged her out, getting in a few more punches along the way.

'Well, well,' Pryce drawled. 'Look who we have here. If it isn't Little Miss Redbreast. That makes two of my men you've killed, girl. Oh, yes, I have heard about poor Pace's untimely demise. Bloody boor, that fellow, so I can see how you might have wanted to kill him. It's what you're doing here that I can't figure out. If it were anyone else, I'd hand them over to my man Egan, have him tickle it out of you. He's really good at getting people to talk. But in your case, I think his majesty would be most disappointed if I passed you on before he got to have a word with you.

'Garth, Doil, load her in the coach with the royals. Just make sure she's properly restrained. I suggest you use shackles. She's a wildcat, this one. Oh, and no more beating her. You don't want to go spoiling his majesty's fun now, do you?'

Now here she was, shackled like a common criminal and sandwiched between the two Ardathian princes. Sitting across from her was Pryce's man Doil, flanked by the queen and her daughter. In one hand he held Rhea's crossbow, keeping it pointed more or less in her direction. The other was busy feeling up the queen under the blankets and furs. He'd started groping her not long after they left Balder's Field, as soon as the exhausted boys had fallen asleep. Rhea had been nodding off herself and only noticed what was going on because, when Doil first touched her, Merys jumped like she'd been stuck with a pin.

'How dare you!' she hissed, her plump, creamy cheeks going all

453

mottled.

Leaning over, Doil whispered in the queen's ear, loud enough for Rhea to overhear. '…not allowed to touch that one over there. But I could tend to your daughter, if that's what you prefer.'

Rhea saw the princess blanch and the courage drain out of Merys faster than the last few sips out of a ripped waterskin. Saw her put up some feeble resistance when Doil grabbed her hand under the blankets and started to force it towards his own crotch.

Rhea knew there would be a price to pay for what she was about to do. Too bad, but she'd had enough of this crap. It wasn't like she cared all that much for Her Sniffy, Better-than-thou Majesty. But *nobody* treated a woman like this in her presence and got away with it. Besides, Doil molesting Merys in front of her own kids – that she simply couldn't tolerate.

Unfortunately, being shackled and all, she wasn't in a position to kill the bloody arsehole. So she did the next best thing. Raised a foot and stomped him in the nuts, hard, giving it all she had.

The breath whooshing out of him in a single, agonized groan, he grabbed at his crotch and doubled over. Forgot all about the crossbow. Before Rhea could get to the weapon, little Alain leaned over and snatched it away. Appeared he hadn't been asleep after all. He raised the bow and pointed it at Doil. Rhea watched his pudgy little fingers tighten on the trigger.

'Don't,' she said. The boy was far too young to start killing people. 'You're a royal prince, remember? Hasn't anyone ever told you about princely honor? Like, the dos and don'ts?' She was improvising here, but it seemed to be working. At least the boy hadn't

454

shot Doil yet. 'Much as this piece of shit deserves to be killed, you should leave this kind of thing to someone whose job it is to deal with such offal. You don't want to go putting a big, fat stain on that honor of yours now, do you?'

'Can I at least shoot him in the leg?' Alain asked. Perky little bugger. Thankfully, Doil was still too busy hurting to think of grabbing the bow back from the boy.

'No. But you can give me that bow, and I'll make sure he behaves himself from now on.'

Reluctantly, Alain handed over the weapon. When Doil was finally done moaning and bitching, he came back up with murder written all over his ugly mug.

'You dirty, shit-eating – '

Rhea trained the bow on his privates.

'Shut it, arsehole. One more word out of you and I'll put you in a world of pain. And this time, it's not going to be my foot hitting you between the legs.'

The incident earned her the queen's respect.

Merys didn't say anything, was probably too mortified even for a simple thank you, but her attitude towards Rhea changed markedly. Where before she'd treated Rhea with royal hauteur – in other words, largely ignored her – now she managed a trembly smile and a look that was probably meant to convey gratitude but only came across as pinched and slightly moronic. Rhea gave her a nod in return, though she still thought the Queen of Ardath was an uppity cow. Little Alain was a bit of all right, though.

There were other consequences to her actions, as she'd known there would be. When next they stopped and Pryce found out what she'd done, he had her dragged out of the coach, trussed up like a feast-day fowl and slung over the back of a horse. Now she *was* cold. And bloody uncomfortable, though that didn't begin to describe what it felt like to be reduced to a traveling sack of meal. And she was worried, because of what Pryce had said before he left.

'See that she's well fed,' he told Garth, her new keeper. 'Keep up her strength. She'll be needing every ounce of it. I reckon his majesty will call for her soon, and I very much doubt it'll be just to have a friendly chat.'

The first time she met Edric was on the night he came into Macsen's tent and took the sword. Back then, he'd struck her as a very unpleasant and undoubtedly dangerous person. But she hadn't been afraid of him. Well, a little bit, maybe.

The next time she saw him, at the parley with the Colors, she got a weird feeling that he'd changed in some profound and terrifying way. Suddenly the man scared her so bad she could have pissed herself. And, for some reason she couldn't yet fathom, he reminded her of the only other person who'd ever made her feel that small and helpless: the sailor from Orr.

What was more, when they dragged her out of the coach after the incident with Doil, she noted that Edric's entire entourage consisted only of Stonebridge, Wystan, Pryce, a dozen men-at-arms and twenty Headhunters. He must have left the rest of his army trailing somewhere far behind. Which meant the bastard was making a run for it. Making it that much harder for anyone following them to catch up before he had them all secured behind Kingskeep's walls.

*   *   *

The first thing Laurin did in the morning after the Dunmarkans had departed was to go and search for Dag and Lil. He didn't hold any high hopes of finding them, but he did owe it to them to at least look. He'd kept a sharp eye out for them last night and seen not seen them pass, but that didn't mean they were still here. Might have ended up in some Dunmarkan cooking pot, for all he knew.

As it turned out, they had – but not in the sense he'd imagined.

After finding the picket lines empty, he was dispiritedly making his way back through the remaining half of Edric's camp when he spied two plump, hairy backsides, one bay, one dappled, protruding from the entrance of a largish tent. A cook tent, by the massive iron tripod standing over a bed of cooling coals outside it. No pot hanging from the chain and hook suspended from it, though. But there was a trail of spilled gruel leading from the firepit to the tent and a great deal of slurping and friendly bickering going on inside, so he reckoned that was where the pot and the rest of its contents had ended up.

Asking them nicely to come out didn't work, nor did slapping their greedy little rumps, and they were wedged in the entrance so tightly there was no getting past them. So he took out his knife, slit the canvas, and there they were, not looking the least bit guilty. Well, gods only knew when they'd last been fed, so he probably shouldn't be too hard on them.

He never did find Rhea's palfrey, but he was so relieved to have the other two back that, leading them over to the Colors' camp, he nearly forgot his other worries for a spell. Those came back with a vengeance as soon as he'd tied up Dag and Lil and told them in no uncertain terms that they'd already had all the food they were getting today.

He was sick with fear for Rhea, furious at bloody Edric, and fed up with having to sit around waiting while the fiendish bastard was putting mile after mile between himself and his enemies. So it was with an almost joyous spring in his step that he went to fetch Dag and Lil after Bryn came out of the war council and told him they were leaving in an hour, and to hell with Edric's terms. Laurin wasn't sure he liked the look on Bryn's face, though. Dark. Grim. Like a man become a little too familiar with dealing out violence and death as a matter of course. Laurin couldn't find his mate from the tunnels in that face. As if that part of Bryn had stayed down there and never come out. Hopefully not. One Avellin trapped forever under a mountain was enough.

As their little expeditionary force gathered before heading out, Laurin was glad to see that everyone he would have wished for was coming along. Even Gale's man Mullin looked like he could take care of himself in a scrape. Hart came as something of a surprise, though. It took Laurin a moment to place her, seeing as she wasn't all rouged and powdered like the last time they'd met: Tilly the whore, who'd slipped him the mysterious note back when he'd visited Sleazetown with Macsen and Rhea. She gave him a wink and a cheery smile, as if to say, 'Don't worry, we'll get this done.'

We'd better, he thought. *Anything else doesn't bear thinking on.*

As if the gods had decided to help speed them along, the weather cleared up. In the course of an hour the clouds departed, leaving

458

behind a clean, blue sky, the late autumn sun bringing a small measure of warmth, if not to the body then at least to the soul. The relief was shortlived.

Turning south at the Burnt Keep crossroads, they found that Edric had left them a little present. Two dead men were sitting propped up against trees either side of the road. Redfern men, by their tabards, probably prisoners Edric had dragged along for just such an occasion. They'd been arranged so they seemed to be staring intently at an object lying in the middle of the road: one of Wystan's bursters. A big one. And the road up ahead was crowded on both sides by low, wooded hills, making it the perfect spot for an ambush. As warnings went, this one couldn't have been any clearer. Scanning the hillsides, Laurin saw the odd bit of yellow and red flash among the trees. Dunmarkan soldiers, no doubt. Realizing the implications, he suddenly felt sick.

Edric did *leave watchers, only not where he said he would. And we're way ahead of his deadline, giving him all the reason he needs to do something dreadful to the hostages. Dear gods, what have we done?*

'It's another feint,' Bryn said, sounding as if he could see inside Edric's head. If he could, then it wasn't something Laurin envied him. Anxiously, expecting the burster to go off any moment, he watched Bryn dismount and walk over to where to the thing was lying. After studying it for a moment, he picked it up and shook it, nearly giving Laurin a heart attack.

'It's got no fusible,' Bryn said. 'And anyway, it's empty. We should check the hills, just in case, but I'm betting there's nobody up there.'

459

Turned out he was right. Someone had gone to the trouble of tying strips of yellow and red cloth ripped from a Dunmarkan tabard to trees and bushes, that was all it was. Only a feint but effective nonetheless. By the time Daven and Mullin got back from scouting the hills, they'd lost well over an hour.

Dusk wasn't far off and they were close to the head of the trail Torvald had mentioned when Catch, riding point, came cantering back.

'Dunmarkans camped up ahead,' he reported. 'Looks like it's their whole damned army sittin' smack across the road. And they got that trail Torvald told us about covered as well. Best we get off the road, in case they come checkin'.'

'Damn!' Iefan said, once they were into the woods. 'Doesn't that bastard ever miss *anything?*'

'Never seen it happen,' Macsen growled. 'Sharp as a gods-damned dagger, that man. Pity the only use he's ever found for those brains is hurting people.'

He sounds exactly like I feel, Laurin thought. *Angry, and getting angrier by the minute. But I guess angry is all right, seeing as the only alternative is giving in to despair.*

Making use of what light there was left, Daven and Mullin went scouting. They didn't get back until well past dark, and the news they brought was fit to rob a man of his last hope.

'The coach with Merys and the kids isn't there,' Mullin reported. 'And there's no sign of Edric or Stonebridge.'

'Or of Pryce and his Headhunters,' Daven added. 'Didn't see Wystan, either.'

'Rhea?' Bryn asked.

Daven shook his head.

'I'm not surprised they're gone.' Bryn's face appeared carved from stone. 'It's what I would have done. Put up a roadblock against any pursuers, and then made a run for it. If Gale can figure out that Kingskeep's the prize, so can Edric. Isn't really all that hard.'

'So what do we do?' Flatside asked.

'Daven,' Bryn said. 'Can you find us and the horses a way through these woods that'll get us past that army?'

'Now?' Daven asked.

'Now. I know it's dark, and I know we could all use some sleep. But if we let this hold us up, we might as well turn around and call the whole thing off. Any chance we might have of getting past them, it's now.'

'He's right,' Iefan said. 'Come tomorrow and daylight, they'll have this place sewn up tight.'

'All right,' Daven said. 'Give me an hour, and I'll see what I can do.' He slipped off into the night while the rest of them hunkered down for the wait.

Laurin fussed over Lil and Dag's cinches, gave them half a carrot each. Then there was nothing left to do but sit tight and fret. Nobody was in a talking mood, and apart from an owl hooting somewhere in the distance and the horses' occasional, soft snuffles and snorts, the night was dead quiet. And cold. Huddling deeper into his cloak, he watched the moon come up, first as a soft glow on the horizon, picking out the wooded ridges to the east in stark silhouette, then as a luminous, perfectly round disc rising over the

461

hills. At least they'd have some light on their way through the forest – if Daven managed to find them one. It would also make them much easier to spot.

He reckoned that closer to two hours had passed when Daven reported back.

'Found us a way,' the woodsman said. 'Game trail from here, and then it's a creek. Best I could do. But it's gonna to be dicey. They got sentries posted all across the valley, an' two of 'em's standin' right by the creek. Gonna have to take those ones out, but gettin' to 'em's gonna be a problem. Snow's startin' to freeze over and turnin' all crunchy like, so under the trees you got either that or dry leaves to choose from, an' the creek's gonna be full in the moonlight by the time we get there. Oh, an' they got scouts out rovin' as well. Heard at least one of 'em sneakin' through the underbrush.'

Daven's report was met with silence. To Laurin's surprise, it was Hart who spoke up.

'Mullin and I will take care of the sentries. Give us a quarter hour, then come on after us.'

Before anyone could think to answer, they were gone. It was eerie. One moment they were standing there, the next they'd simply vanished with hardly a rustle as if they'd simply become part of the forest. Laurin blinked, but all he could see were trees and patches of snow dappled in shadows and moonlight. Still full of surprises, was Tilly the whore.

Daven's game trail wasn't much of a trail at all.
By the time they reached the creek, it felt to Laurin like he'd led

462

Dag and Lil around half the trees in the forest. Not to mention tripping over roots and getting slapped in the face by low-hanging branches. But it got them there, was what counted. The creek was another matter. As Daven had said, it was fully in the light, and the water softly rustling along the pebbly bed didn't do much to mask the sounds of all those hooves and feet splashing through the shallows.

Of a sudden Laurin felt terribly exposed, like he had a target painted on his back and arrows might come flying out of the woods any moment. Nothing for it, though. His neck hairs standing on end, he forged ahead.

They'd gone roughly a couple hundred yards when Hart reappeared out of nowhere.

'Sentries are taken care of,' she told Bryn, whom everyone, Iefan included, seemed to have accepted as leader of this expedition. 'Mullin's going after the scouts, so I reckon we won't be seeing him for a while. Any road, the way's clear.'

Laurin half expected to find the dead sentries floating in the water but saw no sign of them. Instead there was a small bridge, a few logs laid over the water long enough ago to have acquired a carpet of greensward. It was Torvald's trail, crossing the creek. A comfortably wide, gently meandering strip of soft forest loam covered in pine needles, it allowed them to travel quietly and with some speed for the next two hours, until it passed through a clearing where Bryn called a halt. None of them had gotten much sleep during the past few days, and they were all in dire need of rest.

Laurin saw to Dag and Lil, had a bite to eat and a sip of water, and was asleep the moment he hit his bedroll, so deeply gone he didn't even dream. Or, if he did, he didn't remember.

*   *   *

Unlike Laurin, Bryn did dream, although his dreams were anything but pleasant. He was caught in the midst of a storm of crows, surrounded by a seething black mass of thrashing wings and hurtling bodies. There were thousands of them, attacking him from all sides, with *Altingal* the only thing keeping him from being hacked to pieces. In his hands, the sword became a whirling, slicing, stabbing blur of bright, merciless steel, cutting the attackers down by the scores and the hundreds. It was both terrifying and exhilarating to watch himself wreaking such havoc – until the true horror of what he was doing hit him like a fist in the stomach when he looked down and saw, not dead crows, but the corpses of men, women, and children lying at his feet.

Then he was back in the paradisian gardens with Cormac – or with what was left of the old man. The king had started to fade since Bryn had last seen him, was fast becoming a translucent shadow of his former self.

He's on the way out, Bryn thought. *I wonder if I'll see him again after this.*

'I hate killing crows,' he told Cormac. 'I'm sick of all the bloodshed.'

'Sick is good,' Cormac said. 'Because the day it stops making you sick is the day you start getting used to it. From there, it's a long and steep descent to a place you definitely don't want to go.'

'But will it ever stop?'

Cormac gave him a level stare. 'It will,' he said. 'But never for

464

good. Nothing ever stops for good. Sooner or later, it all comes back around. That's what it means to be king: you get one thing done, and already a dozen more are standing in line waiting for you. More often than not, bloodshed is one of them.'

'Why me?' Bryn asked. 'Why not somebody else? Somebody who actually likes doing this kind of stuff.'

'Likes it? That would be your brother Edric. Should be all the answer you need to that part of your question. And as to why you? It's the Blood, lad. It takes what it needs without consideration, without patience or mercy. The Blood decides how and where those of us who belong to it may best serve its purpose. Meaning, you don't really have much of a choice in the matter. The best you can do is stay sharp and look out for the traps, so as not to end up like Edric. Or like myself, for that matter. Wanting too much of a good thing can be as bad as the opposite, especially if your motives aren't quite as pure as you'd have yourself believe.

'Now – I'm about to move on, and we won't be seeing each other again, least not this side. You'll be on your own from now on, my boy. And let me tell you, sitting in The Big Chair is the loneliest line of work there is. So before we part – and for what it's worth – here's a bit of advice from an old hand.

'Once the throne is yours, you'll find yourself surrounded by people clamoring for your attention, asking favors of you, expecting you to take sides, vying for your good graces, fawning, flattering, plotting, backstabbing, trying to outsmart you and seeking to exploit your every weakness. Beware of them all, especially those who would have you believe that you're something more than a mere mortal, that your role is to rule instead of serve. In my experience,

465

they're worse than the ones who simply want you dead.

'My point being: keep your friends close. Find yourself a good woman. Have children – and I don't mean just for the sake of begetting heirs. Surround yourself with as many good people as you can find. They may at least in part make up for all the bad ones you'll be forced to deal with.'

'You still think this is going to work?' Bryn asked.

He never got an answer, because suddenly the whole garden was swaying like a ship in high seas, trees, pavilions, trellises and statues toppling and crashing to the ground as Edric came stomping into the dream, tall as a god, his every step shaking the ground. Seeing him here in this place, Bryn felt a fear greater than anything he'd ever known. It made him want to kill Edric for good, eradicate him from existence. He attacked, and was immediately swept up by Edric, whose strength *was* that of a god, overwhelming, crushing, irresistible.

Next he knew, he was jerking awake, still fighting for his life, his hands clutching Edric's throat. No, not Edric. Gradually, Ham's face came into focus, red as a beet, eyes bulging, mouth gasping for air. Shocked, Bryn let go.

'Gods, Ham! I'm so sorry! Did I hurt you? Are you all right?'

'S'all right, m'lord. No harm done. Musta been a mighty bad dream you was havin'. Reason I woke yer, his grace said to tell yer it'll be getting' light soon, reckoned you'd want to get an early start.'

'Yes. Thank you, Ham. Can you see to the horses?'

'Already done, m'lord. A spot o' breakfast, an' we'll be ready to go.'

466

The incident left Bryn badly shaken, worse than any other horror this bloody war had thrown at him so far. No time to think what it meant, he told himself, although, deep down, he should have known better.

* * *

30

Rhea recognized the village.

It had been their first stop when she'd come the other way with Laurin. With a chill, she realized this would be their last night on the road. Tomorrow they'd reach Kingskeep.

When Garth led her into the inn's common room and she saw Edric, Pryce, and Wystan warming their hands by the hearth, she could have screamed with frustration. Here were the very three men she needed to kill, all in one place and within spitting distance, and she couldn't do a thing about it. Wystan gave her a dark look, Pryce a sardonic smile. Edric simply ignored her, though he was the one she wanted to see suffer most. Because she knew who he was now – ever since she'd met Gale back in the Dunmarkan camp after the battle and had finally gotten him to solve the last remaining riddle for her.

'Oh, lass,' Gale had said. 'Are you sure you want to go down that road? There are other things you could do with your life, you know.'

'Yes, I'm sure. And no, there aren't. Not before I've seen this through to the end.'

469

'All right, then.' He sighed. 'Just don't hold me responsible for the consequences. So. It's not the letters 'S' and an 'I'. It's the numbers five and a one. Pretty much the simplest code there is. So simple it makes one wonder why they bothered at all. Try substituting the numbers with the corresponding letters of the alphabet.'

'E,' Rhea said. 'And A.' She got it then. 'Gods, am I ever stupid! Edric Avellin! I should have figured it out ages ago.'

'In truth, I was rather glad you didn't,' Gale said. 'And I'm still not sure I should be telling you now. But someone does need to kill that man. Unfortunately, with your friend Bryn gone, candidates for the job have become thin on the ground. Do promise me you'll be careful, though, and not go barreling in like a fury unleashed. Although the most likely outcome is still you getting yourself killed, you might want to at least give yourself a chance to get the job done first.'

'But why Edric? Why would he have bothered when he had Pryce to take care of his dirty work?'

'Ah, lass, this is where we get to the heart of the matter.
'And let me assure you, it's not pretty. To call it bitter irony would be a vast understatement. Because, you see, Pryce had no idea what your parents were up to. None at all.

'What really happened was this: one day, Edric saw your mother when she came to the keep to visit your grandfather. No doubt Edric's was a sick and crippled version of the real thing, but I do believe it may have been the only time in his twisted life that he felt something akin to falling in love. He wanted her, wanted her badly, and the fact that she was married and a mother didn't give him pause, nor did it stop him. Instead, he tasked Pryce with sending a couple of Headhunters to take her and bring her to him.

'Only they botched the job. Went after her and your father, likely because they were too lazy or arrogant to wait for a chance to catch her alone. From what I heard, your father must have fought like a lion. In fact, you can stop looking for Charis Carr, the woman who was Pace's partner that night, because she's dead. Your da killed her while trying to protect your mother.

'Sadly, he wasn't able to keep his beloved safe, and Pace ended up killing them both. Afterwards, he and Pryce doctored the story before presenting it to Edric, who otherwise would have had Pace's head for failing to deliver the prize.

'Remember that night we all met in Macsen's tent? Though he hid it well, Edric recognized you on the spot, knew exactly who you were. And judging by the way he looked at you, I'd say it was it was a good thing you left for the Bent that very same night.'

Since then, Edric had been at the very top of her list.

Garth steered her up the stairs and down a short hallway on the second floor. The room he led her to was large and ornately furnished, the kind of accommodation an inn this close to the capital would reserve for noble guests. There was a four-poster bed, a writing desk and a wardrobe, even a commode.

A pair of saddle bags hung over the back of a chair. They were made from beautifully tooled leather and embossed with the lion rampant. Edric's, no doubt.

Garth manhandled her onto the bed. She fought, tried to wriggle off the other side. Not a chance. He caught her, straightened her out, pulled her bound hands up over her head and tied them to the head-board. Secured her feet as well.

'My, aren't you the big, brave hero,' she sneered. 'Tying a help-less woman to a bed so another man can rape her – that must make you feel so manly and strong.'

'Shut your piehole, whore,' Garth hissed, leaning so close to her face she could smell the foulness on his breath. 'Pace was one of ours, and you killed him. So rot in hell, and I hope you take a long time getting there.'

'After you, asshole,' she said, wishing he'd come a little bit closer so she could bite off his nose.

Instead, he grabbed her between the legs and gave her crotch a painful squeeze. Waved a long-dagger in front of her face.

'It was me, I'd fuck you with this. I'd even go so far as to suggest it to his majesty, except I'm sure he'll think of it all by himself.'

'That's because both of you are dickless pussies who can't get it up any other way,' Rhea yelled after him as he walked out the door. The moment it closed behind him and she was alone, her courage collapsed like a stuck bladder.

I am not going to cry, she told herself. *I am not going to cry, and I am not going to think about what's coming. I am not going to cry...*

Maybe the endlessly repeated mantra had a calming effect, maybe it was sheer exhaustion, or maybe it was some deep-rooted instinct for self-preservation taking a hand – in any case, she fell asleep.

And woke to find Edric standing over her, looking down at her

472

like a butcher studying on how to best carve up a side of beef. His face showed no expression at all, but the eyes were another matter. She could see something worse than death lurking in there, something that scared her beyond anything she'd have thought possible.

He sat down on the edge of the bed. Took her face in one hand, turned it this way and that, like an artist looking for the best angle of light. Unable to help herself, she flinched under his touch, tried to pull away.

'Don't worry, little bird,' he said, his voice sounding odd, as if several different persons were speaking at once. 'I won't kill you. But I won't lie to you either: I will hurt you. Then perhaps I'll let you heal for a bit. Or not. And then I'll hurt you again. I will hurt you in all the places you can think of, and in every place you can't. I will burrow into your body, and eventually into your soul.

'That is what awaits you, little bird. That, and more. Sooner or later you'll come to welcome my ministrations, to thank me for them, even. And that will be a good thing. Because the fact that I'm not going to kill you means there is a whole lifetime of pain awaiting you. So, what do you say, little bird? Shall we begin?'

'Go ahead,' Rhea said. 'Just be advised I'm going to kill you. Slowly. Everything you do to me, I'm going to visit on you twice and three-fold.' Useless bravado, but it was all she had left.

Now there was a knife in Edric's hand. It was small, the size of a pen knife, but it looked very, very sharp. He started cutting through the laces of her leather jerkin.

Edric had laid Rhea's breasts bare and was working on the laces of her trousers when someone knocked on the door. Clearly annoyed,

473

he stopped cutting.

'What is it?'

'Urgent news, your majesty.' It was Pryce. Even shouting through a closed door, the man managed to sound bored.

'Come in, then,' Edric said.

'Sorry to disturb,' Pryce drawled, stepping into the room, his glance brushing over Rhea just short of a leer. 'Cuthbert's back from scouting our backtrail. Unfortunately, it appears Strong and the Bailon boy haven't been dawdling. Cuthbert says they're less than two hours behind. Camped for the night. If they get off to an early start, they could be here by daybreak.'

Bryn! He's alive! Rhea thought, her heart doing a somersault. *And he's coming for me!*

A look at Edric told her he was weighing his options. Would he decide to make a stand, or run for Kingskeep? She hoped for the former, wanted him to stay and fight. She'd seen how Bryn and Iefan had handled themselves in battle. Just the two of them were a force to be reckoned with, and surely they hadn't come alone.

Edric disappointed her by slipping the little knife back into his pocket and issuing a string of orders to Pryce.

'Have Garth come and fetch the girl. Put her in the coach with Merys and her brats, but make sure she's securely bound. Then pick your best men and have them set up an ambush. The rest of us are leaving. Now.'

*   *   *

Three days on the road to Kingskeep, and Anuun was ready to give up. He'd reached a point where he had to fight for every step, where

474

he dreaded the prospect of having to get up again even before he sat down to rest, which he got to do seldom enough as it was. Truth be told, he'd gone so far beyond the limits of his endurance, all he wanted to do was crawl into a hole and die. Then, on the third night out, he finally succeeded in dreaming the Spear.

In the dream, he was back in the Ice Wastes – only it all looked terribly wrong. Everywhere around him, patches of sooty mold polluted the pristine, white snow. Gripped by a nameless dread, he watched the corruption continue to spread until only the few square yards of snow he was standing on remained untouched.

Suddenly it was as if a door opened inside him, releasing knowledge he hadn't even known he possessed. Sure of what he had to do, he knelt and thrust his arm deep into the snow, feeling around with his fingers until they met something solid. A length of wood, it felt like, and strangely warm to the touch.

Pulling it free, he saw that it was the shaft of a spear. Hands trembling with urgency, he took the point Wanderer had given him and joined it to the shaft. The two were a perfect fit, the pieces coming together as if fused by magic. Then, guided by the same, inexplicable sense of knowing, Anuun thrust the spear point first into the snow– and watched in awe as the white began to recover and spread with amazing speed, consuming the rot like a wildfire ripping through dry brush.

For the first time in weeks, he woke feeling rested and refreshed. Not up to his old form but a far cry from yesterday's near break-down. That evening he stayed up late, working the length of ash he'd cut on the second day out into a shaft worthy of a Spirit Spear.

Now, on the eve of the day that would see them to Kingskeep, he sat by the fire, joining the perfectly rounded and smoothed wooden shaft to the obsidian point. Unlike in the dream, it took more than just a thought to fasten the one to the other.

Thankfully, the dwarf had everything a man traveling in the wilds could possibly need stowed away in that seemingly bottomless pack of his, including pitch glue and strips of rawhide.

Laurin was still up, sharing the fire with Anuun. As were Flatside and Bryn, the one smoking his second pipe of the evening, the other staring into the flames as if he expected them to hold the answers to all their problems.

For a wonder, Anuun didn't mind the company. Enjoyed it, actually, in a quiet way. Because, over the last few days, something he'd never have reckoned with had happened: like Wanderer before them, these humans he'd been traveling with had somehow found their way into his heart, until he'd begun to consider them not merely comrades but friends.

For an even greater wonder, from what he could tell the feeling was mutual. Much as he yearned for the Ice Wastes, he didn't look forward to parting company with these men. Of late, the peace and quiet he'd always cherished above all else was beginning to look more and more like loneliness than like blessed solitude.

Bryn worried him, though. He could see a great capacity for goodness in the young man, but the way he'd clenched himself around his purpose made Anuun think of someone caught in the grip of a grim, mailed fist. Slowly, drop by drop, it seemed to be squeezing that very goodness out of him. Anuun hesitated to consider what kind of a man Bryn would become, should he continue to

476

walk down this road.

'Flatside?'

Laurin must have had similar thoughts, for he broke the silence with a pointed glance at Bryn. 'I've been wondering. How did Catch come by his battle name?'

'Well, now,' Flatside said around the stem of his pipe. 'That I can tell yer, seein' as I was there mysel'. Happened close to thirty years ago, durin' the border wars with Harad. 'Cept fer the sergeant, we was all still green younglin's, though we reckoned we was hard men 'cause we'd already had a coupl'a brushes with the enemy. Truth, it was more tradin' insults from afar than actual fightin'. That day, we was feelin' even grander 'cause this kid from up north just joined our company. Looked like he was barely fifteen and straight off the farm, so right away he got stuck with the name Yokel.

'As it happened, it was the same day we first ran into some serious bastards. Me, a bloke called Walder, an' Yokel was fightin' close t'each other, when suddenly this great big bruiser comes trompin' up. Blighter was all plated up like a noble, swingin' a bastard sword in one hand an' a fuckin' mace in t'other. All I'm thinkin' is, how'm I gonna get outta this alive, when that idiot Yokel goes chargin' right in. Right off, he gets his sword busted in two, and then knocked clear off his feet for his troubles.

'Now Walder goes pokin' the big guy with his spear. Big guy doesn't like it, gets pissed, ends up stabbin' poor Walder in the gut an' then takin' his head clean off. I'm next in line, an' I can already see this is not gonna end well for me. In fact, I'm good as dead when of a sudden Yokel's back in the game.

'An' what does the madman do? He grabs Walder's head by the hair, swings it around, and throws it right in the big guy's face, yellin' "Catch!"'

'Before the Harad man knows what's hit him, Yokel's up an' runnin', with Walder's spear wedged tight under his arm. Ran the fucker through an' through, he did, plate, mail, guts an' all.

'Stopped callin' him Yokel that day, an' he's been Catch ever since.'

Anuun was contemplating whether asking Flatside how he'd come by his own name would be considered prying when, quiet as a shadow, Mullin slipped out of the dark under the trees and joined them by the fire.

'Got news, my lord,' he told Bryn, who came out of his dark reverie like a man just arrived from a far distant land. 'Edric's less than two hours ahead of us, in a place called Far Greening.'

Bryn stared at the man as if he were seeing him for the first time. 'Two hours. And we're less than a day from Kingskeep.' Abruptly, he stood up. 'We have to leave immediately. This is our last chance to catch them.'

'Horses are done in,' Flatside said. 'We'd not get a mile out of 'em afore we rode 'em into the ground.'

'So we'll go on foot.' It didn't look like Bryn was going to let anything stop him. 'If we leave now, we can still get there in time.'

'Afraid not, my lord,' Mullin said. 'They must have been watching us as well. Leastwise they were just about to move out despite the late hour. No way we can catch them before Kingskeep. What's more, it looked like some of them were staying behind, most likely

478

to set up a nasty surprise for us.'

'You're saying that's it, then?' Bryn asked, looking like he would have gladly strangled the messenger. 'We've lost? Because once Edric reaches Kingskeep, he'll have every gate and sally port barred tighter than a gnat's arse. There will be no way left for us to get in.'

'Beg to differ, my lord,' Mullin said. 'There's always a way, long as you know where to look. Happens I do. So does Hart. As a matter of fact, we can't just get you into Kingskeep without anyone the wiser, we can get you right into the keep. Provided you can handle heights, that is.'

'I can,' Bryn said. 'And I will. So tell me about it.'

'You sure about this, mate?' Flatside asked Mullin when he was done explaining. 'Just hearin' you talk, my nuts've already shrunken by half.'

It was a sentiment Anuun could readily share.

*　　*　　*

31

Scary climbs had been a necessary part of Laurin's job, but Mullin's way into the keep was fit to give even a seasoned Waylen nightmares.

They couldn't afford to have Edric's men tailing them, nor was there time to spring the trap and take them out, so they'd given Far Greening a wide berth. Leaving the road a mile short of the village, they skirted along the edges of meadows and fields, always staying well inside the treeline.

The second and final time they left the road was five miles outside of Kingskeep, Mullin leading them along a series of woodsman's trails to a clearing and a dilapidated barn deep in the shadow of the Steps.

'This is where we leave the horses,' he said. 'Anything you don't absolutely need, leave it here as well. Place we're going, the last thing you want is unnecessary gear weighing you down.'

Reluctantly, Laurin left his pack behind, but not before taking out a couple of things that he thought might come in handy and were small enough to stow in his belt pouch.

From the clearing, it was a short walk to the foot of the first Step. Everywhere else, it was a mild evening carrying a premature promise of spring. Here, in the angle formed by the Godswall and the northern side of the Steps, winter still held sway. Suddenly Laurin found himself crunching through ankle-deep snow, his breath pluming white in the ice-cold air.

Looking up, all he could see of the castle above was the outer wall, and beneath it a slope that looked to be near vertical and at least five hundred feet high. Naked rock, much of it sheathed in ice, alternated with bands of snow-dusted scree. Not even a mountain goat would venture that climb. Not even a crazy mountain goat with a death wish. So he was mightily relieved when Mullin led them farther left to where the first Step curved around towards the second – until they stopped at the foot of a couloir, a narrow slash in the mountainside that to Laurin looked even deadlier than the rest of this bloody hill.

'Well, bugger me an' my uncle,' Catch said, studying what lay ahead of them, his face pale and grim like everybody else's. 'Flatside, old lad, I'm callin' dibs on this one. Meanin' I get to go first. Can't have yer smelly backside fallin' in my face.'

'Fine with me,' Flatside said. 'But just so we're clear: you fall, I ain't catchin' you. All I'm gonna do is stand aside an' watch yer sorry arse go bangin' by.'

As it turned out, the gorge was climbable, if just barely.

A staircase of sorts made of jumbled boulders and up to man-high steps of sheer rock, most of it was either slicked by water and a carpet of reddish, stinking algae or covered with a thin sheet of ice.

One wrong step, one slip, and in all likelihood you'd end up back where you started – but not before every bone in your body had been smashed to bits on the way down.

Halfway up, bathed in sweat from sheer terror as much as from the exertion, Laurin's panicked mind latched onto the question of how they were supposed to scale the castle wall, provided they ever made it that far. He spent the rest of the ascent fighting off the image of having to climb back down this chute of horrors, reckoning it would probably be easier to simply jump and have it over with.

It was one particular fear that proved unfounded, as he saw when they reached the foot of the keep proper. There was a large, round opening in the base of the wall overlooking the couloir, protected by a massive iron grate that looked to be firmly anchored in the surrounding masonry.

'This is where the keep's waste is dumped,' Mullin explained. 'Every so often, they flush it out with water from the reservoirs, meaning this next bit is going to be a little dicey. There's irons driven into the tunnel walls every ten feet or so. You hear water coming, grab on to one of those and pray it's just somebody emptying their chamber pot.'

'Now he tells us,' Ham said, looking ill. 'What woulda happened if they flushed the damned thing while we was still down the couloir?'

For an answer, Mullin gave him an eloquent shrug. Then, stepping up to the wall, he removed several loose stones from the edge of the opening, allowing the grate to swing open on creaking hinges.

'Emergency escape route,' he said with a grin. 'Though I doubt anyone's ever been hard enough pressed to actually consider using it.'

The tunnel floor was slick with algae, and there was enough of an incline to make every step a balancing act with a quick slide and then a five hundred-foot drop awaiting outside. Thankfully, it was only about thirty yards to a set of iron rungs and another grating, this one set in the ceiling, then they were out of the sewers and on the castle's lowest level of storerooms and dungeons, looking down a dank, low-ceilinged corridor that was lit by a single, smoking torch. Either side, iron-banded doors stood open on empty cells.

Laurin was about to send his sincere thanks to the gods when he heard the scrape of metal against stone somewhere up ahead. It was the only warning they had before all hell broke loose.

*   *   *

Bryn heard the scraping sound as well.

It was immediately followed by the thump of a crossbow being fired. Almost simultaneously, a bolt slapped into the wall mere inches from his head. His first thought was that Gale had betrayed them, and that Mullin had steered them into a trap. Not a heartbeat later, the man proved him wrong by stepping in front of him and taking a bolt meant for Bryn. Beside him, Flatside gave a pained grunt, following up with a heartfelt curse.

'Into the cells!' Bryn shouted, grabbing Mullin and dragging him out of the line of fire as more bolts careened off the walls and ceiling. Flatside, Macsen, and Laurin piled in after him; the others sought cover in a cell across the hallway.

'Macsen, old boy!' one of the attackers shouted. 'Did you really think I wouldn't know about that rat hole you came in through?'

484

'It's Pryce,' Macsen told Bryn. 'I should have known. Mullin should have known.'

'No use blaming Mullin,' Bryn said. 'He's dead.'

'You can surrender,' Pryce shouted. 'Or you can rot where you are. I don't care either way, just so you understand that this is as far as you're going.'

'Damn, but a crossbow'd come in handy right about now,' Flatside said, sounding shaky.

'You all right?' Bryn asked.

'Took one in the shoulder. Reckon I'll survive.'

'I think I can do better than a crossbow,' Laurin offered, fetching something out of his pocket and holding it out for Bryn to see.

'Where the hell did you get that?' Bryn asked, staring at the small burster in Laurin's hand in amazement.

'Filched it when we were opening up the tunnel back on the Bent and Wystan wasn't looking,' Laurin said. 'I've got two of them, actually. Brought flint and tinder as well.'

'Good man. Let's do it.'

Moving over to the door with Laurin, Bryn saw Iefan staring a question at him from across the corridor. 'Burster,' Bryn whispered. 'Stay back.' Giving him a nod, Iefan retreated deeper into the cell.

Laurin struck a light, lit the fusible, and Bryn lobbed the burster down the hallway, praying it would go far enough. In the enclosed space, the explosion was deafening, instantly filling the hallway with billowing clouds of dust and smoke. Bryn risked a peek. For a wonder, the solitary torch was still burning, casting a muted halo in the dust-laden air.

Drawing his dagger, he slipped out through the door, Macsen

485

hard on his heels. Iefan and Catch joined them from the other side, Iefan grabbing the torch in passing. With the dust obscuring the view and their ears still ringing from the explosion, there was no way of telling how much damage the burster had caused.

A gruesome sight met them when they reached the spot where it had gone off. The bodies of a dozen men, some whole, some in parts, were strewn across the floor, blood and gore splattered all over the blackened walls. Only one of them was still alive, likely because he'd been standing a ways behind the others. It was Pryce. He was conscious, and didn't look like he was too badly hurt. A few broken ribs, by the cautious way he was breathing. Macsen went down on one knee beside the Lord Executioner, setting the point of his dagger to the man's throat.

'Don't,' Bryn said. 'This one is Rhea's.'

Macsen looked up, gave him a hard stare. 'She'd say that, wouldn't she? Just so happens I don't want her to kill him.'

Bryn surprised himself by saying, 'Neither do I. But she still needs to make that decision for herself.'

'All right, then,' Macsen relented. 'We'll lock him up in one of the cells. First, though, he'll answer a few questions.'

'Ask away,' Pryce wheezed, not quite managing his usual, languid tone. 'This should be fun.'

'Where's Edric?' Macsen asked.

'Good one, old boy. Where do you think he is? Up in his chambers, fucking your little girl. Horny bastard couldn't wait to stick it to her. I'd wager that right about now she's hurting a lot worse than I am.'

486

Bryn reckoned Macsen would have killed the man then, if Hart hadn't shown up with a ring full of keys. 'Here,' she said, holding it out to Macsen. 'Pick a cell, and then let's go get her.'

'And Merys?' Macsen asked Pryce. 'The children?'

'Back there.' Pryce gestured. 'Few doors down. Intact, as yet. Not happy with the accommodations, though.'

Ardath's royal family was where Pryce had said, huddled together in a corner on a pile of rotting straw. All four of them were pale, frightened, dirty, but alive and unharmed. Leaving Iefan, Catch, and Flatside to deal with them, Bryn and the others moved on, aware that a single wasted moment could make all the difference between finding Rhea alive or... No. He was not even going to consider the alternative.

'Edric will have guards patrolling the keep,' Hart cautioned. 'We should split up, double our chances. Macsen knows the way as well as I do.'

'She's right,' Bryn said. 'Ham and I will go with Hart. Daven, Laurin, with Macsen. Gods be with you.'

'And with you, lad,' Macsen said. 'Let's go get the bastard.'

In the heat of the moment, none of them realized that Anuun had gone missing.

Hart stuck to dusty hallways and narrow back stairways used by servants, if at all. 'Not the shortest way,' she said. 'But short doesn't necessarily mean quick.'

Bryn could only trust that she knew what she was doing.

Apparently she did, for she got them to within ten yards of the door to Edric's chambers before trouble caught up with them in the shape of six heavily armed guards rounding the corner behind them.

'Go, m'lord!' Ham urged. 'Hart an' me'll hold 'em up.'

A nod from Hart, and Bryn sprinted for the door. He found it ajar. Dagger in one hand and *Altingal* in the other, he nudged it open with his foot. Peeked. Saw an empty anteroom. No place for a man to hide. The next door was ajar as well. It opened onto a sitting room. A few pieces of dark, heavy furniture, ancient and probably quite uncomfortable. Nobody there either. A door led off to the side, probably a privy. No time to check. Next was a study, spare and uninviting as the other rooms, and again, empty. It was here a terrible suspicion befell him: what if Pryce had lied? Edric could be anywhere in this vast, sprawling keep. He might even be laid up somewhere in the city, for that matter.

One last door. Like all the others, it was off the latch, almost as if someone were expecting him, making it easy for him, leading him on. He kicked it open.

Behind it was a bedroom.

Rhea was there, lying naked and spreadeagled on the bed, wrists and ankles tied to the bedposts, belly and thighs bleeding from at least a dozen cuts. As far as Bryn could tell, she was unconscious. Edric was standing beside the bed with his back to Bryn, a sword dangling from his right hand in an almost casual manner.

'There you are, little brother,' he said, his voice crowded with a chilling multitude of personalities, an aura of darkness hanging about him like an evil fug. 'I've been expecting you. You're late, but not too late for the grand finale.' He turned around, gave Bryn a cold stare from black eyes roiling with shadows. His codpiece was undone, his cock huge and stiff as a flagpole. 'I was just about to fuck her ragged.' He gestured at Rhea with the sword as if it were merely a riding crop. 'Of course you're welcome to watch. But first, I do need to ensure you don't get up to any foolishness.'

With his free hand, he lifted the oaken nightstand from beside the bed, hefting it as if it weighed less than a feather, and threw it at Bryn with enormous force, hitting him square in the chest. Every last bit of breath knocked out of him, Bryn went down in a welter of splintered wood, his already bruised ribs screaming in protest.

Then Edric was standing over him, sword in one hand, a heavy brass candlestick in the other.

Bringing up *Altingal*, Bryn managed to block Edric's blade with half an eyeblink to spare. Still on his knees, desperately straining against Edric's brutal strength, he realized he was still holding the dagger. He stuck it into Edric's thigh just as the candlestick came whistling down and caught him full on the left shoulder. He felt something break, and his arm went numb. Scrambling backwards and onto his feet, he watched Edric pull the dagger out of his flesh with the indifference of a man who didn't feel pain. There was no blood either, only a black, tarry smear on the blade. Bryn could think of only one explanation for what he was seeing: his half brother wasn't just a vicious, murdering fiend – he was also deep into some sort of sorcery.

A white-hot rage suddenly boiling up inside him, Bryn went on the attack. And found that the King of Dunmark was a master swordsman.

Easily fending off *Altingal*, Edric grabbed an ornately carved,

489

high-backed armchair. Swung it at Bryn with inhuman strength, time and again, smashing stuff left and right, a candlestand, a chest of drawers, an escritoire. Ducking and weaving, Bryn was forced to retreat. He managed to put a table between Edric and himself, a move that bought him only scant moments. Edric merely raised a foot and gave the table a kick, sent it crashing into Bryn, who nearly went down again. In the face of Edric's inhuman strength and ferocious violence, Bryn's confidence began to crumble. Whatever Edric had done to himself, whatever dark magic inhabited him, he was in a league Bryn had no hope of matching, perhaps not even with *Altingal*'s help. Then he remembered the dream, the one where he'd fought against Edric and lost, and all hope deserted him.

Batting the table aside, Edric closed in, raised the chair high.

Vaguely, Bryn registered movement behind Edric.

Then suddenly the tip of an obsidian spearpoint was protruding from just beneath the king's breastbone. Edric looked down at himself. Raised his gaze, stared pitch-black hatred at Bryn. Uttering a savage bellow, he threw the massive chair and missed, shattering a wall mirror instead. The spear did seem to be giving him trouble, though. Dropping the sword, he tried in vain to reach behind his back and grasp the shaft. Anuun, standing behind him, gave it another shove and a twist.

Edric's opened his mouth as if to say something, perhaps utter a curse. Nothing came. Instead, his mouth just kept on opening, wider than any human mouth had a right to. Staring into that dreadful maw, Bryn saw throat muscles convulse. Then a sudden a stream of dark, viscous fluid poured forth, splattering the floor. Immediately, the stuff began to consolidate, quickly rising up as it gained shape. Moments later, a fully formed… thing stood staring at Bryn from a single, red eye, arm-like appendages equipped with wickedly sharp implements already reaching out to gut him.

He hadn't the vaguest notion of what he was looking at. He'd seen drawings of demons in books, and he remembered reading that they were apt to enter and exit their human hosts through the mouth, but those were all hideously ugly creatures, more or less man-shaped in appearance and covered in warts and spikes and what have you. This thing was all smooth surfaces, hard angles and sharp edges, as if it were an animated, freakish suit of armor forged by an insane weapons smith in the midst of a bad seizure. No time to figure it out. Whatever it was, it was about to kill him.

Praying that what Cormac had said about the sword being a weapon against dark magic was true, he swung *Altingal* into the side of the thing's boxy helm – or head, no telling which of the two it was.

The moment the blade touched the creature, there was a silent explosion of black light – if such a thing could be said to even exist. Blown off his feet by the force of it, Bryn was flung against the wall. Next he knew, he was lying prone, his cheek pressed against cold marble, dazed and hurting all over.

Something was blocking his view. *Altingal*'s hilt. And something else right behind it. A pair of boots. Large boots. Expensive boots. Numbly, he groped for the sword, his fingers closing around the hilt just as he was suddenly grabbed by his hair and yanked upright. Edric still had the spear in him, but he'd somehow managed to break off most of the shaft. He looked ill, deathly pale, yet the flat, black eyes staring into Bryn's were filled with a murderous rage. His free hand was inches from Bryn's throat, ready to strangle him. Straining, as if something were holding him back.

'Let go the sword, little brother,' Edric hissed. 'Let it go, or I'll kill the girl.' He dragged Bryn closer to the bed.

'You want it?' Bryn said, suddenly remembering the sailor's reaction to *Altingal*. 'Here.' Twisting around, he drove the blade deep into Edric's stomach, right under the ribs, angling it upwards towards the heart.

Screaming like a man doused in boiling oil, Edric let go of him. Withdrawing the sword, Bryn saw smoke pour from the wound, from Edric's mouth, from his eyes. He was clawing at himself as if he wanted to rip out his insides, howling like a lost soul. Which he was, Bryn suddenly understood with terrible, blessed clarity. In that very same instant, something inside him gave way, making room for a great pity, and grief for what could have been, both so immense they brought tears to his eyes.

The rest was an act of mercy.

Bryn said, 'I forgive you, brother.' He didn't know if Edric could still hear him, but the words needed to be spoken. Then, once more, he chose 'Shortening the Odds'. Executing it perfectly, he released his poor, twisted sibling from his suffering for good and all.

Bryn found neither satisfaction nor relief in what he'd done.
Instead, he felt sad, and infinitely tired, a great bleakness descending on him like a weight placed there by the gods. Wearily, he

shook it off, forced himself to move – and nearly stumbled over Anuun, sprawled on the floor in a way that didn't encourage much hope.

I'll see to him in a moment. But first, Rhea.

She was still unconscious. Drugged, maybe, though it didn't seem like Edric to spoil his own fun by putting a victim under. She was hurt, she was bleeding, and she was incredibly beautiful. Carefully, he gathered up the bedsheets and wrapped them around her. And a blanket, because she looked so cold.

Suddenly she opened her eyes. Shuddered. Shuddered again when she sat up and saw Edric's body.

'It's all right,' he said, laying an arm around her. 'It's all right. He's dead. It's over. He can't hurt you anymore.'

Then he was holding her in both his arms, her head ducked into his shoulder, her whole body shaking and shaking until finally something gave way and she cried against his chest with great, heaving sobs, clinging to him like a lost child.

'You came for me,' she said when she'd finally cried herself out.

'I came,' he said. 'So did your grandda, and Laurin.'

'Grandda,' she said, untangling herself from him. 'Is he here?'

'He's here,' Bryn said, suddenly remembering that the two of them weren't alone in the world. Faintly, the sound of clashing steel could be heard from the hallway. The fighting wasn't over.

'I need to go,' he told her. 'Stop them from killing each other out there. Will you be all right if I leave you alone for a moment?'

'Go. But be safe.'

Anuun was stirring, he noted in passing.

He found Ham and Hart holding the door to the hallway. Macsen and Daven were close by, engaged with a second group of men-at-arms, and he caught a glimpse of Laurin lurking behind them, ready to swing his axe at anything that got by them. The men outside were all Guard, which was perhaps the reason why they seemed to be fighting with only half a heart.

Protecting a cruel and ruthless king was one thing – doing it over the dead body of their beloved and feared First Sergeant was another. Time to put an end to it.

'Stop!' Bryn shouted, shouldering past Ham and Hart. 'All of you, stop, and lower your weapons. Edric Avellin is dead. I am Bryn Avellin, son of Seorus Avellin, rightful heir to the throne of Dunmark.'

They heard him. And they obeyed. Briefly, he marveled at how easily it had gone, until he noticed them staring at his right hand, their eyes wide with wonder and awe. What held them captive wasn't his hand, he realized a moment later, but what was in it. *Altingal*. The blade was glowing a bright amber – like the sun when it was about to set. Or rise.

He held it high for all to see. 'This is *Altingal*, Cormac Avellin's sword. Eight hundred years ago, it helped win the Battle of Simbalan and rid the world of Aelfin Malamut. Ten days past, it saved the kingdoms from something easily as dangerous. And today, it freed Dunmark from a man who should have never had to sit the throne.

'First Sergeant,' he went on to address Macsen. 'See to it that the word is spread throughout the keep: no more fighting. Then I suggest you step inside and greet your granddaughter, who is as well as we could have hoped. We'll also need a healer for our friend

Anuun, seeing as he's not in a good way.'

*   *   *

32

Much as he wanted to be with Rhea again, Bryn decided to give her and Macsen a moment alone. They were family, after all, whereas to Rhea he was... what? Something, he hoped, though under the circumstances most any shoulder would have sufficed for her to cry on.

Patience, he counseled himself, when suddenly there was another explosion inside. Could Laurin have accidentally set off his second burster? But no, he was right there, looking as alarmed as everyone else. Fearing the worst, Bryn hastened through the empty antechamber and into the sitting room. It was empty as well, though the privy door was now standing open.

He found Macsen in the study, lying in a crumpled heap by the near wall, a fistsized rent in the front of his hauberk, tendrils of smoke rising from the padding underneath. Also present in the room were Stonebridge and Wystan.

'I knew I should have checked the privy,' Bryn growled, suddenly in a killing mood again. 'Looks like a couple of floaters found their way to the surface.'

'Lord Bailon,' Stonebridge said. 'If the smell doesn't agree with

497

you, it's because you've stuck your nose into things that are none of your business. I suggest you surrender, hand over your weapon, and perhaps I'll allow you to skulk back to whatever pigsty in Ardath you call home.'

'Or what?' Bryn had a distinct feeling that *Altingal* made both of them uncomfortable, though where he thought he detected avidity in Stonebridge, in the Black it looked a lot more like fear. 'You'll have your pet magicker throw me one of his bursters, like he did with Macsen?'

'You think I'm stupid?' Wystan snarled. 'Only a fool would use bursters at such close quarters.'

'Then I suggest you two surrender before I lose patience with you.' Bryn raised *Altingal* threateningly, just to see their reaction. It was as he'd thought: Stonebridge looked hard put not to reach for the sword and wrest it from Bryn's grip; Wystan recoiled as if someone had waved a poisonous snake in his face.

'Kill him,' Stonebridge ordered the Black. His greedy little pig's eyes remained fastened on the blade that was still glowing with an inner fire.

Wystan brought his hands together, kneading the air as if he were fashioning an invisible snowball. Rhea appeared in the bedroom doorway, wrapped in a blanket and holding the blackened dagger Bryn had used against Edric. He gave her a slight shake of his head. *Stay out of this.* Hoped to gods she'd heed him.

Meanwhile, a ball of dense, black smoke had formed between Wystan's hands. So the creep did have magic, and not the nice kind, either. The attack came with a swiftness that left Bryn no time to react.

One moment Wystan was staring down at the dark shape between his hands, the next it came flying at Bryn as if shot from a catapult. But instead of hitting him square in the chest as it should have, the Black's missile was yanked off course in midflight, *Altingal* rising up to meet it with Bryn's hand merely a passenger on the hilt. Amazed, he watched the sword absorb Wystan's magic, the blade going dark for a moment before it resumed its amber glow.

He raised *Altingal* further, the point aimed at Wystan's heart, saw mortal fear in the man's eyes. Bringing the steel closer still, Bryn though he could see tenuous threads of the same black stuff Wystan had used to make his missile coming out of the man's body, as if the sword were drawing them out.

'Don't!' Wystan screamed. 'Stop it! Get away from me!'

Gently, Bryn touched the point to Wystan's chest. For long moments, the blade went dark. When it lightened again, Wystan sagged, looking utterly deflated, a man bereft of everything he'd held dear. Almost, Bryn felt sorry for him.

'Give it back,' Wystan begged. 'Give me back my magic, and I'll do whatever you ask. I could kill Stonebridge for you, if you like.'

'You vile, traitorous – ' Stonebridge looked ready to kill.

'If I wanted his grace dead,' Bryn cut him short, 'I could make him so without your help. I might consider offering another deal, though. The bursters. Have you told anyone else how to make them?'

'No,' Wystan groaned. 'But I'll tell you. Anything. Everything. Just give me – '

499

'Have you written anything down? A recipe, a manual perhaps?'

'No. Far too dangerous. Someone might steal it. The knowledge is all in my head.' Wystan stabbed a finger at his temple. 'Safe. All yours, if you want.'

'That's good,' Bryn said, hardening his heart for what he had to do next. 'Because I do want it protected. Unfortunately, there's only one way of keeping it safe and out of the hands of others like you. I'm sorry, but there won't be a deal.'

He made it quick. A sudden push on the blade, a stab to the heart, and it was over. Brutal, sickening, but necessary. No doubt someone else would come up with a version of Wystan's bursters sooner or later. Hopefully later. Until then, Bryn aimed to spare the world this particular atrocity.

'And you, sir,' he addressed Stonebridge, who stood there fuming, a man still refusing to accept that his fortunes had just taken a sharp turn for the worse. 'It was you behind Wystan's mischief all along, am I right? I'll wager your plan was to get both Edric and myself out of the way, and then take the throne for yourself. I suppose you can demonstrate a bloodline that would lend at least some credence to your claim.'

'An excellent claim,' Stonebridge said defiantly. 'And one that has the merit of benefiting the kingdom. As opposed to handing the throne to a fledgling pretender who happens to have unrightfully acquired an ancient Dunmarkan heirloom. Stolen it, I should say. By rights, you should be hanged for grave robbery.'

'By rights,' Bryn said, '*you* should be hanged for treason. Fortunately for you, I'm done with killing for now. Which means you'll be gracing Kingskeep's dungeons with your presence for a very long time.'

'We'll see about that,' Stonebridge hissed. 'If you think this is over, you're sorely mistaken. You can impress these simpletons with the bloody sword all you want, but you'll never hold on to the throne without the support of the South. And I *am* the South. So – '

'Take him away,' Bryn told the men of the Guard who'd come up behind him. The healers had arrived as well, he saw, tending to Macsen and Anuun – which meant they must both still be alive. Rhea was still standing in the doorway. She'd dropped the dagger, he saw. He was just in time to catch her before she collapsed.

* * *

It was the Spirit Spear that led Anuun to Edric.

Standing amidst the human wreckage in the dungeons, he suddenly felt an irresistible pull that left him no choice but to follow it. Certain as it was about its destination, it didn't seem quite sure how to get there. It must have taken him on a somewhat circuitous route – at least he had to bull his way past a gaggle of soldiers fighting with Ham and the woman Hart.

As it was, he arrived not a moment too soon. Edric was about to drive Bryn into the floor with an enormous monstrosity of a chair. With no time to waste, Anuun skipped any issues of fairness and rammed the spear into Edric's back. Giving it another shove and a twist as Edric tried to reach back and get a hold of the shaft, Anuun felt the spear reach deep inside him, taking back the power it had loaned him and throwing every last bit of it at Edric.

Next thing he knew, the floor was rushing up at him. Somehow

501

he must have missed it, for instead of a jarring impact there was only silence as he fell into soft, deep darkness.

Some time later, he awoke to find a stranger kneeling by his side, feeling his pulse and shaking his head. 'Don't know what's wrong with him,' the man said to someone crouching next to him. Laurin, looking terribly distraught.

He's worried for me, Anuun realized. How very good of him. I should tell him...

'Ice,' he murmured, hoping they'd understand him. 'Iceling... too long away... never make it back... die.'

'Ice,' Laurin said, his mien suddenly brightening. Anuun saw him cast a glance eastward, as if he were able to look through the castle's walls and see what lay beyond and above the great Godswall. 'If it's ice you need, my friend, then I know exactly where to find you some.'

'River won't do,' Anuun whispered. 'Need lots...'

'Oh, I reckon there's more than enough of it up in the high Caerrocks.' Laurin gave him a grin. 'How about a glacier? Will that do for a start?'

It would. Anuun gave the dwarf a nod and a weak smile before he passed out again.

Next time he came round, the first thing he noticed was a refreshing chill in the air. And a smell of snow. He saw a deep blue sky overhead, and the faces of several men bobbing in and out of view. Realized they were carrying him somewhere on a stretcher. Nearby, someone was whistling a merry tune. Laurin, no doubt, guiding them along paths no one knew better than him.

Of a sudden Anuun's heart was filled to bursting with a new and wondrous feeling. He reckoned it must be love. Love for this selfless little man who was doing his best to save Anuun's life; love for the friends he'd shared so much with over the past days and weeks; love for life itself. It was then he knew he wasn't going to die. At least not just yet.

*   *   *

33

Sitting in The Big Chair was the loneliest line of work on earth, Cormac had said. For Bryn, those words looked to be fast becoming hard reality, seeing as his friends were deserting him one by one. After receiving a bird from Owain Cullan with a message saying that things were under control in Cullamor, Iefan had accompanied Merys back to Ardath – which was as it should be. He'd promised to return to Kingskeep for the coronation ceremony, now less than a week off. Bryn dreaded the prospect of making a spectacle of himself, and would have gladly done away with the pomp and circumstance, but Torvald, one of the few who'd stayed on, had strongly counseled for it.

'The people need to see it happen,' he said. 'And they need to be impressed with the whole nine yards. Like it or not, it's what they expect. And you need to make an impression. Holding Stonebridge hostage is not going to buy you the South. Neither is flaunting the trappings of power, I'll grant you, but not doing so would make you appear weak in their eyes. Foolish as it seems, it's how their minds work.'

Torvald's support was proving invaluable, and his tireless efforts at diplomacy were already bearing fruit: he'd persuaded at least some of the southern nobles to attend the ceremony, though in each case the commitment had come with a price. Bryn thought them all petty, avaricious fools, though he was coming to see that dealing with their likes was part of the cost of being a king. How all of this benefited him was something he had yet to discover. Not at all, he suspected, Cormac's rant about the Blood and shouldering burdens taking on new and poignant meaning.

Anuun seemed to have taken well to the glacier, but he was still recuperating and wouldn't be coming to Kingskeep any time soon. The day after Laurin returned from the Caerrocks, Bryn summoned Guildmaster Firth.

They had a quiet talk with the man, Bryn offering him a choice between guaranteeing Laurin's safety or losing the Guild's charter in Dunmark, a choice Firth found easy to make. With that out of the way, the little man begged Bryn's leave and departed the very next day, all fired up over a rumor he'd heard about a small colony allegedly founded by retired Waylens and other Small People in a secluded valley somewhere in the southern Caerrocks. It would probably be months before Bryn saw him again, if ever.

The one person who did sometimes keep him company after a fashion was Edric's daughter Wilda. She'd taken to sitting quietly in a corner of the audience hall, watching him with those large, dark eyes that seemed to miss nothing. She was a weird one, no doubt about it, but weird in a way he found strangely endearing rather than irksome. He suspected that if he ever got to talk to her before she slipped away like a shy little animal, he'd discover a person who was as sensitive and intelligent as she was... well, different.

Torvald had arrived with a weeks' delay in the wake of Edric's army – now Bryn's army. Gale came with him, and immediately asked for an audience. Bryn thought he knew exactly what the man wanted, and reckoned Gale knew that he knew. Once Gale had been settled into a chair in front of a warming fire in the small audience hall, Bryn skipped the pleasantries and came right to the point.

'My lord Gale. I'm of two minds what to do with you. Should I have you hanged for treason, or should I thank you and welcome you back into the fold?'

'I'm well aware of the dilemma I pose, highness.' Gale gave a wry smile. 'As you can imagine, I'd much rather offer you my continued services than get acquainted with the sharp end of a rope. I wouldn't presume to expect your trust, but I do have hopes of obtaining your forgiveness.'

'We'll see. You can start by confessing your sins. I want the truth, and I mean all of it. I'd strongly advise you to proceed on the assumption that I already know a great deal of it. Lie to me, hide something from me, and I promise you'll regret it.'

'I appreciate the warning, highness, but I'd not begin what might become a fruitful collaboration by attempting to deceive you.'

Fruitful collaboration.
The man had balls, that much Bryn had to give him. 'Very well, then. I'm listening.'

'If I may, I'll begin with the Sweepers,' Gale said. 'More specifically, Garamon.'

507

'Garamon, yes. That was you, wasn't it?'

'How did you know?' For once, Gale looked surprised.

'An educated guess. And a bit of research. What you said that night on the Bent got me thinking. I remember you stressing the point that you served the kingdom's interests, not Edric's. Another thing I found interesting was that the Sweepers seemed never to have lacked for funds. Put that together with the fact that you were Lord Treasurer, and it was only logical to have someone go over your books.'

'You found that I'd been diverting monies from the royal coffers,' Gale said.

'Yes, though it took a good deal of digging. Interestingly enough, you took none of it for yourself – unless you've got a small fortune stashed away somewhere no one's thought to look.'

'I can assure you I haven't. Every penny of it went to the cause.' The way he said it, with a hint of pride, Bryn was inclined to believe him.

'Well,' Gale went on, 'I'm glad that's out of the way. Because the next one is going to come a bit harder, I fear. It concerns Mistress Redbreast, and it's obvious her wellbeing has become a matter close to your heart.'

'What about her?'

'She didn't tell you? Amazing girl. I suppose I owe her one. Here it is, then: I sent her after Edric, told her he was the one who was responsible for having her parents killed. In my defense, I can only say that you were presumed dead at the time, and there appeared to be no one else willing and able to take on the job.'

'You *sent* her? That doesn't sound much like the Rhea I know.'

'You're right, of course. She wouldn't let herself be *sent* by anyone, would she? I should have said, I *pointed* her at Edric – though only after some very persistent questioning on her part.'

'All right. I can see how she wouldn't take no for an answer, especially where the death of her parents is concerned.'

'And it was I who alerted Torvald to the fact that Edric burned his villages.'

'I'd say well done to that. What else?'

'There is one more thing,' Gale said. 'When Edric found out about you, he asked me to – '

He was interrupted by a knock on the door. It was Torvald.

'Sorry to interrupt, highness, but it appears Pryce and Stonebridge have escaped.'

Descending to the dungeons to have a look for himself, Bryn found two dead gaolers, an empty cell, and no clue as to how Pryce and Stonebridge had gotten away, except that they must have had help from outside. But the problem wasn't Pryce or Stonebridge, it was Rhea.

Only a few days ago, she'd been down to see Pryce. When she returned after a very tense half hour, she announced to Bryn's great relief that she'd decided not to kill the man. Knowing he would spend the rest of his life in prison was good enough for her, seeing as he'd only been carrying out the orders of the person who was really responsible for the death of her parents, and of so many others: Edric, whom she couldn't reach anymore because Bryn had killed him, a fact she'd pointedly mentioned when he'd visited her sickbed.

Other than that, Bryn's visit had been trying for both of them. She seemed withdrawn, perhaps embarrassed because he'd seen her in a moment of weakness. The fact that Macsen had died of his injuries after two long days of suffering surely didn't help either. Then again, maybe it was something more complicated, and he was simply too thick to get it.

He, on the other hand, was bursting with the need to let her know how he felt about her but had the sense to know that this was entirely the wrong moment. The question was, would it ever be the right moment?

Pryce and Stonebridge's escape changed all that.

He knew it the moment he saw her approach him in the hallway outside his rooms. She was wearing a new set of leathers, deep maroon instead of Headhunter black. The color suited her well, and he had to admit that, sadly, so did the purpose that drove her. Much as he would have liked to see her wearing a dress and the crown of the Queen of Dunmark, it was a dream – one that wasn't likely to come true anytime soon. Probably never.

'I'm going after Pryce,' she informed him. 'Can't have him and Stonebridge running loose. There's no end to the trouble they might cause.'

'I was hoping you'd stay,' he confessed, unable to stop himself. 'Is catching them really all that important to you?'

'I'm doing it for you, too,' she said. 'You've got enough on your plate as it is, what with cleaning up Edric's mess and winning over the South. So I thought I'd at least take Pryce and Stonebridge off your hands.'

'That's very thoughtful of you, though in truth I could use a hand right here in Kingskeep, seeing as most everyone else seems to have left. And besides, I – '

'I'll be back,' she cut him off gently, surprising him by stepping close and reaching up to cup his cheek. 'I need to find Pryce, and I also need some time to myself. But I *will* be back.'

She gave him a look that was softer than any he'd ever seen from her. Then, rising up on her toes, she kissed him square on the mouth. Her lips on his were warm, alive, and full of promise, making his longing for her almost too keen to bear.

'Be well,' she told him, gifting him with a smile that didn't quite chase the shadows from her eyes. For the first time, he realized that she had the cutest dimples when she smiled – probably because it was the first time he'd seen her smile. It nearly shattered his resolve not to break down and beg.

'You too,' he said, clasping his hands tightly behind his back lest they betray him. 'And please, take care of yourself.' Then she was gone.

For a wonder, even though the person he wanted most to hold on to had just walked out the door, he suddenly felt happier than ever before in his life. Granted, it was a bittersweet sort of happiness, tempered by loss, but he'd take it any time. She had promised to return. And she would. For another kiss like that, he'd wait for however long it took her to find her way back to him.

*   *   *

Part of Rhea wanted nothing more than to stay in Kingskeep with Bryn. She couldn't. Not after what had happened with Edric. It

511

made her feel so unspeakably tainted. Worthless. Dirty. A kind of dirty that no amount of water and soap could remove. So, using Pryce as an excuse, she fled, taking with her the vague hope that time might heal what nothing else could.

Because she'd come to understand something important: killing Pace should have been a turning point – and she'd missed it. Laurin had seen it, but she'd been too pig-headed to listen to him. She should have stopped then, should have let go of the past and given herself a chance to move on. She hadn't, and perhaps running into Edric had been the price exacted for stubbornly clinging to old hurts and to a need for revenge that served no one, least of all her dead parents. Now, she understood at least part of what had driven her.

Strangely enough, it was seeing Pryce in his cell that had finally opened her eyes. He was exactly as she remembered him – and not. The same arrogant drawl, the same uncaring, fuck-the-whole-world attitude, but of a sudden he seemed... reduced, shrunken, not nearly as impressive or important as he thought he was. The prison he lived in wasn't this cell in Kingskeep's dungeons, she realized – it was who he was: someone who'd long ago lost the capacity to change, to become anything else than what he'd made himself into. Which was why, when she heard that he'd escaped, she wasn't angry or disappointed. Because she knew he'd be taking his prison with him wherever he went.

Maybe, for her, it wasn't too late. It shamed her to admit it, even to herself, but she'd been on her way to becoming someone like Pryce. Gods be thanked, she'd woken up in time. Figuring out Pryce, she'd understood something about herself. Maybe, some day, she'd even manage to comprehend Edric, and thus rid herself of him and of the terrifying images that haunted her even into her dreams.

Images of Edric standing over her, absently testing the little knife's blade with his thumb while he talked to himself in multiple voices, as if he were several persons sharing a single body. Discussing amongst themselves how best to cause her a maximum of pain and suffering while keeping her alive.

Images of Edric cutting her: the cuts he made were mostly small and shallow, but she saw the terrible hunger burning in his eyes, saw the hand wielding the knife shake with the barely restrained urge to stab, rend and gouge with total abandon, to yield to the beast inside him and transform her into a bloody mess of dead flesh.

Sometimes, she wished he had. Because then she'd be feeling nothing now, not the pain of losing Grandda, not the regret for having left Bryn like she had, not the loathing and anger and the overwhelming hurt that made her want to just break down and cry like a lost little girl.

She didn't. Hadn't done it when she was little, wasn't going to start now. A true Redbreast went down fighting, not blubbering. But she wasn't going to go down, not if she could help it. She'd get through this, one way or another. She would. She had a promise to keep.

*　　*　　*

One more hill to climb, then Laurin should be able to get his first good look at the valley. Finding the elusive community of little people was proving harder than he'd thought. This was the third

513

such place he'd come to, and there was no telling what awaited him beyond that rise. Twice, he'd found a homey little village nestled among the foothills of the southern Caerrocks, and twice his heart had leapt with joy, only to plummet when it turned out the inhabitants were entirely ordinary big people, and not a single dwarf among them.

Coming out this way, he'd fought a long and difficult battle with himself over whether to stop by the farm and visit his folks. He hadn't been back since that day twenty years ago when Master Crowlin had taken him away, and he feared that digging up old memories would cause him and everyone else nothing but pain and discomfort. What if they felt they needed to make an embarrassing show of gratitude for the money he'd sent them all these years? Or worse, started treating him with deference, like he'd become someone better and more important by making his way out there in the big, wide world? Terrifying thoughts, all of them. He went anyway.

He found Da and Ma at the old place, bowed by age and a life's worth of hard work but still in good health and better spirits. When Ma hugged him to her bosom, smelling of hay and freshly baked bread, for a moment there he felt as if he'd never left. Looking mightily pleased, Da clapped him on the shoulder, man to man, before fishing a hanky from the pocket of his many times patched work pants, blowing his nose and dabbing at his eyes while mumbling something about the cold making them tear up.

Workday or no, by evening the whole family was gathered for a festive dinner, brothers, sisters, inlaws, and a horde of nieces and nephews who called him Uncle Laurin and couldn't hear enough about how he'd fought in the Battle of Three. Although he tried to minimize his role, they somehow got it into their heads that he'd sent the Nordsmen packing practically single-handedly.

He was pleasantly surprised to hear that his brothers had put the money he'd sent to good use. They'd bought the neighboring farm when it had come up for sale, and they'd also leased water rights from the local lord and built a small but thriving sawmill, a business in which it turned out he was a silent partner, with every penny he'd invested accounted for and all debts squared away.

At some stage during dinner, Da banged his cup on the table, shouting for silence.

'I used to joke that Laurin here worked for one and ate for three,' he said when the hubbub had died down. 'Well, I have to say that ain't entirely true no more. He's done more than his fair share of work these past twenty years, and he's helped all of us get through some pretty tough times. Believe it or not, he's even fought and dined with kings.'

Working up to the high point of his little speech, Da made a dramatic pause. Seeing that everyone was getting ready to raise their cups and cheer, Laurin reckoned he would be the one needing a hanky any moment now.

'He still eats for three, though,' Da finished up, getting a round of hearty laughter.

Of a sudden Laurin was very glad he'd decided to come. There was no denying it: he was happier than he'd been in a long time. In fact, he almost managed to get a grip on his stupid little heart and forget Rhea for a little while.

515

Almost there, now.

So far, things looked promising. The trail leading up from the lowlands looked well traveled, and there was a first, faint trace of wood-smoke on the air now that he was close to cresting the hill. Didn't mean it was the place he was looking for, though he had a feeling this might be the one. If not, he'd just keep on looking. It wasn't like he was pressed for time, or had anything more important to do.

*   *   *

Many miles away, in the wee hours before dawn, Nudd Wiggin was dragging himself along a dark, deserted street in the great city of Orr. That he'd made it this far at all was nothing short of a miracle. But, somehow, after the disaster with fricking King Edric he'd managed to get a handle on Scour's leftovers, enough to hold most of himself together on the long trip west. Nonetheless, it had been an ordeal the likes of which no man with a lesser purpose than Nudd's could have survived.

Right from the start he'd been losing pieces of himself left and right, splotches of black sludge marking his trail. In the beginning he'd been meticulous about stopping to pick them up, patting them back into place wherever he seemed to be sporting a noticeable dent. They had a tendency to fall off again sooner or later, and somewhere around Landing things had gotten to a point where he just couldn't be bothered anymore.

He was already used to traveling exclusively at night, seeing as people didn't react well to the sight of someone who was entirely black – not to mention that Scour had taken all those superhuman powers along with it when it abandoned ship, leaving him helpless to defend himself even against a bunch snot-nosed, clod-throwing brats who'd assaulted him one evening near Tirlangan. One such utterly humiliating experience was all it took to turn him into a nocturnal creature, skulking along byways and hedgerows while all his many enemies lay safely abed.

As if losing so much of his power and substance wasn't frightening enough, he also found it increasingly harder to hold on to any kind of coherent shape. Not only did his body – or what was left of it – begin to throw him off balance by producing sudden bulges at the most unfitting moments, it also developed a disconcerting habit of growing useless appendages in the weirdest places. And, obviously determined to torment him, it did so with frustrating irregularity. No sooner had he gotten used to, say, a third arm attached to his left arse cheek, than it was reabsorbed and something equally useless and annoying appeared elsewhere instead.

It was enough to drive a man insane – and in fact he strongly suspected he already was – but he was *not* going to go out without having gotten at least one small taste of his due revenge, and *fuck* the gods and anyone else who thought they could take even that away from him. Someone would suffer, if it was the last thing he did.

Almost there now.

Only a few more yards left to go until he reached the doorstep of the house Master Brychan and his daughter Dilys lived in. No way he could get inside, not the shape he was in – no pun intended. Not a problem, that. All he had to do was wait for morning to arrive. Dilys was always the first one out, unlocking the front door and stepping out to empty her and her accursed father's chamber pots into the gutter. No problem at all. In fact, Nudd could use the time to get some rest. He was past exhausted. No harm in closing his eyes for a moment or two.

*   *   *

At the crack of dawn, Dilys, née Brychan and now more or less happily married Wolsey, turned the big key and unbarred the front door as she did first thing every morning. Stepping out into the street with the first of three chamber pots – she now had her husband's nightsoil to dispose of as well, and the petty curmudgeon would no more pay for a maid than her miserly father did – she noticed something that immediately had her up in arms. Not two yards from her door, some inconsiderate *wretch* had dumped a whole barrel full of some black, sticky, evil-smelling... *stuff.*

Woe to whoever did this, she thought angrily. *I'll have the bailiffs chase them down, and I don't care if they have to interrogate every last nightsoil man in the city. Needs be, I'll have them make whoever it was lick their vile leavings off the cobbles with their tongues.*

Then, in a fit of spite, she dumped the contents of all three chamber pots on top of the black, stinking stuff, thinking, *Crap to crap. Might as well make the cleanup worth their while.*

Already feeling better, she went back into the house, slamming the door behind her for good measure.

*   *   *